What readers are saying . .

"*Stani and Emily first meet. . .in the wonderful book* **Hearts Unfold**. **Heart of My Own Heart**, *a sweet sequel which continues the story of their romance, details their first year together as a married couple.*" "*Another lovely book by a very talented author.*"--Sherri

"*The story was engaging, touching, and left me wishing I had more to read after I finished. I loved the chemistry between Emily and Stani.*"—Tamia (Tennessee)

"*A truly special journey of the heart. An inspiring story of faith and love.*"--Chris

"*Karen Welch has written a very special love story.*"--Martha

Heart of My Own Heart

A novel by

Karen Welch

Copyright © 2012 Karen Welch

All rights reserved

This book is a work of fiction. Names, characters, places and incidents are either the product of the author's imagination or used fictitiously. Any resemblance to actual persons, living or dead, business establishments, locales or events is entirely coincidental.

Cover photography licensed through Getty Images, Inc. USA.
Photo credit-Tetra Images. Photographer Rob Lewine.
Cover design by C.W. Ferris.

This book is dedicated to Mary Rudershausen, the epitome of an intelligent, courageous and gifted woman. Over a lifetime of teaching and mentoring, Mrs. Rudy inspired countless young people to pursue their dreams, and her memory lives on in their achievements.

*"Heart of my own heart, whatever befall,
Still be my vision, O Ruler of all.*
Be Thou My Vision—Ancient Irish poem

Prologue

Two days married and already it seemed so natural to wake next to him, to hear him sigh as he rolled closer and his arm circled her waist. Emily smiled as Stani mumbled her name and his lips found her ear. But another moment and his soft breathing told her he'd drifted off again.

Today they would leave the safety of this place for that other world. Her valley home had become his now, but they might never be free to stay here for very long. That other world, of concert stages and recording studios, of endless travel and late nights that all ran together in a hectic blur, would be their home for most of the coming months. He wanted to take more control, he said, so they could come home more often, but she knew that at least for now, he had no real choice. Bookings and contracts, and Milo, would see to that.

It would be fun, she had told him. They would be happy anywhere as long as they could be together. An adventure like nothing she'd ever known. But in her heart she knew what that other world had the power to do to him. Out there he drove himself too hard, sought to meet every demand, to satisfy every request, to prove over and over that he was what they said, the most brilliant talent of his generation, the prodigy who had grown into a superstar.

Carefully, she turned beneath his arm, until she could see his face on the pillow beside her. Years ago, she had watched over him through that terrible night, praying only that he would live. Now she prayed for more, that he would live a life full of love and laughter, the life he wanted, not the live expected of him. He wanted a family, and a home built on the faith he had so recently come to. That other world would only grudgingly allow him those things. It would be her job to see that he never lost sight of what was important, that the spotlight never blinded him to all he had learned here in the simplicity of her valley.

In his sleep, he pulled her closer, and she gladly obliged, laying her head on his chest and letting her hand run up into his hair. Whatever she needed to do for him, no matter where it took her or how much she had to learn about that other world, she was prepared to do it.

He had read the words at their wedding that for both of them said it so clearly. "Where you go, I will go, and where you lodge, I will lodge."

Chapter One

Emily had changed. Nothing drastic or disturbing, Stani admitted. But this amazing woman, his wife, was definitely not the girl he had fallen in love with. Subtle changes that must have occurred during the first weeks of their marriage, and yet he had failed to recognize the astounding transformation until it was well under way. When he asked John if he'd noticed, since he was after all with them every day and night, and he was also a trained observer of human behavior, his only response had been an ironic grin.

"Sure it isn't just your imagination?" The question set him back, and he considered the possibility that was all there was to it. But no, he insisted, she was definitely different. "Different how?" He had the distinct feeling John was baiting him, but he continued to mull over the idea that his wife might be turning into someone he had never known.

In the first place, she rarely blushed anymore, and could hardly be described as shy or retiring these days. Rather, she seemed significantly more self-assured, at times even a bit commanding, as in the case of that officious desk clerk in Milan who had insisted they would have to wait an hour before their suite was ready for occupancy. With a beguiling little smile, Emily had pointed out that her husband had a rehearsal in less than two hours and would require a place to rest in the meantime. And surely there was another suite, even perhaps a larger one, available. Stani had watched in amazement as the clerk sputtered for a moment before returning her smile and arranging for their luggage to be taken to the best rooms in the house.

Then there was the way she dressed. Granted, most of her clothes had been purchased in Paris during their honeymoon, a far cry from Martha Jean's Boutique on the little courthouse square. When he had promised her a wardrobe suitable for the European tour, she had sweetly informed him that she understood she needed to be at least as well dressed as he was. They had visited all the finest shops and even some of the top fashion houses. Emily hadn't even questioned the cost of the items she favored, which had surprised him. But even more shocking had been her choices. The girl who preferred blue jeans and classic styles in conservative cuts and colors had come away with a rainbow assortment of sophisticated suits and dresses, elegant and often revealing evening gowns and a selection of lingerie and nightclothes that made her husband blush. Furthermore, to these she added not only the jewelry he chose for her, but an ever growing collection of imaginative accessories, beaded vests and flowing scarves, not to mention the hats, which she claimed were more for the purpose of disguise than fashion.

She did her hair differently, too. Its dark length was pinned up in a variety of elegant styles for evening, often with a jeweled comb or a flower tucked in somewhere. In the daytime, rather than leaving it to fall around her shoulders, a style she knew he preferred, she opted for the sleek knot at the back of her head which she had worn when nursing. More practical, she insisted, and it could be accomplished in less time than it took him to style his own signature auburn curls. Even her makeup, previously reserved for special occasions and then barely perceptible, was more sophisticated. A nod, she told him, to the society they moved in. She couldn't expect to win the approval of his colleagues and patrons looking like the simple little country girl she had been. Now, as the wife of classical superstar Stani Moss, she had a role to play. And for this stage, carefully applied cosmetics were essential.

Of course, in their private hours together, the few they could snatch between travel and work, she was the sweet, loving girl he adored. At least most of the time. But there were those other times, those astonishing moments when this woman, his wife, came into his arms with a flare of passion that stunned his senses and took his breath away. This Emily, insistent and insatiable, appeared when he was least prepared, thrilling him with her creative and uninhibited approach to intimacy. She had little regard for the hour or the demands of his schedule, case in point, that afternoon in Rome, when he had very nearly missed a rehearsal after she chose to "thank" him for the gift of a string of black pearls. Or those nights after concerts, when he should have collapsed, exhausted, but rather found himself finally falling asleep at three in the morning after hours of intense, and often athletic, lovemaking.

When he tried to explain the changes—to himself since John was no help—he was hard put to define them. It wasn't so much that Emily was different; it was that she was *more*. More at ease in his world, more confident of her place in his career driven life, more comfortable at his side in the limelight. And she was more intensely spiritual as well as sensual, more attuned to his every need, more in step with his moods. She was a free spirit, moving with effortless grace and shining with a brighter light. At the same time she was completely in control of their transient lives, always ready to go to their next destination, on time and impeccably organized. Nothing she hadn't been all along, he decided, just more so.

He was considering the changes as he waited for her to return, staring out the window of their hotel rooms in Brussels. They had been married a month, to the day. He had expected her to be waiting when he returned from the morning's radio interview, and was disappointed and a little hurt to find her gone. Another change, he wondered. Would she start to go out alone in foreign cities now, without so much as telling him her plans? Was she suddenly so independent that she would expect him to fend for himself, while she kept to her own schedule? He was preparing to fall into a self-pitying sulk, when she swept through the door, her hands full of shopping bags.

"I didn't know where you were." Did that sound accusing? "I missed you." No question *that* sounded forlorn.

"But I told you I was meeting someone for lunch. Remember, the wife of your old friend Yuri?" She stood in the doorway, a vision in dove gray that turned her eyes to sparkling smoke; a long fitted coat and a wide band that held her hair back from her face. At least today it was hanging down her back, he noted. And she was undeniably beautiful, her cheeks flushed and her eyes shining. "I told you last night, I wanted to thank her personally for those amazing Florentine goblets they sent us as a wedding present. *And* I learned she's an American, too. Turns out she grew up on a farm in western Maryland. How's that for small world?"

Stani watched her unbutton the coat, shrugging it off her shoulders to reveal a brilliant tapestry tunic of red and silver over slim black trousers. "Sorry, I forgot. That's new, isn't it?" Now he sounded suspicious, he realized.

"What, the coat? Yes, I saw it last week and decided I'd like something warmer before we head farther north. I know I didn't really need it, I have that beautiful fur you bought in Paris, but the truth is," she paused, pulling off the band and shaking out her hair, "I rather fancied the color. Do you like it?"

He smiled in spite of himself. "You're starting to sound like a Brit, love."

"Well, in case you hadn't noticed, the two charming gents I travel with are both Brits. I guess you and John are rubbing off on me. Now answer the question, do you like my new coat?" She joined him at the window, sliding her arms around his waist and gazing into his eyes, no doubt taking the measure of his mood.

"Yes, it's lovely. I fancy that color on you as well. It turns your eyes that very warm shade of gray. But I was referring to this. Isn't this new, too?" He touched the collar of the sparkling tunic.

"I picked it up in Venice, actually, but this is the first time I've worn it. Do you like *it*, too?"

He considered for just a moment. "It's spectacular, but hardly the kind of thing you used to wear. I miss that lovely girl in the alpine sweater who swept me off my feet."

Without hesitation, she took his face in her hands and kissed him, exactly as she had done that first time. "I'm right here, Stani. I haven't gone anywhere, you know." She turned and taking his hand, led him to the sofa. "Why on earth would you be missing me?"

Before he knew it, he was stretched on the cushions, his head cradled in her lap and she was winding her fingers through his hair in that way that set his nerves tingling. "You've changed since we've been married. I've been trying to figure out just how."

She laughed softly. "I haven't changed. I'm just growing. Did you really think that girl in the alpine sweater was the woman you would need as your wife?"

"Of course I did. She's the woman I love."

Her brows flew up sharply. "Are you saying you don't love me anymore?"

"No! I love you more than ever. But you're different. . .how can I put this, you're *bolder* these days."

"Bolder. You mean I'm not hovering in the shadows anymore, not so intimidated by all these famous people you call your friends? Or do you mean I'm flashier, wearing these wonderful new clothes and the ridiculously extravagant jewelry you keep giving me? Or maybe I'm pushier, seeing to it you're treated properly, like the superstar you are?"

He grinned. Somehow the fact that she knew she had changed made it all right. "Precisely. Not to mention the way you insist on dragging me to these receptions you know I've always avoided. And making them seem like fun. And then there's your habit of making friends with *my* friends. They think I was intentionally hiding you away until we were married. You've become something of a flirt, darling girl. Not a thing you ever were before."

"All just good fun. And look at it this way. If you were a lawyer or a stock broker, I would need to make friends with the other members of your firm and particularly with their wives. In our case, the wives of your musician friends will hopefully become my friends too. At least we have things in common, like never getting to stay in one place very long and competing for attention with Beethoven and Mozart. And everyone's been so nice to me."

"Because you've charmed them all, my darling. Along with the photographers. I'm starting to feel a bit like the man who accompanied Emily Moss on her first trip to Europe."

"Poor Stani, you don't really think I'm stealing your spotlight?" Her hand had wandered down to his chest, tracing the line of buttons on his shirt.

"Not that I'd mind." He lost his train of thought, as her fingers slid between the buttons. "Emily, I have a rehearsal in two hours, you know."

She gave him a smile, one he'd come to recognize, full of promise and sparkling with anticipation. "Yes, darling. I know. Two hours. It's our anniversary, remember? We have just enough time to celebrate."

Chapter Two

In the first days of their honeymoon, John Kimble had tried to stick to his promise to leave them alone. The very definition of a honeymoon, according to the old dictionary at the farmhouse, was "a trip or time spent alone by a newly married couple directly following their wedding." He'd checked, when he had too much time on his hands before the wedding, and pointed out to Stani that nowhere did it mention the bridegroom working every night. The two weeks in Paris, before the concert tour officially began, would be their one shot at any real time alone.

But after several days, he'd begun to worry. They should have called for the car by now, gone out to eat or sightsee. Surely they hadn't gone out alone. Stani would get them lost for sure. While it was just like him to lose track of time and place, John had expected better of Emily. Milo had phoned, giving him the perfect excuse to intrude on them. They needed to be warned that a session with the Paris press had been arranged for late next week. And Milo was miffed because apparently they had told the desk to hold their calls. Didn't Stani realize, he asked in that tone that never required an answer, that he still had work to do and this was after all the first stop on the tour, not just a place to hide away? The press was clamoring for an exclusive interview with the newlyweds and he'd made all the arrangements. *Without* consulting Stani, John added to himself.

As he went up in the elevator, John debated how to best broach the subject. Not that Stani would be surprised. Milo was always open to any opportunity for good publicity, and this would no doubt get their pictures all over the papers, saving the need for promotion; although he suspected the tour was already sold out. In the three years he'd been traveling with Stani, John had rarely seen less than a full house anywhere he performed.

Three years, once Stani was able to travel again, and for John this was the opportunity to do what he knew he wanted to do for the rest of his life, watch over Stani Moss. That little boy he'd first been hired to herd around London had grown into an international superstar by the time he'd rushed to New York after hearing of the car crash. The boy had barely escaped with his life, and during the months of struggle to recover the use of his arm, John had formed the firm conviction that he would never allow Stani to go off on his own again. In many ways, Stani was his family, a replacement for what he'd lost all those years ago. He wasn't about to let anything happen to him again.

Still, when he knocked at the door to their suite, he felt very much out of order. They would call if they needed him, and apparently, they had yet to need him. What he saw when the door finally opened was proof that these two had been doing just fine on their own. Two people who for four days and nights had been doing what two people on their honeymoon might be expected to do. The evidence was everywhere, in plain sight. The elegant rooms which had not seen the services of a maid in days, the room service tray from some recent meal, apparently breakfast, and through the open door, the big carved bed covered with tangled sheets, the surrounding floor littered with discarded clothing. As a detective, if he'd been called to this room after some crime had been committed, there would have been no doubt what had been going on here.

They took the news well. Emily even expressed excitement at the prospect of the interview, which produced a quizzical glare from Stani. "He might have waited. Or at least asked me first."

John pointed out that Milo hadn't been able to reach them. "Someone asked to have your calls held?"

Stani blushed. "I forgot. It's been three days since we checked in. We lost track of time, I guess."

"Four days, if anyone's counting. Well, I'll let you get back to whatever it was you were doing." He gave a long look at Stani's black silk robe, and the matching white one his bride wore. "Not needing to go out for anything, I suppose?"

Two pairs of eyes, gray and brown, stared at him with identical disdain. "No, I thought as much. Well, you can call me if you change your minds. I'll get things set up for this interview. And you might think about taking Emily shopping, like you promised, lad. I don't mind that she only brought one little bag, but it hardly seems fair to drag her all over Europe without any clothes."

They had called the next day, ready to make the rounds. And he saw right away the changes in Emily. Changes he had expected. The girl would see it as her responsibility, taking care of Stani and being the kind of wife he needed in this crazy life of his. And she had never, as far as he had seen, been one to shy away from responsibility. If Stani was confused by this new woman who was his wife, John was sure the changes were all for the good. The lad would just have to give himself time to adjust.

During the days in Paris and the following weeks on the road, John watched the two of them with barely concealed amusement. Stani was clearly more distracted than usual and not by the music now, by his wife. Emily, on the other hand, had taken her customary practical approach to the rigors of travel, making sure everyone was comfortable and Stani in particular was as free from stress as anyone could be, given the kind of pressures built into his job. She seemed eager to tackle the challenges of this new role, acquainting herself with his colleagues and establishing herself as a visible partner in his heretofore solitary life. In the midst of travel and work, she even found time to nurture their shared faith, continuing their ritual of reading scripture together and on the rare Sundays they were not on the road, locating a church for morning worship. John was both pleased and proud to watch her set to work. He'd always believed Emily would be the thing to settle the lad down, give his life some meaning. Now Stani might have a real chance at living what he liked to call the life of a man, rather than throwing all his energy into his career.

It occurred to John more than once that with Emily along, Stani might not need his services to the extent he had in the past. But when he suggested the same, over dinner in Brussels, they immediately dismissed the idea.

"Oh, no, you won't get away that easily. Besides, I won't always have my wife's undivided attention, you know. Once the babies start coming, I'll be just another face in the crowd." Stani glanced over at Emily, who was busily arranging the room service tray to suit her preferences, and there it was again, that foolish grin that spoke volumes about his feelings for this strange new woman, his wife.

"Babies? Not yet, surely. Can't you at least wait until we get back to London? I don't much like the idea of foreign doctors messing about. Childbirth is risky business."

Emily turned her smile on him, that knowing little upturn that said she was indulging his foolish concerns. "Don't worry, John. I promise I'll try to wait at least nine months. But seriously, we could never make it without you. I wouldn't have a clue about getting us all over the world. My talents lie much closer to home, the simple things, you know. Besides, you'd miss us, wouldn't you?"

He had to smile back at her. "I suppose. And it's no end of fun watching him play lover all over the place." He gave a little nod in

Stani's direction.

"You have to stick around for the sake of the violin. And Milo counts on you to keep me out of trouble. To keep both of us out of trouble, I guess. He still thinks I'm ten and can't cross the street alone."

"Nonsense, darling. Milo is well aware that you're your own man now. He's certainly kept his distance these past weeks."

"He's otherwise occupied with Lady Marcia, I expect. We'll see him soon enough." John didn't miss the little jab Stani gave his salad. He wasn't sure if it was meant for Milo, or his newest protégé, but either way, he knew Stani wasn't looking forward to the next stop on the tour, when they would be joined by Milo Scheider, manager, mentor and on occasion, manipulator extraordinaire.

Emily lay listening to Stani's breathing long after he'd fallen asleep. It was an old habit now, listening to him breathe. A simple, routine kind of thing in the midst of this life where little was ever simple or routine. All those years ago, in the terrifying hours after she'd dragged him into the safety of the house and sat watching over him, willing him to survive, she had listened for every breath, terrified it might be his last. Now, with his strong warmth pressed beside her, the listening was a comfort, a reassurance that he was hers, now and forever.

He had said she was changing. He was right, of course. She had to change, to grow into her role as his wife, to learn the complicated ins and outs of this world of his. She wanted to fit in, to make him proud and most of all to protect him from the things here that so easily harmed him. Back home in the safety of her little valley, he had learned to live a different kind of life, simpler and less driven. He had grown into a man who reached out to others, who relied on his new-found faith for guidance, and had become part of a community that respected him for himself, not for his music. In this world, his world, he worked too hard to please and to keep up the pace of touring and performing. The effort drained his energy and lowered his mood. He grew tense and weary and eventually fell victim to self-doubt. She had seen it all last spring when she'd joined him on tour in England. She'd learned a lot, and now, as his wife, she intended to use her position to shield him.

Of course she would change, now that she was free herself. She had tried to tell him, the night before their wedding, that finally she felt free to join him in this life. No longer bound by grief and what she now knew to be a misplaced dedication to keeping the past alive, she was free to give herself to their future with all her considerable energy. It was her duty to keep him well and happy, to see that he loved and laughed with her every day, to give him something of that simpler life in the midst of this other world.

There would always be things that threatened his peace. Too much work, too much travel, not enough time to relax and recover from the soul-draining performances, and of course, Milo. They had come far in the time she'd known Stani, made great strides toward a more equal partnership. But for Milo, Stani would always be that one great opportunity, and for Stani, Milo would always be the force that drove him too hard. The habits of a lifetime were not so easily broken, and for Stani, despite all Milo's best efforts, the conflict had yet to be resolved.

She raised her head from the pillow to study his profile in the dim light. He was so beautiful, as he had always seemed to her. That first night, bruised and battered as he'd been, she had seen the beauty in his face, the sensitive, vulnerable boy behind the man. Without knowing anything about him, she had recognized that he was exceptional, someone to be loved and protected. And now he was hers to do just that.

She smiled, recalling the look in his eyes earlier, a look that said he couldn't quite understand. "You're bolder." Bold was exactly what she wanted to be. Brave and strong, fierce enough to stand between him and whatever threatened his happiness. There would always be the demands, the stresses, the too often self-imposed pressures of his career. There would always be Milo, pushing Stani toward greater success. She could only hope to be a distraction, a balance to those things, and bolder was definitely a start.

Milo would join them in Amsterdam, and for Stani, that signaled the end to the relative peace he'd enjoyed. On their second night in Brussels, he stated plainly that he was arming for battle. When Emily suggested he was only looking for trouble, he scoffed.

"Milo may have mellowed about some things, but the music will always be a tug of war for us. He's already completely involved in this recording deal with Marcia. More skirmishes ahead, love, you can be sure. But at least I have you to bind up my wounds now."

"Marcia. I guess I've been trying to forget." For an instant, a shadow darkened her eyes, and then she flashed him a sly smile. "I'm not afraid of her, *or* of Milo. Just let them try to disrupt our little bit of heaven."

"Ah, my fierce little wife. But seriously, Marcia seems to have become a pet project for Milo, and she's a lot prettier than I am." Punching his pillow, he stretched on the bed and stared up at the ceiling, apparently visualizing the enemy.

"Oh, I don't know about that. You're beautiful, remember?" When she was standing over him, her dark hair haloed by the light and the satin of her gown shimmering across every line of her body, he groaned.

"Come here, you. Why would I waste a thought on her, when I have you here?" Drawing her down to sit on the bed, he raised himself on one elbow and studied her face.

"Lady Marcia Strathmoore-Finch." She spoke the name grimly, and then chuckled. "To think I was jealous of her, with her flowing blonde hair and her overflowing bodice. I thought she wanted you, and what she really wanted was a recording contract. Not that she wouldn't have you, if she could, I'm sure." She eased herself down beside him, resting her head on his chest.

"Emily. . ." he made an attempt at severity, when in fact the sensation of her body aligned with his was constricting his breathing in the most pleasant way possible.

"Yes, Stani?" When he didn't answer, she raised her head to meet his teasing eyes. "What?"

"May I make love to you now? Or would you prefer to discuss Marcia some more? What about her glamor and her talent and what was that word you used, her shapeliness?"

He was gratified by her exasperated moan, and the way her mouth closed over his in one of those long, sweet kisses that so often opened the way to much, much more. No need to worry that Marcia Strathmoore-Finch, or any other woman, could ever be a threat to his fascination with this marvel that was his wife.

Chapter Three

Stani had been right about Milo's passion for his newest client. When he first committed Stani to an appearance with the daughter of a prominent arts patron in London the previous spring, it had been primarily a favor for a friend. The Earl of Strathmoore was indulging his young daughter's whim to pursue a career as a pianist. He had approached Milo with the request that Stani, at the time riding the extraordinary wave of attention following the release of his *Mozart My Way* recording, appear with her in recital. The result had been a stunning pairing of two charismatic and attractive young artists, and Milo had been easily convinced that not only would a joint recording further launch Marcia's career, but it could only serve to enhance Stani's image as well.

If the truth were known, Milo had been in search of another young talent. Stani, who had absorbed his vast energies for so many years, was now taking control of his career, moving in directions of his own choosing and limiting Milo's influence. Marcia, although hardly the prodigy Stani had been, was talented and appealing and captured Milo's imagination. There would never be another Stani Moss, another such phenomenally gifted child who would turn the classical world on its ear, but Milo would never stop striving to take the music he loved to a wider audience, and a pretty young blonde at the keyboard might be just the thing.

By the time they met in Amsterdam in early November, Milo had already been to London, and he was full of the news that Marcia had signed the contract to record with Stani. She had requested a meeting to discuss the music when they stopped over in London at the end of the month. "Her father asked if you would be willing to do a short series of recitals, prior to the recording's release. Nothing formal has been arranged, but I thought it safe to say you would agree."

"I see. So I'll have to be in London at the end of January. When will I be free to go back to New York? I've been talking with Jana about recording my sonata. I can only give Marcia so much time,

Milo. Don't forget there are tour dates in the States set for next spring."

It took only a calculating breath before Milo responded. "You'll be able to do it, Stani. As for Jana, I'm sure she'll make herself available whenever you want her." He could certainly speak for his wife. Jana had, after all, been willing to give up her solo career to work beside Stani during his childhood. Jana, they both knew, could be counted on to do what made everyone most comfortable. "You should certainly be able to return to New York by April."

Emily heard the ragged sigh, before Stani countered, "Mid-March, at the latest. We plan to go home in April for a few weeks. Please don't make commitments without consulting me, Milo. I have my own life to consider now." Reaching for his hand under the tablecloth, Emily gave it a gentle squeeze. The visible tightening along his jaw signaled his mounting frustration.

"I'm sure it can all be arranged to your satisfaction. But we must remember that schedules have to remain flexible if you want to take advantage of these opportunities, my boy." There it was, that subtly prodding reminder that had heretofore ruled Stani's life. Milo, at the same time controlling and encouraging, pointing out ever so politely that he knew what was best.

Emily felt Stani stiffen, and took note of the grimace that twisted his face. His voice, when he spoke, was soft, almost hushed, as always when his emotions were running high. "Recording with Marcia is an opportunity for her, not necessarily for me. I'm doing this as a favor for you, Milo. But I can only do so many favors, and even then I have to have some say in their scope." He took a deep breath, and raised a hand to his left temple. "But let's not discuss it further tonight. I haven't had a night off in over a week. I intend to spend this one with my wife." When he turned to her with a smile, Emily saw the darkening in his eyes, a sign of the growing pain in his head. "If you'll excuse us, I think we'll get a little air and then retire. John, would you mind walking with us? You know how I tend to get turned around in these narrow streets." Out of the corner of her eye, Emily took a moment to check Milo's reaction to their abrupt departure. No indication that he'd seen the pain in Stani's eyes, or noticed the weary edge in his voice.

Once on the street, John draped an arm around Stani's shoulders. "Let it pass, lad. He's just doing what he still sees as his job."

"I know that. But when will he recognize there are limits? I've told him, the final decisions have to be mine. He doesn't listen." Again the hand went to his temple, as if to ward off some anticipated blow.

"Stani, let's just walk and try to relax. You've been working so hard. Can't we take advantage of this time off?" Emily took his arm, setting her stride to match his.

"I'm sorry, love." His lips twisted in a wry grin. "I took the bait, didn't I?" As they walked on in silence, she knew he was still mulling over the conversation. "He's right, you know. Schedules do have to remain flexible. And they can be adjusted. I just don't like being told I'll do things without being asked first. Stubborn, I suppose."

"Stubborn has its merits, darling. Stubby would tell you that. And I've been accused of a little stubborn streak myself." He managed to smile at the reminder of the old white mule who was such a treasured part of their life on the farm.

"Perhaps I should take a page from Stubby's book and just lay back my ears when Milo makes me mad. Or give something a little kick." He tried to laugh at the image, but there was no mistaking the resulting wince. "Ah, well, I'm sure it can be sorted out. Milo will eventually get used to doing things my way, or I'll get used to doing them in spite of him."

"That's a good boy. Now if you don't mind, I'd like to go back to the hotel. I think we're due for an early night." She'd been watching his face for the pallor that foreshadowed a migraine. "John, I think we might want some soda and ice on hand tonight. Could you see to that for me?"

Stani smiled ruefully. "Can't hide anything from you, can I?"

"No. And you shouldn't try to. But I wish you could avoid getting so upset with Milo. I know he would never intentionally cause you this kind of pain." She found herself hoping they would meet up with Milo on the way back. Would he better understand the power he had over Stani, if he saw the pain in his eyes now?

She had helped him onto the bed by the time John brought the ice and soda. Stani swallowed the aspirin without opening his eyes and lay completely still while she applied ice to the scar just above his ear, where the headache always seemed to focus. She thought he might have drifted off, until he stirred, reaching up to lay his hand over hers, pressing it closer to his temple.

"Any better?" The slightest shake of his head answered. "Please take the medication, Stani. It won't hurt for you to sleep late tomorrow." She knew he would resist as long as possible, hating the effects of the narcotic pain killers. When he finally mumbled his agreement, she went in search of the pills.

When he had undressed and crawled beneath the covers, he seemed to drift into a restless sleep. Once the drugs took effect, he might sleep for hours. They would leave him groggy and probably not very happy in the morning, she knew. At least they were not due to leave Amsterdam for two more days. He should be fully recovered by the time he had to perform again. She touched his cheek and smoothed the hair from his forehead, wishing that she could have done more for him. There might never be a way to avoid the conflict that led to these headaches. Not as long as he reacted so strongly to Milo's pressuring. If only Milo could see him now, as she did, laid low by his inability to argue for what he wanted. If he would just give Stani permission to say no, to stand up to him in a disagreement, Milo himself might be able to ease the situation.

Just about to ready herself for bed, she was startled by a knock on the door. Stani had heard it too, he stirred and his eyelids fluttered open for a moment. "I'll get it, darling. You go back to sleep."

When she opened the door a crack, peering out cautiously, Milo greeted her with a smile. "I failed to give Stani the list of music Marcia sent for him to consider. I hoped I might speak to him about it." He looked beyond her into the room, and Emily stepped aside. The door to the bedroom was open and she knew he would be able to see Stani on the bed. As she watched for his reaction, his eyes widened suddenly and he pushed his way past her, dropping his briefcase, and letting out a low cry of warning.

When she turned, Stani was just rising unsteadily to his feet, his head rolling dizzily from side to side. In two strides, Milo had reached him, catching his arm and easing him back onto the bed. For an instant, as their eyes met, Stani seemed to struggle to recognize the man hovering over him.

"Here now, Stani, just lie back. You need to rest, my boy." The tone was at the same time firm and gentle, and Emily was surprised to see Stani obey, falling back on the pillows and closing his eyes.

"Now you see why he hates to take the medication." She stood by as Milo drew up the covers, carefully folding them across Stani's chest.

"Another migraine?" Milo spoke just above a whisper. "But he seemed fine at dinner. What causes these to come on so rapidly?"

Taking his arm, she led him to the doorway. "Tension," she said simply.

He stared back at the still figure on the bed. "Are you saying I caused this?"

"It's not entirely your doing. When Stani feels you're pushing him, ignoring his wishes, he can't bring himself to stand up to you. If he knew how to argue with you, even get angry and shout at you, it would be better for him."

A thoughtful hint of a smile lit his eyes. "Stani shouting at me would be something new. But he can always refuse. He has every right to say no to any suggestion I make. He should know that."

"I'm afraid he still hears your suggestions as demands."

He seemed to mull over what she'd said, gazing back into the bedroom. Without a word, he returned to the bedside, standing over Stani for several minutes, finally laying a hand lightly on his shoulder. "I'll talk to him when he's recovered. I'll try to explain to him that old habits are hard to break, perhaps for both of us. I accept that he's in control of his career now, but at the same time, I still have some responsibility to help him. We should be able to work together, shouldn't we? Without this sort of thing?" He took his hand away, but not before giving Stani's shoulder a gentle squeeze. Something about the gesture moved Emily, raising a lump in her throat at this side of Milo she had never seen.

"I hope so. If you can help him, maybe he can at least learn to say no to you." She smiled wistfully, her eyes going to Stani's sleeping face. "Maybe even get angry and shout at you. He's learned to do a lot of new things in the past year."

Milo let out a long sigh. "I would never knowingly hurt him. *You* know that, don't you?"

"I do, but now we have to convince Stani."

"Maybe together, you and I, we can do that. Will you work with me, Emily?"

She met his eyes, noticing for the first time how weary he seemed, and nodded. "For him, of course I will."

<hr />

Stani slept for almost ten hours, but his sleep was restless, and as a result, Emily kept watch most of the night. When she ordered breakfast late in the morning, he came to the table in a dismal mood. After only a cup of tea and few bites of toast, he pushed back his chair and went to the window, gazing out with a long sigh. "I had the queerest dreams. I hate that drug. It does things to my brain."

"It'll wear off soon. What sort of dreams?"

"I was still recovering, after the accident. For a long time, I had trouble with balance, dizzy spells. I dreamed that I fell and Milo picked me up. He was so gentle, standing over me. He never did that, you know. He never took care of me. I had John for that. Milo would hardly come near me, almost as if he were afraid of me. Or repulsed by me." Dropping his head, he ran his hands into his hair.

Going to him, Emily slid her arms around his waist. "It wasn't a dream, Stani."

"What do you mean?"

"Milo was here last night. You tried to get up. He helped you back to bed. And he was gentle."

He turned, looking into her eyes. "And he was talking? Something about explaining things to me?"

"Yes. Give him a chance, Stani. You still have a lot to learn about each other, even after all these years."

He eyed her skeptically for a moment. "And you had nothing to do with this?"

"If you mean did I call him, no. He just showed up at the right time. But it was good for him to see you like that. I'd been wishing he could understand the effect he can have on you. He really doesn't know how easily he upsets you." Tenderly, she ran her fingers across his brow, smoothing away the furrows. "Now will you try to eat a little more? And then I think we should go back to bed for a while. I didn't get enough sleep, playing nurse to my favorite patient all night."

"I don't have to be somewhere today? I'm sure there's something I have to do." He was visibly struggling to clear his head, running his fingers through his hair again.

"Not until late afternoon. You have an interview here in the hotel, but by then you should be fine. More food and more rest. That's all you need."

"More wife. You're the thing I need most." He sat down, letting her fill his plate and pouring himself more tea. "And I suppose I should talk to Milo at some point. Let him explain things to me?"

"When you're up to it. No rush. I expect Milo's thinking things over this morning, too. Now eat. Wife's orders."

Chapter Four

By the following morning, Stani seemed back to normal. He was determined to get any conversation with Milo behind him before his next performance. "I think I'll invite him to lunch, just the two of us. You won't mind, will you, love?"

"Not at all, but if you come back with a headache, you can be sure I'm going to sit the both of you down and we're going to settle this once and for all. You two are supposed to be partners, which implies equality."

He chuckled, drawing her into his arms. "That sounds very much like a threat. I take it you expect us to settle our differences like gentlemen. Or is twenty paces at dawn an option?"

"Oh, no. No weapons. Just remember both of you are working for the same thing. Stani Moss, our generation's greatest violinist. He deserves the best the two of you can do for him." She kissed his cheek, hugging him tightly. "Be brave, darling. But be fair. Milo cares so much about you."

"So you keep reminding me."

With John as guide, Emily went shopping while Stani and Milo met for lunch. She told John of her hope that Milo at last understood how Stani reacted to his overstepping the boundaries of their partnership. "I really believe he just gets carried away with what he considers opportunities. And Stani might see them the same way if Milo didn't ram them down his throat."

"Maybe they need to take you on as a third partner."

"Maybe they already have. I told Stani that if they don't get it worked out today, and stick to their agreement from here on out, I'll do whatever I have to do to get them to see eye to eye."

John snorted. "Good luck. I've been watching those two for years, and so far, an uneasy truce is the best they seem to manage. Since Stani started to come into his own, Milo can't seem to adjust. And I think he's tried. But if you could see the change the way I do, in Stani, I mean. He's gone from just doing whatever he's told to resisting everything Milo puts to him. In Milo's defense, Stani has been hard to judge at times. A third vote at the table might make the difference, especially such a level-headed one."

"Thank you, John. But I think I'd rather stay out of it, if I can. Besides, I may soon have more pressing responsibilities." She pretended to be absorbed in the clocks on display in a nearby shop window.

"Such as?"

"Oh, you know, changing diapers and midnight feedings." In spite of herself she grinned at up him, watching the look of confusion that slowly turned to realization.

"So soon? I thought just the other night you said. . . ."

"I didn't want to say anything in front of Stani. He already has too much on his mind."

"You are being careful, girl? Stani told me there were some concerns. You even saw a specialist before you were married, I remember."

"And he told me as far as he could see, I was fine. But why do you think I'm telling you? I know you'll watch out for me, John." She hoped her smile was sufficiently confident.

♥

At her first sight of Stani, stretched on the couch with an arm over his eyes, she braced herself for the worst. But he looked up with a one-eyed grin when she laid a gentle hand on his hair. "Hello! I thought you'd never get back. You must have seen every shop in the city."

"Not every one. We had to eat, you know. So, how did it go?" Perching next to him, she studied his face for clues.

"Let's see. Milo apologized, a milestone in itself. Then he implied that I wasn't holding up my end of the partnership. He said I should never just accept his suggestions, that I should question them more. He said I let him take advantage of me."

"Milo said that?" She couldn't hold back a grin.

"Oh, there's more. He said you had suggested I might let myself get angry when I disagreed with him, and if that would help, I was free to do so. He'd rather have me shout at him that see me with a migraine. I nearly choked on my salad! The very idea of his encouraging me to throw a temper tantrum! What on earth did you say to him the other night?"

"Only that it might be better for you if you could get angry and shout at him, rather than keep everything inside and end up with a headache. I can't believe he actually took it all to heart."

"He also said that I could refuse any of his suggestions and he wouldn't be offended. He admitted that he gets carried away with all the opportunities, but he knows I can't be expected to take on every offer. He pointed out that soon I may have a family, and won't want to spend so much time working."

"Sounds as if he's thought of everything."

"There was something else. Something he's never talked about before. He told me he was terrified when he thought I might fall. He says he still has nightmares about the accident." Sudden tears welled in his eyes. "Why is it so hard for me to accept that he does care?"

"I don't know. He couldn't make it clearer, could he?"

"No. And I'm going to try to remember what he said today, the next time I feel he's pushing. It's my own fault, isn't it?"

"He's given you permission to disagree with him. If you don't, then yes, it's your own fault. Even John says you've been hard to judge since you declared your independence. Isn't it possible you've been imagining that he was overstepping, when he didn't mean to be?"

"Are you finding fault with your husband already." He grinned, reaching up to pull her closer.

"If it's in his best interest, I have to be objective, don't I? You're still perfect, don't get me wrong." As she kissed him, she glanced at her watch. "And now my darling husband, it's time for you to get ready do what you do second best."

"Second best?"

"Play your violin. You have a concert tonight, remember. After that, maybe you'll feel up to doing what you do *best*."

"And just what is that?"

"Make love to your wife, of course."

Chapter Five

Stani was ready to go home. Even though London was only a part-time home, at least he would be under his own roof. And there were no more concerts. They would be in one place for ten days, with at least some semblance of a regular schedule. He had been worried that Emily was getting too tired. She'd had a mild case of food poisoning in Copenhagen and it had seemed to linger, affecting her energy and her appetite. She'd been sleeping more than usual, too. He was tired himself, and could well understand how wearing such a long tour could be. At least now they could get to bed, in the same bed, at a decent hour most nights.

Emily had also begun to complain about too much restaurant food, saying she was looking forward to cooking their meals again. He'd teased her that she was gaining weight, and she'd accused him of stuffing her with too many rich desserts. He knew her weakness, she reminded him. Nothing but simple home-cooking for them now, she promised. It would be good, he thought, to live like real people for a change. He was ready to sit by the fire and hold his wife in his arms, just the two of them alone for hours on end.

But there would still be work to do, of course; meetings with Marcia and her father, along with the producer. And the photo shoot for the record jacket had already been scheduled. He dreaded it; all that time posing with Marcia. He would take Emily along, just for good measure. He might be in need of protection from all that blonde enthusiasm.

Emily was anxious to get to London, as well. Her suspicions confirmed, she planned to see a doctor before the flight home. She felt well enough, a little tired and a few bouts of nausea, especially when the odors of certain foods were present. Restaurants were a problem at times. Now she could avoid so much rich food and have time to prepare meals that at least sounded more appetizing. She was hungry much of the time, but at the sight of the food she craved, her desire for it seemed to vanish.

She had talked with John about finding a doctor, and he was doing some research. Since they'd be back in London during the next few months, she wanted to be sure to find someone to follow up with her then. She had insisted that John not mention anything to Stani. He had a full schedule while they were here, and besides, she wanted to wait until they were at home in the valley, before she told him the news. She had it all planned, just the way she would tell him. He should have time to enjoy the moment, not rush off to some appointment as soon as he'd heard.

They settled into the house, with only a day to rest before Stani began the round of meetings. She laughed as she unpacked her clothes in what last spring had been his bedroom. "Remember how embarrassed I was that Jana thought we were sleeping together? And how tortured we were, being together so much of the time?"

"Just take me and be done with it." He stood behind her, gently easing her jacket from her shoulders. "That was by far the most shocking thing a woman had ever said to me." He began to kiss her neck, his hands wandering around her waist. "If you said those words to me now, I might be inclined to oblige you, my love."

"You are the most obliging of husbands, Stani. But tonight I think sleep might be best for both of us. You have a busy week coming up."

"What about you? Do you have plans for these days in London, while your obliging husband keeps his nose to the grindstone?"

"Christmas shopping. I hope to get it all done and shipped before we leave. And I want to look over the house, think about what I might want to do when we come back in January. It's a wonderful house, but if we're going to spend time here, there are a few things I might want to change. With your permission, of course." Stani had been slowly undressing her as she talked, and now she turned in his arms. "Have you heard a thing I said?"

"Of course. You're going shopping and then there's something you want to do to the house in January." He looked up from the lace veiled softness in the open front of her blouse. "Emily, you're the most beautiful woman I've ever seen. But how is it that you're growing more beautiful all the time?"

Wrapping her arms around his neck, she rested her head on his shoulder. "I guess it's all the attention I get from my husband." Gently, her fingers began to weave into the thick waves at the back of his head.

"You're sure you just want to sleep tonight?" There was no mistaking the huskiness in his voice.

"Eventually."

The photo shoot was scheduled for Saturday morning at Marcia's home in Kensington. The music room had been described as huge, with the grand piano situated in front of towering windows hung with red velvet draperies. It would provide the perfect ambiance, Marcia had said, and she would not feel so self-conscious posing in her own home. Emily had laughed outright at the idea of Marcia experiencing any sort of shyness, given her lack of inhibition on the concert stage.

Stani had been given specific instructions on what to bring, tails, of course, and something casual. As they dressed that morning, he grumbled at having to make a decision. "Marcia said jeans and a white shirt, or all black. Which do you think would be more likely to be taken seriously?'

Emily, lounging on the bed watching him stare into his closet, was already dressed, and she noticed that his eyes repeatedly went to the deeply ruffled neckline of the blouse she had chosen to wear with a tailored black pantsuit. Clearly, he found the view preferable to the rows of slacks and sweaters in his own wardrobe. "I wish we were taking pictures of you today. You look good enough to eat."

"Thank you. Maybe you'll be able to take your eyes off Marcia this time. And I think all black. It certainly fits your image. And your closet's full of it. Black will stand out against those red drapes she was cooing about. And for goodness sake, don't forget your shoes!"

He laughed, taking one last look at the enticingly visible curves before turning back to the closet. "We're using the same photographer, you know. Marcia was impressed with the Mozart cover."

Now it was Emily who laughed. "Marcia and every other woman in the world. You promised you'd never do that again, remember?" The stir over Stani's image following the release of his Mozart variations had very nearly overshadowed his debut as a composer. In particular, the fact that he had appeared barefoot on the cover had resulted in his being acclaimed not only as a superstar, but as a sex symbol.

He blushed to the roots of his auburn curls at the reminder. "Never fear, but this may be humiliating enough, just being photographed alongside Marcia. She has a way of making everything seem somehow provocative."

At the puzzled little frown on his face, Emily giggled. "I'll be there to protect you, darling. Don't worry. But for goodness sake, try not to smile at her so much. She's easily encouraged, you know."

When they arrived at the imposing townhouse, which Marcia had described as a "coming out gift from daddy," and were led to the music room by a very gracious housekeeper, Marcia was already deep in conversation with the photographer. Her father, Lord Strathmoore, greeted them warmly, offering tea and leading Emily to a chair. "You can watch from here, my dear. These things do take some time, I understand." As he directed Stani and John to a room where Stani could change, Emily thought he seemed the sort of man who might be more comfortable in a less elegant setting. The deep tan on his rather homely face suggested hours spent in the out-of-doors, far from this sort of grandeur.

As Stani followed her father out of the room, Marcia called to him. "Let's do the formal wear first, Stani. I thought we'd do some of both and see what we like best." Clearly, she had a vision for what she wanted, Emily mused. The shy little girl of that first rehearsal was apparently gone forever. She was dressed today in a clinging gold gown designed to show off every one of her abundant assets to fullest advantage, her blonde curls cascading over the expanse of bare white skin. Unconsciously, Emily tossed her head, drawing the length of her own straight dark mane over one shoulder. When she realized a moment later what she'd done, she laughed to herself. No more need to worry about Marcia capturing Stani's attention for long. He seemed to be more attentive than ever these days. She wondered if he might have sensed the changes in her, without even knowing her secret.

While they waited for Stani, she noticed the photographer turning his lens toward her. After a few minutes, he approached and clicked several frames. "You're a great subject, in your black and white. Have you ever done any modeling?"

She laughed. "No. And I bet you say that to lots of women. A good line to drum up business."

"Maybe. But in your case, I'm serious. If you wouldn't mind going over there by the window?" He followed her and continued to focus, taking a number of shots before Stani returned.

"Your wife is a photographer's dream. Get in there with her and I'll take a few of the two of you."

They stood together in the soft morning light, framed by the huge windows. With a minimum of direction, the photographer captured them in a sequence of poses, finally instructing Stani to kiss his wife as if he really loved her. Stani laughed. "Easy enough."

"I'll get you copies of these. No charge. But you might think about letting me do a layout of you two. I'm sure one of the pictorials would love it. Two beautiful people in love and one of you a superstar. I promise I'll make it painless."

Marcia had been waiting with a patient smile glued to her face, but now she took Stani's arm and led him to the piano. He unpacked his violin and stood ready for direction. Returning to her chair, Emily settled in to watch what promised to be an entertaining production. Aware that she was suddenly very hungry, she sipped the now tepid tea, hoping to still the gnawing in her stomach. There were scones on the tea tray and she nibbled at one, as she watched the photographer work. He was really very good, she decided. The way he posed the two of them, Marcia with her golden beauty against the black of Stani's tailcoat and the deep red of his hair, created an instant work of art. They stood back to back, then leaning against the piano, framed by the windows, and finally with Marcia at the keyboard and Stani with his violin tucked, bow raised. There was no denying they made a handsome pair. Emily found herself wondering if these pictures might not prove to be almost as sensational as that other one, of Stani in his billowing white shirt and his bare feet, had been.

When the two of them went off to change, the photographer, who introduced himself this time simply as Nigel, asked if he might get one more shot of Emily. He led her to the piano and without a word, put his hands on her waist and lifted her onto the closed keyboard, positioning her feet on the bench. He seemed to effortlessly drape her over the instrument, arranging her hair over one shoulder, adjusting her arms and legs until he was satisfied with the result. While Emily was fascinated by the ease with which he worked, she was at the same time embarrassed by all the attention and felt a rise of color in her cheeks. Marcia's father was standing by watching with interest, and even the housekeeper had come to observe from the doorway.

Nigel instructed her not to smile, just to stare into the lens with "those amazing eyes." He clicked off several frames, then suggested she look off into the distance. Her gaze fell on Stani, just returning to the room. He paused, flashing a grin at the sight of her. In spite of Nigel's orders, she returned his smile. "Gorgeous!" The camera clicked again, and Nigel held out his hand to help her down. "I think we caught something special there. You were glowing!"

She felt herself blush again. "I've never done anything like that.

You made it surprisingly easy."

"You're a natural. If you ever want to make up a portfolio, I'd love to work with you."

Emily made a little face and laughed. "The last thing I have time for is having my picture taken. But it was fun. Thank you." She went back to her chair, aware of Marcia standing by waiting to take center stage again. Now dressed in a very tight white slacks and a fuzzy white sweater, she was barefoot. Stani was in black, the slim trousers and V-neck sweater that had been his daytime uniform for years. The tiny gold cross, his last year's birthday gift from Emily, could be seen against the dark copper curls in the V, and he had pushed the sleeves of his sweater high on his forearms. He was utterly masculine standing next to the petite Marcia in her soft sweater, her hair tumbling around her shoulders. Nigel was clearly excited by the possibilities.

The poses were more intimate now. He seated the two of them back to back on the piano bench, instructing Marcia to hug her knees to her chest and lean against Stani, then folding Stani's arms over his chest, and pressing their heads close together. The effect was such that Marcia appeared sweetly kittenish, while Stani was stern and strong. Nigel next set Marcia on the keyboard, moving Stani between her knees. She draped her arms around his neck and placed her face close to his. When the camera lens clicked, Marcia was smiling impishly, her cheek pressed against Stani's.

As she watched, Emily was aware of a growing queasiness. She was painfully hungry, and the dry scone seemed to stick in her throat. She sipped the last of the cold tea and knew without a doubt that she was going to be sick. As quietly as she could, she rose and dashed for the door, where the housekeeper stood watching.

The woman seemed to know instinctively what she needed, leading her swiftly to a powder room off the hallway. As Emily retched over the toilet, the housekeeper pressed a wet towel to the back of her neck, introduced herself as Mrs. Dowd and clucked her tongue sympathetically. "Poor dear, how far along are you?"

When she could speak again, Emily tried to downplay the episode. "It was just a little bit warm in there. I'm fine now.

But the knowing smile said she hadn't been in the least convincing. "Haven't told him yet, dear? Well, he'll guess soon enough, if he has eyes. You're the very picture of a mother-to-be. That's the glow that young man was talking about. Now you just come with me and I'll fix you a nice cool drink. Are you at all hungry? Sometimes a bite to eat will settle things down." She led the way to the kitchen, chuckling as she went. "I remember when her ladyship was first expecting little Marcia. Sick, oh my word! Couldn't eat anything but wheat crackers for weeks. Wheat crackers and ginger ale."

When Stani came in search of her, she was seated at the kitchen table with a chicken sandwich and a tall glass of club soda. "Are you all right? I couldn't imagine where you'd gotten off to!" His worried look faded when he saw the sandwich. He would not question her ever-present appetite, she knew.

"I was hungry. Mrs. Dowd was kind enough to fix me some lunch. Are you all done?"

He rolled his eyes. "Yes. I can't imagine we'll use any of those last shots. They had nothing to do with music, I'm sure. I'll help John pack up my things and come back for you. You're sure you're okay? Marcia thought you looked ill."

"I'm fine. You know me, just starving." Over Stani's shoulder, she caught the amused gaze of the housekeeper.

"All the same, I wish you'd see a doctor. Whatever you ate in Copenhagen seems to have affected your appetite in the strangest way. You're either not hungry at all, or starving." He left the room and Emily stifled a giggle.

"I don't think he has a clue. Do you think it's wrong not to tell him?"

"He's certainly in for a shock when you do. Men can be such slow tops about such things. But he seems a nice boy. He'll be happy, won't he, about the news?"

Emily smiled. "Oh, yes. He'll be happy. He's been talking about babies for months. He just doesn't seem to know anything about how they get here."

Chapter Six

Stani had another meeting scheduled on the following Monday afternoon with Marcia and her father. John had made an appointment for Emily to see a doctor he'd been assured was the best to be had, using Stani's name to get her in on such short notice. When Stani kissed her goodbye that morning, she felt just a twinge of guilt. It would be unfair, she told herself, to distract him when he was so involved with this project. When she was sure and when they had more time, then she would tell him.

Dr. Hennessy was a pleasant, down-to-earth man who reminded her a little of Dr. Maurice, the trusted specialist who had cared for her mother during the years of recurring illness. He had seen many women through safe deliveries and nothing seemed out of the ordinary in her case, except that she must be mistaken about her date of conception. He was certain she was at least ten weeks along. She told him that that was highly unlikely. Ten weeks ago, she had been a new bride, barely on her honeymoon. He had smiled knowingly. "Either you and your husband are both very healthy, or you are going to have an exceptionally large baby. Of course, there's always the possibility of multiple birth."

"Multiple, as in twins?"

"At least. We'll just have to wait a bit longer to see, won't we?"

He had assured her that she could travel safely until the end of the second trimester, but that by then Stani would have to learn to do without her for a while. He also suggested she be prepared for the possibility of a Cesarean section. "You're a very slender young woman, and your pelvis is narrow. Just be open to the idea. It's quite the rage with wealthy women these days."

She made an appointment for January and left the office wishing she'd brought Stani with her. Hearing the doctor confirm what she already knew had been more unnerving than she'd expected.

When John asked if all was well, she smiled and said of course. When he asked again, this time in a tone that reminded her he was a cop and knew a half-truth when he heard one, she replied, "Yes, everything is fine. But now I know I have to tell Stani. I shouldn't have done that without him."

"But you're well and there's no problem with the baby?" John stumbled over the last words and shook his head. "That sounds terrifying to me. I can only imagine how it will sound to Stani."

She laughed, patting his arm. "You'll get used to it. And yes, we're fine. He said I can travel without any fear, at least for a few more months. Let's go home, John. Suddenly, shopping has lost its appeal."

A large manila envelope had been left on the doorstep. It was hand addressed to "Stani and Emily," and in the upper left corner was a stamped logo, "Nigel Barton, Fine Photography." She glanced up and down the block, wondering if the person who had delivered it might still be there, and to her surprise, a car parked across the street suddenly sped away. Coincidence, she thought. If Nigel had been the one to bring these pictures, he would have stayed to visit, hoping to persuade her to pose for more, no doubt.

The photographs were impressive. Once again Nigel had proven himself an insightful artist. Just as he had previously captured Stani's inherent sexuality, now his camera had brought into focus the two of them at this precise point in their life together. These images, taken when their first child was just beginning to grow inside her, depicted precisely the love they shared at this moment in time. He had forever captured the intimate gleam in their eyes, the tenderness of their smiles for one another, and the perfect symmetry of their bodies as they stood in each other's arms.

Stani phoned to say he was going to have dinner with Milo. "I'm sorry, love, but if I finish tonight, I can have all of tomorrow free. Don't wait up for me if you're too tired."

"I'll wait up. Just don't be too late."

She took a long bath, trying to calm the nerves that gnawed at her stomach. She had imagined them curled together on the couch before a crackling fire in the front room of the farmhouse, in the same place Stani had first told her he loved her. But she knew she couldn't wait. She needed his support, and he needed to know he was going to be a father. Just how one said the words, or even made the implication, she wasn't at all certain. But she was sure she didn't want to be retching over the toilet when he came home.

She had just tied the sash of her robe when she heard Stani come in.

Going to the dresser, she picked up her hairbrush, taking deep breaths and saying a little prayer for good measure.

He came into the room, his step light and a smile on his face. The look in his eyes, when he caught sight of her, turned decidedly warm. "I'm glad you waited up." He came to stand behind her, meeting her gaze in the mirror. "Did you have a good day?"

"Yes, and you?" She was aware of the sudden pounding of her heart, and wondered if he might not be able to hear it.

"Fine. Got lots done and now I can stop wondering what new surprise Marcia may have waiting for me. We gave the final list to the producer. No more debating what might best show off her skills or shortage thereof." He took the brush from her hand and began to slowly run it through the length of her hair.

"So now you're all mine again?" Her lids drooped with pleasure.

"All yours." Lifting the hair to one side, he laid a kiss on her neck.

Emily untied the sash and shrugged the robe off her shoulders. When it fell to the floor at her feet, a little chill ran through her. This would be the moment. In the soft light, the sheen of her nightgown accentuated every curve. There was no hiding now. He would see for himself. She watched his face, wanting to remember the instant he realized.

His eyes half closed, he was preoccupied with slowly running his hands down her body. As his fingers encircled her waist, gliding along the silky gown, they came to rest just over the barely perceptible little bulge. She felt him draw in his breath as his eyes widened, scanning her reflection. Down and then up to meet her face. She smiled as his color deepened, then paled. His lips parted as if to speak, and closed abruptly. He was holding his breath, she realized, the look of confusion turning to wonder. Laying her hands over his, she pressed them to her body. "Say hello, Papa."

He gasped for air. "Emily, how? When?"

She laughed softly. "I don't think I have to explain how, do I? And as to when, apparently very quickly. The doctor swears I'm ten weeks along."

"Doctor? You've seen a doctor already?"

"Just today. I wanted to tell you after we were home again, but I couldn't wait any longer. It's growing too fast."

Now he was staring at her reflection, understanding for the first time the changes he had found so enticing. Again his color rose. "And all this time, you've let me make love to you. Is that safe?"

"Of course it is."

"And you didn't have food poisoning?"

"No. Misnamed morning sickness, it seems to happen any time. It should get better soon. Usually after the first three months, it goes away."

"Three months? Ten weeks? When is it due?" He was slowly grasping the reality, trying to come to grips with what this meant for their lives. The misty image of sweet little infants was now a solid roundness in his wife's belly, heart-stoppingly wonderful and frightening at the same time.

"June. Which means we'll have to be settled in New York this spring. I think that would be the best place to have it."

"June? That's just next summer!"

She laughed again. "It only takes nine months, darling." Turning to put her arms around him, she urged him toward the bed. "You look as if you need to sit down, Stani. Is it really such a shock?"

"I've been blind, haven't I? I should have known. I'm so sorry, darling girl. Here you've been ill and I've been dragging you around with me. We should go home now, so you can rest. Or is it safe for you to fly? Maybe we should stay here." His thoughts were racing now.

"No, of course we're going home. The doctor says I can fly until at least six months. Stani, I'm not ill. I'm pregnant. There's a big difference."

"He thinks you're all right? No problems?"

"I'm fine. He thinks we might have a big baby on the way. But it's too early to say. In the meantime, all I have to do is eat right and take my vitamins. And apparently educate my husband on this new subject. Never had a pregnant wife before, have you?"

He grinned. "Hardly. Are there books for the totally ignorant expectant male?"

"I'm sure there are. But you'll learn soon enough. Now that I can share all the midnight cravings and strange little sensations with you. John thinks you'll be terrified, but I know you'll get used to it."

"John knows?" His grin turned to a frown.

"I had to have someone to watch out for me, didn't I? I was trying to spare you, darling, until I was absolutely sure. You've had so much on your mind."

He pulled her into his arms. "Oh, Emily, you should have told me. Nothing I had on my mind could have been more important than this. This is my child, too, remember? I may be ignorant, but I want to be with you every step of the way." He drew back, laying his hand over the little bulge again. "My child. My own family. Do you know how incredibly wonderful that is?"

"Yes, I think I do. I knew you'd be happy."

"Happy?" His smile was so unequivocally loving, as he looked again at the roundness beneath his hand, she felt tears welling. "First you love me, want to share this crazy life with me. Now you tell me that as soon as we made love, we created this new life. Happy is hardly the word for what I feel. John's right, it's terrifying. And utterly miraculous." Gently, he gathered her to him, easing her onto the bed at his side. "I promise, there is nothing more important I could ever think about, no music, no schedules, no concerts, nothing. Do you understand? I want to know everything, the minute you do, about this baby. Don't protect me from this, please?"

"I promise. Now, will you kiss me? And then I think I'd better eat something. Or I may be dashing to the bathroom again."

"Ugh! Are you saying I should have been grateful for a little protection?"

"Too late now. Your days of blissful ignorance are over, my darling husband. How do you feel about black olives and chocolate ice cream? I've been craving some all night."

Stani had been impressed with the photographs. So much so that when Nigel called to say he had contacted one of the major pictorial magazines and they were interested in doing a piece on this latest phase of Stani's life, he agreed to talk with him about the idea. It would involve an interview and photo shoot, which could be done when they returned to London in January. Milo thought it an excellent idea, coming at a time when Stani would be performing with Marcia and ahead of the release of his own compositions in the following months. The human interest aspect of his happy life as a newly-wed and expectant father could only enhance his image.

"He's already looking forward to having this new angle to exploit, but I think he's also genuinely excited for us. I know it would be pure publicity, but it might also be fun. At least we'd have a choice about the photographs that are printed, instead of being at the mercy of the photo hounds. And I don't mind my fans getting a close up look at my bride." They had finished dinner and retreated to the little sitting room, settling in front of the empty fireplace. After several days of rehearsals with Marcia, Stani was looking forward to spending a few hours at home with his wife.

"Even if your bride is starting to look a bit thick around the middle? At the rate I'm going, by January, there'll be no hiding this little lump." Emily patted her waist fondly.

"By January, you'll be even more beautiful, if that's possible. You're sure you'll feel up to it?"

"Of course. I'm feeling a little better already. I told you, after the third month, this silly nausea should go away. And that's only a couple more weeks, if the doctor knew what he was talking about. By January, I'll be back to normal. Just eating for two, which won't be at all unusual."

"I just worry that you'll overdo. All this traveling, and Christmas coming up. I know you and Christmas, Emily. None of that wearing yourself out, do you hear? Have you finished your shopping?"

"Yes, sir. And this year, I'll have no opportunities to volunteer, no cherubs or Christmas Families. Just a stopover in New York, and then home, where I promise to let my idle husband wait on me hand and foot. How does that sound?"

"Perfect. If only I thought you'd stick to it. Don't force me to lock you in the house and turn away all visitors. And you know everyone will be coming in the front door unannounced as soon as they hear you're home. Especially once the news gets out about this little lump." He laid his hand on her belly as though to protect it from too many curious neighbors.

"It'll be so good to get back home. But first we do have to see about the loft while we're in New York. I hate to think of all that needs to be done. And then there's a lot I want to do here, when we come back. For a woman who never stays at home for long, I have an awful lot of decorating to do. Did you ask Milo about the furniture here?"

"He says the house was furnished when he bought it. It was purely an investment he made when he saw how much money I was making on that first tour. You're free to do what you want. He has no interest in anything here."

"Not even Beethoven? I thought surely he'd have some attachment to him." The bust, which stood guard in the foyer, seemed to be the only original touch in the otherwise unimaginatively decorated house.

"Apparently not. But I kind of like him. He's very imposing, right there by the front door."

"Then he can stay. I'll have plenty to keep me busy, while you and Lady Marcia go off on your little tour. Unless you want me to come along and protect you."

"Ha! She's not interested in my body. Only my reputation. And John can keep me safe, I'm sure. But I don't much like the idea of leaving you alone. I think we'll hire a housekeeper as soon as we're back. A kindly lady to watch over you, with orders to keep you from lifting anything heavier than a feather pillow."

"And we'll have to think about a nanny. We'll need someone who wants to see the world from the inside of a hotel room."

Stani shook his head, grinning. "You realize I will have gone from being a complete loner to a man with a family and herds of staff in just over a year. What have you done to me, Emily?"

"I think I fell in love with you. You don't really mind, do you?"

"Not at all. I'm just a bit overwhelmed by all this domesticity. And I never had to think about being someone's employer. How does one go about finding housekeepers and nannies, anyway?"

"Ask John. He seems to be very good at such things. He not only found me a doctor, he did a background check on him and set up the appointment. He'll know what we should do."

"Can he find decorators and furniture movers, too? Not to mention we'll need a gardener. Have you seen how everything has grown up out back? How much does a gardener get paid, or a housekeeper, for that matter? And then there's all the baby gear to buy. Do you know where to shop for that sort of thing?" He stopped to look down at her. "What are you giggling about?"

Emily struggled to bring her laughter under control. "You, Stani. You, suddenly realizing what it means to have a baby. It changes everything, doesn't it? It's easy to talk about being parents. But the truth is it's not just the baby. It's all that comes with it, houses and helpers and gear. Kind of scary, isn't it? But there are months yet before we need all those things. Let's just relax and enjoy this time, when all our baby needs is you and me loving it." She drew his hand back over her waist. "And each other. I love you so much, Stani."

"I never thought I could love you more than I did when we were married, but now I don't believe there's any limit to how much love can grow. I want so much to take care of you, work hard for you and give you everything you need. You have to tell me how to do that. Teach me how to be the best husband and father I can be."

"You'll do just fine. But there is one thing you could do for me tonight."

"Anything." He looked into her eyes expectantly.

"I'd really love a ham sandwich. And maybe some strawberry ice cream. I'm starving."

He laughed, hugging her close. "No olives?"

"Ooh, no. I'm off olives. But a couple of those gherkins, you know, the little sweet ones, might be nice."

Chapter Seven

By the time they reached New York in early December, Emily indeed seemed to be over the nausea, but she was tired much of the time. She had slept during most of the flight from London and then taken a nap before dinner. They postponed a trip to the loft until the next morning, and after a hearty meal in the hotel restaurant, Stani had tucked her into bed by nine o'clock. He made phone calls, setting up necessary meetings with various people, worried that he might have to leave her alone too much of the time if she wasn't up to going out. Responsibility weighed heavily on his shoulders, as much as he welcomed it. Inept, he admitted. He had no training for such things, and his brain seemed to be too easily overwhelmed with the mix of doing what he wanted for his family and what he knew he must do to meet the demands of his career.

The morning dawned gray and rainy. When they arrived at the loft apartment which had been their wedding gift from Milo, the place they had so clearly envisioned as their home in the city, they were both disheartened by the sight that met their eyes when the elevator doors opened. The cavernous space, with its exposed ductwork and huge windows, was cold and echoed uninvitingly. In the center of the floor was a disorderly pile of shipping boxes, containing the assortment of wedding gifts they had hoped might inspire the eventual décor of the apartment.

"We don't even have a bed or a chair, Stani." Emily stood at the edge the room, reluctant to venture too far inside.

"I know, darling. It's a lot to think about." For once, he was at a loss to offer any sort of encouragement. The undertaking seemed too huge to attempt even under the best of circumstances. One glance at the troubled look in her eyes and the droop to her shoulders was enough to prompt him to take her arm and turn back toward the elevator.

"Maybe we should hire a professional. Would that be too extravagant?" He thought he detected the faintest note of enthusiasm in her voice.

"Of course not. If that's what you want. And we can always stay at the hotel, when we come back in the spring. You'll have time then to decide."

"You're right. I'm just so tired now. By then, maybe it won't seem so enormous. But it would be lovely to just have it all done. Wave a magic wand and just move in." Looking back, she heaved a long sigh.

Steering her onto the elevator, Stani laughed softly. "Alacazam? Don't worry about it now, darling girl. We'll sort it out later. Let's have lunch and then you can take a nap, while I go off to meet with your favorite conductor. Do you think Bernie will be surprised to hear I'm going to be somebody's father?"

Stani had given it a good bit of thought, debating both sides of the issue before calling Peg. He had hoped for the day when he would not automatically turn to her, when she would not seem to be the obvious answer to his problems. But at this juncture, when there were several reasons her particular talents would perfectly mesh with his needs, it seemed foolish to look elsewhere. She would certainly be more than willing, given their history, to come to his rescue once again. When he'd phoned her at home, she'd expressed both surprise and delight, and insisted that of course, he must come right over. She couldn't think of anyone she'd rather spend her morning with.

He wasn't sure why he hadn't told Emily or John where he was going. Of course, they wouldn't have seen anything wrong with his turning to Peg for advice. No matter that at one time he and Peg had shared a more intimate relationship. Emily knew very well that was long past. No matter the somewhat awkward fact that Peg and John had for a time been likewise involved. John would be the last one to expect Stani's association with Peg to end on that account. Stani had always, and probably *would* always, rely on Peg for certain things. Now, as he took a cab to the familiar address, he felt just the tiniest bit uncomfortable. It wasn't that he had anything to hide, other than the fact that he hated to admit Peg Shannon was the only woman in New York with the perfect mix of brains and generosity to satisfy his present set of dilemmas. It was just that he would have much preferred a more public meeting, rather than find himself knocking at Peg's door on a rainy morning, entering to the haughty greeting of her butler, and being shown into the private sanctum of her sitting room, where she would no doubt meet him with her customary warm welcome. Peg, if the truth be told, represented the past Stani often wished he'd never lived. And yet he felt sure she had a well-defined place mapped out in his future, one he would most likely be grateful for, regardless of the discomforting reminder of her presence there.

Just as he had expected, Peg had all the answers easily at hand. When he left their meeting, he felt he had accomplished a great deal. Not only had they discussed and narrowed down the list of potential officers for the board of directors of his newly formed charitable foundation, but Peg had agreed to contact the individuals on his behalf. "I know these people personally, Stani. It'll be much simpler for me to talk with them. Most of them owe me a favor or two, anyway."

"You know how pathetic I am at talking to strangers. You're saving me a lot of stammering over the phone to people who may or may not even know who I am."

Peg had laughed. "Of course they know who you are. Stani, get used to it. You're a famous man. These people will be flattered you even asked them to do this job. You're not some teenaged wonder boy anymore. You've made your mark."

He had been embarrassed by something in Peg's tone, as if she might wish he *were* that boy. That boy she had first taken on as a hopeless misfit in the elegant world of classical performance, and transformed into the showman he was now; that boy she had taken into her bed, as if sexuality were one more subject to be taught, along with poise and style. Now, as they sat together in the same room where they had shared many of those early lessons, Stani forced himself to believe that she must have put all that aside, as he had, and was prepared to go forward as though nothing more had ever existed between them.

He reminded himself that she was an expert at this kind of organization, and he needed her help now. When he told her so, she laughed again. "I'd hate to think I'd done all I could for you. We made a good team, Stani. Surely we can still work together on whatever terms your life now dictates." There, she had said it as plainly as was necessary. The past was what it had been, but she could adapt to his future, in the name of their friendship. He gave her a grateful smile, hoping that was sufficient response to her gesture.

"There's one more thing you might be able to help me with, actually. How would I go about finding a decorator to do some work on the loft?"

"What needs to be done?" There was an unmistakable spark in her bright blue eyes.

"Pretty much everything. I'm afraid it's going to be more than Emily can take on just now. I'd like to at least have it livable by the time we come back in March. You know, a bed and a place to sit. And a table to eat on. But by then, I'm sure she shouldn't be worrying about things like shopping for furniture." At the questioning raise of her brows, he grinned. "She's pregnant, Peg. Due in June."

The resulting squeal brought the butler shuffling past the door. "Oh, my God, Stani! That's wonderful! And of course she shouldn't have to worry about anything. I'd love to help. I can take care of everything for you." She turned to a fresh sheet on her notepad and clicked her pen in preparation. "Just give me an idea of what you had in mind for the apartment."

He tried to think of anything they had talked about. "We sent a lot of the wedding gifts, art work and books and dishes. The painting you gave us. I guess we thought they might inspire something. They're all piled in the middle of the floor now."

"What style does Emily prefer? Modern, French Provincial, English Country?" Peg smiled encouragingly, as he wracked his brain.

"Antiques. She likes antiques, the sort of thing at the farm. She said they came from France with someone in her mother's family. And she liked the antiques in the London house, too. And the bed in our hotel in Paris." He was warming to his subject. "She was wild about that. One of those carved affairs that curve around at the head and foot. You know the sort of thing. And I know she loves red. The drapes in the front room at the farm are a sort of garnet color, which she said was her favorite."

"Surely not all red?" Peg was rapidly making a list.

"No. But deep colors. Her bedroom was done in gemstone colors. The curtains were sapphire blue, and there was a quilt with red and purple and gold. But she did the new kitchen in yellow." He held out his hands, at a loss for more.

"So it's safe to say she likes color, as opposed to neutrals, and antiques as opposed to contemporary furniture."

"I suppose so. Will a decorator be able to tell anything from all that?" He looked at her list, which was amazingly long.

"Oh, yes. Don't worry about a thing. I can handle this for you, Stani. When you come home in the spring, you'll have a place to sleep and sit and eat. I promise. Do you have a budget in mind?"

"A budget?"

"How much do you want to spend? How priceless do you want these antiques to be?" Peg grinned at his confusion.

"Not priceless. But nice certainly, good quality. And I think things that children can't hurt. Sturdy. Easy to keep clean. Don't you think?"

"Childproof." Peg wrote the word in big letters across the top of the page.

"Just have the bills sent to the office here. I'll let the accountant know what I'm doing. Here's the address and the agent's number." He took her pen and added to the bottom of the list. "If there are questions, just write to me. We'll be in Virginia until mid-January, then in London. I don't know how to thank you, Peg. I haven't a clue how to go about this sort of thing, but I know Emily will be relieved to have it done. She said she wished she could just wave a magic wand and move in."

"Consider it done. And just concentrate on taking good care of her, Stani. She's that perfect partner I knew you'd find some day." Again, something in her tone suggested she recalled the moment she had first told him that. A natural lover, she had said. Someday, she had assured him, he would make one special woman the finest of partners. She had been in his arms that afternoon in London, just after they had first become lovers. Now she smiled and a little shudder lifted her shoulders. "A father, Stani. You'll make a wonderful father, I just know it. I'm so happy for you."

He left the brownstone thinking what an exceptional woman Peg Shannon was, finding himself grateful, as he had always been, for her devotion to him and relieved that there would be no tension between them now. If there had been, he would have found a way to manage without her special talents, but the thought was more than a little bit daunting. As it was, not only had she relieved him of the burden of soliciting help from strangers, but she would contact a decorator. When they came back to New York, he would be able to surprise Emily with the results. Of course, if she didn't like what had been done, it could be changed over time. But at least there would be a home to come to, not just a hotel suite. He could picture her smile and the sweet kisses he would enjoy for having pulled off such a thing on his own. His step was definitely lighter, as he entered the hotel again.

When he let himself into the suite, he was met by two pair of expectant eyes. For just an instant, he focused on keeping the story straight. Not to say too much, but there was really nothing to hide.

"Well, lad, you certainly gave me the slip this time. What had you up and out so early?" He had the instant impression that John was speaking for the two of them. Emily, curled in an armchair with a cup of tea, still in her robe, was merely staring, waiting.

"I had a meeting with Peg this morning. About the foundation. You remember, love, I told you I wanted to get some names from her. When I called her she suggested I come to the brownstone." He looked meaningfully in John's direction. "I thought you might prefer not to go, so I called a cab." The point was clearly taken.

"Satisfying? Your meeting, I mean." Carefully setting her cup on the table next to her chair, Emily stretched her arms above her head, lifting her hair and letting it fall in a smooth cascade around her shoulders, a gesture she knew could take his breath away.

He grinned. "Yes. We accomplished a lot. The board of directors should be in place by June, so that we can award the first scholarships. The Haynes-Moss Foundation for the Arts will finally be up and running. Of course, you may have to vote in absentia this year." Crossing the room, he pulled her to her feet and into his arms. "You're looking much brighter this morning. Feeling better?"

"Oh, yes. And I'm sick to death of just hanging around here. What are you doing for the rest of the day?" Her arms twined around his neck, her fingers ruffling his curls.

"Errands. Manny and Marius. Want to come along?" He lifted her hair, nuzzling her ear. From his chair, John let out a humph. Not precisely disapproving, just reminding them they were not alone before things got out of hand.

"I suppose you'll want me to drive you. I think I'll just go downstairs, until you two are ready." He left, not sure they had taken notice.

While Emily dressed, Stani stretched on the bed watching. As she turned in front of the mirror, studying her profile, he grinned. "You're not worried about losing your figure, are you?"

"No. But I am worried about not being able to button my winter coat. Maybe Manny could make me something. I doubt I'll find anything full enough off the rack. I think I'll ask him. And I want to get my hair cut, too."

For a moment, he was sure he had heard wrong. "No! Oh, Emily, not your hair!" He was on his feet beside her, his hand going protectively to the dark length.

"Not all of it, silly. But at least a few inches. It takes so long to dry. And it's gotten so heavy I can hardly put it up anymore. You'll never miss a few inches, I promise." The toss of her head effectively ended the discussion.

At Manny Weinberg's little shop, they were met with the usual warm welcome. While Manny fitted yet another in a long line of tailcoats and chatted with Stani about the European tour, Emily browsed the bolts of fabric. Finally deciding on a royal blue boiled wool, Manny took pencil and paper and sketched a long coat, high-waisted with a full skirt and, after a moment's consideration, added a fluffy fur collar. "Gray fox, I think, to match your eyes. And a hat, too, yes?" Manny studied the sketch over the top of his glasses, finally nodding. "Stunning. We'll cut in plenty of fullness, so you can wear it all winter. What do you say, Stani?"

"Gorgeous. One of a kind."

"And the coat, do you like that, too?" Manny grinned, watching fondly the way his young friend stared into his wife's eyes. After a moment, he went on. "I might suggest something else for you, Mrs. Stani. I could make some nice trousers and jackets for you as well. Like what you are wearing now, but with room to grow." He eyed her black slacks and long plaid vest.

Stani was immediately taken with the idea. When Manny had been told of Emily's condition, his smile had been momentarily tearful. "Such happiness, Stani, after so much hurting. I remember so well how it was, when you first went back into the concert hall. But now you are well and happy and soon you will be a papa!" He knew the clothes would be sewn with genuine affection. At his nod, Manny pulled out swatches for Emily to consider, reminding her of how damp and cold England could be in winter. "Nice soft worsted. And silk shirts, full here, you see." He demonstrated on his own rotund middle and Emily giggled.

"Bigger, I think, Manny. Just to be sure."

When the choices had been made, they had rushed to the hairdresser, laughing that the baby was already costing then a sizable sum. "But you'll be the best tailored mother-to-be in London, darling girl. No one else will have such a distinctive wardrobe. And there'll be a little love sewn in for good measure. He's a nice man. We've been together for a long time. Now about this haircut. Can't I talk you out of it?"

"No, I don't think so. We'll see what Marius recommends. He does such a good job with your hair. You should trust him to do the same with mine."

"He doesn't know how beautiful yours looks spread on the pillow beside me. And I'm not about to try to explain that to him."

Marius, who came from the back of the salon with a crow of welcome, listened for only a moment before clapping his hands at Emily's request. "I knew one of these days all that weight would be too much. Of course, we'll cut it, my dear. Stani, shame on you! How can you ask her to carry pounds and pounds of hair on that slender little neck?" He was rapidly steering Emily into the chair, snapping out a cape and sweeping it over her with a grand gesture. For a moment, he lifted and eyed the thick length of hair, tilting his head first this way and that. Drawing his shears from his shirt pocket with a flourish, he held them high, as if waiting for some lightning bolt of inspiration.

Before Stani could protest further, the cutting had begun. Inches of hair lay on the floor, leaving a sculpted mane that reached just below her shoulders, angling appealingly around her face. "I feel like a new woman. And see Stani, there's still plenty of hair to spread on the pillow." She smiled impishly, tossing her head.

The hairdresser turned to Stani with a decidedly smug grin. "You see, Stani, I still know what's best. Remember when you first came to me? Those ghastly curls all over the top of your head? And I turned you into an Adonis, didn't I?"

"I feel so much better, Stani. I think the worst of the morning sickness is over. But all this running around has worn me out. I think I need a nap." Emily laid her head on his shoulder with a yawn. "I had the most unpleasant dream last night."

"What about, love?"

"I thought we were at the farm. When we walked in the front door, the house was full of cobwebs and everything was covered with inches of dust. I guess it's just my guilty conscience, reminding me that I haven't been there to take care of things. We'll have to clean house as soon as we get home." She let out a long sigh, her face grim. "I'm going to need your help. This little lump is sapping all my energy, I'm afraid."

Once she was tucked in bed, Stani's thoughts began to churn. Home, the place they had left as newlyweds three months ago, was waiting for their return. Not just the house, but the community that was so much a part of Emily's history, and so much a part of his own future. As if in answer to the unformed questions, the image of Jack Deem's weathered face crossed his mind, that wise, all-seeing smile in his eyes. Jack, of course, was the one he should turn to. Not only would Jack have the answers, but he would be the one who would most want to know the reason Emily needed help cleaning the house. Why this one time, the highly symbolic act of caring for her beloved home could be entrusted to someone else.

It had not occurred to him to warn anyone of their arrival. Maybe Emily had written, he wasn't sure. But there were things now that needed to be done, and Jack was the one to get the process started. When the familiar voice at the little sheriff's office answered, Stani could picture Jack picking up the phone on his cluttered desk and leaning back in his chair as they began to talk, as if it had only been yesterday when they last met.

"We'll be leaving New York on Friday morning. I know James is taking care of the grounds, but would it be possible to hire someone to clean the house before then? Emily's worried it will be full of dust and spiders." He waited for the expected reaction.

It took a moment, as Jack's chuckle faded. "Why can't she clean it herself? She's pregnant, isn't she?"

"She's doing fine, Jack. She just tires easily. All she seems to do right now is eat and sleep. But everything's going well. So, can you find someone to get the house opened up for us? And is there some way someone could shop for food? As I said, she eats round the clock."

Another long moment passed, when Stani could picture Jack absorbing the news. "I'll take care of it. You're sure she's all right? She's seen a doctor?" Jack, more than anyone else, would worry.

"I promise you, he said she's fine."

"You two didn't waste any time, did you?" Jack would forgive him, but not before reminding him of his own culpability. Emily's well-being might be his responsibility now, but he knew Jack would never really let go of her. He'd been watching out for her far too long to ever completely relinquish the job.

"Apparently not. How's everyone there?" Better to move on, let him come to grips with the news. He would not be completely reassured until he saw for himself.

"About like usual. Bobby and Ruthie Dixon are having a bad time of things, though. I was just over there yesterday. In fact, I think I'll get Ruthie to clean for you. She's trying to pick up work wherever she can. Bobby got hurt on the job, had to have back surgery. Now it looks like he won't be able to go back to work for the county. Things are pretty rough for them right now."

"How's little Emily doing?" The baby, born on Christmas Eve in the back seat of the sheriff's cruiser, named for the nurse who had delivered her in the pouring rain, had been such a defining factor in his own spiritual journey. He felt a particular bond with the Dixons, although he knew little of their actual circumstances.

"Growing. Pretty little thing. And those brothers of hers are crazy about their little sister. They're a nice family. Just seem to have hit on some bad luck."

"It'll be good to get home, Jack. Back to the real world again." When Stani hung up the phone, he let the flood of guilt wash over him. During the months of touring, he'd lost touch with the reality of life in the place he had learned to call his home. He hadn't given any thought to the lives of those people in the valley who had made him feel so welcome. How could life treat some people so harshly, when others seemed to simply fall heir to wealth and comfort? He thought of Marcia, so secure in her position, a position she had done nothing to earn. Was he guilty of the same kind of assumption?

Going to the bedroom door, he peered into the dimness. He needed to talk to Emily, to ask her what he should do to ease the suffering of her little namesake and her family. But she was sleeping soundly, curled on her side with one hand tucked beneath her cheek. Stani was struck with how vulnerable she seemed, and the desire to protect surged within him. A man needed to provide for his family, he thought. What could be more frustrating than losing the ability to earn a living and care for your wife and children? Bobby had been a hard worker, always ready to help his neighbors. Now he was forced to sit by and see his family suffer. Stani remembered so clearly that night almost a year ago. Ruthie and Bobby, working together to bring their child into the world. The look of wonder and joy at the baby's cry and Bobby's pride at the first sight of his newborn daughter.

Looking down on Emily's sleeping face, he knew he had failed. His world, with all its privileges, had crossed paths with that other world of hard-working, honest-living people who struggled to make a decent life for themselves. Yet in a few short months, he had almost forgotten the value of the lessons they had taught him.

Turning from the bedside, he went in search of John. It was time to pack. It was time to go home, to celebrate Christmas and reconnect with the community he had promised to be part of when he had taken his wedding vows. The sound of Jack's voice, speaking from the real world, had reminded him of the truths he had seen there. He felt an urgent need to be there again, before he completely forgot all he had learned.

Chapter Eight

It was nearing sunset when they pulled through the gate. Every window in the house was glowing, and the sheriff's cruiser was in the driveway. Emily had slept for much of the trip, but now she was awake and watching wide-eyed for that first sight of home. "Oh, Stani, look! It's like the house knew we were coming!" Indeed, the big frame house, with its deep porch and graceful dormers, seemed to reach out to them, solid and welcoming.

Jack was standing in the doorway, a broad grin stretching his face. "Well, Jiliand Emily, just look at you. Less hair and more of everything else." In the look that passed between them, Stani saw the questions, the love and concern, and finally the shared joy.

"I'm barely three months and not supposed to be nearly so big yet. People will be counting, won't they?" She stayed in Jack's arms for a long moment, savoring the familiar scents of home in his weathered jacket.

"You're not worried about people talking, are you? All they'll talk about is how happy you look. I take it this boy's been showing you a good time?" He shook Stani's outstretched hand, searching his face as well.

"Of course. But it's so good to be home. Let us in, won't you? I'm ready to see my wonderful new kitchen again."

Stepping aside, Jack let her pass. The room seemed to explode with voices. For a minute, she stood blinking, as the sea of smiling faces came into focus. Beside her, Stani put out an arm in support, his face breaking into an astonished grin. "Welcome home!" Jack said near his ear.

In the general din of greetings Emily was passed from one pair of waiting arms to another and Stani found his back pounded repeatedly in welcome. Laughter at the success of the surprise rang throughout the house. Sara McConnell, the soft-spoken wife of the pastor, held Emily for a long moment, nodding with a knowing smile as she gazed into her face. Martha Jean Clark likewise gave her an appraising look up and down, but Stani knew it had more to do with prospective wardrobe needs. Coming up beside him, Pastor Mike laid a hand on his shoulder and said fondly, "She looks wonderful, Stani. You've certainly been doing something right!"

The crowd seemed to part, admitting a tall, rugged figure, his arms full of firewood. In the doorway James McConnell paused, his piercing blue gaze meeting Stani's for a discerning instant. Then a smile crinkled at the corners of his eyes. "Didn't think we'd just let you sneak in without making some noise, did you?"

"Come into the dining room. We'll get dinner on the table right away. You look a little peaked, Emily. Are you feeling all right?" Sara had taken Emily's arm, with a questioning glance at Stani.

"She just needs feeding. Her last snack was two hours ago."

"Does everyone know already?" she asked in a whisper.

Sara nodded. "I'm afraid secrets don't keep for long around here. Jack couldn't rest until he told everyone he saw. And of course, once the news reached the post office. . . ."

Emily looked around the room, until she spotted the postmistress and grinned, her eyes suddenly bright. "Myrtice! I should have known. Thank you, everybody! What a wonderful way to come home!" Turning back to him, she whispered, "And thank you for telling Jack. Remind me to reward you later."

When everyone had finally gone, leaving a spotless kitchen and a refrigerator full of food, John unloaded the car and trudged toward the stairs. "I think I'll sleep in tomorrow, if that's all right with you. This country air, not to mention that meal, reminds me of how tired I am after herding you two around for three months."

Stani looked up from the fireplace, hanging the poker back on its stand. "That's what comes with age, my friend. I myself am raring to go. James and I are going to make some deliveries in the morning. The Christmas Family boxes are packed and ready, he says. You can stay here and keep my wife company. And keep her from getting into trouble. No housework and no cooking. D'you understand, my love?"

Stretched on the couch, her eyelids heavy, Emily extended a hand in his direction. "You're going to leave me so soon? We just got home, Stani!"

"Only for a few hours. You'll be asleep anyway, I expect. James is picking me up at eight."

She smiled sleepily. "In that case, you can go without me. This little lump doesn't get up that early." She gave her waist a fond pat. "I can't believe everyone knows, and I haven't told a soul. I guess they would have noticed at church Sunday, anyway. Martha Jean is bringing out some things from the shop tomorrow. She says I'll have to wear my bathrobe otherwise. My slacks won't zip anymore, Stani. We may be having an elephant instead of a baby."

He joined her on the couch, lifting her head onto his lap. "It's just because you were so deliciously slim to start with. I think it's very attractive, all these lovely new curves you're growing."

From the foot of the stairs, John cleared his throat loudly. "I'm probably going to wish I'd stayed in New York, aren't I? Permission to retire, sir." He started up to his room.

"Permission granted. But you haven't lived until you've experienced Christmas here in the valley, John. Miracles happen every hour, right darling?"

"Oh, yes, if not more often. Now what was that you were going to remind me of? Oh, I remember. Your reward. Would you like it here, or in the bedroom?"

Chapter Nine

Stani was up at dawn, making tea and watching the light spread over the wintry landscape. Cup in hand, he went out to say good morning to Stubby, who last night had blinked at them in the light from the house, as if to say they might have waited until daylight to disturb him. Now he allowed his ears to be stroked and accepted a lump of sugar from Stani's open palm, not exactly enthusiastic, but at least forgiving of their neglect. The old white mule, past the time of pulling a plow, but none the less a vital member of the family, stood at ease by the fence, as Stani stared across the frosty lawn. "We're going to have a baby, Stubby. One more change around the old homestead, eh?"

Apparently lured by the sound of his voice, the two fat gray tabby cats Emily had whimsically named Heathcliff and Catherine came from the barn, rubbing against his ankles in greeting. He knelt to give them each a smooth, noting that either James had kept them very well fed, or the rodent population had suffered greatly the past few months. "Taking care of business, are you, kitties?"

With one last stroke of the mule's soft muzzle, he stood in the cold wind for a time, looking over the long steep hill that led down to the springs. Four years now, since he had wandered blindly to this place, his life very nearly lost and most certainly found in that climb. The tingle along his spine and the sting of tears in his eyes had little to do with the chill morning air.

He looked in to be certain Emily was still sleeping when James pulled into the drive. When he kissed her outstretched hand, she stirred, sighing softly. He shrugged off the temptation to join her and headed for the door. There were things to do. He only prayed he would know how to go about getting them done.

James, who had turned to serving his childhood community following a tour of duty in Vietnam, had told him he planned to deliver the food and gifts donated for the sheriff's department's annual holiday drive. In particular, he was going to deliver to the Dixons, intending to also see to any chores around the place that might be too heavy for

Ruthie to do alone. Stani had recognized the challenge in James' direct gaze. Here was his opportunity, if he was man enough to take it on. He and James had developed a mutual respect during the past summer, but Stani knew James still doubted his ability to actually become a part of this rural community, where neighbors watched out for each other and gave of not only their earnings but themselves in answer to one another's needs.

Now, as he climbed into the battered pickup truck, James tossed him a jacket. "You can't load firewood in that fancy overcoat, man. I brought this one of my dad's, just in case. If you're going to help folks around here, you've got look the part. You're not some fancy fiddle player here." He grinned, offering an open sack of donuts.

Stani, started to refuse, then thought better and took a donut. "I've been thinking about that very thing. I want to help, but I have no idea what to do."

"You'll learn. Stick with me today, and I guarantee you'll see things you've never seen before. Can you leave Em alone for a few hours?"

"John is there. She'll be fine. Now that she's home, I hope she'll start to feel better. She says the nausea is passed, thank goodness. This is something else I've never seen before, pregnancy. Life is full of surprises."

James laughed. "You're right there. Did Em tell you Penny's coming next week?"

"Really?" He wondered for a moment if she had told him, but decided it didn't matter. James seemed in a rare mood to talk, so he would just offer a sympathetic ear. When James had met Penny Riley, just before the wedding, the instant spark between the two had shocked and pleased Emily. That her childhood friend and her college roommate still had a number of obstacles to overcome before they could be happy was an ongoing cause for prayerful concern. "How are things with you two?"

"Slow. I've been up to Boston twice. Met her folks. As I said, slow."

"Problems?" He found his eyes riveted to the winding road that was carrying them higher into the hills than he'd ever been. The terrain was rough, with thickly timbered slopes rising on either side of the deep ditches bordering the narrow tarred strip. He wondered how the road fared in bad weather. It seemed barely passable now in places where the paving had broken away along the shoulders.

"Maybe," James was saying. Stani turned his attention back to the conversation. "She said they weren't going to encourage her to get serious about the son of a Presbyterian minister. She's hoping they'll see she's already serious and come around."

"So she's coming here for Christmas? That should tell them something. How will you handle the two faiths? I assume at this point you're planning a future together?"

James drew a long breath, staring straight ahead. "I can't convert. At least I don't think I can. I'm still trying to get my faith legs back under me, if you know what I mean. I don't see that it should be necessary. But I would never ask her to leave her church. I've told her, if it's going to be a constant source of grief for her, I'd rather she let me go now. But that's not what she wants. And obviously, it's not what I want. Penny is such an amazing girl, strong and smart. Not to mention sweet and funny as all get out. I've never been in love, but I know this has to be what it feels like."

Stani couldn't help grinning. "I'd say so. Correct me if I'm wrong, but you find yourself thinking about her all the time, talking to her in your head no matter what you're doing, and wanting more than anything to feel her in your arms. And the least little thing, some scent or sound that reminds you of her, can send you off into a daydream." At James's responding grin, he chuckled. "It's love all right, my friend. The most wonderful, terrifying, life-altering thing that can ever come over a man. Congratulations."

But James's face suddenly assumed a more familiar grim expression. "It just seems so unfair. She's been through so much, losing Frankie and being alone all this time. The two things that kept her going were her faith and her dedication to her family. Now those are the very things that could stand in the way of her finally being happy. I don't want her to have to choose me over what's always mattered the most to her."

Stani studied his profile. James was so much in love that he was willing to sacrifice his own happiness for Penny's peace of mind. He wondered whether he would have been as unselfish, if faced with the same kind of issue. "She and Emily are a lot alike. Those were the things that sustained Emily through her own grief."

"If her parents could only see how much I care about her, maybe they'd get used to the idea of her marrying a non-Catholic. I know they want her to be happy. But I can't just march into their house and tell them how I feel." James hesitated, his eyes narrowing to a steely blue stare. "Stani, I knew those guys, the boys like Frankie. Decent, honest kids from good families who just did what they were told to do. I know the kind of life she would have had with him, how he would have taken care of her, loved her and respected her. She still deserves that, even more so now, after all she's done on her own. I think I can give her that life, in fact I think it's my *duty* to give her that life. I was one of the men who gave those boys their orders. They called me 'sir' and did whatever I told them to do." He clenched his jaw until the muscles knotted beneath the thick sideburns. "This is a chance for me to make up for at least one of them who never got to come home. It's like God sent me this way to redeem myself. How do you explain that to someone?"

He took a minute to reply, waiting for the thought to form. "You just explained it to me. Maybe you can't march in and tell Penny's parents your feelings, but could you put them in a letter?" It was a wellspring of insight, seeming to come from somewhere outside himself. "When I first found Emily, she suggested we write to each other. I think she was sure at that point we'd never see each other again. But it was in those letters that I could say things I would never have been brave enough to say face to face. Not at first, anyway. And I think it was the same for her. If you could write to Penny's parents, tell them on paper what you feel, it might give them a chance to think, before they decide you're wrong for her."

James was silent for a time, steering the truck carefully along the rutted roadway. "Nothing to lose, I guess. You really think they might understand?"

"I do. And I can't believe, when you put it the way you did just now, that anyone could question your sincerity."

The truck slowed to a halt at the top of a long hill, where a small gray house stood in the clearing. Smoke churned from the chimney and at the door, three little boys stood watching expectantly. Stani saw Ruthie come up behind them, smiling and waving and pulling them back into the house to quickly close the door.

"Kids letting the heat out." James grinned. "Come on in and say hello. We'll unload in a minute and then I'll get to work. Maybe you should sit and visit for a while. Might be a real education for you."

Inside, the entire family was gathered in the one room that served as kitchen, dining and living room. Added to the already crowded space, a cot in one corner allowed Bobby to join his wife and four children in an area most people would have found unbearably close quarters. And yet the scene seemed instantly welcoming. On the wood-burning cook stove, a pot of something savory simmered, infusing the room with a pleasantly rich aroma. At the kitchen table, a checkerboard held a game already in progress. Near the cot, the smallest of the boys was busily moving a toy truck along an imaginary roadway. Nestled in the crook of her father's arm, Emily, now almost a year old, was watching with wide, appraising eyes as the two strangers entered her domain.

Ruthie was quick to offer them a seat, pulling chairs away from the table. "Robbie, Wayne, you can finish your game later. Let the gentlemen sit down. Mr. Moss, we hadn't expected to see you here. James didn't say he was bringing company with him."

"He didn't know until last night. And Ruthie, please don't call me 'mister.' My name is Stani, which I know is a bit odd, but it's the one I'm stuck with." He turned his attention to Bobby, lying flat on his back on the cot, his face turned to watch the activity. "I was sorry to hear you've been laid up, Bobby. James tells me you're able to get around a bit now."

"An hour, morning and evening. Not much, but it's a start." Bobby smiled, holding tightly to the baby, who was making an effort to climb down from her throne.

"I know a little about slow recoveries. They can try your patience, can't they?" Stani studied the curious little girl, whose eyes were clearly focused on his hair. "Emily has certainly changed since I saw her last. Three months makes a big difference, doesn't it?"

Managing at last to wriggle free of her father's grasp, Emily dropped to the floor on sturdy legs. After a tentative start, she took quick steps across the room, stopping squarely in front of Stani, gazing up at the top of his head.

Bobby chuckled. "She likes your hair. She notices everything, that one does. She just started walking good last week. Walked earlier than any of the boys did." He was obviously proud of his daughter, his face beaming as he watched her cautiously reach out to Stani.

"May I pick her up? She won't mind?" Stani held out his hands, looking to Ruthie for permission.

"Sure you can. She'll let you know if she doesn't like it. She's not timid at all."

He lifted her in his arms, marveling at the lightness of her little body. Her hands immediately reached toward his hair, touching it gently. Her lips formed a perfect O and then she smiled, looking him directly in the eye. "Hello, Emily. Do you approve of my silly hair?"

The eldest boy, who appeared to be about eight years old, came closer, holding out a hand to safeguard his sister if this clearly inexperienced stranger should let her fall. "She likes bright things, lights and colors. Mama says it's 'cause right when she was born, the ambulance was coming with all its lights flashing." The boy's tone was profoundly serious, but Stani chuckled at the memory he called to mind.

"That's right. I was there, you know. I remember, she cried and the siren blared at exactly the same moment. It was an amazing thing."

"Mama says you come from the same place as the Queen of England." The boy slid a little closer, putting a hand on the baby's back, but keeping his eyes fixed on Stani's face. Ruthie made a move as if to discourage such boldness in her son, but Stani smiled reassuringly. "Did you ever meet her?" the boy went on, continuing to study him as if to discern his true identity.

"The Queen? No, I've not had that privilege, but I did meet her son and daughter, quite a long time ago. I had to play my violin for them, and afterward they came by to say hello."

Now the boy screwed his face into a frown. "You had to? Mama said you get paid to play music. How come they *made* you play for them?" He was clearly suspicious, prepared to question Stani's credentials.

"Well, you see, I was very young, and they asked me to play for what's called a command performance. If I had said 'no, thank you,' they might never have asked me again."

"You talk funny, you know that?" Finally a grin, displaying several missing teeth, indicated they might be friends after all.

"Yes, so I'm told. That's what comes of being born in England, I expect. What is your name, if I may ask?"

"Robbie Joe. Robert Joseph, really. I know your name. It's Stani Moss. You married Miss Emily Haynes after she saved your life." He paused, as if unsure of his next move. Then with head high, he said proudly, "I play the fiddle too."

Emily was sitting contently on Stani's knee, examining the silver buttons on his coat sleeve. In the corner, James was talking quietly with Bobby. Ruthie had carried the smallest boy to the kitchen sink, where she was gently washing his face and hands with a rag. The middle son, who appeared to be about six years old, had picked up a schoolbook and was sitting close to a window, silently moving his lips as he read with great concentration. A chill touched the back of Stani's neck. He had been delivered into a world of new images, each marvelous in its own simple way. Now the earnest boy in front of him had revealed his most treasured secret and stood waiting for his reaction.

"Do you really? Who taught you to play?"

"My granddaddy. He plays real good, except he has rheumatism now. But he can still show me things."

"Do you have a fiddle, Robbie Joe?" He glanced around the sparsely furnished room.

"No, sir. I play my granddaddy's when we go to visit. Mama says fiddles cost more money than Daddy used to make in a whole year, before he couldn't work no more."

"Robbie Joe!" his mother chided softly from across the room.

"*Any* more. Sorry, Mama." He turned back to Stani. "I bet you have a bunch of fiddles, don't you?" Emily wiggled around to look at her brother, reaching out to touch his face with exploring fingers. He took her hand and held it gently, smiling back at her. Then he looked up to Stani for an answer to his question.

"A few. How old are you, Robbie Joe?"

"Eight years old. But I'll be nine in February. How old are you?"

Stani grinned. "Twenty-five. Old. But when I was your age, I took lots of lessons, learning to play the violin. It's hard work, you know. But if you really want to learn to play well, you have to take lessons."

"Where do you get lessons? They don't teach stuff like that at my school." Robbie took the baby in his arms, hugging her against his chest. "Mama, Emily messed her diaper. She smells something awful."

"I'm so sorry, Mr. . . .Stani. Here, Robbie, let me have her. And stop pestering Mr. Moss with all those questions."

"No, no, I'm fascinated, Ruthie. It's always good to meet a fellow musician."

James, making his way to the door, stopped to grin down at Stani. "If you two musicians wouldn't mind continuing your discussion outside, I could use some help with a few chores. Robbie Joe, can you show me where your Daddy keeps his chain saw?"

When a substantial pile of firewood had been stacked by the door, and the contents of the truck had been unloaded, James suggested Stani go inside and continue his visit while he checked under the house for a suspected frozen drainpipe. "Robbie Joe, take Mr. Moss inside and offer him a glass of water. He looks worn out with all this hard work. Fiddle players aren't used to chopping wood, you know."

Bobby was sitting at the table, watching solemnly as Ruthie prepared lunch. The two smaller boys were on the floor, rolling a ball between their outstretched legs, while Emily sat nearby following the movement of the ball back and forth across the space. For the first time, Stani noticed that the children each wore several layers of clothing. Ruthie was likewise wearing a pair of corduroy trousers under her dress, as well as a heavy sweater. Now that Bobby was out of bed, he had wrapped a blanket around his shoulders and drawn another over his lap. Coming in from the cold, Stani realized the room was not much warmer, with only the heat from the cook stove creating a capsule of warmth in the kitchen space.

Robbie Joe poured water from a pitcher and brought it to Stani. "Your son's a hard worker, Bobby. He put me to shame out there."

"He's my right hand, for sure. And he does real well in school, too. Maybe someday, he'll be able to make enough money to take care of his parents in their old age. Right, Robbie Joe?"

"Yes sir, Daddy." He went to his mother and whispered something, pointing to Stani.

"Oh, Robbie, I don't think Mr. Moss has time for such things. We'll have to see about that later."

"Just ask him, Mama. Please. Like you always say, he can only say no."

His curiosity aroused, Stani spoke up. "What is it, Ruthie? How can I help you?"

"Oh, Robbie has this idea of taking music lessons. He only sees his granddaddy once in a while, you see." She paused, obviously embarrassed, and brushed at the unruly sprout of hair at the back of the boy's head.

Robbie turned with pleading eyes. "So maybe could you give me lessons? Just one, even?"

Without an instant's hesitation, moved as much by the look of doubtful expectancy in the mother's eyes as by the eagerness in the child's voice, Stani replied, "Why, I'd be honored, Robbie Joe. I'll tell you what. If it's all right with your parents, I'll arrange for someone to bring you to my house one day next week. How would that be?"

The smile on the boy's face, and the light in his mother's eyes raised a sudden lump in Stani's throat. But Bobby shook his head. "We can't pay for lessons, Robbie, you know that. It wouldn't be right."

"Please consider it a gift to me, Bobby. I don't have the opportunity to teach often. It would be a real treat for me to spend some time with the boy. How about Monday afternoon? Could you spare him for a few hours then?" Across the room, the baby suddenly clapped her hands and crowed with laughter, drawing everyone's attention. Stani let out a responding chuckle. "It seems Emily likes the idea just fine."

Chapter Ten

In the truck, Stani plied James with questions. Why was the house so cold? Were those oil lamps in the room? Wasn't there electricity to the house? He couldn't make sense of what he'd seen.

"Turned off. Bobby's been off work for three months. They couldn't keep up with the bills. Same for the fuel oil. Can't run the heater without oil or electricity. Can't have running water either. They use the old hand pump to get well water. They're behind on the rent too, he told me."

"They pay to live in that. . .shack? Oh, it's clean and homey, but the roof looks as if it might be about to fall in and there are broken windows. I did recognize the cardboard taped to the windows. What sort of landlord lets a house get in that condition?"

"You'd be surprised. There are lots worse around here."

"Can they afford to buy food?"

"Fortunately, Bobby raised a big garden last summer and Ruthie was able to save it, can the vegetables, dry some fruit. Jack has made sure they had what they needed from the food pantry, or bought it for them himself, if the truth were known. I know for a fact he buys milk for the kids. Ruthie knows how to stretch a dollar, but there are few of those coming in. She's been picking up work, cleaning and washing and ironing for some of the ladies in town. But she can't leave the kids much, at least not until Bobby can get around more. I was trying to talk to him about applying for some kind of assistance, disability or even welfare. He won't hear of it. He says he'll find some way to support his family again, as soon as he's back on his feet."

"About that. Shouldn't he be getting some kind of therapy? He'll never get better just lying around. After my injury, I went through months of therapy. Surely back injuries require that kind of thing too?"

"If he accepted assistance, he would get at least a little of that. But without money coming in, they don't want to get into debt for things they know they can't afford."

"So he risks being crippled for the rest of his life?"

"Could be. But he's determined he'll work again. And I don't want to discourage him. People overcome all sorts of disabilities when they want to badly enough. The shame is he didn't buy the health insurance his job offered. Figured he needed the cash income, I guess. They let it lapse after Emily was born. Now they have hospital bills they can't pay, and no money coming in to keep up with their expenses. The last thing they want is more debt."

Stani tried to imagine facing such an endless sequence of obstacles. Not only did Bobby face a doubtful future for himself, but he had five other lives to consider. And he so obviously loved his family. He and Ruthie were devoted parents who were encouraging their children toward a better life. One accident, one moment in a lifetime, could irreparably alter the future for all of them. As he considered the bleakness of their situation, James was talking about mutual need.

"I'm sorry. What's that you were saying?"

"I said there might be a solution to the problem, for you and for Bobby. Bobby needs a job, one he'll be able to do without too much heavy work, and you're going to need a caretaker."

"A caretaker?" He had the thought that James had suddenly begun speaking in a foreign language.

"At the farm. I'm not going to be around here much longer and you need someone there full time anyway. As much as you're going to be away, the place will go down fast without a full-time caretaker."

"First of all, where are you going?" He was still struggling to follow the turn in the conversation.

"Boston, if my plans work out. I want to go back to school and get my social work degree. I'm looking for jobs in Boston now, so I can work while I'm in school. By spring, I hope to have something nailed down."

"I see. So how does this help Bobby and Ruthie?" He began to suspect that James had already worked out a plan, before they'd even paid their visit today.

"The way I see it, you need someone to live on the place. You need a cottage for that someone to live in. There's plenty of land to put down a mobile home, or even build a house. The advantage to a mobile home is it's quick to set up and comes furnished. I figure three bedrooms will work for them. That gives Bobby and his family a decent place to live, gives him a job he'll be good at, and keeps your farm in good shape. The other advantage to you is that Bobby is a really fine gardener, and he could do what Em had wanted to do herself."

"Revive her father's gardens."

"Exactly. So everyone benefits. Ruthie can keep the house clean, so Em won't worry about it. It'll be ready for you whenever you can come home. With a baby on the way, that should mean a lot to her. She's going to want to get back here whenever she can. I can't see a drawback, unless you can't afford it." He glanced at Stani with a grin.

"That's almost funny. We were just talking about needing housekeepers and nannies. Now you've convinced me I need a caretaker. All of a sudden I feel like a man with a lot of responsibility, when barely a year ago, I was just starting to think about asking Emily to be my wife. It's been a whirlwind for sure. And now I'm going to be a father, don't forget that." He sighed deeply, gazing out at the bare trees passing the window. "How do I make it happen, James? Tell me what to do."

"Talk to Em first. It's her farm, after all. But I think she'll go for it. Then I'll take you to look at mobile homes."

"Before we talk to Bobby? Are you that sure he'll agree?"

"If he knows you're going to hire somebody, no matter what, I think he'll jump at the chance. If he thinks you're doing this as an act of charity for him and his family, he'll turn it down. Get the house first, then we'll talk to him."

"What about therapy? How do we get that for him? And the electric turned on, and heat and water to the house? And the rent paid?"

James grinned. "I'd say Father Christmas is going to have a busy time of it next week. Don't worry, I'll be with you every step of the way." He slowed the truck to a stop inside the gate.

Stani stepped out, turning back to James. "Oh, and there's one more favor I need. Can you bring Robbie Joe to me on Monday afternoon for a violin lesson?" He ran a hand through his hair, trying to sort his whirling thoughts into some semblance of order. He needed to talk to his wife, but there were three cars in the driveway, including one he recognized as Angela Salvatore's. Not much chance he'd get any time with her just now.

"You got it, buddy. See you in church tomorrow?"

"You don't know how I'm looking forward to it. I need to have a word with God, up close and in person, about all this he's asking of me this Christmas. Last year, I was the one receiving the blessings."

Again, James' face spread into a grin. "You still are, man. You still are."

It was hours before Stani had a chance to tell Emily about his morning. Angela stayed until late afternoon. As Emily's godmother, she clearly felt herself entitled to the privilege of monopolizing her company, even while others came and went. And Emily had seemed so happy, enthroned by the fire surrounded by her visitors. When he'd arrived, she had smiled brightly, informing him that lunch was in the fridge and, he felt, scarcely acknowledging his presence. He'd been relieved to find John lounging in one of the overstuffed chairs in the sunroom, an open book in his hands, a cup of tea on the table nearby. At least here was someone to talk to.

"You look beat. What have you been up to?" Glancing up from his book, he barely seemed to take the time to make such an assessment.

"Chopping wood. And seeing the world. The real world." Taking one of the sandwiches from the plate in the refrigerator, he sank into the other armchair, stretching his legs on the ottoman near the wood stove. "It's good to be home. And Emily looks wonderful today. I knew just being here would do her good."

John's face clouded suddenly, and he looked up again, this time laying the book aside. "Speaking of home, I have some news. Milo phoned. Seems there's been someone hanging around the London house. Apparently the neighbors had called the police several times about someone climbing the garden fence, looking in the windows. Then Milo surprised someone in the conservatory when he came in the other night."

"What? Housebreakers?" He set down his plate, an uneasy feeling rising in his chest.

"Nothing stolen or vandalized, as far as the police could tell. Although the latch on the gate to the alley was damaged. They're going to put a watch on the house in case this person comes back. Any idea if anyone might have been taking an interest in you, or in Emily, anyone hanging around when you were there? Emily didn't mention anything, did she?"

He tried to think through the haze of the past few weeks. If only he hadn't been so caught up with Marcia and Milo. "No. There was nothing. You were with her some of the time. You didn't see anything, obviously."

"What about that photographer? He seemed *very* interested in her that day at the shoot."

"Nigel Barton? But we've used him before. He seems like a nice guy. Certainly not the type to peer in windows."

"Still, I'm going to give his name to the police. Have him checked out. I haven't told her. I wanted to wait until you were here."

"No! I don't want to upset her now. I'm sure she doesn't know of anything that could help. She would have told me, or you, if anyone had been hanging around. It just doesn't make sense. We were only there for a little over a week. And she didn't go out on her own much, not the way she did last spring." He was searching his mind for any reasonable explanation, some obvious answer to calm his rapidly growing uneasiness.

"Could something have happened then, that she didn't think was important?" John was thinking out loud, staring into the distance.

Stani shook his head. "Nothing I remember. John, you're scaring me. You think this person knows who lives there? That he might have been watching her all along?"

"Calm down, lad. I'd just like to know more about where she's been, who she might have met up with. We'll have to talk to her, before we go back. In the meantime, the police may find something there. I'll give them the photographer's name. And tell them that she was all over the neighborhood last spring. Guys like this are usually better known than they think if they hang around the same area for long." He paused, hoping to see that Stani was reassured by his words. "Maybe I should go back early, do a little poking around myself."

"Let's wait until after the holidays. As you say, the police may find him." He looked toward the front of the house, listening to the sound of laughter and women's voices. "This is just the kind of thing I worry about. Here, she's so secure, and she doesn't understand that out there, everyone's a stranger."

"Try not to worry. If you're all worked up over this thing, she'll know something's wrong. Leave it to the police. She may never need to know anything about it."

"You're right. I have other things here to take care of, anyway. Now, if you'll excuse me, I'm going to take a long, hot shower. Maybe after that, I can get a moment to talk with my wife. I need to tell her we're going to have another busy Christmas this year." He walked through the kitchen, running his hands through his hair.

He showered, hoping to wash away the anxiety, relieve himself of the nagging fear that twisted in his chest at the thought of some faceless threat. He tried to return his focus to all he had seen just that morning. God had shown him a glowing opportunity, and then this unsettling thing from the world out there had overwhelmed his response. As he studied his reflection in the mirror, his eyes went to the words written on the wall by Emily's mother, the passage from Philippians she had relied on during years of illness. "Have no anxiety about anything, but by prayer. . ." he read aloud. He cast his gaze heavenward. "Easier said than done."

When he was finally able to talk to Emily, he was convinced he had put aside his fears. He told her about all he had seen in the little house that morning; her beautiful namesake, who was fascinated by his hair; the serious young boy who had asked such pointed questions, and then revealed his desire to play the violin. "It was all so amazing, seeing the way they live, how close they are. I think I failed to notice how cold the house was at first, because everything seemed so warm. Does that make any sense?"

"Of course it does. I wrote to you, didn't I, about my visit there. No matter the conditions, they've managed to make that house a real home.

"But now things are much harder. They don't have any way to keep paying their bills. James told me the whole situation, and then he told me how to fix things. For them and for us." He grinned, as he began to explain James' plan, point by point.

Emily laughed when he concluded by telling her that he was going shopping for a mobile home next week. "James will make a great social worker. And he's not a bad salesman, either."

"You agree with his plan then? It is your farm, after all."

"Of course I do. When you got to the part about Bobby planting the gardens, I was sold. And it'll be nice to think that there are children on the place all of the time. Who would have ever guessed last Christmas Eve that the baby who popped out into my arms would someday be living here? Oh, Stani, I think this is wonderful! Just more of our miracle, right?"

"That's what I hoped you'd say. And there's more. Penny is coming here to spend Christmas with James. He's moving to Boston next spring."

"Goodness. They didn't waste any time. I have news, too! Jack and Martha Jean are getting married. She wanted to know when we'd be back, because they want us to read at their wedding. Of course, I'm supposed to pretend I don't know when Jack finally gets around to telling me." She snuggled closer to him, curling at his side. "And we'll be having guests in London, in February."

"Guests?" He stiffened slightly at the mention of London. He had forgotten, for a time, that there was anything but the fullness of their life here.

"Lil and Charles are taking a trip to Europe, riding the rails all over. Not a luxury tour, by any means, according to Angela. But they'll be stopping off with us before they go home. Won't that be fun, to have them visit us in our house there? Finally connecting our two worlds. I can't wait to show Lil where you proposed to me in the dark."

He grinned at the picture of Lil Salvatore, Emily's tiny whirlwind of a godsister, and Charles Evans, her solemn, introverted boyfriend, riding the rails all over Europe. The continent might never be quite the same after such an invasion. "We'll have to show them a good time, won't we? Wine and dine and the like. How are they affording to take such a trip on the combined salaries of two second chair violists?"

"Angela says Charles is very good at managing money, and he's insisted Lil put some aside too. That took some doing, I'm sure. Lil is what's known as a one paycheck wonder. She's always tapped out by the day before payday. Nice to know Charles is such a good influence. Love, I guess, has inspired Lil to tighten up her shopping habits. Maybe I'll treat her to a little excursion in London, though. I can only imagine what she could do to Harrod's!"

He pulled her close, wrapping her in his arms. With the image of Emily on the streets of London, the shadowy threat again invaded his mind. "You know how much I love you, don't you? I want so much to take good care of you."

She turned to face him, clearly gratified by his devotion. "Of course I do. And we take care of each other, remember?" Her response was one of those long, sweet kisses that reminded him of the comfort and peace she had brought to his life.

Chapter Eleven

They attended church, ate lunch at the cafe and took a long nap together. "Sundays here are so different from any other day of the week. A day of rest, not a travel day, or a performance day. I need more of these Sundays." Stani had felt truly relaxed all day, storing up energy for the week ahead.

"Hard to come by in your world, darling. Just enjoy them when you can get them. And by the way, Jack should be here any time. He said he had another surprise for us. We should get up." She stretched, rolling on her side and sliding an arm across his chest.

"You make that very unlikely, when you do that. Did I tell you how lovely you looked in your new dress this morning? Very Madonna like." Martha Jean had provided a flowing dress of deep blue, with a belt that tied above the waist. The dress had only emphasized the little bulge, and Stani had felt a glow of pride, standing next to his wife in church. "I think I like pregnant women. Especially the one who's carrying my child."

"Speaking of Madonnas, we *have* to get the house decorated for Christmas. We need a tree and some greens, not to mention deciding what we're going to have for Christmas dinner. I haven't even looked at the presents I had shipped from London, much less wrapped any. Oh, Stani, where am I going to find the energy to get all this done? Just thinking about it makes me tired." She stretched and settled more firmly against his side.

He had decided another doze might be just what they both needed when sounds of activity in the next room sent him leaping to his feet. "Sounds as if Jack's here. Come on, let's see what sort of surprise he has for us this time."

With slightly less alacrity, Emily slid off the bed and picked up her hairbrush from the dresser. "It sounds like he's brought an army. What on earth is he up to? Surprises, indeed." But the sparkle in her eyes betrayed her excitement.

"It's Christmas, darling girl. Surprises abound!"

They were treated to the sight of Jack, assisted somewhat awkwardly by John, wrestling a large fir tree through the front door. Behind them Martha Jean, her arms full of trailing cedar, issued a stream of directions. At Emily's squeal of welcome, Jack laughed. "Figured I'd better get this done for you, before you tried to do it yourself."

"Oh, Jack, thank you! I was just moaning about how much we have to do."

"Now sit down, Em, and tell me where the decorations are. You can supervise. And Stani, honey, we're going to need some Christmas music." Martha Jean carried her load to the dining room, brushing past John as she went. "John, I bet you make a wonderful pot of tea. And I know there are Christmas cookies in the kitchen. Come on, fellas! Let's get this party going!"

Laughing, Emily let Stani lead her to the couch. "Ask and ye shall receive?"

"More like drop a hint around Martha Jean and the job gets done." Stani grinned broadly. "Miracles every hour, love."

Chapter Twelve

Stani's mind was churning with words and ideas he'd never known existed. He and James had first talked with Jack, who James said would know how to provide the things Bobby and his family needed without it seeming like a handout. The plan had fallen into place with little or no effort. Jack would tell Bobby and Ruthie that he had received a donation from a long ago resident of the community, specifically for a deserving family which might otherwise have a less than merry Christmas. He would use the money to pay their delinquent bills and take care of their back rent, paying it in advance for another month as well. He would also arrange for a therapist to visit and evaluate Bobby's condition. If therapy was recommended, he would tell Bobby it had been authorized by the county. "Which it should have been. He'll never know it wasn't paid for due to the fact that he was injured on the job. We'll just be righting a wrong, one case at a time." Jack had tallied up the amounts needed and Stani had written the check.

Next, they had visited the bank. Stani had authorized James as his agent to purchase and set up a mobile home on the property. He had a sheaf of papers for Emily to sign, but Emory Harris had been willing to let James go ahead with obtaining permits and making the necessary contacts before the holiday closings slowed the process. "You know we don't stand quite so firmly on ceremony here, Stani. Just get these back to me when Emily's had a chance to sign them. And congratulations! When the time comes, I'll be glad to talk with you about setting up a college fund." There was a twinkle in the banker's eyes, as he offered his usual hearty handshake. Stani left the bank feeling once again that he was genuinely accepted as part of this remote community, a thoroughly gratifying thought for a man who had never had a real home until his arrival here.

Finally, they had driven to the dealership located out on the highway, just so Stani could get an idea of what he was buying, James said. "I'm betting you've never been inside a mobile home."

"I'm not even sure what one looks like. It won't really be mobile, will it? They won't be able to drive it anywhere?"

"That's a camper you're thinking of. You'll see. This is a real house, just comes in pieces all ready to put together. We'll make sure it's set up good and solid, so it won't blow away if another windstorm tries to take the place down."

Stani gave him a hard look. "That sort of thing wouldn't strike the same place twice would it? I'll never forget the damage it did, to the house or to Emily." He shuddered at the fleeting image of Emily's body beneath the fallen tree that summer night. The house had suffered significant damage, and he had stayed on much longer than originally planned, watching over Emily's recovery and learning a number of valuable lessons about this place he would call home.

"Not likely. Still, up on that rise, it pays to spend a little extra for the best. Are you prepared to shell out for your caretaker's cottage?"

"Whatever it takes, James. You know I'm not going to scrimp on anything that will be part of our farm. Only the best. Just lead me to it." Our farm. He hadn't said the words quite like that before. It sounded so fine he said them over and over again in his head, until he found just the proper ring. Valley Rise Farm, proprietors Stani and Emily Moss. A sudden inspiration struck him, which he filed away, thinking he'd talk to Emily about it later.

In the model home, as James pointed out the various features, Stani tried to visualize the Dixon children playing on the carpeted floors, or sitting on the big, overstuffed couch. The kitchen was a marvel, compared to the primitive space Ruthie was accustomed to. James pointed out that the bathrooms, both of them, would be a vast improvement over the outhouse and washtub they used now. "You mean they have to go outside, even the children?"

"Indoor plumbing may be all the rage in the rest of the country, but up there, it's only something in other people's houses. And if they have it, much of the time, the pipes freeze and break, because the houses are so poorly heated. These kids are going to have a lot to get used to."

When the deal was finalized, Stani was amazed that a home, a real home with all the basic amenities, could be purchased for such a price. Of course, James cautioned him, there was the work to be done on the land, plus the foundation, and the septic and water lines. "You still have a ways to go." Not wishing to show his total ignorance of what was involved, Stani had merely nodded knowingly. Something in James' eyes had told him he wasn't fooled at all.

James dropped Stani at the gate, promising to have Robbie Joe there by three. Climbing out of the truck, Stani let out a sigh of relief, turning back to James with a grin. "After all this education, I'm ready to get back to what I know. A boy with a violin, that I can relate to."

Emily had been wrapping gifts. The dining room table was littered with paper and ribbon, and the heap of packages under the tree was growing. When he found her in the kitchen, hands covered with flour, he chided her for overdoing things.

"I'm fine. All of a sudden, my energy seems to have returned. And I've been craving cinnamon bread for days. How was your shopping trip?"

"Very enlightening. Thank God for James McConnell. And Jack, of course. Without them, none of this would be happening. Are all the men in your part of the world so practical?"

"Not only the men. The women can accomplish a few things on their own, too, don't forget."

"Never. Now sit down, woman, and let me make you some lunch. I can at least do that much." He looked around the gleaming kitchen. "We are so blessed, aren't we? Did you know the house Bobby and his family live in doesn't even have a bathroom? Why, even our flat in East London had a bathroom. I thought we were poor, I suppose because my mother was always telling me we were. We were well off, compared to those kids. And they are happy in spite of it. I wish I could have said the same for us. Poor Mummy, she must lack some essential gene for enjoying life."

"I've never heard you call her that before." She hesitated to say he rarely mentioned his mother at all.

"What, Mummy? I don't think of her as that often. She hardly seems real to me anymore. I was only eight when she let me go to live with Jana and Milo. I rarely saw her after that, and it was always disappointing when I did. I suppose some women just aren't equipped to be mothers." Setting their sandwiches on the table, he slid into the banquette beside her. "Others, however, like the mother of my child, are infinitely well-equipped." He dropped a kiss on her shoulder. "How is our little lump, by the way?"

"Fine. I think since it has more space in my new clothes, it's growing faster. I hope Manny has those things ready for me before we go back to London. Otherwise, I won't have anything to wear for the photo shoot."

Stani realized he'd forgotten the planned magazine layout. "Maybe we should postpone that. Who knows what the weather will be like, that time of year. I can't have you out in the cold, posing for photographs."

"I don't think Nigel would expect us to stand around in the rain. And I don't think it would be fair to postpone. He counts on jobs like that to make a living. I'm sure there's bound to a good day or two, even in January."

"We'll see, darling. Now eat your lunch. I'd hoped to sit by the fire and relax with my wife before Robbie Joe gets here. It *is* all right with you for him to use your father's violin?"

"Of course it is. If I let one prodigy use it, I have to let them all. Right?"

Stani tucked Emily in for a nap and sat down to wait for his student. Somewhere in the recesses of his memory, the image of himself as he had stood before Milo that first time had been fighting its way into his consciousness. His mother was standing nearby, watching. He knew what was expected. If this imposing man, seated behind the big, carved desk, was impressed with his music, it would please his mother. If he wasn't impressed, they would go home and be unhappy, both of them. His mother had told him how important it was to play his best, because this man could make them rich.

He had played his best, and Milo had smiled. They had gone home, but his mother had not been happy. Instead of pleasing her, somehow playing well for Milo had resulted in his mother's giving him away. It had been a cruel trick of some kind. He had done his best for her, and she had abandoned him. He could remember as if it had been yesterday, how it felt to be eight years old, discarded by his only parent, wounded and confused. His heart went out to Robbie Joe, coming to stand in front of a stranger to play for the first time. There would be no cruel tricks played on this boy, he vowed. If he had talent, he still deserved the life of a boy, before he became a violinist.

Robbie Joe arrived right on schedule. His face was shining clean; clearly it had been scrubbed by a mother's loving hand, and he was wearing what appeared to be his Sunday best. When Stani took the violin from the case, the boy looked it over carefully. "That's a little bit different from Granddaddy's. Fancier, and shinier, too."

Stani explained to the boy that the violin had belonged to Emily's father. He had loved it and played it for many years. It was very special to Emily, and must be handled with great care. But by the same token, he went on, a violin can only know it's loved if it's played from time to time. So she was happy to let Robbie Joe play it, knowing he would take the greatest care of it. "It may sound a bit different from your grandfather's fiddle, too. Each violin has its own voice. Listen." Stani played a few measures of a folk tune he thought might be familiar to the boy.

"I know that song." He was holding his arms at his sides with great effort, his eagerness evidenced by the gleam in his dark eyes as he looked up to Stani.

"Would you like to hold it? Show me where you put your fingers." With a shiver of his own anticipation, Stani passed the violin to the boy's waiting hands.

Emily was aware of soft voices and bursts of music drifting in and out of her dreams. At one point, she heard Stani's laugh, a crow of delighted surprise. The boy's voice was earnest, and when he played, she sensed the same sincerity. Eventually, she got up and went to the door, listening for the right moment to join them. Stani was sitting in the armchair, while Robbie Joe stood at attention in front of him. Both faces wore the same intense expression. They turned when they heard her step, two pairs of brown eyes, startled by the intrusion from outside their little sphere.

"Robbie Joe, play that again, just for my wife. She's a very fine audience." Stani leaned back in the chair, a fond smile lighting his eyes.

The boy played the melody, note for note, just as he'd been instructed. He kept his eyes closed, a frown creasing his brow as he drew the bow over the strings. Emily felt a chill along her spine, sensing that she was witness to a profound moment in this child's life, and in her husband's as well. When he had ended the piece with a little flourish, and stood gazing expectantly into her face, she clapped her hands softly. "That was marvelous, Robbie Joe. If I hadn't been watching, I would have thought that was my husband playing. You must be a very bright student, to have learned that in just the past hour."

He grinned, the gap in his teeth a startling contrast to the previously serious demeanor. "I didn't learn it, ma'am. I just heard it."

"Robbie Joe, I think now you should have a glass of milk and a slice of my wife's famous cinnamon bread before James comes to take you home. My wife tells me it's hard work, playing the violin. We violinists must keep up our strength." Stani rose, taking the instrument from the boy's hand and laying it gently in the open case. Urging him toward the kitchen, he looked back at Emily. "Incredible!" he whispered, shaking his head, the glint of an unshed tear in his eye.

"He has to have lessons, as soon as possible. Will Angela know of a teacher? Someone willing to travel here, obviously. I'll pay for it, until we can present him to the foundation for a scholarship. I'm not a teacher, but until we can get him one, I'll work with him." Stani was pacing up and down in front of the hearth, propelled by his excitement.

"Stani, please sit down. You're wearing a hole in the carpet. Have you thought that you might want to talk with his parents about this, too? You can't take over his life, you know."

He paused, wheeling around to her with a horrified look in his eyes. "No! That's not what I mean to do at all." He took a deep breath, then rushed on in a different tone, as if justifying his earlier reaction. "He has a family who loves him, and I think will encourage him. I just want to see him develop his talent. And he has talent, Emily. You heard him. He has to learn to read, but he should do that quickly. I did. And he wants it so much. He loses himself in the music completely."

"The way you did? Stani, this child has talent, yes. Maybe a great talent, I don't know. But he isn't you. Encourage him, teach him, but remember to let him be Robbie Joe."

He came to sit beside her, staring into the fire. "I can see myself, at his age, so clearly. I swore, before I even heard him play, that I wouldn't let him be treated the way I was. Then I was inspired to do just what Milo did. Take his talent and leave the boy to run behind."

"And yet you care about him, just the way Milo cares about you. You would never intentionally do anything to hurt him."

Stani dropped his head in his hands. "Is this some lesson I needed to learn? I had to step into Milo's shoes to see how easy it is?"

She ran her hand along his spine. "You're not Milo, darling. And Robbie Joe isn't you. But if it helps you understand Milo and yourself better, then maybe it is the lesson you needed."

When he spoke again, his voice was low and thoughtful. "I'll talk with Robbie, and his parents. Find out what they would like to do. If they want lessons, we'll find a teacher. The foundation can pay for them. But if he wants to play baseball, he's free to do so. Or if he wants to be a farmer, that's fine too. And the next time I get furious at Milo for all the things I think he's done to me, I'll think about Robbie Joe and what he made me feel today. Little boys with violins are hard to resist, aren't they?"

Emily pulled him into her arms, ruffling his hair. "Haven't I told you that, over and over again?"

Chapter Thirteen

The week before Christmas was filled not only with holiday preparations at the farm, but with an onslaught of various workmen and an invasion of rumbling trucks and earth-moving equipment. Stani was astonished with how rapidly the work had begun. A site for the new home had been chosen on the west side of the house, just at the edge of the woods, close to the now overgrown furrows of the former garden. From the window, as he sat at his desk, he could watch the progress.

As he worked on lessons for Robbie Joe, writing out exercises on the yellowed staff paper left behind by Emily's mother, he thought he could sense her nearby, encouraging him in his efforts. "A passionate teacher," Angela had once described her best friend. Lilianne Haynes had left a lasting legacy as a musician, and here in this space which still housed her beloved piano and the music she'd collected over the years, Stani imagined her spirit smiling at his struggles. He had never really taught anyone anything, he realized. But he had been taught by the best. Perhaps he could at least inspire Robbie until a real teacher was found. Music was the one area in which he felt some confidence in his own knowledge. So much that was going on around him was completely beyond his experience, and he welcomed the chance to spend time in the simple act of penning notes on paper.

So much had happened so quickly, Stani had struggled to absorb the details. He and James had returned to the Dixon's home, two days after Robbie's visit. By that time, the electricity had been turned on, a tank of fuel oil had been delivered and a therapist from the tri-county hospital had paid a call. Ruthie was beaming, as she offered them coffee and cookies, and they joined Bobby at the kitchen table.

"The therapist has ordered a brace," Bobby reported. "She thinks with that, I'll be able to walk around better, and she said I can do some exercises here at home to strengthen my back. She says it's healing up real good. But I've gotten weak, staying in bed." His eyes were brighter, Stani noticed, and there was a hint of optimism in his voice.

When Emily crept over to Stani and climbed to her feet, pulling up by his trouser leg, Bobby grinned. "She wants to get up there to your hair again."

"My hair seems to attract beautiful girls named Emily." Stani lifted the little girl, studying her face. She was blond, like her father, with bright blue eyes and rosy cheeks. She reached immediately to his hair, making a little oohing sound deep in her throat. "Sweetheart, you sound like just a dove that coos outside our bedroom window in the summertime." She laughed, whether at his comment, or his hair, he couldn't be sure, but the sound was so delightfully pure, he chuckled in return.

"I won't tell your wife you've been flirting with another girl," James teased. He turned his attention to Bobby. "Sounds like you might be ready to look for a job, soon. Any idea what you might want to do?"

Bobby looked suddenly grim again. "I can't go back to the county. They require a man to be able to lift fifty pounds. I've never done anything else, except farm work when I was just a kid. That doesn't pay enough to support a family the size of mine. I'll just have to see what kind of odd jobs are available, I guess. With Ruthie cleaning and doing laundry, we might scrape by."

"What if I told you there might be a caretaker's job, on a farm? Keeping up the place, taking care of the yard and house, watching out for a little livestock, nothing heavy, but a good bit of responsibility. In the summer, you could plant your own garden, along with one for the homeowner."

Bobby seemed cautiously interested. "You know of something like that? Around here?"

"Yes, I do. But you'd have to live on the place full time. There's a new double-wide, right there on the land, big enough for a family." As Bobby looked questioningly at Ruthie, James added, "The house has two bathrooms."

Watching the silent communication between the couple, Stani tightened his grip on the squirming toddler, holding his breath in anticipation of Bobby's next question.

"Who would I be working for?"

"Emily and Stani."

Bobby's eyes turned to Stani, full of suspicion. "You really need somebody there full time? Or are you just looking to help us out? Because of Emily there?"

Stani flashed a smile, setting the baby on the floor. "As lovely as she is, and as much as we feel we have a very special connection to her, Emily here can't really do the job I need done. Unfortunately, my work keeps us away from the farm too much of the time. And my wife is expecting now. With a family of my own, I'll have to work even more. I need to know that when we can come home, the place will be in order, the house kept clean, and so forth. Plus, we have that old mule to look after. He's very special to my wife, you know. James assures me you are an excellent gardener, and of course, my wife would be thrilled if the farm could produce again the way it did when her father was alive. So you see, Bobby, you'd be the perfect man for the job. I have the need, and you have the skill. I know it might be inconvenient for you to have to move your family, but I think you'd find the compensation fair. You would live there rent free, all utilities provided, and I could pay you and Ruthie each a salary in exchange for the work you would be asked to do." He looked from one serious face to the other. "I understand if you need some time to think it over."

Finally, Bobby took a deep breath, looking straight at his wife, and said, "No, I think we can give you an answer now. I won't be able to do much for a month or two more. And then I may still be a little slow. Right now, I can't even help Ruthie pack things up to move. But if the job was still available in, say, February, I'd be real glad to come to work for you, sir." Stani refrained from glancing at James, but he was sure there was a look of triumph in his eyes.

There were details to be worked out; and with more than a little input from James, he was able to discuss them with his new caretaker with what he hoped sounded like the appropriate authority. The discussion had just ended when the three boys came in from playing in the yard.

"Ah, just the young man I'd hoped to see. How are you, Robbie Joe?" Stani held out his hand and the boy shook it solemnly. "I wanted to have a word with you before I talked with your parents." Robbie immediately sat down at the kitchen table, looking up at him expectantly. Pulling a chair close, Stani took a seat opposite. "Robbie, if you could have lessons on the violin, real lessons from a real teacher, would you be interested in learning?"

"Yes, sir. But I don't have a fid...violin."

"That could be taken care of. But you must understand, learning is hard work. You would have to practice for hours, playing music you might not necessarily like. To please your teacher, you would have to be willing to give up some of your play time. It won't always be fun, but if you want to play really well, you have to do what your teacher asks of you. Do you understand?"

"Yes, sir. But Daddy says we can't pay for lessons."

"Ah, well, I have a solution for that. I know of a place where you can get money for lessons, a scholarship, it's called." He looked up at Ruthie, who had come to stand behind her son, listening closely to the conversation. "Just like a college scholarship, but for music students. As long as you work hard at your lessons, and your teacher sees that you're making progress, this place will pay for everything you need."

"You really think he can play that well? It would be worth asking for money to get him lessons?" Bobby asked.

"Yes, I do. Right now he plays by ear, from memory. But when he learns to read music, I believe he has the makings of a fine musician. *If* that's what he wants, and what you want for him, of course."

Ruthie laid her hands on the boy's shoulders, giving them a squeeze. "Son, do you really want to learn?" For the first time, Stani noticed that Robbie and his mother shared the same dark, intelligent eyes, speaking eyes that held a wealth of emotion in their depths. Now as she gazed at her son, the love and concern reflected in her face stirred something deep inside him. This was the way a mother looked at her child, with her heart in her eyes. Never had he seen that look on his own mother's face, he was sure.

Robbie Joe had seemed to think for just a moment, but now he spoke up clearly. "Yes, ma'am. And I promise, I'll work hard. And keep up my chores and my school work, too. Please, Daddy. I'll still be your right hand, I swear." The pleading eyes went from one parent to the other, and Stani realized he was watching them with much the same expression.

"Would he have to pay back the money?" Bobby wanted to know.

"No, not at all. And if he decided at some point he didn't want to continue, that would be all right too. There's no obligation. It's designed simply to encourage young people like your son to develop their talent."

Bobby looked to his wife again, that same silent communication, and finally met Robbie Joe's anxious stare. "All right, son. If you're willing to work that hard, then go ahead. Maybe God gave you a gift you're supposed to share. Like Mr. Moss here."

Stani felt his face spread into a relieved grin. As Robbie hugged his father and mother, little Emily raised her arms, asking to join in the celebration. Lifting her off the floor, Robbie swung her around until she squealed with pleasure. Once again, Stani had the sense that he had been delivered into this place for his own enlightenment, his eyes opened to wonders he had never known existed.

Once back in the truck, James clapped him on the shoulder. "Congratulations! You just hired yourself a caretaker *and* got yourself a protégé! Not a bad day's work. How many times did you rehearse that little speech you made to Bobby?"

Stani grinned. "Quite a few. Thanks for writing it down for me. I'd never have known how to say all those things. Do you think it would work as well on prospective housekeepers and nannies?"

James laughed. "You'll do okay, now that you've got the hang of it."

Stani shook his head, heaving a long sigh. "I feel as though I'm living someone else's life. How did a kid from a council flat in East London end up living like landed gentry?"

"Are you saying you grew up poor?" James urged the truck out of the yard, throwing a surprised glance in his direction.

"Not exactly. When I was eight, just the age of Robbie Joe, I went to live with Milo and Jana. Compared to what I'd known up until that, they seemed wealthy. It was a long few miles from Lambeth to Pimlico, I can tell you. Of course, once I started making money, our situation steadily improved. I had everything anyone could want, in terms of material things."

"What happened to your parents, if you don't mind my asking?"

"My father left when I was an infant. My mother. . .well I suppose you could say I was more than she'd bargained for. When she found Milo, and he became my manager, she was more than happy to give me up. Fortunately, Milo and Jana were willing to have me. It was hardly a normal family, but it was better than I might have had."

"Wow. I guess I just assumed you were their son, or adopted anyway. Penny told me Milo wasn't always so hot on Emily. That sounded just like a father to me."

Stani breathed another long sigh. "I suppose. Maybe when we're parents, we'll understand why they think they should have control over our lives. I can tell you that already my feelings for that little lump in my wife's belly are extremely protective."

When they reached the farm, James went to inspect the worksite while Stani went in search of Emily. She was in the sunroom, sitting with a cup of tea and a stack of Christmas cards. Immediately, she demanded to know the outcome of his visit with the Dixons.

"Amazing! See how much you can accomplish on your own? I'm

so proud of you, Stani."

"Ha! If James hadn't told me exactly what to say, and you hadn't reminded me that I can't just take control of a child's life, nothing would have been accomplished at all. But it was quite an experience. Every time I go there, see that family together, it's like a vision of something I never thought existed outside of books. Like the Cratchits, or some other incredibly loving fictional family. Will we be like that, do you think? When we have a herd of little lumps, all tramping around the world with us?"

"Of course we will. 'Love that binds,' remember?" Smiling, she fingered the engraving on her wedding ring. She slid into the corner of the armchair, patting the cushion. When he had settled beside her, he gazed down at his own gold band.

"'All things in harmony.' Not just inspiring words, but something real to be achieved. I still have so much to learn about love, in spite of all you've taught me. The love of a family, the concern and respect they have for each other. In the harshest of circumstances, Ruthie and Bobby have remained the best of parents. What allows some people to do that, when others just cut and run?"

With her eyes full of understanding, she nestled her head on his shoulder. "It's not in their grasp, not without a lot of faith, both in themselves and the plan for their lives. But others step up to fill the gap, at least in most cases. You've been blessed Stani, the same way I've been, with people who took on the job of being family where there wasn't any." She was silent for a time, and he had the sense she was facing memories that would no doubt always haunt her here. Just as he still grappled with his past, Emily must find herself confronted at times with all she'd lost, especially in this place she loved so much.

With a little sigh, she straightened. "I'm going to have lunch with Jack tomorrow. I think he may finally have found the courage to tell me he's getting married. Then Penny gets here, and there's always somebody stopping in to visit. Before we know it, Christmas Eve will be here. Do you think tonight we could just be at home, staring at the tree and the little crèche figures marching to Bethlehem? With so much happening, we haven't had much peace or comfort, have we?"

"No, but we've had our share of blessings and miracles, I'd say. Was it really just a year ago, I came here to tell you I wanted to marry you and God spoke to me so clearly? And then little Emily made her dramatic entrance?"

"And I fell apart all over you and you took such good care of me? Yes, it was just last year. And this year is turning out to be just as full of wonders." She laid her hand over the bulge at her waist. "And just think, next year, we'll have even more to celebrate."

He nuzzled her hair, chuckling. "Let's get this year behind us first. I'm already a bit overwhelmed. Since this will be our only Christmas as newlyweds, let's make the most of it."

When James came to the back door, intent on giving a progress report, he was treated to the sight of the two of them twined together in the big chair. He paused, considering whether to leave them alone, or interrupt the obviously tender moment. If it had been Penny next to him in that chair, her hands in his hair and his lips on hers, he would have been less than pleased by any intrusion. He backed slowly down the steps and made his way to the truck. What did they care about water lines and septic tanks, anyway?

Chapter Fourteen

Jack had said very little during the drive into town. As Emily laughingly described Stani's efforts to grasp all that was involved in setting up the mobile home, he smiled absent-mindedly. Once they were seated at a table in the little cafe, he seemed to have difficulty meeting her gaze.

"Jack, is there something you want to tell me?" She grinned in spite of herself.

He shook his head, smiling sheepishly. "I didn't know it would be this hard. It's not as if you'll be all that surprised, I'm sure. I guess telling you makes it more official somehow."

"Yes?"

"I'm going to marry Martha Jean. In the spring. And we wondered if you and Stani would read at the wedding. Sort of the way you did at your own." The words seemed to stick in his throat, bursting forth in short breathless croaks.

"Of course we will, just as long as you do it early in the spring. I won't be traveling much after April, you know. But for you, of course we'll be here. Congratulations, Jack."

"You don't think I'm too old? I mean, after I've waited this long, it hardly seems practical."

"Practical has nothing to do with it. If you and Martha Jean want to be together, age means nothing. I know she'll take good care of you. And you of her." Reaching across the tablecloth, she laid her hand over his.

"She's a good woman, Em. Down to earth, independent. She has lots of common sense." As he spoke, she couldn't avoid the obvious. The contrast was stark, as if he had intentionally chosen a woman as different as possible from the one he had loved all those years.

"Just what you need. I'm so happy for you, Jack." She hesitated a moment, studying his still handsome face. "And Mother would be happy too, to know you'll finally have someone who loves you." Her eyes filled with tears as he looked up in surprise. "I know she was concerned that you never married. She wanted you to be happy, you know?' When he looked away, his jaw tightening, she went on softly. "It's all right, Jack. I guess I always knew how you felt about her."

He took out his handkerchief and passed it to her. "Don't have one of your crying spells now, please. I might have to join you." She dabbed at her eyes, smiling. "You're an amazing girl, Jiliand Emily. Do you read everyone's mind as easily as you do mine?"

"No. But we've been together my whole life, Jack. You're my third parent, remember?"

He grinned, and she was thankful the moment had passed and they could move on together. "Does that mean I'm going to be a grandfather now?"

"Absolutely. Our children are going to be overloaded with grandparents of all sorts. Americans, Brits, Hungarians. Neither of us had grandparents, you know, so we're looking forward to seeing all of you loving our babies."

"You're sure you're all right? I'm going to worry, no matter what you say, but tell me anyway."

"I'm fine. Much better now that I'm home. The world is an exciting place, for a while. But we were both in need of some peace. Stani maybe even more than I was. He works so hard out there. He demands so much of himself. He hasn't exactly slowed down since we got home, either. But I'm so proud of what he's doing here."

"So am I. He and James McConnell make quite a team."

She nodded, her brows shooting up in a knowing arch. "James tells Stani what to do, and Stani does it."

Jack laughed and patted her hand. "Sort of like marriage, right?"

Chapter Fifteen

Christmas Eve dawned cold and cloudy. There was snow to the north, and preparations were being made for a white Christmas. Emily had decided on a traditional English dinner, roast beef and Yorkshire pudding, with a few equally traditional Southern dishes thrown in for good measure. The number of guests kept fluctuating, and she planned for twelve, just in case everyone invited actually showed up. With Angela and Lil driving over from Charlottesville and Charles Evans coming from Richmond, the weather might well cut the numbers in the party, but she was determined to be prepared for a full table. The house had taken on an air of festive anticipation, with the scents of evergreen and cinnamon in every room. This Christmas would be a time of both old and new traditions, their first married Christmas. The very idea made her want to dance to the holiday music that played on the radio in the kitchen.

"You're going to overdo, Emily. Why not just have roast beef sandwiches and a nice big salad? That way I can at least make the salad." Increasingly, Stani felt the need to curb her overreaching enthusiasm. As always, she was determined to throw herself wholeheartedly into this, her favorite time of year. The countertops were lined with tins of homemade treats, which would be shared with their guests, and he had noticed her sampling the variety with regularity. Her energy seemed to have risen to its normal level, and the queasiness had been replaced by an extremely healthy appetite.

"We don't eat sandwiches on Christmas Day! That's what we eat for the rest of the week." She arched one expressive brow and he took the meaning to heart. Emily knew best how to enjoy this holiday, while he was still a novice at the celebration. "Now, if you'll help me clean the house today, tomorrow we can just put the roast in the oven before we leave for church. Dinner will practically make itself. You'll see. It'll be wonderful."

"Let me get Ruthie to clean again. I'm sure she could use the money."

"No. It's Christmas Eve. She'll want to spend the day with Emily. It's her first birthday. We can do it. We managed just fine last summer."

"Last summer you weren't pregnant." He caught her in his arms, as she headed for the closet under the stairs. "No vacuuming! Sit!" Laughing, she took his face in her hands, kissing him hard.

"Oh, good grief! Don't you two ever stop?" Penny Riley stood framed in the doorway, her arms full of packages and an expression of disapproval on her pert features. "I thought you might have gotten that out of your systems by now." She laughed, a warm throaty laugh that seemed to originate in the depths of her tiny form. Five foot two and barely a hundred pounds, Penny nonetheless brought a compelling presence to any room.

"Never! What are you doing here so early? I thought you and James were coming after lunch." In the midst of hugs, Stani took the load from her hands and Emily helped her out of her coat. "Look at you! Do you always dress for success, even here in the hills?" Penny was indeed wearing the tailored jacket and silk blouse portion of her corporate lawyer's uniform, along with blue jeans and high heels.

"Hey, this is my casual success look. Besides, my old W and M sweatshirts are getting pretty ratty these days. And I might point out that little number you're wearing isn't exactly faded overalls." She gave Emily another hug, brushing at the deep red pile of her gold embroidered caftan.

With a grin, Emily drew the folds of the robe taut across her waist and turned her profile to Penny. Words were unnecessary as their eyes met, Penny's growing slowly wider in realization.

"Already? Good grief, Em! The last time I saw you, you were barely married!"

"We didn't waste time. Now come and sit and tell me what's going on. All James said is you were coming to spend Christmas with him. And where is he, by the way?" Dropping onto the couch, Emily pulled Penny down beside her.

"He had to make some kind of emergency trip to Charlottesville, he said. So I thought I'd just come up here and spend the time with you two. I'm not interrupting anything important, I hope." Penny looked to Stani, who had gone to the fireplace to poke at the blaze. "Nothing you can't resume at a later time?"

"Perfect timing, actually. I was just about to tie my wife to a chair, before she could go on a cleaning spree. She seems determined to wear herself out today. Just keep her there and visit with her, won't you?"

"Gladly. But if you need help with anything, I can do that too. I need something to do to feel useful." For the first time, Emily sensed Penny might have come in search of a sympathetic ear or two.

"Maybe later. First I want to know what's been going on. I keep feeling James is avoiding telling me something." She waited, watching as the smile faded from Penny's eyes and she seemed to be composing her response.

"It's pretty simple, really. James and I are in love and my parents have chosen to ignore it. They won't accept that I want to marry a man who's as committed to his faith as I am to mine. We know we can work things out, but they won't even talk to me about it." She looked from one to the other, her eyes filling with tears. "Any way I look at it, I'm going to hurt someone I love. I never expected them to be so stubborn about a thing like that."

"But they want you to be happy. Surely they'll come around. Maybe they just need to get know James better." Emily put an arm around Penny's shoulders, and Stani took a seat nearby, leaning close in support.

Looking from one pair of concerned eyes to the other, Penny shook her head. "They won't even try. He's come to Boston twice now. The first time, they were painfully polite. The second, my dad didn't even come home in time for dinner. It's obvious they're just hoping we'll give up. I think my mom might be a little more inclined to accept him, but she'll never go against my dad. He wasn't even speaking to me after I told them I was coming here for Christmas. What am I going to do? James is the best thing that's come into my life in years. I can't let him go, and I can't turn my back on my parents, either." Giving way to tears, she buried her face in her hands.

Stani went to his knees in front of her. "Penny, James talked to me about this, too. He's as unhappy about it as you are," he said softly, laying a hand on her arm.

"I know. He even told me to let him go, if this was going to be such a problem. That just made me even more certain he's the man I want to spend my life with. There has to be a way to resolve this, I just haven't found it yet." In typical Penny fashion, she wiped her face and took a deep breath. "I'm not going to let it spoil my time here. James' parents have been so kind. They've made me feel like one of the family already. His dad said he'd pray for us every day, and for my folks, too. And his mother is without a doubt the sweetest woman I've ever met. This is going to be a wonderful Christmas, I know. I just had to get that out of my system. Now what is it you need so desperately to clean, Em? I could use something to keep me busy until James gets back."

"Where exactly did he have to go? I'm surprised he would leave you on your own."

"I have no idea. Last night we talked for a long time, past midnight. I slept late, and when I got up, he had left me a note. He said he'd been inspired by what I said last night, to forgive him for running off."

Stani chuckled. "What on earth did you say that inspired him to run off?"

"I told him about the advice Emily had given me, when I was here for your wedding. About not hesitating. You remember, Em."

"Failure is in the hesitation." Emily smiled knowingly at Stani. "I told her two very wise men had taught me the truth of that. Sounds as if James may have taken it to heart. I guess you'll have to wait and see, won't you?"

"In the meantime, give me something to do, please! I can't sit around wondering. I'd rather scrub floors!"

When John returned from town with the grocery order he'd been dispatched to pick up, the house was sparkling, and the three of them were laughing around the kitchen table.

"Looks like the Christmas spirit has arrived early. Judging by the weight of these sacks, you must be planning to feed an army tomorrow, girl."

"Just a small one. If only the snow will hold off, so everyone can get here." Peeking into the first of the bulging sacks, she oohed at the contents. "Look at this roast! Mr. Brown has outdone himself."

"That little market is quite a place. The proprietor said to tell you 'Merry Christmas,' and he sent you this, 'specially for you, he said, straight from Scotland." He produced a tartan tin, which Emily took with a smile.

"He's been sending me this every year since I was a little girl." As she continued to peek into the sacks, her eyes lit up excitedly. "Penny, if you really want to stay busy, we could get started cooking now. This will be my first Christmas dinner in my new kitchen. And now that I'm not feeling queasy at the thought of food, I'm dying to cook again." Watching her pull things from first one bag and then another, enthusiastically examining each item, Stani laughed.

"I don't know whether to be relieved that you're feeling so much better, or worried that you'll hurt yourself banging around among the pots and pans."

"I can't hurt myself, Stani. Not with you and John and Penny here to help. The more we get done today, the less we'll have to worry about tomorrow. Now which one of you big strong men wants to help me heft this gorgeous roast out of the sack? Penny, there's an apron hanging there by the door. Don't get yourself all messy." She looked up just in time to see the first snowflakes drift past the window and her eyes clouded. "Oh, dear. I guess we'll have a white Christmas after all."

Coming up behind her, Stani slid his arms around her waist. "Don't worry, love. At least this time, I'll be right here with you, standing on my own two feet." They stood gazing out across the yard for a moment, picturing the very different scene that Christmas four years ago. "Now, tell us what to do, my darling girl. We are your humble servants."

When James came in search of Penny, he found the farmhouse filled with the sounds and smells of Christmas. Music blared from the stereo in the front room, and he had only to follow the aroma of baking bread and the seductive scent of cinnamon and apples to find the merry little group gathered in the kitchen.

"Ah, James. Just in time for lunch. Come, have a seat next to this lovely lady and I'll make you a sandwich." Stani rose from his place, taking note of the intense expression on his friend's face. Under normal circumstances he would have expected James to instantly comment on the somewhat unusual attire of the ladies at the table. Penny was now wearing one of Stani's old work shirts to protect her silk blouse, and her high heels had been abandoned for a pair of much too large bedroom slippers borrowed from Emily. On one cheek, she sported a becoming smear of cake flour. The lady of the house presented a charming picture of domestic efficiency in her elegant velvet robe, topped by a voluminous apron complete with huge ruffles at the shoulders, and her hair had been caught up in a haphazard ponytail. Stani had just been teasing them about their holiday fashion trends when James entered.

But James seemed oblivious, marching straight up to Penny and holding out his hand. "Will you come with me into the other room, please?" was his only greeting.

Her eyes wide with a mixture of anxiety and interest, Penny took his hand and followed him wordlessly through the French doors, which

James ceremoniously closed behind them.

They watched from the kitchen, helpless to do otherwise, as the scene in the sunroom played out. When James had urged Penny to sit on the ottoman, he dropped to one knee in front of her, very deliberately reaching into the pocket of his worn fatigue jacket, and drawing out and opening the lid on a small black box. Stani heard Emily's gasp, no doubt in response to the emotions that crossed Penny's face as her eyes went from the box to James' face and back several times. Reaching out, she ran her hands into the long dark hair and pulled him close, at which point Stani let out his own breath, a sigh of relief that once again a man's soul-baring declaration had not been spurned.

When it became obvious that James had proposed and been accepted, judging by the tender if somewhat awkward embrace that went on for several minutes, John cleared his throat and pointed to the front of the house. "It seems they might want a bit of privacy, if you two can tear yourselves away," he whispered sharply.

Emily wiped at her eyes, as the three of them settled around the fireplace. "I guess James did take my advice to heart. He didn't seem the least bit hesitant just then."

"My knees are weak, just from watching him." Stani grinned, taking a seat beside her. "That was a bold move. James took a bit of a risk, don't you think?"

"I seem to recall a certain violinist taking a similar risk last Christmas. At least James appears to have asked Penny, rather than informing her of his intentions." Smiling into his eyes, she tenderly brushed at the stray curl on his forehead. "Either way, it's a risk worth taking, wouldn't you say?"

"If it weren't snowing, I'd consider taking a walk. There's no end to the pairing off around here. I heard that even the sheriff's taken the big step." Despite his words, John seemed content to stretch his legs toward the hearth. "You don't suppose there's something in the water supply?"

Glancing at her watch, Emily frowned. "I hate to disturb them, but my pies should come out of the oven now. I'll just tiptoe in there and try not to gawk." She shook her head slowly, as she started toward the kitchen. "Imagine, James proposing to Penny. In our sunroom. On Christmas Eve. Miracles, for sure."

For the first time, Stani Moss performed in the church where a year earlier he had begun his own journey to meet the Christ Child. On the night of their return to the farm, Pastor Mike had asked if he would consider playing at the Christmas Eve service and he had immediately agreed. Now, as he sat with Emily and John in a pew full of friends who had been strangers a year earlier, he knew he had completed that journey. Watching the cherub choir, now under the care of Sara McConnell, seated around the crèche just as they had been with Emily that night, he felt the same tingle of anticipation. Glancing at her candlelit face beside him, he saw much the same emotion shining in her eyes, and the corners of her mouth were turned up in that sweet, tranquil smile he so loved. Beyond her, James and Penny sat hand in hand, their eyes meeting briefly as if to confirm the step they had taken together such a short time ago.

At the rear of the already crowded church, a whispered commotion could be heard. Turning, Stani saw that Jack had arrived and was ushering in a group of late arrivals. Leading the way down the aisle, he was followed by Bobby, walking slowly and leaning heavily on a cane. Next to him, Ruthie carried little Emily, who gazed down on the faces along the way, her eyes bright with curiosity. Three little boys followed, Robbie Joe bringing up the rear. Stani watched their progress, as Jack brought them straight to the front of the church, where they filed into the pew directly opposite. From his seat on the aisle, Robbie Joe looked across at Stani and smiled his brightest gap-toothed grin. As he turned to leave, Jack laid a hand on Stani's shoulder. "Merry Christmas, son."

The organ began to play, as the last of the congregation filed in, and when Pastor Mike took his place in the pulpit, a chill touched the back of Stani's neck. "This is the night of brilliant stars and heralding angels. This is the night of humble shepherds and watchful wise men. This is the night of our Savior's birth. Let us worship God together, on this night of miracles."

Stani listened to the scriptures and carols, Emily's hand tucked securely in his. At the appointed time, he rose and took his violin to stand near the manger. Aware of the wide-eyed cherubs, watching from the other side of the crèche, he smiled. Then closing his eyes, he played. What Child Is This?, a tune as familiar as his own breathing, tonight infused with a new spirit. When the choir joined him, the music soared, swirling within the little church to draw in every listener. In his mind's eye, he saw Emily, her eyes glistening in the candlelight, her hand resting lightly over their unborn child. His heart swelled in his chest, filled with more love and longing than he could ever have imagined a year ago, when he had stood at the back of this church and for the first time recognized the voice of God speaking so clearly.

When he returned to his seat, he met the gaze of the little boy opposite, a gaze so full of awe that he felt another shiver of emotion. For a long moment, he stared at Stani as if seeing him for the first time. But when Stani smiled into the dark eyes, Robbie returned an adoring grin and darting across the aisle, threw himself into Stani's arms. Wordlessly, he gathered the child to him, momentarily overwhelmed by his own response. This boy, so earnest and open, would never understand the power of his simple gesture. But for Stani, who had yearned for the courage to show the same kind of gratitude to the man he most wanted to please, Robbie Joe's arms, tightly hugging his neck, were the finest Christmas gift he could ever receive.

Chapter Sixteen

Emily smiled sleepily at the twinkling tree lights. "Do you think Christmas Eve will always be this special for us? I can't imagine anything better than tonight. But next year, we'll be somebody's parents."

"Somebody's parents." Leaning over her lap, he whispered, "Did you hear that? You're just 'somebody?' Surely we can do better than that, Mother."

She ruffled his hair, laughing softly. "Only he, or she, knows for sure. Do you have names in mind already, Papa?"

"Of course. I think Ludwig might be nice, or then again, Felix. Elinora has a nice ring to it, or maybe Giselle."

"What, not Stanley? Or just plain Jane?" She settled herself against his side, drawing his arm around her neck. "What if it were twins? Freddie and Eddie, or Cindy and Mindy?"

"Twins? Two? Good lord, Emily, you don't really think it could be twins, do you?" He turned to stare into her face, his eyes suddenly dark and wide.

"The doctor did mention the possibility, based on the size of this little lump of ours. I suppose we'll find out soon enough."

He was silent for a time, considering the idea. "Two of everything, times three nurseries. That's a lot of baby gear. Good thing their father makes a decent living."

Emily snorted softly. "Is that all you can think of, the expense? What about twice the number of dirty diapers, twice the midnight feedings, twice the sleepless nights, diaper rashes and first teeth? Good thing their mother is going to have lots of help from their father."

"I still like the idea of having just one baby at a time. That's terrifying enough. I think I'll stick with that thought until we know for sure."

"Wasn't it wonderful to have all of the Dixons there? Emily has grown so fast! I still remember what she looked like, all wet and wrinkled, there in the back of Jack's car."

"And now she's bright and beautiful. I hope our daughter likes me as much as she does."

"Daughter? What happened to Felix?"

"Makes no difference. But my son is not going to be beautiful, you understand that don't you? It's bad enough that you label me so inappropriately. My son will be handsome. My daughter will be beautiful, like her mother. Got it?"

"Yes, sir." Snuggling closer, she sighed contentedly. "Do you realize it's almost Christmas? We should go to bed. Christmas Day falling on Sunday makes for early rising. Look outside and see if it's snowing again. I'm so glad it stopped, so we could at least get to church tonight." Stani reluctantly rose and went to the window, peering out into the darkness.

"Looks like we might escape the worst of it. Still only a dusting on the ground." He stood over her, holding out his hands. "Come on, love, let's spend this Christmas Eve in our own bed. No more sleeping on couches for us. Romantic it may have been, but now I have the right to sleep next to my wife in wedded bliss." Pulling her to her feet, he drew her into his arms. "Merry Christmas, my darling girl. Blessings abound."

When Emily was sleeping soundly, Stani left the bed. Shrugging into his robe, he tiptoed barefoot out of the room and made his way to the kitchen in the darkness. It would be nearly seven in the morning, he reckoned. Early, but surely not too early. When he heard the voice answer at the other end, he hesitated for just an instant. "Milo? I hope I didn't wake you."

"Stani, is something wrong? Emily's all right, isn't she?" He sounded sleepy. And alarmed.

"We're fine. Perfect, in fact. I just wanted to wish you and Jana a Merry Christmas."

"Oh. Merry Christmas to you, too. And to Emily, of course. What time is it there, Stani?"

"After midnight. I was awake, thinking. Milo, thank you for everything you did for me. I know it wasn't always easy between us. But I am grateful. I hope you know that." He wasn't sure what else to say. Or if Milo understood how much he meant to convey with those few words.

The pause at the other end might have indicated many things, but when he spoke again, Stani was sure Milo's voice held more emotion than he would have been willing to admit. "I'm the one who is grateful, Stani. When you have a child, you'll understand that. I only hope you'll be better able to show it than I could. Now go back to bed, my boy. Don't leave that lovely girl alone for too long."

Emily rolled over and snuggled against him when he slipped beneath the covers. "Where have you been?" she sighed.

"I called Milo to wish them a Merry Christmas."

She raised her head to meet his eyes in the dimness. "Miracles?"

"Most definitely."

Chapter Seventeen

Emily was in the kitchen just after dawn, humming along with the carols on the radio as the bacon sizzled and when Stani crept up behind her at the range, she let out a little sigh. "You didn't really think you could startle me? I could feel you coming all through the house."

"Feel me?" He lifted her hair and nuzzled her neck, his hand finding the little bulge at her waist.

"You're radiating something this morning. Christmas joy, maybe? I could hear it echoing in your footsteps." She turned in his arms, a twinkle in her eyes. "Besides, I heard you banging around in the hall closet. What is it you have hidden in there, anyway?"

"Christmas surprise. But not until after breakfast." His kiss was meant as a reminder of all the past breakfasts they'd shared, including the one on Christmas morning only a year ago.

They didn't rush through the meal, and John joined them while they were still at the table, pouring a cup of tea and helping himself to a chunk of cinnamon bread. "What's on the agenda this morning?"

His eyes widened as Emily went down the list. Open a few gifts, dress for church. Have a quick lunch after church, then start dinner preparations, which would involve a list of things all its own.

"No just sitting around the fireplace with our feet up? Yesterday was hectic enough. I could use a day off."

Their voices rose in unison protest. "John, it's Christmas Day! This is the real celebration. Friends and family all gathered for a meal, music and gifts. Tonight, when we're all so full we can't move, *then* we'll sit by the fire." Emily was on her feet, pulling at Stani's hand. "But right now, I want to show you something, darling. In fact, if I don't, I'll just explode. Get your coat. Hurry!"

Laughing and rolling his eyes at John, he let her lead him to the front door. "Really, love, you want me to go outside *now*? It's snowing!"

"Only a little flurry. And there's nothing much on the ground. It won't take long!" Her excitement was tangible, as she bundled into her coat. And it was infectious. He realized his own heart was racing as he did the same.

He took a moment to tie her muffler high around her ears. "Are you sure you can't just *tell* me what it is I'm supposed to see, without running out into the yard yourself?"

She grabbed his hand and pulled him through the door. "No! I want to see your face."

He followed her across the yard toward the gate, struck by the stark winter scene that spread in every direction from the high ground on which the house was situated. Beyond the surrounding valley, the distant ridges were nearly obscured by a blue haze. The ground underfoot was covered with a light dusting of dry snow, and huge flakes drifted lazily through the air. Near the gate, a lone pair of cardinals took flight, their bright wings a startling intrusion of color into the gray landscape. The silence was profound, and he took a moment to appreciate the peace of this place. And then Emily pulled him through the gate and came to an abrupt halt, steering him around until he stood facing the house again. The satisfied smile on her face suggested they had reached their destination, but he couldn't imagine what he was expected to see.

"Look, Stani!" She nodded toward the fence, or was it meant to be toward the house? Still, he couldn't grasp this marvelous thing she was showing him so proudly.

Finally, his eyes fell on the sign. The large oval that bore the name of Valley Rise Farm. It had been newly painted, the letters a fresh, crisp green against the white background. Beneath, scripted in red, were the names of the farm's proprietors. Now, instead of the former "J.E. Haynes," it read "S. and E. Haynes-Moss." When he couldn't find words, she hugged his arm and said softly, "James brought it out and hung it last night. Do you like it? I decided to use our names the way you did for the foundation."

He took another moment to recognize what this really meant to her. It was her farm, her legacy from her parents. Now she was adding his name to the most treasured thing in her life. "I love it, darling girl. You know, I even had a thought about it, when we were shopping for the caretaker's home. But then I decided it was too much yours to ever change it. Haynes has always been here, and for some chap named Moss to move in was just too overreaching." He wrapped her in his arms, staring into the intense gray depths of her eyes.

"Not overreaching at all. It's yours now too. It's *ours*, Stani. And that J.E. Haynes person is gone forever." Her kiss was deep and sweet and for a time he was lifted off the cold hillside, swept away by the miracle of this girl in his arms, who carried his child deep inside her, whose love had brought him to a place he could call home.

"We should go inside, love. It's too cold out here for the mother of my child. Besides, I have something for you, too. Although, I'm afraid it will pale in comparison to a farm."

Back inside, warming her feet near the fire, Emily waited impatiently for her surprise. When Stani held out the long blue box, she grinned. "Miss Marshall, I presume?"

"Of course. This year she already had a selection of things picked out for me to choose from. Sort of the 'Emily Moss Collection, by Tiffany's' I suppose. But this was by far her favorite. Merry Christmas, darling girl."

John heard Emily's gasp and squeal of delight all the way in the kitchen. He arrived in the front room in time to see Stani fasten the gift around her neck and accept the long, tender thank you kiss. From what he could see, the boy had indeed done well for his bride's first Christmas. The wide choker of delicately set rubies and diamonds suited Emily to perfection. Of all the numerous pieces of jewelry she'd received in the past months, this one was by far the most beautiful, and he suspected the most expensive. His security guard's sensibility reminded him that not only was he responsible for a million dollar fiddle, the girl's jewelry case represented yet another valuable to be guarded. But the sight of the two of them locked in each other's arms with those radiant smiles on their faces, he felt sure, represented the most priceless treasure he could ever hope to protect.

By dinnertime on Christmas Day, which had been set for five o'clock, it was evident that Mother Nature was in a benevolent mood. While occasional flurries came and went, there remained only a picturesque dusting of white on the landscape, and the roadways were unaffected. At Stani's insistence, Emily had taken a brief rest after lunch, but nothing, she declared, would prevent her from being in the kitchen, at least supervising the final preparations. When the first of the guests arrived, Angela and Lil making their usual exuberant entrance just after three, the aroma of roasting meat had filled the house, blending with the scents of evergreens and a blazing oak fire.

Stani was struck once again by the charm of the dynamic mother-daughter duo. As he took their coats, he marveled at how much alike they were, with their long dark curls and black eyes. Angela, though her hair was now streaked with bands of silver, was still as slim and lovely as her daughter, and just as animated. Stani noted with amazement that they never really stopped talking or moving, infusing their energy into the very air. Both gifted musicians, they also shared a certain mystical quality, and Emily had more than once suggested they might be just a little bit psychic. Angela in particular left the impression that nothing escaped her keen gaze, while Lil seemed at times to see beyond the obvious with an uncanny inner vision.

Now Lil hugged Emily and smiled up into her face, a sparkle of mischief in her eyes. "You didn't waste any time, did you? You know you're going to be the world's best mother? You had plenty of practice, mothering me."

"I would resent that if it weren't true. Even when you were just little girls, Emily was always leading you around by the hand." Angela eyed the two fondly and held out her arms. Stani watched as the three of them hugged in a little circle, once again thinking that he loved Emily's family, even as he admitted their vibrancy and enthusiasm could at times be intimidating. Thankfully, they both approved of him, Lil in fact being what Emily termed his biggest fan. And Angela had made it clear from their first meeting on Christmas Day a year ago, that she wholeheartedly supported his pursuit of Emily. Had the opposite been the case, he would have faced a formidable opponent.

"Stani, my dear, why is there no music playing?" Angela asked now, her black brows arching sharply as she rolled up her sleeves in preparation for kitchen duty. And obediently, he went to do her bidding, wondering that she hadn't demanded he play for them himself. Angela, as Emily so aptly put it, was a force, plain and simple.

As Emily resumed her work in the kitchen, Angela and Lil were assigned the duty of setting the table. The meal would be served buffet style, she had decided, using her mother's French china and crystal. An antique linen cloth was brought from the sideboard, and Lil took on the task of ironing, standing at the board in the sun room, where she could be part of the lively conversation in the kitchen. While Stani and Emily worked side by side, Angela polished glassware and John sat at the table with a cup of tea, carefully staying out of the way, and clearly hoping to avoid any sort of culinary duties.

"It's a treat to just watch all this work going forward, and know the experts are on hand." He had taunted Stani earlier about his enlistment into the catering corps.

"I actually enjoy it, you know. Not many other jobs include such lovely co-workers."

"Save your strength, John." Angela gave him a sharp look. "We'll need fresh troops for the cleanup brigade."

When the table was set, Lil posted herself at the front window, watching anxiously. "Charles should be here by now. I hope he hasn't forgotten how to get up here. He isn't very good with directions."

"Oh? And this is the man you're going to cross Europe with?" Angela teased.

"You can't take a wrong turn on a train, Mom. For the millionth time, we'll be just fine." A car coming through the gate caught her attention. But a moment later, she turned away in disappointment. "Emily, here comes a carload of people."

Mike and Sara, with Penny in tow, joined the crowd in the kitchen, spilling over into the sun room. As Stani added wood to the stove, he noticed Penny sitting on the ottoman, stroking the upholstery thoughtfully. "Fond memories?" he said softly as he walked past.

Her smile was radiant, as she looked up. "Oh, yes! What a Christmas this is turning out to be!"

Stani laughed. "You're right about that! And where exactly is your fiancé?"

"He said he had some 'folks' to check on. I don't know how he's ever going to leave this place. He has a whole host of 'folks' he seems to be watching out for." The proud gleam in her eyes said clearly how she felt about James' informal mission here in the valley.

Martha Jean appeared in the kitchen doorway, announcing proudly, "Look who we found out on the highway!"

Jack, his arms full of various parcels, came through the door, Charles Evans close behind. "This young man was sitting at the bottom of the drive. Apparently the map someone drew for him got turned upside down, and he was about to head back for Richmond. Luckily, we came along just in time." He looked pointedly at Lil, grinning broadly.

By the time James arrived, dinner was ready to be served. "Sorry, Em. But I had to get Mrs. O'Neill's water running. Pipes froze solid last night. While I was up on the ridge, I stopped in at the Dixons'. That's one happy bunch up there tonight! Warm house, plenty of good food and the kids all got something new to play with, *and* to wear for Christmas. Thanks to the Christmas Family boxes, not to mention that anonymous donor, this is the best Christmas they've ever had." He took a moment to drop a hand on Stani's shoulder. "Blessings all around, eh, man?"

It was a very different Christmas, Emily thought, as she sat watching the faces around the table. Different in so many wonderful ways. The house was filled with the people she loved most. Her husband, her godparents, her friends, old and new, all gathered around this table, laughing and talking. Angela was deep in animated conversation with John. As James and Charles laughed over some shared joke, Penny and Lil looked on affectionately. Mike and Stani were talking seriously, their heads close together. And Sara, with a sweet look of satisfaction, was watching as James, still laughing, reached over to drape a long arm around the back of Penny's chair.

Not exactly the solitary life she had imagined, Emily thought. So different, in fact, that it was hard to believe she had really expected to be happy with that life. She looked at Stani, his bright head bent to catch something Mike was saying, as a roar of laughter went up from the other end of the table. Love, quite simply, had changed everything. And not just for her, but for most of the others here as well. She had seen the look in Lil's eyes, when Charles walked through the door. And Penny and James seemed to have put aside their worries, determined to create as many happy memories as possible while they could. Even Jack and his fiancée were holding hands, Emily noticed, as Martha Jean explained something about their wedding plans to Sara.

Stani looked up and their eyes met. She sighed, smiling down the length of the table. He knew what she was thinking, she was sure. That all this was possible only because he had come back to find her. That all the happiness and promise gathered at their table was in some way connected to the moment he had walked up on her porch and taken her in his arms. He smiled, that beautiful flashing smile that today she knew was meant only for her. While the conversation and the laughter continued, he rose and came around to her chair, drawing her to her feet. Without a word, she took his face between her hands and kissed him. The room fell suddenly silent. Softly at first, and then with increasing enthusiasm, their guests applauded.

It had been a perfect Christmas, they agreed. Curled together in the big sleigh bed, both pleasantly exhausted by the long hours of celebration, they talked softly of the joy around their table tonight. Tomorrow, the work would resume on the building site, with the mobile home due to be delivered by the end of the week. If the weather cooperated, it would be ready for occupancy by the week after New Year's. And then they would have to begin packing for the return to London. "It'll be over too soon, Stani. You won't have had any time to rest. What you're doing is wonderful, but you were supposed to be relaxing here."

"But the rewards outweigh any effort I'm making. And besides, James is doing all the hard work. All I've done is sign some papers. And learn a great many valuable lessons. That seems to happen to me, every time I'm here. If I could only remember all of them, when I get back to that other life. Keep reminding me, will you, when I get so caught up in all the unimportant things, things that have nothing to do with the real world?"

"Maybe just a picture of Robbie Joe would do the job. He seems to have shown you a lot about what really matters."

Stani smiled, the image of a gap-toothed grin floating past his mind's eye. "So he has. Blessings come in the most unexpected packages, don't they?"

Chapter Eighteen

The call came just after breakfast. Peg's father, Michael Shannon, after suffering years of failing health, had died quietly in his sleep on Christmas Night. Peg had been in Florida with him, and she had called Stani before leaving for New York. She wanted him to play at the funeral, which was scheduled for Friday morning at St. Patrick's. Emily heard him saying, "Of course, I will. Just tell me what you want, anything. I'm so sorry, love. I know how close you were," as she walked into the kitchen. When he hung up the phone, she waited for him to explain.

"I'll have to leave on Thursday. And I suppose John will have to go with me. I don't like leaving you, though." He turned to the window, gazing toward the ditches that stood waiting for the work crew to return. "So much going on, and now this."

"I'll be fine, Stani. Penny will still be here. Maybe she can stay with me. When will you be back?" She poured herself a cup of tea, sitting down at the table.

"Probably not before late Friday night. We'll fly out of Washington, I suppose." He turned abruptly toward the front of the house. "I need to talk to John. And then I have to see what else James needs me to do, before I go. I also need to talk to Robbie Joe, to let him know we think we've found him a teacher. Angela should be calling in a day or so, but she was sure she knew someone who would come out here. And then I'll need to get him an instrument. Maybe I could do that while I'm in New York." He paused, catching sight of the expression in her eyes. "What's wrong?"

"Slow down just a little bit, darling. You have three days to get things done. I'm sure you have time for another cup of tea with your wife, before you run off to save the world. Besides, John isn't even up yet. Please sit down, just for ten minutes?" She patted the seat beside her, and he retraced his steps.

"I'm sorry. When I heard Peg's voice, she sounded so needy. I guess I overreacted, didn't I?"

"Maybe a little, but only because you care. I wouldn't expect any less. You're sure you don't want me to go with you?"

"I don't like you traveling unnecessarily. It'll only be overnight. As long as you promise to be good."

"Of course. And it'll give me a chance to spend more time with Penny. I've been thinking that I should make plans for the nursery before we leave. Maybe she and I could go to Charlottesville, check out some baby furniture, if I can tear her away from James."

Stani frowned. "Only if the weather is perfect. Promise me."

"I promise. Really Stani, you can't lock me in the house until the baby comes. I'm fine, and now that my energy seems back to normal, I have things to do. Please stop worrying about me. Stop worrying about everything."

He stood up suddenly, heading out of the kitchen.

"Where are you going?" she called after him.

"To the bathroom, to read the wall."

The trip to New York had been accomplished without too much effort, thanks in large part to John's insistence that he take care of everything without any interference from Stani. "You've never dealt with trips before, why start now? Just let me do my job, lad, while you do what you have to here. And you might try getting a bit of rest before we go. Didn't I just see you rubbing your head? A migraine comes on, and Peg will have to make do without you."

The funeral mass for Michael Shannon had been uplifting, paying tribute to a man who had dedicated much of his life to helping others. Many of those present had benefited from his generosity, including musicians who joined to share their gifts in a final show of gratitude. Peg had asked that Stani play Vaughn Williams' Lark Ascending, a piece he had always loved. The stillness of the packed church, and the tangible emotion evoked by the music had soothed his own soul and left him with an overwhelming sense of communion and comfort. But the final musical tribute, sung by a noted operatic baritone, a rendition of a hymn entitled Be Thou My Vision complete with accompanying bagpipes, had proved to be the most inspiring. As he listened to the hymn, the words struck him with startling clarity, seeming to speak directly to his need for guidance. His life was moving in so many new directions, with responsibilities he'd never been prepared to assume. The hope found in the hymn's simple phrases had reminded him that no matter what lay ahead, if he kept his heart open, he would be shown the way.

To his relief, Peg hadn't insisted that he remain long at the gathering following the service. John had been able to arrange for an earlier flight, and they would arrive at the farm just after dark. He would have the entire evening to spend with Emily, something he knew he was in sore need of. In the few hours he'd had in New York, he'd managed to purchase a violin for Robbie Joe, which he felt sure would bring out that wide-eyed grin as a reward. He'd stopped in at the tailor's and was anxious to tell Emily of the surprisingly beautiful things Manny would shortly be shipping to her. He'd even checked on the loft, and while the pile of boxes was still in the middle of the floor, the garden had been tended and seemed adequately prepared for winter. Now he was ready to go home. A night away from Emily had left him longing for her; her smile, her voice and most of all her presence beside him. He had slept poorly, and he intended to tell her how much he'd missed her warmth, and the little sighing sounds she made in her sleep. He smiled to himself, imagining the welcoming arms he knew were waiting for him.

Emily had enjoyed her day, but she was well aware it had sapped her energy. With Sara and Penny, she'd gone to Charlottesville, intent on at least doing research into furnishings for the farmhouse nursery. After lunch at Salvatore's, Angela had joined them and they had visited three different shops during the afternoon. It was her first venture into the world of bassinets, cribs and changing tables. The variety of intriguing accessories for the modern infant left her wondering how the average family could afford more than one child. The four of them had spent hours investigating the options, and she had a sheaf of brochures stowed in her purse to show Stani, although she'd already decided what she liked best. He would be tired, she knew, arriving home so late, and she would wait until tomorrow to begin the discussion.

They had returned just before dark and Sara had insisted on her staying to supper at the parsonage. It had been good to sit and visit in the familiar kitchen, and she had enjoyed a long talk with Mike, catching up on the happenings in the community over the past three months. It was past eight when Sara drove her home, and she was feeling the effects of such a long day. She would take a leisurely shower and then sit by the fire until Stani came home. The thought of going to bed alone again was not in the least appealing. Tonight she would wait to feel his arms around her before she fell asleep.

When they pulled through the gate, she was amazed to see the house ablaze with light. "Stani must have gotten in early! Oh, I'm so glad! Now I won't have to try to stay awake." Laughing, she got out of the car. "Thanks, Sara! That was so much fun!"

She could see Stani standing in the doorway and her pulse quickened in anticipation. But as soon as his face came into focus, it was clear there was something very wrong. Before she could open her mouth, he pulled her into the house, closing the door firmly behind her.

"Where on earth have you been? I've been frantic! I even called Jack!" His eyes were dark with anxiety, his hair in wild disarray.

She stared at him, blinking. "Jack? Why?"

"Because I was sure something had happened to you! When I got home the house was dark and there was nothing to tell me where you were." He spread his arms in a gesture of helpless frustration.

"But I told you I was going to Charlottesville shopping. And you weren't due to get home for hours. Stani, I was just having dinner at the parsonage. There's nothing to be so upset about." As she started to move past him, taking off her coat, the phone rang. She reached to answer it, sure she knew who was calling. "Yes, Jack, I'm home." She smiled into the receiver. "No, I was just having supper with Mike and Sara. Just a little miscommunication."

When she turned back to Stani, hoping to see a smile of relief, he walked away from her. Going to the fireplace, he laid an arm on the mantle, staring down into the cold ashes. "You frightened me half out of my mind, Emily. What do you expect, when I come home and you're gone like that? I imagined every possible sort of disaster."

Fighting back tears, she forced herself to answer calmly. "I had no intention of frightening you. I would have been here waiting for you if you hadn't gotten in early. But, Stani, you can't go to pieces every time I leave the house. I'm a responsible adult, not some child to be watched over. You have to trust me to take care of myself." Not merely tired now, she was painfully weary, and keenly aware of the distance between them. "I'm going to take a shower. You look tired. Maybe you should get ready for bed, too." With a last look at him, standing with his shoulders hunched, head down, she went into the bedroom.

Stani stood for some time, staring blindly into the fireplace. His heart had stopped pounding and now he felt cold and completely spent. Just a short time ago his mind had been racing wildly, but now he couldn't seem to form one coherent thought. Slowly, as if sleepwalking, he went through the house, turning off lights. He knew that John had been on the landing when Emily returned, but he had no desire to go up and report to him what had proven to be the simple explanation for her absence. When he'd been searching frantically throughout the house and even in the darkness of the yard, John had tried to tell him there would be just such a reasonable solution to the mystery.

At last, with nowhere else to go, he went into the bedroom. The shower was still running, the bathroom door tightly closed. On the bed, laid open and propped on his pillow, was Emily's Bible. It took only a moment for him to recognize the passage, which seemed to jump off the page to meet his tired eyes. The verses from Psalms, which he had chosen for her to read at their wedding because they spoke so eloquently to her belief that a loving God had been protecting him, saving him for a better life on that night four years earlier. "The Lord will not let your foot be moved, and the One who watches over you will not sleep. The Lord shall preserve you from evil; the Lord shall keep you safe. The Lord shall watch over your going out and your coming in, from this time forevermore."

He stayed there by the bed, reading the words over and over, branding them into his memory. She had left him a reminder, even when he had so obviously hurt her, of the faith in the living, caring force that had brought them into this shared life. Only hours earlier, he had been moved to acknowledge the power of that force as a guiding vision, a reassuring light along the strange new paths opening to him. Then in an instant when fear—and most likely the memory of that horrible night after the windstorm—had overwhelmed him, he had completely lost touch with the truth.

When she finally came out of the bathroom, wrapped in her old flannel robe, her hair damp and tousled, he was still holding the Bible under the light of the bedside lamp. He looked up slowly, afraid of seeing the hurt that had clouded her eyes earlier. "Please forgive me?"

She smiled gently, nodding. Without saying a word, she came to him, her arms going around his shoulders. For a long moment, she studied his face, seeming to search for something. Her hands went to his hair, tenderly twining into the wild curls. Soft kisses fell along the line of his brows, down his cheeks and finally she kissed his lips, tentatively, then with increasing demand.

He had never held her closer, never been more affected by the feel of her in his arms. "I love you, Emily. Maybe too much. It isn't that I don't trust you, or know how capable you are of taking care of yourself. It's that I know I can't survive without you. Don't you understand it's me, my weakness, my pathetic inability to live in the world that terrifies me?"

Laying her fingers on his lips, she made a soft shushing sound. "Don't talk that way about my husband. He has more faith than that. He knows that whatever comes in life, God will always provide the strength he needs to meet it. He has learned to look to the hills. Tonight he lost sight of that, for just a moment. But my husband will find his way back to the peace and comfort of this place."

Much later, when she had fallen asleep after hours of the tenderest kind of lovemaking, he lay awake thinking. He knew that in part he had reacted so unreasonably tonight because he was apprehensive about the return to London. John had told him on the flight home that the police had failed to find any evidence that might lead them to the person seen prowling around the house. He would have to question Emily, he said. She might remember something from last spring, someone she had met in her ramblings in the neighborhood. Besides, John insisted, she couldn't be kept in the dark. She had a right to know what had happened and that this person might still be watching for their return. The thought made his stomach twist with fear. If even some imagined threat could make him wild with panic as it had tonight, how would he be able to deal with this vague, but none-the-less flesh and blood menace that might be waiting for them there?

In the morning, he and John had agreed, they would sit down with her, tell her what had already happened, and warn her of what might be ahead. And he would have to trust her, let her take part in her own protection. She would settle for nothing else, he knew. His wife had strength and courage far beyond his own. Tonight she had reminded him of his vow to take advantage of all his new faith afforded. She had reminded him that it was human to give in to doubt and fear, but only momentarily. And she had reminded him of where he must turn to find whatever he needed to sustain him, whether in the safety of this valley or in the turmoil of that other world they lived in.

Chapter Nineteen

Emily had listened calmly to what John and Stani told her. She tried to retrace her steps during those days in the spring, when she had explored the streets, walking for blocks in every direction from the house. There was no one that stood out, she was sure. There had been elderly men and women, who sat on the same bench or outside the same doorway every day when she passed. There had been clerks in the shops, students around the university beyond the Museum. But no one had seemed to take any particular interest in her.

She agreed the fact that he had been there more than once was disturbing. And, she admitted, it was unsettling to think that he might have chosen their house specifically. But with John there, and the police involved, she would not live in fear. She would be careful, watchful. But there was no reason to lock her in the house, or prevent her from going about her life as she had before.

"Stani, you had already decided to hire a full-time housekeeper. Why not prepare a room for her, since we're going to make some changes anyway? Wouldn't having someone there all the time discourage this sort of thing?" Her mind was turning to practical ways to keep life going forward normally.

"That sounds reasonable. The more people in and out of the place, the less likely anyone is going to come around." John understood that Emily was also looking for ways to calm Stani's obvious anxiety. He couldn't fault Stani for being concerned, but living in a state of constant worry would only cause more problems for them.

Emily smiled thoughtfully. "What I really need is another John. One very capable man who can do whatever the moment calls for. Bodyguard, baggage handler and houseboy, all rolled in to one."

John blushed a little and laughed. "But with two good eyes. I realized last night when Stani was tearing around in the dark out there, I wouldn't be much good to him in a situation like that."

"She has an idea, though. She does need her own bodyguard. You have to be with me so much of the time, we need another man, just to look out for Emily, drive her around and stay near the house when you and I are away from home."

"I still have a few mates in London, PI's and security types. I could make a few calls. As to the houseboy bit, I do know of one particular lad, a young hot shot of a PI when I first came to London, though he's probably forty by now. For the past several years he worked for some sort of aristocrat, some aged duke or such. He did everything from cooking and cleaning, to gardening and chauffeuring. He used to say he might as well have been married to the chap, the way he depended on him for everything. I ran into him last spring and he gave me his address. Seems the old man had died and left him a nice little legacy. He'd be just the type you need, assuming he wants to do a bit of work again."

"Call him, John. Call everyone you can think of. If I knew she was in hands as capable as yours, I'd rest a lot easier." Stani persisted in pacing back and forth in front of the hearth, as if the movement helped relieve his tension.

"Maybe John should go on to London now, so he can find someone for the job. And he could do a little snooping on his own."

"I suggested that earlier. What do you think, lad? Can you spare me here? I admit I'm itching to have a look around for myself."

Reluctantly, Stani agreed. "You're sure we can fly back on our own? I'm as bad as the old lord, I'm afraid. I never go anywhere alone anymore."

"You won't be alone, darling. I'll be with you, and I flew to Berlin alone, remember. Believe it or not, people far less intelligent than yourself do it every day."

When John had gone off to make arrangements for his return to London, Emily pulled Stani down on the couch beside her. "Were you really tearing around outside in the dark?"

"Yes, I was. I went a little crazy when I came home and you were gone. It brought back an unfortunate set of memories. And I had forgotten all about your plan to go shopping. I was just thinking about getting back here and holding you in my arms. I know it was foolish, but consider it the measure of my devotion." He lifted her hand, kissing the scar that still marred her palm, the look in his eyes meant to remind her of what had happened in the yard that summer night.

She reached out to caress his face. "I'm not going to end up under another tree, darling. I'm pretty confident that lightning rarely strikes twice, anyway. But it was more than just that. You've known about this other thing in London for days, haven't you? And it's been eating away at you. Stani, why didn't you tell me? No wait, I know. You were protecting me. That's why you shouted at me when I came home last night."

"I did not shout at you! I never shout!"

"I know, but you did your version of shouting. I know what it means, when your voice gets very soft and low like that. You're about to explode. All in the name of protecting me."

"You said I was forgiven. Do I need to apologize again?"

"Only if you want to kiss and make up the way we did last night. But we should probably wait until bedtime. All those people working out there around the mobile home, someone's bound to interrupt us." When he gathered her close, kissing her tenderly, they heard John's footsteps on the stairs.

"Ah, and I'll have to be sure whoever takes the job has a stomach for romance. Not everyone can tolerate so much billing and cooing, you know." Not at all to his surprise, they seemed to ignore him completely.

Chapter Twenty

Standing at the bedroom window, Emily had a clear view of the new caretaker's residence. Nestled against the woods, it seemed to fit perfectly into the landscape and its architecture appeared designed to complement that of the farmhouse. "It looks as if it's always been there, Stani. I can't imagine a better place for it."

He chuckled as he came to stand behind her. "According to the crew, it was a feat of gargantuan proportions to set it in place. They would have been much happier to have dropped it by the gate."

"James says he'll build a nice big front porch for the children. When we come back in April, we'll have neighbors. Lots of neighbors." The smile in her eyes told him she was visualizing children running and playing in the yard.

"April. Wedding bells." He circled her waist, letting one hand rest over the little bulge.

"Jack getting married." She shook her head slowly at the thought. "You know he came to see me yesterday. He'd heard about the prowler. I told Penny, who of course told James, who told his dad, who mentioned it to Jack, assuming that he already knew." She sighed, still gazing across the yard. "He wanted to be sure I knew how to be safe in a big city."

"What was his advice, other than to avoid them entirely?"

"Be vigilant. Don't overlook little things, like a parked car, or someone who seems out of place. And most of all don't trust anyone."

"Good advice, I'm afraid. With the possible exception of the man who loves you."

"I refuse to live in fear, Stani. I love London. I'm not going to stop doing the things I enjoy there."

He shuddered involuntarily. "Let's not talk about it now. Let's enjoy the time we have left here. Show me your ideas for the nursery. We have all afternoon, just you and me. Let's daydream for a while." He pulled her toward the doorway of the little adjoining room.

They spent an hour, measuring and picturing various layouts. The idea of a baby taking up residence in the house in just a few months pushed back the shadow of that other thing that threatened their peace. By the time they brought their first child to this place they loved, all of that would be behind them. The mystery would be solved and their lives would be forever changed by the miracle of a new life.

They packed to return to England as the Dixons began to move the first of their things into the caretaker's cottage. As the children stowed their few toys and put away their clothes in the new dresser drawers, Emily packed her new wardrobe, just arrived from Manny with a note wishing her good health. She was enthralled with the clothes he had created for her; impeccably tailored, yet unquestionably feminine, with little touches of trim and color. Her favorite was the evening suit fashioned like a tuxedo with satin lapels trimmed in black pearls. The white silk blouse was cut low, with a row of soft pleated ruffles in the neckline.

"Marcia won't have anything like this, I'll bet." She was admiring herself in the mirror, modeling the outfit for Stani's approval.

"Marcia would look like a penguin in that. It calls for a tall, slender, if slightly pregnant beauty to pull off such a creation. I must say, Manny certainly took note of just what would suit you, darling. These are exquisite. Let's see that gorgeous coat."

When she had put on the royal blue coat, with its fur trim, he whistled appreciatively. Tucking her hair under the matching hat, she twisted and turned to get the full effect. "I hardly look like myself. This is as good as a disguise, don't you think?

"Don't go getting any ideas, Emily. You will be escorted, like it or not. Maybe John can find you some handsome but disinterested man to act as your bodyguard. Someone who's taken a vow of celibacy, preferably." Drawing her into his arms, he took her hat and tossed it onto the pile of clothes laid out on the bed.

"I'm supposed to be packing, Stani." He had rapidly relieved her of the coat, and was preparing to start on her jacket.

"I'm only helping, love." The sound of children's laughter startled them. Through the window, they could see three little boys running across the yard. Quickly, Stani went to close the drapes. "I suppose we'll have to get used to that, won't we? No more privacy for us."

With a little smile she opened her arms. "When has that ever bothered us?"

Chapter Twenty-one

Privacy in the London townhouse would be a rare commodity as well. By the time they returned, not only were Milo and Jana still in residence, but John had secured the services of his old friend, George Bertram, to act as bodyguard and general escort for Emily. In addition, a housekeeper, Mrs. Winslow, had been hired. A recent widow, she was more than willing to leave her now lonely flat and stay overnight whenever needed. Congratulated on his rapid achievements, John had chuckled.

"I used my best sales techniques. Painted a pretty picture of the two helpless newlyweds I'm so devoted to. Not to mention the more than attractive wages I was able to offer. Milo said I was to spare no expense, as long as it gave you and Emily some peace of mind. Bertram said he'd play bodyguard and chauffeur, as well as putter in the garden, but he wasn't keen on housework. And Mrs. Winslow is a right motherly type. When I told her Emily was expecting, she got very close to teary-eyed. They should make a good team. She'll spoil him, I expect, and he'll be his usual ingratiating self."

"Just as long as I can still use my kitchen. You did make it clear I still intend to do the cooking?" Emily sensed these two experienced domestics might easily assume any control she had imagined she had over her own activities.

"Oh, yes. But you're not allowed to go to the market alone. Bertram has instructions to be at your side the moment you set foot out the door. He has a good eye. If there's anyone out there, he'll see them. And I expect Mrs. Winslow has all the protective instincts of a tigress."

Determined to make the best of her situation, Emily stated her intention to begin the planned refurbishment of the townhouse, declaring that she hoped Mr. Bertram wouldn't object to shopping for draperies and bedding.

"Oh, never fear. He's the domestic type, for sure. He told me he's just done over his little cottage. Went on in rather too much detail. He may well be able to direct you to the best shops for what you need."

When she had gone upstairs to unpack, John took Stani aside. "I've talked to the police and done a little poking around. I did some checking of my own on Nigel Barton. He's pure as the driven snow."

"It could be anybody, John. Thousands of faceless anybodies. How do we narrow that down?"

"One at a time I'm afraid. Or we may never know. He may just vanish and never be heard from again. But in the meantime, she's safe with Bertram. Get on with your work, and your life, Stani. And let her do what gives her pleasure. No more panics, lad."

"I'll try. Now you'd better introduce me to my new staff. I'm ill-equipped to play master of the house, but I'll give it my best shot."

Emily settled into a routine, accompanied by the ever-present Bertram. A tall, handsome man, graying slightly at the temples, always impeccably attired, it was clear that he enjoyed their conversations as he accompanied on her on her errands and shopping expeditions. George Bertram, she learned, had found his last employer when he'd been hired to make inquiries into the disappearance of a number of rare books from the Duke's library. The investigation had taken some time, and when he had finally determined that the culprit was in fact a family member, the Duke had rewarded his success, and his discretion, with a very pleasant post as his personal assistant.

"The old gentleman was lonely more than anything else. He had plenty of household servants to tend to his needs. But he missed his late wife, and I think I took her place in many ways. He relied on me to choose everything from his neckties to his bedroom décor. I was with him for almost eight years, and he was very kind to me. I think he considered me practically one of the family." Emily had been touched by the wistful tone in his voice. He might at first impression seem slightly stuffy, but she felt confident that beneath that very proper exterior beat an equally warm heart.

They agreed to disagree on terms of address. He preferred simply Bertram, to "Mr. Bertram" or the completely unacceptable "George." On the other hand, Emily laughingly told him she would not answer to "Mrs. Moss" or "Ma'am." "I'm an American, Bertram. It would be too strange for you to address me so formally. My name is Emily, and I would be much more comfortable if you would use it. Just think of me as, say, your niece, can't you?"

"I've never had a niece, ma'am. But if you refuse to answer to anything else, I shall try to accommodate you." When she reminded him that John called her "Emily" or even on occasion, "Girl," he grimaced. "Don't mistake me, John Kimble is as fine a man as any I've had the pleasure to know, but he persists in rubbing everyone's nose in his middle class mannerisms. And your husband, if you'll pardon my saying, treats him like anything but an employee."

"My husband treats him like just what he is, the best friend he's ever had. When you know us better, you'll realize we are far from your average, conventional household, Bertram. You may as well join in the fun."

With Mrs. Winslow, she had less success. Accustomed to working for upper middle class families who demanded a certain level of respect, she found it impossible to treat her current employers with anything less. While she admitted that they were young enough to be her children, she insisted that she would address them as Mr. and Mrs., or at least sir or ma'am. But as the days passed, and she and Emily spent more and more time together in the house, she fell into the habit of using terms of endearment more often than not.

"Would you like for me to make your bed now, my dear, or will you be going back for a little more rest?" she would ask at breakfast, when Emily had been out late the night before with Stani at the recording studio. Or "Will the dear boy be home in time for tea today, do you think?" after Stani had left for another interview with Marcia, promoting the recital tour.

Emily laughed that they hadn't hired a household staff, they'd gained an even more extended if unconventional family. "Are there really so many unattached people out there, ready to become aunties and uncles to the rest of us poor orphans? It's heartwarming isn't it, the way they're ready to take us under their wings? Mrs. Winslow even insisted on polishing Milo's shoes for him last night, after he splashed in through the rain. I think she just needs someone to look after. And Bertram is the sweetest man. And so debonair! He opens car doors with the most elegant flourish. I really do feel like aristocracy. If only all this weren't necessary for such an unpleasant reason, I'd say I could get used to the spoiling." They were dressing to go to dinner with Milo and Jana, who were returning to New York the following day. After two weeks of this new lifestyle, they had admitted to enjoying the new routine, even with the loss of their previous privacy.

"I don't mind spoiling you, darling girl, for whatever reason. Just don't begin to compare me to the amazing Bertram. He could play

Cary Grant more convincingly than Cary Grant himself. I've never known anyone quite so impeccably upper middle class."

Giggling, she put her arms around his neck. "But Stani, it was your elegance that first attracted me to you. Your beautiful manners and your oh, so lovely accent. Bertram has nothing on you. And he can't even play the violin." She kissed him, a smile on her lips.

"So you're happy with your new companions? And you don't mind not being on your own?"

"No, at least not for just a few weeks. It's sort of fun to play the grand lady. But remember, I'm still that farm girl from the valley of love and delight. This is just pretend."

Stani groaned, pulling her down onto the foot of the bed. "I don't suppose we could pretend we've forgotten about this dinner, could we?"

"No, of course not. But we have at least a half hour before John said he'd be ready to drive us." She offered her face for his kiss, but his eyes widened suddenly. Listening, they heard the soft knock repeated on the door.

"I have your little snack, my dear. I thought you might like it while you were dressing." The sweet voice of Mrs. Winslow sounded from the hallway. "And I brought a bite or two extra, in case Mr. Moss might like to join you."

Chapter Twenty-two

John had spent his free time canvassing the neighborhood, with guidance from Emily as to the places she had frequented during the spring. While no one emerged as a suspect, he had begun to form a picture of a certain individual who aroused his curiosity.

He laid out note cards and in large letters, wrote various names and places, along with terms of description gleaned from informal interviews with shopkeepers and other business people. Like pieces of a jigsaw puzzle, he moved them around on his desk, looking for anything that might resemble a pattern. When names, places and words began to repeatedly line up, he took the cards upstairs to Emily.

She saw at once what he was trying to do. "These are names of boys who did odd jobs around the shops, deliveries, cleaning and such, a few hours a week," he explained. "Boys who worked off the books, for a little cash here and there. You can see the similarities." He showed her the ones he had already eliminated, those who failed to fit the pattern in any way. Boys from families known to the proprietors were also set aside. What remained was a group of four, with very similar names and descriptions. All had worked at some time or other for businesses Emily had frequented. All but one, a boy named Will Harrison, who had worked in Nigel Barton's studio.

Emily pushed the cards around on the kitchen table. Softly, she read aloud the information on each card. "Will Harrison worked for Nigel beginning early last spring, cleaning the studio and making deliveries. He left in December. Willie Harrington worked for the cleaning service at the same time, washing windows, doing yard chores. He left last June. Will Harriman worked at the parish thrift shop, doing odd jobs off and on during the spring. He's been back several times looking for work, but only stayed a week or two at a time. A boy named just William, or Willy, no last name, made deliveries for several of the shops, including the butcher's shop and the grocer's. He hasn't been around since last fall. All of these boys are in their late teens, all small or average in size, all described as shy, quiet and having curly hair, some light brown, some dark, some not sure what color." She raised her eyes to John's face. "This has to be just one boy, right, instead of four? One boy that no one really got to know. A boy no one even looked at closely, or knew by his proper name." She picked up one card, turning it over in her hands. "What about Nigel, surely he could give you a description of his Will Harrison?"

"His was the best, but still, no address, no idea of family. He just showed up looking for work on a day when Nigel needed him. He says the boy was bright enough and had a driver's license although Nigel never actually remembers seeing it. He cleaned the lab, took out the trash, and made deliveries in Nigel's car. Then in mid-December he disappeared. No notice, never came to pick up his last few hours' wages."

"And he's never come back to any of these other places? What about the thrift shop? It says he came and went there." She was searching her memory for a face, a boy at the kitchen door with the groceries, someone she must have seen more than once.

"I asked them to call me if he came back there. They seemed the most concerned about him, wondered what had become of him." John was pushing cards around now, too. Emily put her finger on one.

"This one said his clothes were always clean. He had to be living somewhere, not on the street. And you would expect he'd be living close to all these places. John, how can he have been right under everyone's nose, but no one noticed where he came from?"

"We can't be sure this is the one, girl. But if you can think of anything, seeing him around, speaking to him, maybe."

She tried to call up a nagging image. What had Jack said about noticing things out of place or a parked car? "What kind of car does Nigel have? You said Will Harrison used Nigel's car for deliveries."

"I'd have to look back at my notes. Why?"

"That day when we came back from the doctor's office. The pictures were already on the doorstep. I remember a car across the street drove away, just as I looked up. That could have been him, couldn't it?" An involuntary shudder lifted her shoulders. "I don't understand. How did he just happen to go from making deliveries around the neighborhood to working for Nigel? How would he have known there was a connection between us?"

"Stani said Nigel took the Mozart cover picture. Maybe Will saw it in the studio. If he'd been working in the neighborhood last spring, he might have seen Stani here. He could even have seen the two of you together. I'm going to talk to Nigel Barton again. It always seems to come back to him. Maybe I didn't ask him the right questions. At the time, I thought he might be our suspect."

"We're supposed to do that magazine layout with him. Stani scheduled it for mid-February. Valentine's Day." She went on staring at the cards. For the first time, John saw a hint of doubt in her eyes. Not quite fear, but clearly concern.

John talked with Bertram about his theory of a shadowy boy, who seemed to weave in and out of the picture. He appeared to have dropped completely out of sight; but if he had so easily gone unnoticed in the past, who could say he wasn't still hiding in plain sight?

"We have been numerous times to the grocer's and such, and I'm sure I've never seen anyone of that sort. But of course, now that I have such a clear description of this lad, there should be no problem picking him out among all the other nondescript curly-haired boys in London." At John's grimace, he smiled confidently. "Don't worry, John. If there's even a hint of a wave on any lad in the neighborhood, I'll see you get the chance to chat with him."

"You'd better talk with Emily. She has her own ideas. In her mind, all she has to do is visit all her old haunts, make herself obvious, and he'll come out of hiding. I don't like the thought of using her as bait, but she could be right. Just stick close to her. He may be harmless, but I can't have her taking any chances. I've guaranteed Stani you can keep her safe, but I'll warn you, she can be a force when she sets her mind on something."

For Stani, the suggestion of a faceless youth lurking in the streets watching Emily was cause for renewed anxiety. Just when he was preparing to leave with Marcia for the promised recitals, the news that John had at last developed a vague description of a boy who might have been stalking Emily all last spring sent him into alternating fits of panic and fury. The fact that Emily herself seemed to be comforted by the thought only frightened him more.

"You can't really believe that just because this person may be young, he's harmless? He might have been watching you, Emily, maybe even following you. He broke into a locked garden to look in the windows. That is not an indication of innocent youth! If anything, it's worse to think that he may be so young. That he's been passing himself off as some poor waif, taking jobs that allowed him to get close to you. Not only is he clever, he's diabolical!"

"Stani, don't get so upset. No matter what, you know Bertram and John are going to get to the bottom of this. And no one is going to get near me. I don't plan to go running up to every delivery boy I see and ask if he's been peeping in my windows. We're all going to be careful. But at the same time, we have to go on as if nothing were wrong. If he's watching, and I said 'if,' he needs to think we're not the least bit suspicious. He seems to have a talent for disappearing into thin air. I want him to come out of hiding, so we can finally get back to our life."

"You terrify me. How can I leave you, wondering what might happen next? I'm going to talk to Mrs. Winslow and Bertram, warn them how fearless you can be."

"I'm not fearless, Stani. But I am determined to help end this nonsense any way I can. Safely, of course. And you can leave me knowing that I would never risk harming our child." She laid her hand on the ever-increasing bulge, a look of hurt and disappointment in her eyes.

Stani insisted on going with John and Bertram to interview Nigel Barton again. He wanted Nigel to see that he was watching him, too. While John had been convinced that Nigel was not involved directly, Stani was still wary of his smooth manner and his desire to take more and more pictures of them. He might not be the one stalking Emily, but he had certainly shown a keen interest in her.

This time John told Nigel the reason for the investigation. When they'd spoken before, he'd implied only that he was looking at anyone who might have been around the house in December. He had merely asked how the delivery had been made. Now, as he spelled out the details, Nigel was clearly shaken.

"You think Will could have done that? He's just a kid. And not a very mature kid. He's shy, awkward, never has anything to say. It's hard to imagine him having the nerve to even knock on somebody's door, much less hang around peering in windows, or follow someone on the streets." He paused, shaking his head in disbelief. Then he turned to Stani, a spark of recollection in his eyes. "Stani, you've seen him. He was at the shoot for the Mozart cover."

"Are you sure?" Stani struggled to recall that day so many months ago.

"He was working for you then?" John seemed encouraged by this turn of events.

"He had just started. He only worked outside the studio when I had a big shoot, like the cover shot. Remember when you had to take off the boots? Will helped you get them off." The boots, those long black boots that had been so unbearably tight. Someone had pulled them off his feet; Stani remembered the relief, but nothing about the person kneeling in front of him.

"Can you think of anything else about this boy? Anything he might have mentioned about his family, where he was living, other jobs he might have had?" John asked, all the while aware of the look on Stani's face.

"No. He didn't talk much. He stammered, you see. The simplest stress would shut him down completely. But at best, he was limited to little more than a few words. He went about his work, and I admit, I never encouraged much conversation. He took an interest in the photographs, I think. He would look them over, like he was critiquing my work sometimes. I'd ask if he approved, and he'd just smile and nod most of the time." He paused, a frown clouding his eyes. "The ones from that last shoot, with Lady Marcia. I don't think he liked them much. And it was just a week or so later, he stopped coming in to work."

"And you're sure you never had any way to contact him? How did he know when you would need him to work?"

"He would stop by each morning. But we usually arranged in advance. I just assumed he lived nearby. He was always on foot. He wasn't living on the street, I'm sure. He was clean, his clothes were decent. My impression was maybe he lived with an elderly relative. But that was just an impression."

"If you think of anything else, you'll let me know?" John rose, scanning the cluttered studio. "You keep the place locked up tight, I'm sure. Did he have a key, by chance?"

"I'd sometimes find him downstairs, when I arrived in the morning. I gave him a key, so he wouldn't have to wait outside." Nigel immediately caught what John was implying. "But I can't imagine he's been back. Like I said, he just stopped coming in."

"Nevertheless, it might pay to change the locks. But at least for now, just keep your eyes open a bit wider?" Leading the way, John went to the door.

"Are we still on for the magazine layout, Stani? I hope this hasn't put you off the idea."

"I admit I'm reconsidering. What do you think, John?"

"Go ahead. You can't hide, lad. And Emily is looking forward to it. Keep it on your schedule, Nigel. At least for now."

On the street, Stani noticed both John and Bertram studying the area. Shops and offices lined the block. Curtained windows and the occasional flower box, now empty waiting for spring, spoke of inhabitants in the flats above.

"Let's walk a bit. See what the neighborhood looks like." John urged Stani along, Bertram bringing up the rear. They were not many blocks from the townhouse, John calculated. It was quite possible a boy who lived in this area could have found odd jobs in the shops Emily frequented.

"You think this Will Harrison is the boy we're looking for, don't you?" Stani asked, as they paused at the end of the block.

"If that's his name, yes, I do. But none of the names I've come up with have any sort of record. We're still chasing a shadow, I'm afraid. At least we know a little more about him, now. If we all keep our eyes open, there's always a chance we'll spot him." John was still gazing discreetly at the windows above the street.

"Or he'll spot us." Bertram came alongside. "At least now he'll know you're back in town, and he'll know you've been to see Nigel Barton." Stani turned to him with a confused frown. "The appointment calendar on Nigel's desk. He'll be sure to be checking it, now that he's seen you here." The confident little smile on Bertram's face was strangely comforting.

Chapter Twenty-three

Stani was committed to eight recitals over the course of four weeks. He and John would be gone no more than three nights at a time. With Bertram and Mrs. Winslow both in the house, now comfortably settled in rooms on the third floor, he was as confident as he could be about leaving Emily alone. He tried to turn his attention to all that was going on, the recording, the concerts and the chaos in his home.

Emily had started in on the changes to the house with ferocious energy. Almost daily, she and Bertram went out in search of this or that fabric, carpet or lamp, returning to report at length on their adventures in various antique emporiums, junk shops and department stores. In some of the less frequently used rooms, furniture had been shifted, and painters were already at work. Emily warned Stani that in due course, their bedroom would be relocated to the one Milo had previously occupied. It adjoined a smaller room, which would, she had decided, make the perfect nursery.

"You're enjoying all this nesting, aren't you?"

"Oh, yes. It's been so much fun. And Bertram has given me lots of ideas for the loft, too. He's really quite talented. When we get back to New York, at least I'll have some notion of where to start."

Stani winced. He'd almost forgotten that he had asked Peg to hire a decorator. He would have to follow up with her, caution her that only the basics would be needed. Emily would want to bring her own style to the place, after all.

"I'm glad you're having fun. Just warn me when you relocate our bedroom, will you? I get confused enough as it is, what with the lounge moving from one side of the house to the other." She had decided, after consulting at length with Bertram, that the virtually unused lounge at the rear of the house would make a much better music room. The dining room furniture had been moved from the front of the house to a more intimate space nearer the kitchen, and the lounge now occupied the large room off the entry hall. It all made perfect sense, as she pointed out. Nonetheless, Stani had more than once found himself staring into an unrecognizable room, wondering which way would lead him to the kitchen. "I'll need a road map to get around the place, as I come and go to these recitals."

"Just as long as you get to the front door, don't worry. I'll be waiting to show you the way. I don't like you going off without me, Stani. What if you get a headache, or need a really good massage? I know John tries, but still, I'd rather be there with you." Their last night together before the first out-of town recital, they had chosen to stay at home by the fire in the as yet undisturbed sitting room.

"I only wish I could be here for your doctor's appointment." He laid a hand gently over the growing bulge.

"I know, but I'm quite capable of telling the doctor I'm feeling fine. And he's quite capable of seeing how enormous I'm getting." She laid her hand over his, resting her head on his shoulder with a sigh.

"You're beautiful. Round, but beautiful. In Manny's fashions, you're turning heads wherever you go. Even Marcia commented on your tuxedo after the recital the other night." They had been to Whigmore Hall again, this time without the bout of jealous tears.

"So did several others. And all the shopkeepers have taken note of my coat. When I tell them my husband's tailor made it for me, they're amazed."

"Do you think the doctor will hear the heartbeat this time?"

"I'm sure he will. You've been reading that book I gave you, haven't you? Are you going to be one of those modern fathers, who changes diapers and takes the baby to the park while the mother goes back to her job?"

"No, I don't think so. I still have to work, you know. And diapers? We'll have to see how much tolerance I have for that sort of thing. I remember little Emily was accused of having soiled her diaper, when I was holding her. Robbie Joe was quick to point out the rather awful stench. I'd never smelled anything quite like it." He screwed up his face at the memory.

"Poor Stani, you have so much to learn. So many new experiences." She laughed up into his eyes. "You'll do fine, darling. Anyway, they say when it's your own baby, the smell doesn't bother you. We'll have to test that theory."

"In the meantime, we have plenty to do. You with the house and me with Marcia's recitals. That magazine thing. And then Lil and Charles coming to visit. They'll have to have a place to sleep, won't they?"

"Two places to sleep. I asked. Lil said two rooms. Of course, after three weeks on their own all over Europe, who knows? He may not be as strong as you were." She snuggled against him, her arms going around his waist.

"No? Maybe Lil won't be quite such a temptress, either. At any rate, we should be prepared. Two rooms ready for occupancy in the next month. Is that doable?" Currently, the second floor seemed to have been invaded by painters, and the hallway was crowded with disassembled beds and mattresses leaning against the walls.

"With all the help on hand, the whole house will be ready by then. I can't wait to take them out sightseeing. And maybe there'll be a concert we could all go to. And I want to treat Lil to a little shopping at Harrod's."

"Slow down, love. You're pregnant, remember? You can't be running all over town playing tour guide. Maybe Bertram could take them sightseeing, at least. He should make a wonderful tour guide."

Emily giggled. "He'd certainly lend an air of authenticity. We'll see how I'm feeling by then."

"We'll see how I'm feeling about you overdoing by then. How's that? I'm being very tolerant right now. But the closer we get, the more I'll worry." He turned her face for a kiss. Worry, he mused, seemed to be just a part of his routine these days.

Every night, he and John talked with Bertram about what he might have seen or not seen during his outings with Emily. And the conclusion was always the same. This mythical boy, whether he was Nigel's former assistant, or not, seemed to have vanished into thin air. He certainly had not been seen lurking around the house, Bertram assured them. Mrs. Winslow was on watch during the day, and with all the workmen coming and going, someone was sure to have spotted an extra boy hiding in the shrubbery. It was Bertram's gut feeling that it would take some break in routine to lure him out.

"If he's watching, he knows by now that Emily never goes out on her own, nor is she ever at home alone. He'll never come around if he thinks someone's going to trip over him on the doorstep."

"If he never comes around, that's fine with me," Stani declared.

"I say we all go about our business. I doubt he's just disappeared, but as long as he keeps his distance, it doesn't matter." John was convinced they hadn't seen the last of him, but with Stani preparing to be away, he saw no reason to cause further anxiety. An old acquaintance from his years in London had been put on watch near Nigel Barton's studio. Already, he'd informed John of several late night visits by a small, curly-haired youth, who used a key to gain entry. There was no need, John felt, to say anything to Stani yet. He and Bertram would be ready, when the time came.

There were letters from home, one for Emily from Boston, and one for Stani, from New York. Stani pocketed his for later, while Emily tore into hers instantly and began reading aloud.

Dearest Em,
There may be signs of progress here. My darling James, apparently at the suggestion of a certain young violinist, has written a letter to my parents. They haven't let me read it, but it has had a very definite effect on them. James won't tell me exactly what he said, but the gist seems to be that he told them how he feels about me, and about our future. He must have said something very moving, because my mom tears up every time she mentions him now. He has been invited, by my parents, for another visit, and my dad promises he'll sit down and talk with him, "man to man."
If you can, coerce Stani into telling you what he knows about this. Not that I want to go behind James' back, but I'm dying to know how he persuaded them to reconsider. When I came home from Christmas with my ring proudly displayed on my finger, they were still ignoring the whole idea. Then suddenly, this letter came and my mom called to say they wanted to talk to me. Dad didn't say much; he never does. But Mom said maybe they had been too quick to judge, that they wanted to get to know James better.
I'm scared to be too hopeful. But at least it's something.
Keep praying for us. We still have a long way to go.
Love to you both,
Penny

Emily folded the paper, eyeing Stani expectantly. "What do you know about this letter?"

"Only that James told me how strongly he felt about their future together and how frustrated he was that her parents had taken such a stand against them. He said he couldn't just march in and tell them how he felt, and I suggested that he might be able to tell them in a letter. I guess he took it to heart."

She put her arms around his neck, kissing his cheek. "Oh, Stani, that was brilliant!"

"It was actually your idea, darling. Remember pen pals? I told

James I'd been able to say things in those letters I would never have had the courage to say to your face."

"And what about now? Can you say them now?" She continued laying little kisses along his jaw, running her hands up into his hair.

"Oh, yes. But not in front of the decorators, love. They'll never get any work done, if you persist in this sort of display." Backing her gently into a corner of the hallway, he gazed into her laughing eyes. "I adore you, my beautiful darling girl," he began warmly. "You and this little lump are the most precious things in the world to me."

From just over his shoulder, he heard a deep, apologetic voice. "Excuse me, sir. Mrs. Moss, did you want the wainscoting done in the eggshell, or the semi-gloss?"

Chapter Twenty-four

The first recital outside of London, in Brighton, went well. Marcia was surrounded by friends who had come to support her and stayed to party. When Stani returned to the hotel, he immediately phoned Emily.

"Tell me everything. What did the doctor say about you?"

"He said I'm fine. Blood pressure perfect. Weight gain normal. That is, normal for twins."

He thought the room tilted just a bit, as he sat down abruptly on the edge of the chair. John eyed him suspiciously. When he tried to form the word into a question his voice wedged in his throat.

"Stani, are you there? Don't faint, darling. Take a deep breath." He distinctly heard laughter in her voice. "There are definitely two heartbeats. Dr. Hennessy was quite certain."

"Two." Instantly, John crossed the room, hovering over him.

"That's right. Two. Twins come in pairs."

"But that's wonderful, right?" The best he could manage was a choked whisper.

"I think so. One for each of us. Is John there with you?"

"Yes, right here." He looked up to meet John's mystified gaze.

"Good. You're going to need him, I expect, to help you get over the shock. I warned you, didn't I? You'll get used to the idea, darling. Now tell me all about the recital. How did it go?"

"Recital?"

"Yes. You did play with Marcia tonight, didn't you?"

"Oh, yes. I did. Emily, are you absolutely sure the doctor is certain? I mean, it's not too early to tell?" He felt as though his ears had been stuffed with cotton, and the room had grown uncomfortably warm. John was standing next to him, still frozen in place.

She laughed, a sweet little gurgle of sheer joy. "He's sure, Stani. We're having twins!"

He jumped to his feet, dropping the receiver. "Twins, John! We're going to have twins! Two babies!" Throwing himself into John's arms, they made an awkward little turn around the floor. From the dangling headset, the sound of Emily's laughter blended with theirs.

George Bertram informed John that he had finally spotted their boy. Outside the parish thrift shop, when he had taken Emily to pick up that red transfer-ware platter she had decided would be the perfect thing for the dining room wall. She was bent, it seemed, on turning that room into some sort of patriotic statement. "Anyway, he was just at the corner, to the north. He saw us getting out of the car, I expect, and stepped around the building. But I saw him distinctly, peering back around."

"Good work. Now we just have to keep him feeling secure enough to come out again. You didn't say anything to her?"

"Of course not. She'd have gone after him, I'm afraid, and asked him what he thought he was doing, peeping around corners. She's fed up with having to ask me to drive her just around the block, you know."

John chuckled. "I do know. But don't let her get past you."

"And am I correct in assuming the two of them are not to be made aware of your theory?"

John shook his head. "If I'm right, there's nothing for them to worry about. But in case I'm wrong, they still need to be on their guard. Just let them go on thinking he's a stalker, rather than a self-appointed guardian."

Stani had read Peg's letter through twice. He was at first confused, and then alarmed. She said the work on the loft was going well. Then she went on to describe the furniture for the living area, leather couches and chairs in dark green. A wall of book shelves was almost complete, as well as a closet built the length of the hallway. She closed by saying she was especially excited to have located a carved French bed, just the sort he had described. Along with the two armoires she'd found, it would determine the décor for the master bedroom. Nowhere did she mention a professional decorator, and she described at length her search all over Manhattan for a refectory table for the dining room.

But it was when he phoned Milo to tell him the news about the twins that he became convinced he'd made a potentially disastrous mistake. After a number of questions were asked and answered pertaining to his announcement, Stani cautiously asked if Milo had spoken with Peg since returning to New York.

"Oh, yes. As a matter of fact, I was just at one of her chamber concerts last week. She told me you asked her to decorate the loft apartment for you. She said it had helped immensely to have a project to take on, just after her father's death. I wasn't aware that you and Emily had decided to have her do that for you."

He wanted to say that he wasn't aware they had either, but instead he changed the subject. Now as he watched his wife joyfully transforming the townhouse, spending hours supervising the hanging of new draperies and the placement of refurbished furniture, he felt a gnawing anxiety in the pit of his stomach. How could he have mistakenly given Peg permission to decorate their new home? What had he said that had made her believe he wanted anything more than the installation of few basic pieces and a good tidying done to the apartment before they returned in March? How could he have so thoroughly misunderstood what she intended to do? And the most agonizing question of all, how would he ever explain to Emily how he had managed to make such an idiotic mistake?

The house was so different now, so much more their own, that Emily spent hours going from room to room, enjoying the results. Without Bertram's help, she doubted so much could have been accomplished. But the final choices had been hers; the warm, rich colors that replaced the bland neutrals, and the welcoming floor plan that invited guests immediately into the house. On the second floor, their new bedroom, decorated in soft greens and deep rose, was a luxurious retreat. And the nursery, pale yellow and green, with its two cribs, brought a tingle of pleasure every time she peeked in the door. The guest rooms, sporting new paint and linens, had been redesigned for traditional country house comfort. Even the hall bath had been updated, with new tile and a fine old clawfoot tub to remind her of home.

In the entry, the bronze bust of Beethoven still resided within the paneled walls, which were now hung with a collection of the soft-toned landscapes Stani so admired. The stairs had been carpeted with a patterned runner, so that the space no longer echoed coldly, as it had in the past. She had been delighted with Stani's reaction when he returned home to find the chaos banished and the rooms ready to enjoy.

"This is amazing, Emily! When I left on Monday, the furniture was still piled in heaps, and there were ladders and tools in every room. Now I walk into an immaculate home, with not a painter or carpenter in sight. Are you sure we're in the right house?" He peered into the new lounge, where tall windows cast soft afternoon light over the elegant furnishings.

"Oh, it's the right house. See, Ludwig is still in the same spot." She pulled him by the hand up the staircase. "And I'm sure no other house on the block has this." Opening the nursery door, she gently pushed him inside. At first, he hesitated, gazing at the soft yellow walls and pastel plaid curtains. Slowly approaching the cribs arranged on either side of the little wardrobe, he paused to study the characters from Winnie the Pooh, hand-painted on the wardrobe's doors, and laid a hand on the rail of each of the cribs. When he turned back to her, there were tears in his eyes. "Do you like it?" she asked softly.

"It's the most beautiful thing I've ever seen. Next to you." She went into his arms, holding him tightly. "Oh, Emily, how can I ever tell you how happy you've made me?"

"That's the thing about love, Stani. You don't have to tell me. I already know."

Lil and Charles had written from Rome and then from Vienna, typical postcards that said how wonderful the city was and what a great time they were having. The only thing they left off was the classic closing, "Wish you were here." As he looked at the cards over breakfast, Stani laughed, saying that he was sure they didn't need the company of two old married people on their big adventure. "If I know anything about Lil, she's leading Charles by the hand, making sure he appreciates things with the proper enthusiasm."

"And probably never letting him say a word. But I think he loves her, and he's been with her long enough to know her by now."

"When are you expecting them?"

"Ten days. Bertram has already drawn up their itinerary. And we have tickets for a concert at Royal Albert. That should give them a thrill. Oh, and Nigel wants to take pictures of us that night, you know, our 'big night on the town' shots."

Stani winced slightly. "When is he planning on coming here? And what did you decide about going outdoors?"

"He's coming to the house on Friday, when the journalist from the magazine is here, and I thought a trip to the Embankment would be nice, since that's actually a place we've been." She reached across the breakfast table to touch his hand. "I know you're not looking forward to this. But let's try to have some fun with it, okay? At least it's something we get to do together. This past month everything we've done has been with someone else. I've spent more time with Bertram than I have you, and I expect you've seen more of Marcia than you have your wife."

Rolling his eyes, he grinned. "I've seen more of Marcia than I ever hoped to see. Her taste in gowns guarantees that. There've been times when I was afraid to look over at the piano."

"Poor Stani, you know you'll miss her when this all comes to an end."

"Speaking of ends, we're invited to her father's country home, for the grand finale of the recital tour. How would you like to spend three days in a real English manor house?"

"Sounds like fun. When?"

"Early March. Just before we go back to New York. No rest for the weary, my love." Glancing at the clock, he pushed back his chair. "I'd better finish dressing. This is release day, remember? Pray for kind reviews. Marcia is expecting raves, and I'm worried she may be just a bit disappointed."

Phrases like "noble experiment" and "promising first effort" seemed to translate for Marcia into glowing accolades. She was not at all disappointed, Stani said, when the recording was only warmly received. While he was praised for his usual brilliant work, he was also congratulated for graciously sharing the stage with an unknown artist whose talents would clearly never equal his own. One reviewer chided Marcia for riding into the limelight on the coattails of her generous partner.

"She and her father both seemed quite happy. They're already talking about another recital tour; solo, thank heaven. I expect if she found the man of her dreams, she'd abandon her so-called career and ride off into the sunset. Unfortunately, he'll have to be rich, handsome and willing to spoil her as thoroughly as her father does. Meanwhile, she's having fun playing at being a musician."

"And she's had such a beautiful playmate. Just look at yourself, darling. Nigel captured all your manly charms." Emily was studying the record jacket. On the front the two were elegant and smiling in formal attire, leaning back to back at the side of the piano, while the reverse of the jacket featured a close-up shot of them cheek to cheek, with Stani looking very stern and Marcia clearly giggling in his ear.

"Ha! Those aren't manly charms, love. That's me glaring at Nigel for putting me in such a ridiculous position. Fortunately, those are two of the less suggestive poses. Remind me next time an offer like this comes along that I'm a solo artist. This has been a lesson in the value of just saying 'no'!"

Chapter Twenty-five

Emily told Bertram she needed at least one more piece of china for the dining room wall. "Another piece of that transfer-ware would be perfect. Let's go back to the thrift shop, just to be sure they don't have more of it hidden somewhere. And I want to go to the bakery, too. I've been craving some of those little éclairs all week."

She found four plates in the thrift shop, and decided to buy the set. When they had been wrapped and placed in a sack, Bertram took them to the car. She browsed for a moment or two more, then decided she'd start off to the bakery, knowing he would catch up with her before she'd gone more than a few steps. Putting on her sunglasses against the glare of the early afternoon sun, she started out of the shop. At the instant the door closed behind her, its little bell tinkling, she saw him, darting around the corner. Or at least she saw the blur of a slender figure, and had the momentary impression of dark curly hair.

Taking her arm, Bertram said softly in her ear, "Just act as if you hadn't seen a thing."

"But that was him! It must have been. Why else would he run?" She was only slightly shaken, but she was thoroughly confused by Bertram's words.

"He'll be gone by now, out of sight. It's best to act as if nothing happened. Let's walk to the bakery and get those éclairs you wanted, shall we?"

She waited until they'd returned to the car. "Now will you please explain to me what just happened? Why didn't you go after him?"

"I think you should have a talk with John. He can explain things to you more clearly than I can. Just let it suffice to say that I knew you were in no danger, and I've been instructed not to frighten him off." With a little smile playing at his lips, Bertram glanced in the rear view mirror. "Thank you for remaining so calm. Some young women would have fallen to pieces in such a situation."

They went immediately to John's basement flat, where she found herself suddenly far from calm. With tears of frustration brimming, she pleaded with him to explain what had obviously been going on without her knowledge.

Carefully choosing his words, John told her his theory. Based on things he'd heard, he explained, between the vague descriptions and the assumptions made, he'd put together more and more details about this boy and the life he might be living, a shadow life.

"He doesn't want to call attention to himself because he's underage, probably without a legal guardian. He worked in places where they gave him things he needed, leftover produce, stale bread, meat past selling. The thrift shop gave him clothes and household bits from time to time. The only place he made any real money was working for Nigel Barton." John could see he had captured Emily's interest. "Imagine this boy meeting someone like Stani. Nigel said he took those boots off Stani's feet. What would Stani have said to him?"

Emily considered. "He would have been his usual gracious self. He would have smiled and thanked him, as sincerely as he would anyone."

"Exactly. He would have made the boy feel that they were friends. Stani does that with everyone, from the stage hands to the concertmaster, the same manner, the same smile. Then imagine this boy sees all those fans hanging around the house if he came here with the cleaning service. He would know where Stani lived. His curiosity would have been aroused when he saw you coming and going from Stani's house, the same as any fan's would have been. But this boy was no ordinary fan, this boy actually knew Stani, or felt he did. He had a special interest in what went on here."

"An interest? In Stani?"

John nodded and went on. "He came here to deliver the groceries, and what might you have done, if you met him at the back door?"

"I would have thanked him, tipped him, said a few words to him." She was trying desperately to recall a face.

"Exactly. You would have been nice to him."

"But I would remember talking with someone like that."

"Nigel says the boy who worked for him stammered, could barely string a few words together. He would never have been able to talk to someone like you, a pretty young woman who lived in Stani Moss's house."

For Emily, John's picture was beginning to come into focus. "You think this boy just has a case of hero worship for Stani? He's just curious about us?"

"I think that's how it started. In the course of just trying to scratch out an existence, this kid may have found something that caught his imagination. Two exceptional people who made him feel they had taken notice of him."

"But why would he have climbed into the garden to peer in the windows? That's hardly friendly."

"Last spring, he could see that you and Stani were happy. He would have seen you go out together, walking to church, going to the Embankment. He was just watching, like we would any neighbors coming and going. But when he saw those pictures Nigel took of Stani with Marcia, he might have been confused. Maybe he was disappointed in Stani. Or he was worried about how you would react to seeing them."

"He delivered them, then sat there watching. That must have been him in the car I saw drive away."

"And he came back later to check on you, but you had gone back to New York by then. Odds are, his curiosity got the better of him, and he took a chance. Climbed the fence and hung around the street at night, hoping to see that things were all right."

"So you think he was just looking out for us?"

"I do. But that's just a theory. Until we can catch up with him and talk to him, we won't know for sure. That's why I told Bertram not to scare him off. He's been around the neighborhood lately, but he seems to vanish without a trace. My only hope is he'll slip up, or gain a bit of courage."

"How did you ever put all this together?"

"I listened to the way everyone talked about this boy. They didn't pay much attention to him, but no one hinted at anything suspicious about him. He certainly had never attracted the attention of the police. Everyone seemed to feel sorry for him, just let him work whenever he showed up. Nigel had the most to say about him. He realized that he was quiet because he stammered. He thought he might be living with someone elderly, someone he was trying to take care of. Nigel trusted him enough to give him a key to a studio full of expensive equipment. None of these things, vague as they might be, seemed to describe a boy who meant anyone any harm and certainly not a stalker. He had plenty of chances last spring to get close to you, and he never once tried to. Only when he thought there might be trouble between you and Stani, then he took a risk."

"But why has he started watching again now?"

"Maybe this explains it." John opened a folder. The recital flyer from Whigmore Hall was on top. They had been posted around the neighborhood in some of the shop windows. Emily even remembered pointing them out to Bertram. Stani and Marcia, standing back to back, smiling warmly over their shoulders at one another. "Trouble in paradise."

Emily had to smile. "Marcia again."

"You can see why he might be worried about you, girl. Your husband's been running all over with this very attractive blond." John grinned, leaning back in his chair. "But it's still a theory. Until we can be sure Nigel's Will Harrison is the same person who climbed the fence and ran away from Milo that night, we can't take any chances."

"How can we do that?"

"I have a plan. I think he may be watching when Nigel takes those photos at the Embankment. If he is, we'll know for sure."

"If Stani knew, he'd never go through with it. He'd cancel the shoot." John could read her thoughts, as she weighed the possibility of finally solving the mystery against keeping the information from Stani.

"It's up to you, girl. If you feel you have to tell him, I'll try to help you explain it to him." He waited, watching what he knew was a battle with her conscience.

Finally, she let out a resolute sigh. "No, we won't tell him yet. But what will you do, once you're sure he's the right one?"

"We'll try to catch him, give him a good talking to."

"But you won't turn him over to the police? If he is trying to take care of himself, he deserves help, not punishment."

John grinned. "Emily girl, how did I know you'd feel that way?"

Shrugging her shoulders, she smiled back. "He's no different from all the other men in my life, all of you trying to watch out for me."

Chapter Twenty-six

The journalist who came with Nigel on Friday morning to follow them through a "typical day" understood perfectly that people like Stani Moss and his wife didn't have many typical days. But she was confident, she told them with a grin, they could construct something that would appear fairly realistic. She had them make breakfast together, something they had certainly done many times, they admitted. At the work table, which she and Nigel carefully staged with eggs and cheese, vegetables and a suitably decorative pitcher, presumably filled with milk, Stani chopped peppers for the hypothetical omelet, while Emily rattled a whisk in an empty mixing bowl. Nigel clicked away, capturing them in charming, if less that practical poses. They sat at the little table overlooking the garden, pretending to chat while sipping tea, again, not an uncommon activity. Finally they went to the music room, where Stani stood in front of the window with his violin, while Emily posed in a chair nearby, struggling not to laugh at his deliberately screechy serenade.

Once the questions had been asked and answered and all the photographs had been taken, Stani admitted the day had been entertaining. "And tomorrow, we get to take a walk along the river, holding hands and grinning at each other." Dinner warming in the oven, and an evening ahead with only the two of them in the house, they had settled in the sitting room to enjoy the fire burning merrily on the little hearth. Emily stretched her legs across his lap, hinting that a foot rub would be gratefully accepted. "I'm so glad to finally sit down. If this bulge gets as big as I think it might, my poor feet are really going to suffer."

As he gently removed her shoes, smiling at the hum of contentment in response, Stani gazed into the flames. "You've worked so hard to make this house a home and we've had so little chance to enjoy it. I hope that will change with time. The idea of actually living in London again is surprisingly appealing. I guess I never realized that I still feel very much at home here. Having my family here, taking the children to the parks, teaching them about my country, that's something I find myself looking forward to."

"Our children will have so many places to call home. I want each of them to be special. Now if I can get the loft ready before they arrive, we can live in comfort wherever we are." She leaned back on the cushions, resting her hands over the roundness of her belly and closing her eyes in contentment.

A knot twisted in Stani's stomach; the loft. He should have called Peg, he knew. He had intended to, but after hearing what Milo had said, he'd been afraid of upsetting her. How could he tell her that she had misunderstood him, or that he had misunderstood her? If she had done so much work already, it was too late anyway. He should tell Emily what he had done. But then she would be upset. He looked over at her, resting comfortably, a little smile curving her lips. He couldn't disturb her peace, not now. At some point he would have to confess his colossal blunder, beg for understanding and forgiveness. He would make amends some way, but now it was only right to let her rest and relax here, where every corner of every room reflected her own good taste.

He stroked her feet, watching the fire morosely. Never, no matter how inspired he might feel, would he take such a thing upon himself again. He had meant well, believing he was saving Emily from the daunting task of creating a home in the empty cavern of the loft apartment. And instead of a loving reward for his efforts, he now feared a torrent of disappointed tears, when she learned he had asked Peg, of all people, to take on the job. How would he face her every day in a home that had been designed for them, at his request no less, by his former lover? The very idea sent a twinge of pain shooting through his temple. Perfect, he thought, a migraine brought on by a stress he could never explain to Emily, as she nursed him through the night.

He felt her stiffen, and looking over saw that her eyes were wide and shining. At her waist, her hands moved slowly in a circle. "What's wrong?"

"Nothing's wrong. Stani, they moved!" The look of wonder on her face, as she met his gaze, sent a cold shiver down his spine. "Right on time. You realize this means they were conceived on our wedding night? On the night we waited so long for. Oh, Stani, you were right. A night we'll remember every day of our lives, the night we first made love." She held out her arms and he went gratefully into her embrace. Any thought of Peg, or the loft, or his own stupidity was replaced with the comfort of Emily in his arms, and the thought that his children, both of them, were stirring inside her beautifully rounded body.

It had been the most normal evening they'd spent together in weeks, Emily felt. After the magical moment when that first flutter of life had stirred, Stani had seemed to relax. For a time, as they ate dinner by candlelight and made love on the couch, she thought he had finally shaken off the pensiveness that had darkened his eyes so often in the past weeks. He was the sweet, loving Stani who took her every whim to heart, who laughed with her and came into her arms with such tenderness. But now, as she lay awake beside him, studying his profile in the dimness of their bedroom, she knew there was something disturbing his sleep. Just as recently she had noticed his hand going so often to his temple, now he tossed and sighed, as if some tension moved through his dreams.

At first, when the recitals had begun and he'd been away from home so frequently, she had attributed the change to concern over the possible return of the prowler. Then she had begun to wonder if the problem might not be connected to the recitals themselves. Perhaps Stani was stressed by so much forced companionship with Marcia, who clearly felt she should be the center of everyone's attention. But his remarks on the subject seemed to reflect his amused disinterest in his stage partner. He found her musically adequate to make the performances enjoyable, but otherwise, hardly seemed aware of her presence. He was focusing most of his energy toward the future recordings in New York, and had even found time for several student workshops along the tour route. Work, Emily had to conclude, did not seem to be the source of his distress.

In the end, she had to accept that whatever was distracting him, he had chosen not to share the problem with her. That alone was cause enough to worry about him. It was not like him to keep secrets. They had vowed to be honest, each seeking the other's counsel and comfort, whatever the problem might be.

Her own conscience was sore at the moment, knowing that in the morning, when they met Nigel at the Embankment, there was every possibility Will Harrison would be watching. Ever since she had told John she would keep his plan from Stani, she had suffered pangs of guilt and doubt. When he learned of their deception, assuming the plan worked, she knew he would be upset with her. While she had rationalized that it would bring this whole ridiculous situation to a close and get their lives back to normal that much sooner, still she dreaded his reaction when he learned the truth.

But whatever was worrying Stani, her instincts told her that she hadn't yet discovered the cause. Every time she saw that darkness in his eyes, sensed the distance between them, she told herself he would eventually come to her with the truth. The longer it continued, the more she craved reassurance that nothing threatened to come between them and the happiness they had enjoyed for such a short time.

Turning on her side to nestle against him, she laid her hand over his heart. In response, he stirred, and a frown crossed his face. She was surprised when his eyes opened, searching the darkness. "Stani, are you all right? If there's anything bothering you, I wish you'd tell me."

He turned his head, meeting her gaze. "It's nothing, love. I miss our peaceful little valley, that's all."

"I miss *you*. It feels as if you're keeping something from me, and we promised not to do that, remember?"

Taking her hand, he raised it to his lips. "I remember." Then with a deep, ragged sigh, he turned away from her. She felt distinctly that a door had closed in her face.

The morning was clear, and the sunshine quickly brought out Londoners who welcomed a break from the raw gloom of winter. As they wandered the paths, Nigel following them with his camera clicking, Emily tried to keep her eyes on Stani. The temptation to search the passing faces and peer behind trees and scrubs was almost irresistible. She knew that John and Bertram were both watching, as they sat on a bench seeming to patiently wait as the shoot progressed. Even Nigel, through the lens of his camera, would be scouting the surroundings for any sign of the elusive Will.

While his smile flashed and he followed Nigel's instructions to pay court to his wife, Stani clearly showed the effects of his disturbed night. His eyes were dark, and his face was lined with familiar signs of tension. She followed the urge to stroke his cheek with a gloved hand, her smile conveying tender concern as she studied his eyes. Nigel, unaware of the reason behind the gesture, was thrilled with the impression. "That is just the sort of adoration your fans will love to see in your beautiful bride. Now, Emily, kiss him as if to make him forget anything in the world but yourself." She obliged, feeling sudden tears burn behind her eyelids. Ducking her head, she hid her face against Stani's shoulder, leaning into his arms.

"Darling, are you all right? Do you want to sit down for a bit?" Instantly solicitous, he tilted her chin for a better look at her face.

"Yes, that might be nice. I'm just a little tired," she lied, fighting for control.

They found an empty bench, and as Nigel continued to shoot, they sat close together, Stani's arm draped around her shoulders.

"Should we stop? Would you like a cup of tea?"

"I'm fine, really. What about you, you look tired yourself."

"Just a bit." He turned to the clicking camera, holding up his hand. "Nigel, would you mind taking a break? I'd like a few minutes with my wife and maybe a cup of tea."

In the distance, Emily could see John and Bertram, coming along the path toward them. From the spring in John's stride, she felt sure his plan had met with success. "You two having fun?" he called as soon as he was within earshot.

"Actually, do you think you could find us some tea?" Stani asked.

When Bertram had gone off to the tea shack, and John and Nigel had stepped away, apparently engaged in casual conversation, Stani turned to her. "Why the tears, darling girl?"

She smiled, somehow pleased to know he'd noticed. "I'm just worried about you, Stani. You've been distracted, and last night you told me a blatant lie. Oh, you may be homesick, but that isn't what's causing your head to hurt."

"I'm fine, love, really. Just things on my mind. Please don't worry. Ah, Bertram, thank you." He passed her a paper cup, blowing at the steam rising from the tea. "Now drink this, and maybe we can get this thing over with. I'm ready to go home, myself."

"*Then* will you tell me what the matter is? Even if it is what you call 'just things' I want to know, Stani." Before he could respond, they were interrupted by John and Nigel. As the final few locations were discussed, she watched Stani's face. He welcomed the change in subject. She could see the relief in his eyes when Nigel asked if they could move nearer the river, to get the view of Parliament as a backdrop. As the five of them walked in that direction, Stani moved ahead, still talking with Nigel, leaving her to stroll along with Bertram.

"You'll be pleased to know our mission was accomplished." Bertram looked straight ahead, a satisfied little smile on his otherwise impassive features.

"He was here?"

"Yes, just behind that bank of shrubbery where the two of you sat down. John spotted him and Nigel confirms he saw him as well."

"What next?"

"He'll have to come out again. Now that we know he's the right boy, John hopes to catch him in the neighborhood. But he's certain you have nothing to fear from him."

"Can we tell Stani now? I'd feel so much better having it all out in the open."

"That's up to you and John. If it took that look of gloom and doom off your husband's face, I'd certainly be in favor. Is he always so Byronic?"

"Not at all. I only hope it was just this boy that's caused him to worry, although I'm not sure that's been the only thing on his mind. But it will be worth having him get angry with me for not telling him about John's plan, just to find out." With a sigh, she squared her shoulders and forced a smile to her lips. "Are we ready to get on with it, Nigel? I may have ten more good minutes left before I need lunch and a nap."

Chapter Twenty-seven

By late afternoon, Nigel had returned to the townhouse, bearing the prints of the morning's shoot. He asked that Stani call John and when everyone had assembled in the lounge, he laid out several of the pictures on the coffee table. "There's the proof, John, in full color. That's Will, for sure."

When Stani turned to him with a look of startled suspicion, John laid an arm around his shoulders. "Lad, there's some news about our prowler. We know who he is and most likely why he was watching the two of you." Confident that he now had Stani's attention, John went on to explain the identity of the boy who had caused them so much needless anxiety.

"This morning, we were able to make absolutely certain that Will is the one. We had set a little trap for him, knowing he was periodically going to Nigel's studio and would see the schedule. We were hoping, if he was the boy who's been following Emily, he would show up this morning to watch the shoot. If he hadn't been the one, there wouldn't have been any way for him to know you'd be there. Sure enough, he turned up just as we'd hoped."

"But why didn't you try to catch him?" Stani was plainly struggling to absorb all he'd been told.

"In a place that size, he'd have outrun us for sure. Besides, do you think your bodyguards chasing down a lone boy would have gone unnoticed? Not the sort of attention you want, is it, lad?"

"I suppose not. What next?"

"We'll hope he appears again, when Emily goes to the market, for instance, and we'll be sure to get our hands on him then. I want to give him a good talking to. He can't just follow people around, no matter how harmless he may be."

"Why can't I just go out on my own? Wouldn't that bring him out?" Emily had been silently watching and listening, admiring the care John had taken to try to calm Stani's concerns.

"No, Emily! You don't know what he might do if he got

frightened!" Stani spun around to her, an unmistakable look of alarm in his eyes.

"He's just a boy, darling. Not even a very big boy." She looked up, smiling, and saw his color rise, as he looked from her face to John's.

"Wait a minute, do you mean you've seen him too?"

"Only once, Stani. I didn't even know he'd been following us until I happened to see him last week."

"And you knew he'd be there today, didn't you? John, why wasn't I told about this?"

"We thought you might not agree to do the shoot, if you knew. It was my choice. John left it up to me." She tried to catch his eye, but he was glaring straight ahead, the telltale muscle working in his jaw.

"Hold on, lad. There's no reason to take that tone. It was important to be sure, and this was the best way to find out. No one was in any danger. Emily thought you'd cancel, and you would have, wouldn't you?" John's voice was low and firm, as he watched Stani's eyes darken with anger.

"I would have, you're right. The thought of being watched from the shrubbery by some obviously unbalanced boy, and all of you knowing about it." He looked again from one to the other, his face distorted with a mix of conflicting emotions. "I need some air!"

They heard the front door slam behind him before anyone moved. When Emily rose to follow, John held up his hand. "Stay here, girl. I'll go. It's me he's angry with."

She had stayed at the window, watching the animated discussion in the street below. When at last John urged Stani toward the steps leading to the basement flat, she gave in to the tears that had threatened since the moment he'd looked at her with such pain in his eyes. Turning, she found herself sobbing in Bertram's arms. "Come now, my dear, you know he'll be back up here on his knees within the hour." He led her to the couch, going back to close the drapes. "Now I'm going to make us some tea. Just sit there and let yourself have a good cry. I find it's often the best medicine."

By the time Stani had reached the pavement, he'd already begun to berate himself. His behavior was unforgivable. How could he have so overreacted? When John had followed him, chiding him gently for going off half-cocked, he had suddenly realized that his anger had been the result of much more than just the discovery of the secret they had kept from him. "My entire life feels as if it's spinning somewhere out of my control. I can't seem to keep my bearings in all of this."

John had suggested they take the conversation to a more private location. In the orderly quiet of his flat, he had encouraged Stani to bare his soul. "All of this *what*, lad, other than dashing back and forth across the country, spending your nights with the very present Lady Marcia, and your wife being pregnant after only five months of marriage, with twins, no less? Your house is full of strangers, and there's been a boy watching your every move for months. Anything else disturbing your peace?"

He had dropped his throbbing head in his hands. "That's the least of it. I could just possibly handle all of those things like an adult. But I've made a horrible mistake, John. And I have no clue what I should do about it." He had confessed all, and in the end, John had nodded his understanding.

"She has every right to be disappointed, not to say furious. But it was an honest mistake, lad, stupid, but honest. We both know how Peg can be. She took you on, from what I hear, and didn't stop until she'd made you over from top to toe. It stands to reason she'd think you wanted her to do the same to your apartment."

"But now Emily is so looking forward to doing up the place herself. How can I possibly expect her to understand? And Peg, of all the women in the world. She bought us a bed, John." He shook his head hopelessly, his pained expression bringing a sympathetic grin to John's face.

"It's time to be honest with her, for your own sake as much as hers. There's no other way. Go up there and confess it all, beg for her understanding, and then let her give you hell, if she needs to. You've earned it, lad."

Chapter Twenty-eight

In the end, it had proved to be a night they would never forget. But when he'd found her alone in the kitchen, pounding bread dough with a tearful vengeance, he had very nearly lost his resolve. She had looked up with swimming eyes, her lower lip held trembling between her teeth. With a gasping sob, she had begged him to forgive her.

For the several minutes, they'd clung together, each trying to outdo the other with remorse. "I'm such a fool! I should never have walked out like that."

"I knew you might be upset, but I'd never have kept it from you if I'd thought it would hurt you so much. The look in your eyes broke my heart, Stani." Dissolving into fresh tears, she'd allowed him to lead her to the table by the window. When he knelt at her feet, kissing her hands and fighting his own tears, she had tried to tell him how worried she'd been about him. Between sobs, she'd confessed that she had feared he was keeping some dark secret from her, and the idea of causing him any more stress had seemed too cruel. "You said there were things on your mind. Please, Stani, please tell me what it is. You've put this space between us that I can't cross."

Those words had completely undone him. There on his knees, he had begged her to forgive him. "I've made such a horrible mistake, Emily. And I've been too cowardly to admit it."

Her eyes wide and dry now, she had waited for him to go on. But his head was pounding so that he could hardly think of words to explain the unforgivable thing he'd done.

"This is about Marcia, isn't it?" she whispered at last.

"Marcia?" He blinked stupidly for a moment, trying to hold on to his churning thoughts. "No, of course not. It's about Peg."

Now it was her turn to blink. "Peg? You've seen Peg?"

"Yes, in New York. I met with her, remember? That's when it happened."

"When what happened, Stani?" She seemed to be holding her breath.

"You were feeling so rotten, sleeping all the time. And the loft was so dismal, do you remember?" At her slow nod, he went on. "I asked Peg to hire a decorator."

"A decorator?" she gasped, finally drawing air into her lungs.

"Yes. But she didn't."

"She didn't?" She shook her head slightly, never taking her eyes from his.

"No." He hesitated, looking away from her expectant gaze. With one deep gulp of resolve, he forced himself to go on. "She took it on herself. Oh, Emily, I'm so stupid. I had no idea that's what she was telling me. She asked me a lot of questions, what colors you liked and what kind of furniture, and she made a list. I thought she was going to hire someone, just to put in the basics, so we'd at least have a place to sleep when we got back. But it turns out she's done up the whole place. How can I ever make it up to you?"

It was then that Emily had started to laugh. His first thought was that she was sobbing again, but as she ran her hands into his hair, caressing his temples, he realized she was shaking with laughter. He pulled away, looking up in mute confusion.

"That's what you were afraid to tell me? Did you really think I'd be angry?"

"Yes! Emily, you don't seem to understand. *Peg* has furnished our apartment. She even bought us a bed, a French bed like that one you were so crazy about in Paris. And she's built walls and book shelves. And a closet." He ran out of words, as her lips closed over his.

"I don't care what she's done, Stani. As long as we get to live there together, I don't care who decorated the place. I thought you were going to tell me some really horrible thing that was going to destroy our happiness forever. If Peg bought us a dozen beds, as long as you don't share any of them with her, I could care less."

He felt the blood rise to his face. "You thought I had *slept* with Peg? Or with Marcia? I'm the one who should be angry! Oh, my silly darling girl! You can't really have believed that?"

"No, but I knew something was causing you to be so withdrawn. I imagined all sorts of things. And when you said you had done something so horrible, what was I supposed to think? Stani, asking Peg to hire a decorator, or even to do the apartment for us herself, is the sweetest thing I can think of a husband doing for his pregnant wife." She kissed him again, and he realized the throbbing in his skull had ceased.

"But you've seemed to enjoy doing over this house so much, I was afraid you'd be disappointed not to do the same there." He was having trouble accepting her reaction. She still didn't seem to quite understand the magnitude of what he'd done. "It won't bother you that *Peg* was the one who did it for us?" One more chance to fully grasp the extent of his blunder.

"Peg has wonderful taste, in furnishings, and in men. Very similar to mine really." She was once again twisting his hair between her fingers, her eyes that entrancing smoky gray. He felt a familiar tingle run through him, as he got to his feet and drew her into his arms.

"I love you. I don't in any way deserve you, but I do love you so much." As he kissed her, she began to push him toward the door. Pausing for a moment by the work table, she stepped out of his arms and with one deliberate sweep of her hand, sent the mound of dough into the trash bin.

"Now, if you don't mind, I want to go upstairs. I'm going to reward you for your brilliant idea. And then I'm going to reward you again, for buying me that French bed. Then maybe you can reward me."

"What would I be rewarding you for?" Her hands in his shirt were a definite distraction, but he was determined to follow her train of thought, as she backed him up the staircase.

"For being such an understanding wife, of course. But don't think I'm letting this happen again. I'm not about to let you go off on your own, not with Peg *or* with Marcia. I'm going with you next week to wherever it is you're performing, and when we get back to New York, any meetings will definitely be for three. None of this would have happened if I'd been with you, Stani. It's obvious you *need* my help." As if to make her point, she relieved him of his shirt, tossing it into the air, where it drifted slowly down the stairwell.

Much later, when they realized they had missed dinner and were both famished, they went back to the kitchen. While the bacon fried and Stani beat eggs in a bowl, Emily stood behind him, her arms around his waist. "I meant what I said, Stani. This should be a lesson to us both. We aren't any good at doing without one another. It only leads to trouble."

"You seem to do all right without me."

"No. I worry. And I begin to wonder what you're doing out there, that makes you come home all tense and Byronic."

He gave a little snorting laugh. "Byronic?"

"Bertram's term. It suits you, I think. Brooding romantic genius. I prefer my cheerful gentleman farmer, you know. But if we have to live half our lives in this world, I'm not letting you out there alone again.

You will just have to submit to your wife in this matter."

Carefully setting the bowl aside, he turned to gather her close. "When have I ever failed to submit to my wife? She is, after all, a force of nature."

Informed that Emily would be joining them for the remaining week of recitals, John had smiled knowingly. "All's well?"

Stani's grin said as much. "The amazing thing is she doesn't think I'm an idiot. She thinks I'm brilliant." He had walked off, shaking his head, to the sound of John's laughter.

Bertram and Mrs. Winslow were to remain on duty at the house, going about their routines as if Emily were still at home. Perhaps Will would come around looking for her if she didn't appear in her usual haunts. "Just keep an eye out. Don't try to catch him. Let's get him good and curious." John was pleased with the idea of Emily being away for a few days. It might actually prove to be the thing that closed the case. If Will had any idea that something was amiss, he might be lured further from his hiding place.

It had also occurred to John that Emily's presence on the trip might prove beneficial in a number of ways. As the weeks passed, he had observed that while Stani seemed oblivious to the fact, Marcia had become increasingly possessive of his time and attention. She insisted on his joining her for dinner before the concerts, along with her ever-present father. He was also expected to attend the receptions afterward, where Marcia clung to his arm, introducing him to her friends and behaving much as if he were her newest acquisition, to be shown off and admired. John had made subtle comments on the subject, but had not wanted to add another cause for anxiety when Stani had seemed ever more distracted.

Emily would see the situation in a different light, John was sure. If Stani really believed he had managed to keep a safe distance from Marcia, his wife might well be the one to point out his error. Before they made that trip to the earl's estate for a long weekend, Emily should at least know what sorts of plans were being laid. And if he knew anything about Emily, John mused, plans were made to be changed.

Chapter Twenty-nine

The first night in Liverpool, after they had settled into their hotel and Emily had suggested room service for dinner, she had already begun to understand where things really stood with Marcia. Little signs, a gesture here and a look there, not to mention her poorly concealed discomfort at Emily's presence on this trip, were telling enough. Marcia might put on a brave front, but clearly she had expected to have Stani all to herself. When Stani had informed her that they would be having dinner in their room, as Emily was tired from the long drive, he had turned away from the phone with a mildly puzzled expression.

"Is that a problem?" Coming from the bathroom, Emily had already dressed for bed.

"Apparently she had ordered the kitchen to prepare lamb chops thinking they were a favorite of mine. I suppose I've ordered them once or twice, but I can't imagine she would have noticed. She seemed really disappointed. Oh, well, I'm sure she's just making a fuss over it. She tends to do that."

Arching her brows, Emily grinned. "Does she? I would never have expected it."

Stani turned his attention to her, fingering the lacey blue dressing gown. "This is new, isn't it?"

"Yes, I bought it just for this trip. I haven't been in a hotel room with my husband in weeks." Her arms around his neck, she breathed softly into his ear. "I've missed that, you know? Cars and hotels and concert halls. And you."

Emily slept later than usual the next morning. Stani ordered breakfast for them, then dressed for rehearsal, laughingly fending off her efforts to delay him. When Marcia appeared at the door, she was treated to the sight of a somewhat disheveled Emily lounging on the couch, while Stani's color was uncommonly high.

"We're going to be late, Stani. I expected you to be downstairs by now." Her tone suggested that this lapse in their routine had ruined her entire morning.

"Sorry. If you'd like to go ahead, I'll have John bring me around." He turned to Emily. "Were you coming this morning, darling girl?"

Standing up, she stretched luxuriantly. "Yes, I think I will. It won't take me long to dress. But, please, Marcia, don't wait for us. I promise I'll have him there in plenty of time." Turning, she walked to the door, opening it wide to give a full view of the tumbled bedding and trail of discarded clothing on the floor.

At each break in the rehearsal, it seemed Marcia had lost her focus. She called Stani to the piano, requiring his advice or affirmation on this or that passage. It was such an old trick, Emily mused, Stani should recognize it by now. But apparently he wasn't in the least suspicious. He lent his support, and the rehearsal resumed. When they were preparing to leave, Marcia reminded him that they had an interview scheduled at two o'clock. "I'll have the car waiting, Stani. Please don't be late." Her little pout seemed to say that she had forgiven him for the morning's lapse.

They joined Marcia and her father for dinner before going to the recital hall. When Emily politely asked how he was enjoying the tour, the earl laughed. "I'm not. Much rather stay at home, but if my little girl wants to play at this music business, I suppose I can go along for the ride. I don't know how you do it, my dear, following your husband all over the world."

With an adoring smile she took Stani's hand. "Oh, it's more than worth it. Traveling to all the romantic cities of Europe, listening to the most gifted violinist of our time, and then going to bed with him every night. What woman could ask for more?" A gurgle of laughter escaped as Stani blushed, and the earl chuckled heartily.

"I see what you mean, dear girl. Never thought of it quite that way."

No one seemed to notice that Marcia had grown very quiet, attacking her dinner with grim intent. But Emily had the thought that the unpleasant twist of her lips as she dug into her trifle was extremely unattractive, somehow reminiscent of a spoiled child plotting her revenge.

Following the recital, they gathered in a luxuriously appointed room for the reception. Almost at once, Marcia came to claim Stani, insisting he must meet some "very dear old friends of the family."

Emily watched as Marcia introduced the distinguished looking couple to Stani, then possessively linked her arm in his, smiling up into his face. When the earl approached with several other people, joining the conversation, she saw Stani searching the room for her. The little quirk of his brows signaled a call for help, and she made her way through the crowd. As she slid in beside him, she took his free arm.

"Stani, darling, I've been looking all over for you. I'm dying for something to drink, but the mob around the bar was too much for me." She realized how ridiculous they must look, each tugging on an arm as Stani tried to disengage himself from Marcia. "If you wouldn't mind, sir, I'll steal my husband for a moment or two?" She smiled at the earl and pulling Stani out of the circle, led him away, certain she could feel Marcia's glare following them to the bar.

"Is she always so clinging?"

"I hadn't noticed. But now that you mention it, she is inclined to hang on the nearest arm."

"And I'd be willing to bet the nearest arm is usually yours."

Emily had been at her most charming, Stani commented much later, when they finally returned to the hotel. "You were the center of attention, love. I'd forgotten how you shine at functions like that."

Slipping out of her robe, she climbed into bed. "Oh, I'm sure I wasn't the center of attention. But with you beside me, people seemed to enjoy being around us. We make a good team, Stani. And I love hearing all the wonderful things they say to you. I'm always so proud." Holding out her arms, she smiled invitingly. "Come to bed, please. You were so beautiful, standing there making love to that violin."

"And you are so beautiful, lying here in my bed. I didn't realize how lonely it's been without you. You're right, you know, we should never be apart if we can avoid it. I feel so much more myself when I'm with you." He gathered her close, smoothing her hair and laying a kiss on her forehead.

"Umm. Do we have to join the others for breakfast? I'd much rather spend the morning here with you. Couldn't we just tell them we didn't sleep well?"

"Didn't we?" He grinned, kissing the hand that had wandered up to caress his face.

"No, I think we were up until all hours, don't you?"

By the time they prepared to return to London, Stani had the distinct impression that Marcia had tired of touring. While her performances had been as lively as ever, she seemed to have grown weary of the required socializing. She had even begged off early from the final reception, claiming she had a headache and returning to the hotel. The next morning, before they departed for London and she headed to the country with her father, Stani commented that the poor girl seemed quite down.

"She was apparently surprised to hear I was coming to the country with you. I was invited, wasn't I?" Emily asked, as they settled into the back seat of the car.

"Of course. Or it was certainly understood that you'd come if you were feeling up to it."

"I'm really looking forward to it. Lord Strathmoore has promised us a tour of his farming operation. It turns out his land is being used in some sort of experimental program, and I'm anxious to see what he's doing. He also told me there's a wonderful old church in the village near the estate. I want to explore a little bit, if you're willing to go with me. It should be fun, don't you think?" As she snuggled against him, he chuckled.

"If it's anything like these past few days, I'd say so." He tilted her face up for a kiss.

"All right, you two." John's laughing eyes met theirs in the rear view mirror. "Just like old times, I'd say."

"Oh, at least. Maybe even better, John. Take the scenic route back to London, will you? Even if we have to stay over at some charming country inn tonight. I'm not in any hurry for this trip to end."

Chapter Thirty

There were only a few days between their return home and the expected arrival of Lil and Charles. When Stani announced his intention to lock himself in the music room and put in some hours on a composition he hoped to record in New York, Emily turned to Bertram for the still-required escort to the various shops. "I have meals to plan and shop for. I know we'll take them out to at least one restaurant, but after traipsing around Europe eating heaven knows what, the poor kids deserve a home cooked meal or two."

As they made the rounds, she kept watch for Will. Bertram had told them he hadn't been seen in the neighborhood since the sighting at the Embankment. "I expect he's wondering about you by now. Let's see if he puts in an appearance, once he sees you've returned."

But there was no sign of him. They could only assume he had given up watching after their departure. Nigel had been instructed to post the scheduled shoot of their evening out, in hopes that Will was still checking in at the studio periodically. John had several lookouts around the neighborhood, but so far, no one had reported seeing the boy again.

"Disappearing into thin air seems to be his specialty. But he's always come back. No reason to think he won't this time. I only wish I knew if he saw that little drama the night after the shoot. If he saw Stani storm out, and you standing there at the window, you'd think that would have gotten his attention."

Emily laughed. "He would have seen me fall sobbing into Bertram's arms, too. And for all he knows, Bertram is just my chauffeur. What must he think of me?"

It was Bertram who was assigned to drive Emily to the station to meet the travelers. Stani had been up much of the night, closeted in the music room, and she had insisted he sleep in that morning. By the time she left for the station, he was up and showered, promising to have lunch on the table when they returned.

"What other woman can boast of a husband who composes brilliant music all night and then gets up and cooks the next morning?" As she twisted up her hair and tucked it into her hat, Stani took the opportunity to lay a kiss on the back of her neck. "Not to mention lavishing said woman with romantic attention."

"Not sure how brilliant the music is, or how much cooking Mrs. Winslow will allow me to do, but the lavishing, you can count on."

"What were you working on last night?"

"The Hungarian nursery piece. But I can't quite pin down the sound I want. Still searching." With a tender kiss, he turned up her collar and steered her toward the door. "Off you go. I know Lil will be glad to see a face from home."

She smiled, a little shiver of anticipation lifting her shoulders. "And I'm going to be glad to see her. No matter what, Lil always livens things up. When we were little girls I always wondered what sort of excitement she'd bring with her to the farm. Now she's bringing it all the way to London! We'll have an adventure or two, you can count on it."

Weary to the bone and in dire need of a hot bath and a change of clothes, Lil and Charles were welcomed on the platform at Victoria Station by Emily, elegant in her fur-trimmed coat, and a tall, dapper man she introduced simply as Bertram. When he attempted to relieve Lil of her backpack and viola case, she protested sharply.

"It's all right, Lil. Bertram is my chauffeur. He just wants to take your bags to the car."

"What happened to John? I thought he drove you guys everywhere." Relinquishing her battered pack with a mumbled apology, she linked her arm through Emily's and followed Bertram, leaving the silent Charles to bring up the rear.

"He's at home with Stani. I've had Bertram with me in London, since John had to travel with Stani on the recital tour. But we'll catch up on all that later. Right now, it looks like you two could use a hot meal and maybe a good long shower. Charles, I like your beard. It's very becoming."

Before Lil could comment, Charles blushed and muttered his

thanks.

"It suits him, don't you think, Lil? Here's the car. Charles, would you prefer to sit up front with Bertram? Lil, get back here with me. I want to hear all about the trip." Herding them along, Emily studied the tired faces. They seemed older somehow, and Lil in particular appeared to have acquired a new layer of confidence. Poor Charles; she mused, he would never be able to stand up to Lil now.

After a long lunch, during which the travelers seemed somewhat overwhelmed by the luxury of home style dining, Stani showed them to their rooms. He was chuckling when he returned to the kitchen. "Mrs. Winslow is running a bath in the clawfoot. I thought Lil was going to start undressing before I could close the door. And I asked Bertram to find some scissors and a razor. He's going to trim up that beard for Charles. Looks as if he hasn't shaved since he left home."

"I guess their travels across Europe were a bit different from ours. Lil practically slugged Bertram when he tried to take her backpack." Emily giggled at the memory.

"I doubt they stayed in many five star hotels, darling. Admit it. Being married to a classical superstar does have its perks."

Going into his arms, she smiled suggestively. "Especially when the superstar is so appealing. I don't suppose you need a nap, do you?"

"Emily, you are insatiable. If I'd known taking you on a road trip would have such an effect on you, I'd have done it much sooner. Now be a good girl. We can't just fall into bed whenever we feel the urge. What will the staff think?"

She was nuzzling his ear, at the same time running an exploratory hand down his shirt front. "Don't you think they'd understand?"

"They might, but I doubt Lil would. I seem to recall she found us a bit hard to take, even before we were married." He laughingly tried to defend himself from her persistent advances. "Emily, don't ignore me. What is it about my shirt buttons that you find so irresistible?"

"Well, I must say, those two want a good cleaning up! And look at all this dirty laundry. I doubt they've a decent change of clothes between them." As Mrs. Winslow bustled past them to the laundry room, she grinned at Emily. "Why don't you two have a nice little rest, my dear? I'm sure your friends won't be down for a while. Not unless they come down in the altogether."

The three weeks tramping around Europe had been filled with

wonderful sights and memorable experiences, but for Lil nothing could have been more beautiful than the sight of Emily standing on the platform, smiling and waving. If her own mother had greeted her, she would not have felt more at home. Even in her glamorous blue coat and fur hat, with her very proper chauffeur in tow, she had been just the same sweet Emily.

Stani, with the aid of the chauffeur, who now seemed to be acting as butler too, had served them lunch, treating them like honored guests and ignoring the fact that they smelled of days without a decent bath. He had wanted to hear about all the places they'd visited, but Emily had reminded him that they would have plenty of time for that, once the "poor kids" had a chance to rest. Now that she was expecting, Emily had become very maternal, Lil had noticed. And Stani seemed even more devoted to her, if that was possible. They were still the same love-struck pair she'd first seen sitting by the fire in the farmhouse, even in this awe-inspiring house surrounded by servants.

The housekeeper, Mrs. Winslow, had taken charge immediately after Stani had shown them to their rooms, drawing a tub full of hot, sweet smelling water and carting off her bag of well-worn clothes to be laundered. She had soaked and scrubbed, and washed her hair twice, savoring the luxury of expensive soap and shampoo. Now, wrapped in the soft white bathrobe Mrs. Winslow had brought for her, she was stretched on the big bed in her room, staring up at the ceiling, feeling thoroughly relaxed for the first time in weeks. After hard, narrow beds and shared baths in cheap tourist hotels, Emily's house might as well have been Buckingham Palace.

She knew that just down the hall, Charles was enjoying the same treatment. Bertram had taken him to his room, and she had heard him leave, promising to return with "something suitable." Charles' one pair of decent khakis had suffered a tear in the seat, and he had been tying a sweater around his waist to cover the hole for the past week. Lil smiled at the thought of his embarrassment, as the hole seemed to grow steadily larger. Charles had been a perfect touring partner, good-natured and patient. They had traveled with another couple, a brother and sister from DC, to take advantage of the double occupancy rates, and Charles had gotten the more difficult of the two. His roommate was perpetually dissatisfied with their accommodations, their meals and even the weather. To make matters worse, his complaints were voiced in a high-pitched nasal whine which Lil had inevitably begun to unconsciously imitate.

As she sank deeper into the softness of her bed, she wondered what

Charles thought of his room. He had been hesitant about staying here, in the home of his idol. Even though they had spent time with Stani and Emily at home in Virginia, Charles was still in awe of the man he considered musical royalty. But she had pointed out that he had no cash left for a hotel, not even a cheap one. Besides, Stani would be insulted if he turned down his hospitality. Charles might be uncomfortable for a few minutes, but she thought he would soon find this accommodation a vast improvement over anything they'd had so far.

Smiling, she remembered Charles' other concern. Would their hosts think them hopelessly old-fashioned, because they didn't sleep together? Some of their friends in Richmond nagged them endlessly because they insisted on paying rent on two apartments, when they could just move in together like most people in their crowd. Lil had laughed, telling him that Stani and Emily had waited until their wedding night, even though they had traveled all over England and even lived together in the farmhouse for weeks after Emily's accident. They would understand, she assured him, both how difficult it was at times and why they had chosen to wait. Charles had blushed the usual bright red, saying only that he hoped she was right. When they'd been ushered to separate rooms without any questions, she hoped he had finally relaxed a little.

Charles could be very uptight at times. He was smart and talented, not to mention good-looking. If he only had a better sense of his own worth, showed more self-confidence, asserted himself more. As it was, he seemed to always be apologizing for something, letting someone else take the lead. She had tried to step back, wait for him to put himself forward, but he had never done so. Someone had to move things along, she thought. And Charles seemed to be leaving that up to her.

She heard Stani's voice somewhere across the hall. The words weren't clear, but the tone was definitely tender. He was obviously talking to Emily, and then she heard a door close and footsteps going toward the stairs. Getting up, she cautiously opened her own door, peering out into the hallway. She was pretty sure their bedroom was the first one at the top of the stairs. Padding across the carpeted floor, she tapped lightly and called out to Emily. When a sleepy voice replied, she looked in. Emily was stretched on the bed, propped on a mound of pillows and she immediately smiled and held out her hand.

"Hi! Come on in. I'm just being lazy."

"You're sure? I just heard Stani leave and thought you might want company." Closing the door, she went to perch on the foot of the bed.

"What's on your mind?" Emily could be uncannily direct at times.

"Nothing really. It's just so good to see you guys. This trip has been wonderful, but I did get a little homesick."

"Of course you did. And how did Charles manage? He's traveled before, though, hasn't he?"

"He was great. He knew how to get around, what to see. But without much money, it can get a little rough. I guess I'm more spoiled than I thought."

Emily smiled. "Well, now we can spoil you some more. How would you like to go shopping tomorrow, my treat? And tomorrow night, we have tickets to a concert at Royal Albert Hall. Beethoven and Dvorak, I think."

Lil felt the unaccustomed sting of tears in her eyes. Gratitude was not something she easily expressed, but now she felt the urge to throw her arms around Emily's neck. Instead, she grinned and said softly, "That sounds like heaven!"

Mrs. Winslow had persuaded Emily to allow her to prepare a proper high tea for her young houseguests. "You should just be sitting down, playing hostess, my dear. No need to wear yourself out in the kitchen."

When they had all gathered in the lounge at five, the tea cart was rolled in, loaded with sandwiches, scones and a decadent-looking raspberry tart. Mrs. Winslow had even included a bowl of fresh fruit, knowing that "dear Mr. Moss doesn't particularly fancy sweets."

Stani grinned down at Emily, as she presided over the table. "Lady of the manor?"

"I might as well get used to letting my staff do things for me. With two babies, I doubt I'll find time to bake scones very often." She passed a cup to Lil, whose eyes had narrowed in bewilderment.

"What do you mean, two babies?"

"Oh, that's right. You haven't heard. I forgot you've been on the road for so long." Looking up at Stani, she laughed. "I hope you take the news better than their father did. We're having twins, Lil."

When the shock had worn off, Lil demanded to know how on earth they would ever travel with two infants. "We had trouble enough keeping up with a couple of backpacks. And I nearly lost my viola twice. Mom told me not to bring it, but I couldn't imagine being without it. I can only guess at the kind of stuff you'll have to carry around for a couple of babies."

"We'll have lots of help. John, of course, and we plan to hire a nanny. We'll manage. But any time you want to come along with us and babysit, you'll be more than welcome. The more the merrier, I suspect."

As if on cue, John popped his head in the doorway. "Mind if I join the party? I heard there were a couple of state-siders up here." His entry was greeted by an enthusiastic hug from Lil and a hearty handshake from Charles. When he had settled in a chair not far from the tea cart, he caught Stani's eye. "Had a bit of news on our boy today. He's been to Nigel's studio, so he knows you'll be out and about tomorrow night. I can't imagine he'll go all the way to Royal Albert Hall, but at least he knows you're home again."

Stani took a moment to consider the news, a scowl darkening his eyes. "Emily is planning to go out shopping in the morning. I should have confidence in Bertram, I suppose?" Perched on the arm of her chair, he draped a protective arm around her shoulders.

"Of course you should. Plus Lil will be with me. And it isn't as if Will's been seen lurking around Harrod's." At the instant spark of curiosity in Lil's eyes, Emily sighed. "I suppose we might as well tell them the whole story. We can't pretend there's nothing going on, can we?"

John gave an abbreviated account of the suspected prowler who had proved to be nothing more than a misguided fan. "Not that he can keep making a nuisance of himself like that. We just have to get our hands on him now. I hate to involve the police at this point. I'm pretty sure we can handle it ourselves."

"So now you see why we have so many people in the house. I haven't even been able to walk to the corner bakery alone. I'll be so glad when this is finally resolved." Emily paused for a second, her eyes widening. Taking Stani's hand, she laid it against the side of her rounded belly. "Can you feel that?" He waited breathlessly, then shook his head in disappointment. "Maybe next time. But that was a really good kick. I guess they want to be free to get out of the house, too." She gave the bulge a consoling little pat.

The conversation turned to the plans already made for the next several days. Bertram had been recruited to take Lil and Charles on a sightseeing excursion on Saturday. Sunday after church, they could pick any of a number of places to visit, again with Bertram as guide.

Passing him a refilled cup, Stani smiled conspiratorially at Charles, who had been listening in virtual silence. "Tomorrow, while the girls are out shopping, I thought you and I might pay a visit to the recording studio. I have a little business to finish up there, and I thought you might enjoy a tour of the place. And knowing your interest in authentic performance, I took the liberty of making a lunch date with Matthew Covington."

Clearly dumbfounded, Charles sputtered a few times and blushed furiously. "That would be incredible, to actually meet him. He's the spearhead of the whole movement!"

"He and I met years ago, when I was here recording. He played cello on a Vivaldi recording for me. Great guy. I told him I had a friend from the States who's as passionate as he is about period instruments, and he's anxious to meet you."

Emily caught the expression on Lil's face, a look of intense gratitude. She squeezed Stani's hand, wanting him to know how proud she was of him for taking such an interest. Charles might be shy and awkward, but he was also a gifted musician and with a little push from someone like Stani Moss, he might find the courage to follow his passion. And with the love of the girl who so clearly wanted to see him succeed, anything might be possible.

Chapter Thirty-one

Lil had been impressed by the ease with which Emily moved through the huge department store, and by the way the clerks and floorwalkers all seemed to know her on sight. The things they bought were put on "Mr. Moss's account" without Emily even giving her name. Insisting that Lil find a new evening outfit to wear to the concert, Emily had reminded her that they would be photographed for some big magazine layout and their names would be included in the captions. "Our American friends, violists Lilianne Salvatore and Charles Evans, fresh from their extended tour of the continent." Emily grinned, as she scanned the selection of gowns. "I want to show you off, little sister. You're the first member of my American family to visit this other world we live in." They finally agreed on a form-fitting gown of deep green with a collar of glittering gold beads. Gold platform sandals and a shawl of jewel-toned paisley satisfied Emily's desire to make Lil stand out in the crowd. "Think how proud Charles will be of you."

Her eyes flying open in horror, Lil gasped. "Charles! He doesn't have anything to wear. He brought a ratty old jacket and tie in case we went anywhere he was required to dress up. Oh, Em, he'll be too embarrassed to go tonight."

"We already have it taken care of, Lil. Bertram is in charge of getting him all fitted out. Don't worry, he'll look like something off the cover of Menswear Daily." She nodded in the direction of the discreetly distanced Bertram, who had been just out of earshot during their browsing. "But it's up to you to be sure he understands it's a gift. Maybe you can tell him Stani would be insulted if he refused."

"Em, you're being so sweet to us. Charles is so excited to be going to lunch with Stani and this Covington person. You can't imagine what it means to him to have Stani Moss make such a fuss over him."

"Oh, I think I can. Now, if you wouldn't mind, I'd like to take a look at what the pregnant ladies are wearing out on the town this season. I've already been photographed several times in the tuxedo we had made in New York. Can't have Stani's fans thinking he's stingy with his wife's wardrobe allowance. But first, it's time for this pregnant lady to eat again. Let's go to the tea room and indulge ourselves. I am eating for three, after all." Laughing, they took the elevator up to the restaurant, where it was clear Emily was equally well known. Lil pinched herself under the tablecloth just to be sure she was really sitting in a corner table at Harrod's with the girl who had grown up on that farm in the valley, the girl who was now married to Stani Moss and living the life of a princess.

The photographer had followed them into the concert hall, constantly moving in circles around them. Lil could tell it made Charles nervous, but she tried to take her cue from Emily and behave as naturally as possible, holding on to Charles' arm and smiling without looking directly into the camera. Stani seemed especially protective of Emily, as if he were afraid to take his eyes off her for a minute. Lil wondered if he might be worrying about that boy who'd been following her. She'd found herself looking around today while they were shopping, even though she knew Bertram was already on the job.

In spite of her initial reaction to Bertram at the train station, Lil had decided he was really all right. He'd done wonderful things with Charles, from trimming his hair and beard to decking him out in style tonight. Charles had never looked so handsome, and he seemed to have accepted all the attention without too much embarrassment. In fact, Lil thought he seemed almost confident, as he leaned over her and commented to Stani about some note in the program. She had the urge to pinch herself again, as she studied his profile in the dimming lights of the hall. The beard did suit him, now that Bertram had worked his magic. And in the perfectly fitted black suit, his tall, loose-jointed frame seemed to take on a new grace. Even next to the always impeccable Stani, Charles was the picture of a well-dressed man of the world.

She inwardly giggled at the irony of this night. They had just spent three weeks tramping around in hiking boots and tattered jeans, eating horrible food and sleeping on lumpy old mattresses. Now they were sitting in prime seats, dressed up like celebrities and in fact having their picture taken for a magazine story about Stani Moss and his bride, who just happened to be her own godsister.

Emily had found a gown of deep red crepe with long tapering sleeves and a neckline that dipped very low in both front and back. The skirt was caught up high at the waist and fell in soft pleats over what she called her not-so-little bulge. She was wearing her Christmas present from Stani, a choker of rubies and diamonds that must have cost several times as much as their entire European trip. When she had come down the stairs tonight, as elegant and graceful as ever, the look on Stani's face had been almost comical. He had muttered something about a stack of cushions and Emily had laughed, putting her arms around his neck and kissing him for long enough that John had cleared his throat and asked if they really intended to go anywhere.

They seemed so happy, but Lil had gathered enough from things Emily said to know that this strange boy had caused a lot of trouble. And she could see how restless Em was, locked in the house and never free to go out on her own. Emily, who had always loved to roam the fields and had written about how much fun it was to ramble around the cities they visited while Stani worked. She had to feel trapped, and all because some kid had decided to watch her from the bushes and follow her in her own neighborhood. And Emily had said plainly that until he was caught and stopped, Stani would never consent to let her go anywhere without Bertram.

That sort of thing came with celebrity, Em had said with a sigh. But it didn't come easily, Lil was sure. As she listened to the orchestra, she kept turning over and over the idea that even though Stani was famous, his family should have the right to at least a more or less normal life. Emily had worked hard to make their home here as comfortable as the one at the farm, but she was a virtual prisoner within its walls. When the babies came, would they have to have bodyguards too, just to go to the park or play in their own little garden?

Glancing over at Emily, she saw her take Stani's hand, the way she had earlier, and hold it to her belly. Suddenly his eyes widened and he smiled that beautiful flashing smile of his. Emily laughed, reaching over to stroke his cheek. Apparently, he had felt the baby, or babies, move for the first time. Maybe they liked Beethoven too, Lil mused. Then she went back to thinking about the injustice of their situation. That one silly boy's fascination with them could have caused them even a moment's unhappiness seemed intolerable. Surely there was something all these people around them could do to bring this kid out in the open. But they all seemed to know what they were doing. Maybe, Lil told herself, she just wanted to see things too simply. She wanted Emily and Stani to be happy. She wanted them to live this enchanted life without Emily having to stay in the house, or Stani wearing that anxious look all the time. Maybe, she admitted, she just wished she could do something to repay them for making these days in London the best of their entire trip.

John dropped them at the front door, the four of them laughing and waving goodnight. Emily commented on the fact that there were no lights in the windows, only the glow from the entrance hall in the fanlight over the door. Just as Stani pushed his key into the lock, the door flew open and a frantically whispering Mrs. Winslow, dressed in her nightclothes, waved them inside.

"He's in the garden, sir! I heard him, just a few minutes ago. I came down for a glass of milk, you see, and I didn't bother to turn on the lights." Stani turned to Charles, at the same time steering Emily toward the darkened lounge.

"Stay here! Mrs. Winslow, watch her. Don't let her move!" As if reading one another's thoughts, Stani grabbed an umbrella from the stand by the door, while Charles picked up a tall porcelain candle stand from the table in the entry. Trailing behind, Lil stepped out of her high-heeled sandals, bending to pick one up as she went and testing its weight against her open palm.

A nervous giggle rose in Emily's throat. "I hope they don't hurt each other!"

In what seemed a matter of seconds, a series of crashes and shouts sounded from the back of the house. Straining her ears, Emily was sure she heard angry squalling rising over the muddle of voices. Lights began to come on as the trio made their way back, with John bringing up the rear. When Mrs. Winslow switched on the lamp by Emily's chair, they were treated to the sight of a small, very unhappy yellow tabby, which John held high by the scruff of its neck.

"Here's your prowler, Mrs. Winslow. These three sent the poor fellow flying over the gate in a panic. Very nearly landed on my head." Stani and Charles collapsed on the couch, red-faced and breathing hard, brandishing their weapons, as Lil cautiously examined the furry culprit and seemed to find him harmless.

"Poor kitty, you were just looking for some dinner, weren't you?" With great care for her dress, she took the terrified cat from John's grasp, smoothing its disheveled coat.

"Oh, I'm so ashamed of myself, my dears. But I was just so sure it was that boy. It must have been that cat, jumping onto the trash bin." Mrs. Winslow seemed close to tears.

Patting her arm, Emily said soothingly, "I'd have thought just the same, Mrs. Winslow. We're all a little jumpy. But now we know we have more than adequate protection, don't we? Did you see the way my brave knight went to battle with his trusty umbrella?"

"Just think of it as a drill, Mrs. Winslow. Next time, we'll be ready, won't we troops? And I must say that was a nice touch with the shoe, Lil." Stani pointed with the tip of his umbrella to the sandal still dangling from Lil's wrist.

"Now that you've all had a bit of fun, what say we release our prisoner? I doubt we can charge him with more than vagrancy." John was brushing at the yellow fur on his jacket.

But Lil had clearly developed a relationship with the cat. "I think we should at least offer him some milk, before we send him out into the night. Come on, Sandy, let's see what we can find in the fridge for you."

As Lil marched off murmuring to the cat, Charles rolled his eyes at Stani. "She has an affinity for strays. She did that with three cats on the trip. For a while, I thought we might be stuck with the one in Venice. But they all seemed to have sense enough to run away from her."

Before long, they had all followed Lil to the kitchen, agreeing that so much excitement called for nourishment. To make amends for causing such a stir, Mrs. Winslow insisted on serving up a late night feast of cold chicken sandwiches and raspberry tart before returning to her room. Seated around the work table in their evening finery, they talked and laughed until well into the wee hours of the morning. Sandy the cat, after a substantial meal of his own, had curled on the doormat and given himself a thorough grooming from top to tail. Now, as the conversation began to wind down, he tucked his nose beneath one paw and went to sleep.

"Looks like you've got yourself a housecat, lad. I remember when you were little you were always moaning that Milo wouldn't let you have a pet." John had observed Stani staring wistfully at the ball of fur blocking the back door.

Stani sighed. "He can't stay." Then looking to Emily, he grinned. "Can he?"

Emily yawned, pushing away from the table. "Only if Mrs. Winslow is willing to look after him while we're away. It's not as if he'll wait for months between meals. You can ask her in the morning.

And now, as much fun as this has been, this mother-to-be is going to bed. What a night! Beethoven, prowling cats and raspberry tart. If we don't all have nightmares, I don't know why not!" She started for the stairs, rubbing her belly tenderly. "Come on, children. Mother is up way past her bedtime."

"I'd better go with her. She's likely to fall asleep in her clothes. Don't forget Bertram is planning to pick you two up bright and early." With a last look at the sleeping cat, Stani followed his wife, who could be heard still talking to herself as she mounted the stairs.

"So, you two had an exciting night in old London town." John seemed in no hurry for the party to end.

"I'll say! But John, I want to ask you something." Lil was still wide awake, although Charles was blinking tiredly over his cup of long-since cold tea. "How are you planning to get this boy to come out so you can actually catch him?"

"Patience, Lil. Of course, it would help if we could get him to follow Emily on the street, but so far, he runs the minute he sees she's not alone. And Stani won't hear of her going out on her own, so don't even suggest it to him. He's probably right. Even the slightest risk is not worth considering, given her condition."

"I just hate it that they have to keep putting up with this. It's not fair." Lil tossed her crumpled napkin across the table for emphasis.

"Fair or not, it won't be the last time this sort of thing happens. It goes with the territory. Stani attracts attention, gets people excited. I've pulled more than a few overly eager girls off him. Even took a pair of scissors out of the hand of a lass who wanted a lock of hair for a souvenir. Now that he has Emily, it's even more important to be careful. Jealousy could be an ugly thing, I'm sure. But this boy, this Will Harrison, just seems to be watching out for her, as she says, just the way all of us are."

Lil shuddered. "They're so happy. And they deserve to be. I just wish there was something I could do to help."

"Lil, I know that look." Charles stood up, eyeing her sternly. "Come on, it's late. Let's go to bed. I want to be able to stay awake tomorrow, you know." Taking her by the hand, he nodded to John. "I'm sure you'll catch this kid. I promise Lil won't get in your way." Over her protests, he led her toward the stairs. "I mean it, Lil. You can't go around thinking you can save the world with a sandal!"

Chapter Thirty-two

When Emily woke the next morning, Stani was just coming through the door with a breakfast tray. It was very late, judging by the light that streamed in the window when he opened the drapes. As she sat up, stretching and rubbing her eyes, he carefully placed the tray on her lap. She eyed the contents suspiciously.

"Unless you've been secretly taking classes, you didn't make this, did you?" She poked at the wedges of golden French toast piled next to circles of bacon and topped with strawberries sliced into perfect little fans.

Smoothing her tangled hair, he chuckled. "Mrs. Winslow. I'm afraid now that she's found her way around the kitchen I'm out of a job."

"I should have known better. But, oh, this is so good!" She licked syrup from her lips, downing a healthy bite of toast. "Did you already eat?"

"Hours ago. I had a perfect omelet, made to order. How are our little acrobats this morning?" He laid a hand over her waist, a tender smile in his eyes.

"They've been up for hours too. But it was so nice to just stay in bed. Last night was a little bit more excitement than I'm used to." She giggled at the memory of Stani wielding an umbrella. "What exactly would you have done if Will really had been in the garden?"

"No idea. But picking him up by the scruff of his neck, the way John did the cat, might have been a suitable starting place. Although if Lil had gotten to him first, who knows what damage she might have inflicted. They're a great pair, Lil and Charles. Up for anything."

"I suppose Bertram's shown them half of London by now. I really should get up. Do you have things to do today?" She was still intently attacking her breakfast.

"Nothing special. I thought I might pamper my wife a bit. Maybe brush her hair and help her dress." Stretching at her side, he ran a finger lightly along her bare arm.

"Umm. Won't Mrs. Winslow wonder if we don't come down?"

"Mrs. Winslow has gone to the market. She plans to prepare another sumptuous tea for our American friends this afternoon. Besides, I made a great deal of noise about being exhausted after our adventure last night and she suggested I might want to have a nap before lunch. Mrs. Winslow is nobody's fool, darling girl. I'd say she and Mr. Winslow had a very happy marriage, judging by that gleam in her eye."

As he set aside the tray and stripped off his sweater, Emily eyed him warmly. "Who was the man who said we couldn't just fall into bed whenever we felt the urge?"

"A very foolish man, no doubt. But one who loves his wife very much. You know I almost wish that had been Will Harrison, or whatever his name is, last night, so we could finally be done with this business. I know you're not happy having all these people in the house, but you do know we're just trying to protect you?" He pressed her head to his shoulder, settling her close to his side.

"I know. Unfortunately, it seems he's trying to do the same thing. You're all working at cross-purposes, you know. If you'd let me go out by myself, he'd be more likely to make himself visible."

"No, Emily. No. You're pregnant, remember?"

"I could hardly forget. I suppose it would be risky. We'll just have to be patient. And let Mrs. Winslow take over my kitchen, and Bertram drive me two blocks to the bakery." With a long sigh, she turned to meet his lips. "Take my mind off it all, will you, Stani?"

"With pleasure."

By the time they had finished their sightseeing, both Charles and Lil were more than ready for a rest. While Bertram had given them ample time to take in the various sights, the Tower of London, Westminster Abbey, and a drive by Buckingham Palace and Parliament, he had also insisted they walk along King's Row and visit the street market in Notting Hill. After only a few hours' sleep, the pair was dragging sadly by noon, and still had a full agenda for the next several hours. By their return at four o'clock, both were prepared to collapse across their beds. But Emily and Stani were waiting in the lounge, anxious to hear about their day, and Mrs. Winslow was already laying out the tea cart.

They were joined by John and Bertram and the conversation

quickly turned to the previous night's excitement. When first informed of the feline prowler earlier that morning, Bertram had merely smiled. But now he heartily congratulated Stani on leading such a bold assault. "In the event Will Harrison ever appears, I'm sure the sight of his idol brandishing a bumbershoot would terrify him half to death."

"In my defense, it was the only thing handy. And I think I might get a little credit for rallying the troops. If this boy is as shy as you say he is, the three of us falling over ourselves out the back door should have petrified him. He would have been at least as easy to detain as poor Sandy was."

"You were all very brave, darling. By the way, did you ask Mrs. Winslow about letting you keep Sandy?"

"They'd already become fast friends, by the time I came down to breakfast. In fact, it was Mrs. Winslow who asked my permission. Being the good sport I am, I agreed to a trial residency." Grinning, he caught John's eye. "Finally I'm the proud master of not only a mule, but a cat as well. My cup runneth over."

Lil had been sitting quietly, half-listening to the conversation and watching the way Emily and Stani looked at each other across the room. Her mind had been turning all day around the subject of Will Harrison. She couldn't help thinking that it should be simpler to lure him out, rather than wait for some chance appearance. Stani was still talking, saying something about having to keep his wife entertained while she was confined to the house.

"John, you know what you said last night? About Emily going out on her own?" All eyes seemed to turn to her, as though she had said something outrageously out of context.

"I said Will might show himself, if Emily went out alone, but I also said it was too risky."

"I could do it." They all continued to stare, but no one said a word. "You remember how people used to always think we were sisters? In your clothes, Em, I could pass for you. I know I could. And I could walk down the street, go to the places you go, and make this kid follow me."

All at once, everyone was protesting. She waited for someone to see that she was right; someone to say it could work. Finally, it was Bertram whose voice cut through the others. "She might just have a point, John. She's a good deal shorter, and her hair's all wrong, but in Emily's coat and hat, and wearing sunglasses, I think she might do."

Emily looked as if she might cry. "You'd do that, Lil? Dress up like me to try to lure him out?"

"Sure I would. If it meant the two of you could stop worrying about him, I'd be glad to."

"Bertram and I would be right out there with her. All we need is for Will to get out in the open, let down his guard so we can get our hands on him. She'd never be in any danger." Thinking out loud, John seemed increasingly taken with the idea.

Charles, who had up until now been standing beside Lil's chair in silence, grabbed her hand, jerking her to her feet and hauling her unceremoniously out of the room. Later, she could never quite remember what had been said, although she was sure he had demanded to know if she had totally lost her mind. But when they returned, she sat meekly and listened as Charles announced to the whole room, "All right, she can do it, on one condition. I have to be out there with you, John. I promise I'll do whatever you say, but I won't let her go out there without me." She had never seen Charles behave so forcefully. And he had never seemed so masculine as when he had stood over her in the hallway,shaking her gently by the shoulders, his eyes full of something very close to passion. Now he was saying that he would lose his mind if he had to sit and wait, knowing she was out there doing something so crazy. He turned to look down at her, and her heart abruptly shifted to a strange new rhythm, so strange that she couldn't think of anything at all to say.

Eventually, as the plan took shape, Emily led her off to try on the blue coat. She gently tucked Lil's hair under the fur hat, and they decided a couple of bath towels would substitute for the bulging waistline. All the time Emily was fussing over her, she couldn't get Charles' face out of her mind. When she was finally dressed to Emily's satisfaction, ready to go back in to show the others, Lil said, in a voice she hardly recognized as her own, "Did you see him, Em?"

Emily nodded, smiling. "He loves you very much, Lil."

"I know. But he's never been so. . .so. . ." For once she was totally lost for words.

"Wonderful?"

She felt her face stretch into what was probably a big, silly grin. "Spectacular!"

After church on Sunday, while they lunched on fish and chips brought in at Emily's request, Bertram went over the plan with Lil. They had decided on Monday morning, a time Emily often went to the shops. He would coach Lil on just what to do. He and John would be in position to watch her at all times. Charles would be posted farther along the street, where he could see her coming toward him. If the plan worked as anticipated, they would catch up with Will from behind, after he had moved far enough away from his usual hiding places.

Stani asked where his place would be in the scheme.

"Right here in the house with Emily," John answered with a scowl. "Don't you think he'd be just a little suspicious if you were hiding in some stairwell, watching your wife walk by? It's not as if he wouldn't recognize you, lad."

"Right. All this cloak and dagger stuff has me itching to get in on the action." Blushing, he turned to Emily. "Just want to do my part, darling."

"I know, Stani. I feel the same way. I want a chance to give this Will a piece of my mind. And then I want to find out what we can do to help him."

"Help him?!" The words came out in a stunned yelp.

"Yes, of course. If he is trying to take care of himself, and he's underage the way John believes, he needs to know there's someone willing to give him a hand." She was calm and matter of fact in the face of Stani's obvious outrage.

"Emily, really? He's caused us nothing but grief, and you want to *help* him? I'd be all for seeing him locked away."

With a hint of that tranquil smile of hers, she said softly, "Let's just wait until he's actually been caught and John's had a chance to talk to him. There's no need to condemn him until we know the whole story."

With a defeated sigh, he took her hand. "Saving the world again?"

"Not the world, Stani. Just one boy. It wouldn't be so different from what was done for you and me, would it?" The expectant look in her eyes, as if he should certainly see the logic in helping this phantom boy who had disrupted their lives for months, was maddeningly persuasive.

Chapter Thirty-three

Bright and early Monday morning, Emily again helped Lil dress and they joined the others in the lounge. Now wearing her platform sandals, concealed by the extra length of a pair of Emily's trousers, she was perfect in every way, Bertram declared. He had coached her on her walk, less purpose, more grace, and suggested she turn up the fur collar a bit to conceal her face. She had been drilled on how and when to go about the stages of her visits to the various shops. With a hug from Emily, and an even longer one from Stani, she was ready.

Bertram dropped her at the grocer's, the far end of her destination. As instructed, she consulted her watch and waved him off. In the shop, she purchased a pound of cheese, which took several minutes to cut and weigh. Tucking it in the string bag Emily always carried, she left the shop, reminding herself not to hurry. Next she walked to the little flower shop, stopping to gaze at the plants in the display window, looking in the reflection for any sign of Will. Walking on, she went into the butcher's shop, inspected the lamb chops and ordered half a dozen to be delivered to the townhouse that afternoon. She was thrilled when the man behind the counter said ever so politely, "Good to see you out today, Mrs. Moss," and told her he'd send round the very best he had.

Back on the sidewalk, she once again looked around and checked her watch. She stood in front of the shop for several minutes, as though waiting for her driver to return. Then with a little shrug, she began to walk slowly toward the townhouse. Just as instructed, she stopped in at the bakery, purchasing a dozen little chocolate éclairs, Emily's favorite. Here too, the clerk called her by name and made a point of carefully selecting the pastries. Carrying the box by its neatly tied string, she set off once again. She knew that in the stairwell up ahead, Bertram would be waiting. John was just beyond, reading a newspaper at the corner bus stop. She had not seen or heard, or even sensed anything that made her believe Will was anywhere in the vicinity, but she went on with the charade, checking her watch again, and glancing behind her as if hoping to see the car. It was then, out of the corner of her eye, that she thought she saw him, walking close to the buildings, his head down. Her heart did a little twist in her chest, but she turned and kept walking, casually gazing around as if she were enjoying this outing in the fresh morning air.

She dared not look in the stairwell, although she wanted desperately to be sure Bertram had seen him too. Up ahead, John had his face buried in his paper, seemingly oblivious to his surroundings. It took all the self-control she could muster to keep walking, swinging the little pastry box. When she had crossed the street, leaving John behind, she strained her ears, hoping to hear sounds of a scuffle, or even a cry from the boy as he was apprehended. But there was nothing except the occasional passing car and the sound of a distant wind chime.

Up ahead, in another stairwell, Charles would be watching. It would be nearly impossible, she thought, to walk past without looking. She was tiring, not from the walk, but from the tension, she suspected, and her feet ached in the high-heeled sandals. Falling into Charles' waiting embrace would be a wonderful way to end this journey, but if the goal had not been accomplished, she couldn't afford to give away the game. Bertram had already said if it failed to work this morning, they would try the routine again in the afternoon.

And then Charles stepped into her path, pulling her into the stairwell and wrapping his arms around her. She started to protest, but her face was buried against his chest. When he released his hold slightly, he turned her so that she could look back down the street. She watched in fascinated silence as John and Bertram, coming swiftly from behind, each seized an arm, nearly lifting the boy off his feet. For a moment, she thought he was going to struggle, but as he met her gaze, Emily's gaze, he seemed to go limp, his head dropping to his chest. She could hear John, his voice firm and reassuring, telling the boy that no one was going to hurt him. Still with his head down, he allowed the two men to lead him back down the block to the parked car.

Charles was still holding her in his arms, and she willingly sagged against him. "Lil, oh my darling, you did it!" She had never heard that tone in his voice before, not even when he'd told her he loved her. That passion, so unlike the often tongue-tied Charles, who seemed to hope she understood without his having to say those words too often. Now he turned her face up to his, gently removing the big sunglasses. "Lilianne Salvatore, you are the bravest, the smartest and the most adorably impossible girl in the entire world. I love you." And then right there in the street, in the middle of the morning, he kissed her as he had never done before; a kiss so powerful it made her knees go weak and left her feeling as though she'd been running for miles. She clung to him, dropping her parcels on the sidewalk, only vaguely aware that the fur hat had fallen off and her hair was tumbling wildly around her shoulders.

They didn't see the smiles on the faces of the two men as the car drove past. Nor were they aware of the disapproving glare from the lady who came out of the house just beyond their stairwell. By the time they began to emerge from that magical kiss, the car was long out of sight. Arm in arm, Charles carrying the cheese and Lil swinging the little cardboard box, they walked slowly toward the townhouse, neither of them feeling the slightest need for words.

For over two hours, Will Harrison was closeted in the basement flat with John and Bertram. At one point Nigel Barton's car pulled up in front of the house and he went down the steps to join them. Gathered in the lounge, Stani, Emily, Charles, Lil and Mrs. Winslow took turns going to the window, as if to catch the boy escaping or see some other visitor arrive. By noon, Emily was hungry and Mrs. Winslow went to the kitchen, returning with a tray of sandwiches and a pot of tea. Everyone ate, with the exception of Stani, who much of the time stood staring out at the empty street, his dark eyes reflecting the intensity of his thoughts.

At last John led the boy through the front door, closely followed by Bertram and Nigel. Standing with an arm firmly around the narrow shoulders, John introduced them one by one. "Will has something he'd like to say to you all."

The boy screwed up his face, and with excruciating effort forced out the words, "I'm s-so s-sorry. I n-never m-meant to sc-scare any b-body." The anguish in his eyes, as he peered at each one from beneath the tangled mass of curls, said much more than he could ever have articulated. He took a deep breath and went on, his gaze now fixed on Emily. "P-please f-for-g-give m-me?"

John patted his shoulder. "That's fine, lad. Will has given me permission to tell you his story. It took a while for him to explain, but he's been honest with us, and we wanted you all to hear what we know about him now. Right, Will?" The boy nodded solemnly, and John went on. As the details unfolded, Stani tried to listen dispassionately.

The never-present father, and the abandonment by a drug-addicted mother; the elderly neighbor who had let him stay in her flat in exchange for what little he could bring in from his variety of odd jobs; it all seemed too much to accept. Will had left school at age twelve, no longer able to cope with his speech impediment and motivated by the need to support himself and his mother. He was barely fifteen when he found work with Nigel Barton, the first stable employment he'd known. In mid-December he had come home one day to find that the old woman he lived with had been taken to the hospital. She had died two weeks later. For a time he had slipped in and out of the empty flat, but the landlord had ultimately discovered him and threatened to call the police. Terrified that he would be turned over to the juvenile authorities, he had taken to the street. On the coldest nights, he had let himself in to Nigel's studio for a few hours of warmth. He had recently found work cleaning up in a pub after hours, his wages a hot meal and a mattress in the storeroom.

"Will admits to hanging around the house from time to time, and although he says he didn't mean to follow Emily, he did walk along watching her when she was alone on the streets. He said it wasn't safe for her to be out there on her own. He was just trying to help out."

As John talked, Will stood motionless, listening to every word as if to be certain his story was told accurately. Now he turned his eyes to Stani, clearly asking him to accept his explanation. Under the pleading gaze, Stani stood up abruptly. He had heard enough. Striding across the room, he took the boy by the arm.

"Will and I are going to have a word in the kitchen." Then with a hint of a grin, he added, "And a sandwich. I don't know about you, lad, but I missed my lunch."

When the look of panic turned to one of relief and unconcealed adoration, Will followed Stani out of the room. After a moment of stunned silence all around, John turned to Emily with a mystified frown. "Well, I certainly never saw that coming."

In the kitchen, Stani indicated a stool at the work table and began to rummage in the refrigerator, all the while talking to the boy who observed him with wide, questioning eyes.

"You know Will, Kimble in there has been watching out for me since I was just a little boy. He's a very good man to have on your side. If he hadn't taken so much trouble to find out about you, most likely we would have called the police. That might not have been the right thing to do, but then following my wife on the street and watching us from the bushes wasn't quite right either, was it?"

At the emphatic shake of the curly head, Stani went on. "Sadly, there are people out there who would do the same thing, meaning to cause trouble. How were we to know you weren't one of those?" Will shrugged his shoulders, never taking his eyes from Stani's face. "We couldn't, but Kimble was pretty sure you meant well. I trust him with my life, so I went along with his ideas." Stani poured a tall glass of milk and setting a loaded plate on the table, he slid it across to the boy with a smile. "Here, see if that's to your liking." Taking his own plate, he mounted a stool. "Now here's the thing I want to know. What do you think we should do next?"

Again, Will answered with an eloquent shrug, shaking his head again. Seizing the sandwich, he began to take huge bites, washing them down with long gulps of milk.

"Do you like living on the street, working in the pub?"

"N-no!" He swallowed hard and attacked the sandwich again.

"I see. Did you like working for Nigel?"

"Y-yes!" Each word was forced out with a grimace.

"If you had a place to stay, a good place with people who'd watch out for you, would you stay there and not run away?"

His expression became instantly suspicious, as he seemed to be considering the motive behind Stani's question. Cautiously, he placed what remained of his sandwich back on the plate.

"I don't mean like an institution. I mean with a friend, like the woman you were staying with before, assuming she was your friend?"

Tears sprang to his eyes, and he shrugged sadly. "Esther."

Nodding sympathetically, Stani waited for the boy to compose himself. "You'd have to promise not to run away, and we'd need to find you some kind of job."

Screwing up his face, Will seemed suddenly eager to speak. "N-nigel s-said I c-can c-come b-back."

Stani's amazement obviously pleased the boy, and he nodded vigorously. "So you and Nigel already have an agreement? That's fine. What about a place to live? Did he offer you that too?"

Now he shook his head "no" and pointed to Stani. "Y-you."

Arching his brows, Stani laughed. "Me? I'm going to give you a place to live, am I?"

Pointing in the direction of the lounge, Will frowned. "K-kimble s-said."

"Really? Hold on a minute, will you?" Going to the hallway, he called to John. "Can I have a word, please?"

When John had joined them, Stani looked at him sharply. "What's this I hear about you giving this lad a place to stay? In my house."

"Ah, well I was getting to that when you two so abruptly left for lunch. I told Will he's free to leave, but that if he does, I'll have to call the authorities. He's not yet sixteen and has no business trying to survive out there alone. But I offered him an alternative. Probation. If he sticks close to me and Bertram, and goes back to his job at the studio, which Nigel's already offered him, we'll just pretend it's all legal-like. Right, Will?" The boy nodded, his expression relieved.

"I see. And where exactly is he going to stay? You *are* going back to the States with us, aren't you?"

"Oh, yes. But for the next few weeks, he's going to bunk downstairs with me. That'll give him an opportunity to prove he means to honor our agreement. Before I have to leave, we think we'll be able to find him more permanent digs." John took a stool next to Stani, settling in to join the conversation.

"I've been telling Will that you were a good man to have on his side. I guess he already knew that."

"Since he's never gotten into the system, I don't see any need for him to now, as long as we can manage to provide for him." John's grin seemed to open the door for Stani to step through.

"Ah, by 'we' you of course mean me. What do you think, Will? Would I get good return on my investment?" At his puzzled look, Stani went on. "Would you work hard, stay off the street, and maybe eventually try to get a bit more education?"

"Y-yes, s-sir."

"And you would only watch my wife on the street if she asked you to?"

"Y-yes, s-sir."

"Well, John, it seems you've already taken care of most of the details. Am I to assume Bertram is in charge of getting this young man cleaned up and purchasing a suitable wardrobe for him?"

"He's already made a list." At Will's skeptical glare, John chuckled. "Don't worry, lad. He's not nearly so posh as he puts on."

There was an urgent scratching at the back door. With a grin, Stani went to let in the little yellow cat, who now sported a leather collar and shiny bell around his neck. "Will, this is Sandy. You and he have quite a bit in common really. Just a few days ago, he was living rough, too. Eating out of trash bins, running from all sorts of dangers. Now he's found some friends, a warm place to sleep and as much as he can eat. Lucky fellow, wouldn't you say?"

Hesitantly, clearly struggling to recall just how it was done, Will Harrison smiled.

Chapter Thirty-four

After Will was led away by Bertram to begin his transformation with a bath and a haircut, John and Stani had remained in the kitchen, plotting the boy's future. It was agreed that they would let Will set the pace, get back to work in the studio and adjust to his new situation. "Security may be hard to understand for a boy who's never known any. We don't want him to feel trapped. One day at a time, I think." John had seen kids like Will, craving a home, but unable to settle down after being on the street.

"You're sure there's no one out there who'll think we've kidnapped him?"

"He hasn't any idea where his mother went, three or four years ago, and she's never been in touch since. It's only because the old lady took him in then that he didn't end up in care. That and his overwhelming fear of being caught and turned over to the authorities. He went home one day and his friend had been rushed to the hospital. He spent days hanging around there, trying to see her without getting caught. By the time she died, he figured Nigel wouldn't welcome him coming back to work. Poor kid, he was afraid to go back to any of his old haunts. We misjudged him on several counts. He wasn't so much trying to avoid us as he was just trying to survive."

"Did he explain climbing the garden fence?"

"He admits to being curious, but mostly he was after the trash bins. He knew we ate well, and he figured if Emily caught him, she wouldn't call the police. He thinks she's something akin to an angel."

"Can't fault him there. I suppose I should tell her we have another mouth to feed now. And I thought it was only in her little valley that things like this happened."

Emily had sent Lil and Charles out to dinner, her treat, in hopes of a few quiet hours with her utterly amazing husband, even giving them her house key so they wouldn't be disturbed in the event they decided to retire early to the privacy of their bedroom. The suspense, as Stani had taken Will off to the kitchen, had sent the little lives within her fluttering wildly in response to her own anxiety. When at last the boy had come out with John, an expression close to a grin on his face, Bertram had marched him off downstairs. No one had as yet explained to her what happened during that seemingly endless time in the kitchen.

Now, finally, they were alone together in the lounge, and she felt suddenly shy about asking him what had actually transpired. Stani sat silently, the little cat curled on his lap, staring into space as though replaying the day's events in his mind.

Deciding that she would have to be the one to start any conversation, she linked her arm in his. "It was a very exciting day, wasn't it? Full of surprises and people doing extraordinary things."

"I wasn't at all prepared," he said softly.

"I wasn't either. Just when I think I know every wonderful thing about you, you show me something new. What was it that inspired you to do such a thing?"

He heaved a long sigh, his eyes fixed on the spot where Will had stood delivering his apology. "It started with what you said, about what had been done for you and me. But I couldn't imagine any similarity between myself and a boy like Will. Then John marched him in, and when he stood there, so clearly terrified but still courageous enough to go through with trying to apologize, things just started to happen to me. It was like seeing myself, stripped of all the blessings that came my way because I could do one thing well. And those words, that touched me so profoundly the first time I heard them, the words of the Charge, started echoing in my head. I could almost hear Mike's voice, 'strengthen the fainthearted, support the weak, and help the suffering;' not telling me what to do so much as reminding me what had been done for me. This boy didn't deserve to be so overlooked, so invisible. You were right, he deserves help. And most of all, he deserves to be seen, to be recognized."

Putting her arm around him, she laid her head on his shoulder. "He's been through so much, and yet he seems ready to trust us. I think behind all that shyness there must a very wise young man."

"Certainly very resourceful. Think how hard it must have been, especially with his handicap, to make his way alone. The boy can scarcely say his own name." Stani grinned. "But he can communicate, in his own way. I learned a lot, without his saying much. We had quite an enlightening conversation. Nigel was right in saying he's bright. He's excited about going back to work in the studio. He and John seem to have formed quite a bond already, but I'm not sure he has as much confidence in Bertram. But you should have seen the look on his face when he met Sandy." He looked down at the contented ball of fur in his lap.

"Sandy?" She stroked the cat, who twitched his ears as if he recognized his name.

"I told him he and Sandy had a lot in common. And for the first time, he smiled. All over his face. It changed him completely, that smile." He shook his head at the recollection.

"Now who's saving the world?"

"Just one boy. This is what you meant about opportunities, isn't it? When they come along like this, you have to do what you can. I think John must have known I would see it that way. Or maybe he thought you would persuade me. Either way, he had already made a deal with Will to stay here until we leave. He said he thinks he can find him a more permanent place by then. Whatever he has in mind, he's put a lot of thought into it. Once again, John Kimble comes to the rescue."

"This house was full of unexpected heroes today. John and Lil, and most of all, you."

He turned to her with a smile in his eyes. "You think so? You've always been my hero, the girl who pulled me out of the storm, and then showed me what living really means."

"Yes, I do think so. And I'm sure there's a boy downstairs who thinks so too."

"I hope he feels that way after Bertram gets done with him. He may not thank me tomorrow for rescuing him quite so thoroughly."

Emily laughed softly, reaching up to brush the hair from his forehead. "I'm so proud of you. You said you thought miracles followed me around, but in the past couple of months, you've saved a whole family, and one very special boy, all on your own."

"I had help. James had things all planned, and so did John, it seems. They're using me, you know?" Shaking his head, he grinned. "And I'm so incredibly thankful to be used. All my life, I've let people take advantage of me, but finally someone is using me to make a real difference."

"When you took Will into the kitchen, I was so shocked. The babies started fluttering around like a whole flock of little birds. Do you suppose it was just that they knew their father had done something wonderful?" She gently ran her hand in a circle over the bulge at her waist.

"More likely they just wondered what all the fuss was about. When Will gave me that look, as if his whole life depended on my understanding, I just wanted to take him in my arms. I've been so angry with him for disrupting our lives, for making me afraid to leave you, and with that one look, I realized he's not so different than I was, just scared and uncertain. Oh, I never had to go through what he has, but I know that feeling, that everything depends on someone's approval. I had to let him know it was all right."

"So you fixed him a sandwich? That's all it took?"

"Well, I talked to him a bit, man to man. I think we've come to an understanding. John thinks it best not to rush him, let him adjust at his own speed. I almost wish we could stay on here a bit longer, just to see how he does, but that's not practical."

She settled against his shoulder, her eyes closing in contentment. "It doesn't matter where we are, as long as we're together. Let's go to the country next weekend, and if when we get back you feel we should stay longer, we'll look at the schedule again. I have to see the doctor once more before we leave, anyway. If we're not back in New York for two or three more weeks, we can still get to Jack's wedding in time. I don't have to do anything to the apartment, remember? My wonderfully thoughtful husband already took care of that. If you're going to go around saving the world, I can at least be a little bit flexible."

Stani gently laid the sleeping cat on the rug, and turned to cradle her across his lap. When she had settled in his arms, he kissed her, a long tender kiss. "Remember, just a few months ago, when we stood up in that little church and promised to love each other for all time?"

"Of course I do."

"Did you have any idea how complicated life would really be?"

"I think so. I was marrying an international superstar, after all. Not just some farm boy from the hills."

"And you were still willing to take me on?"

"More than willing. I'd say anxious. I'd waited long enough, hadn't I?"

"So no matter the crazy schedules, the constant moving around, the endless number of people in and out of our lives, this is the life you really wanted?"

"Oh, no. I wouldn't say I wanted all those things." She slipped her fingers into his shirt, caressing the place just over his heart. "But I so wanted the man who went with all those things. And I got him."

With another kiss, he settled deeper into the cushions. An hour or two of just holding his wife in his arms like this would be the perfect end to this life-altering day.

There was a sudden commotion at the back of the house, as shuffling steps were heard coming up the stairs from the basement flat, while at the front door, the sound of the key grating in the lock was accompanied by voices raised in greeting. From his spot on the carpet, Sandy rose straight into the air, his fur bristling and his back rising in an angry arch. As Bertram appeared, with the red-faced but now very well-groomed Will in tow, Lil and Charles burst into the room hand in hand, their faces flushed with laughter. With one loud yowl of displeasure, the little cat shot from the room.

As he admired Will's new clothes and haircut, and listened with a smile to Lil and Charles tell of their wonderful evening out, Stani mused that if he were only at liberty to do so, he would follow Sandy's example. Instead, he sat calmly next to his wife, imagining what it would be like to grab her hand and drag her up the stairs to the relative sanctuary of their bedroom. From the gleam in her eye, as she sat listening with that sweet hint of a smile on her lips, he suspected she might be imagining the same thing.

With only one more day in London, Lil seemed to want most to spend time with Emily and Stani, declining Bertram's offer of more sightseeing. She wandered the house, peering into various rooms, while Charles declared he wanted to take in at least a quick overview of the British Museum. When Emily asked if everything was okay with them, Lil had merely smiled and said everything was great.

After assessing her options, Lil asked if she might use Stani's music room for a while. It had been hard to find a place to practice during the trip, viola solos not being all that widely appreciated, and she thought she'd like to spend a little time with her instrument. If they didn't object, of course.

Recognizing that Lil was in something of a mood, Emily insisted she practice all she liked. When the door had closed, she turned to Stani with a knowing smile. "She's always been that way, since she was just a kid. That viola is her best friend. She can saw away for hours, given the chance. I think it drove her father and brother mad at times, but for Lil, it's the best possible cure for whatever ails her."

"And what exactly is it that ails her today?" Stani listened as the vaguely mournful sound drifted through to the kitchen.

"Oh, I expect she's thinking that the adventure's about to end, that life is waiting for her at home. And that life is at best uncertain. She and Charles may be in love, but there's no clear path to their future." Reaching across the table, she laid her hand over his. Her smile was a radiant reminder of how blessed they had been, to find their own clear path. "It remains to be seen how two violists can find happiness together. I think Lil knows that only too well."

In the music room, Stani's work in progress lay on the desk. Lil's eyes fell on the staff paper, scanning the lines of melody he had already written out. The title across the top read "Jana—Something from Home" and as she stared at the page, the urge was irresistible. Tentatively, she began to play, and after a false start or two, the tune seemed to find its way into her consciousness. Melancholy even in its simplicity, a sweet, innocent tune that at the same time held a very mature tone of longing and regret, it somehow made her want to cry.

When Stani came to the door, and after listening for a moment, gently opened it, she turned, sensing his presence but continuing to play to the end of the measure. "I hope you don't mind. It just looked so interesting, I wanted to give it a try. What is it?"

He smiled, his eyes dark with a look that made her skin prickle. "Something I've been struggling with, until I heard you play it. That was remarkable, Lil. You've just given me the voice I was searching for. Thank you."

She wasn't at all sure what he meant, but that look in his eyes was enough. As it had several times before with Stani Moss, something extraordinary had happened once again.

Lil and Charles left London on Wednesday, by which time Will seemed to be settling into the household. He had already become the object of Mrs. Winslow's maternal focus, and in return, he had eagerly taken over a number of her daily chores, among them putting out the garbage and sweeping the front stoop. He and Bertram appeared to be getting on well enough. While John accompanied Stani to the country, Bertram would stay in the flat with Will, during which time he planned to work on refining the boy's personal habits. Routine use of a toothbrush and comb, he insisted, as well as a more restrained approach to his meals, would make the boy much more appealing.

John laughed that for a boy who had gone completely unnoticed for so long, all this attention must be at least a little confusing. But it was clear that Will knew who was ultimately responsible for his new security. His eyes followed Stani's every movement, as if he were watching for the smallest opportunity to show his devotion. John had the persistent thought, as he observed the two of them, that while he was quietly proud of Will's response to their efforts, it was that little red-haired boy he had taken on all those years ago that gave him the sense his own life had not been entirely misspent.

Chapter Thirty-five

Three hours outside of London, the country home of Edmond Finch, the fourth Earl of Strathmoore, stood in the midst of prime farming land. The house itself, a rambling mid-Victorian mansion built along more or less neoclassical lines, was of little interest to the earl. The land, his prized cattle and the cultivation of various experimental crops were the primary focus of his attention. Until his daughter had decided to pursue her musical career, he had been content to let her spend her time in London, while he lived the solitary life of a country squire. It had been Marcia's idea to refurbish some of the rooms and turn his quiet home into a weekend retreat for her friends. Now she wanted to throw a house party for twenty and give her final recital with Stani Moss here. He had dreaded the thought, until he had discovered that Moss's lovely little wife had a passion for agriculture.

While Marcia fussed over every detail of the guests' accommodations and the extravagant meals, her father made arrangements for a tour of the farms. After the recital on Friday night, most of the guests would be involved in various forms of mindless recreation for the remainder of the weekend, but the earl planned to take the Mosses on an extensive viewing of his barns and fields. He was mildly annoyed with Marcia when she persisted in pestering him about some old manuscript in his grandfather's long neglected library. The thought of that collection of moldering books and documents always caused him a pang or two of guilt. "I've no idea where the thing might be, if it even exists. And why would you have such an urgent need for it now, anyway?" he asked when she insisted again that he help her search for the paper.

"Because I read in one of his interviews that Stani has a special love of Wordsworth. I want to show that manuscript to him, as a special treat while he's here. I'll just have to search for it myself." She had stomped off to the library, as if he had sent her to the coal mines. He'd overindulged the girl, he admitted, after her mother had left him for that Canadian salmon tycoon. She was all he had in the way of family, and although she took shameless advantage of him, he let her have her way in most things. But he had no intention of wasting time poking through old papers looking for something he wouldn't recognize if were lying on the breakfast table in front of him now. He'd lost enough time following her all over the country these past weeks. The spring planting had started without him, and he was glad to finally get back on the land again. The thought of showing off his fields to Moss and his charming American wife took the edge off his irritation at having to feed twenty ungrateful people for three days.

It was late afternoon before they arrived. There had been delays getting out of London; and by the time they were well on the way, Emily had needed to stop for a bite to eat. If Marcia was upset that the planned rehearsal would have to be postponed until after dinner, she did not let on. She greeted them warmly, personally showing them to their rooms. The spacious bedroom with its little sitting room and adjoining bath was the most comfortable in the house, she assured them, and she had chosen it especially with Emily in mind. "I know how you need to rest during the day. This is in a very quiet part of the house, so no one will disturb you."

As they dressed for the evening, Stani laughed that a map of the floor plan might be helpful. "I'm not sure I'd ever find my way out if I took a wrong turn. Maybe we should drop breadcrumbs when we come back from dinner."

There were six at the table for dinner, as they were joined by Evelyn Bellamy, a warmly smiling, if singularly plain woman who had been Marcia's first piano teacher and lived in the village near the estate. When John was introduced as Stani's bodyguard, she had asked with a look of mild surprise if he seriously believed Stani would be in any danger from the guests this weekend. With a knowing grin, John had replied, "You never know who might be plotting to snatch him away."

After the meal, during which the earl had regaled them with stories of Marcia's childhood, the rehearsal began. Two new pieces had been selected for this recital, given the intimate nature of the audience, and again Marcia insisted Stani stay close by, frequently pausing to ask for his guidance. Emily noticed with some amusement the frown that crossed Miss Bellamy's face, as she watched her prized student floundering.

As the evening wore on, Emily found herself stifling the urge to yawn, and finally, when they paused for a short break, she asked if she might be excused. While Stani walked with her to their rooms, he confessed that he thought Marcia might be playing her little games with him again. With a laugh, Emily patted his arm. "Might be? Darling, the Helpless Female is the oldest game in the book. Unfortunately, I never learned to play it. Maybe I should suddenly forget how to open a door, or tie my shoes."

As he swept open the door for her to enter, he caught her hand. "You know I prefer my females strong and tender." Pulling her into his arms, he kissed her gently. "You get ready for bed, and I promise, if I have to plead a migraine, I'll be back in half an hour. Silly girl, maybe I should suggest she practice on her own, if she can't get through the piece. I'm sure that's what her piano teacher wanted to tell her."

It was over an hour later when Stani finally returned. Emily had already dozed off, her book failing to keep her awake. As he quietly undressed, she watched through half open lids, smiling to herself. It was no wonder women found him desirable. Poor Marcia couldn't help being affected, watching him night after night on stage. However, she thought, as he slid into bed, drawing her into his arms, poor Marcia would have to accept that he was already taken. And that his wife was not about to share.

By Friday evening, the house was full of people, most apparently already acquainted with one another and accustomed to this sort of weekend entertainment. While many knew who Stani was and were eager to meet him, others merely seemed amused by Marcia's debut as a serious musician and viewed Stani in much the way they did her piano, as just an accessory. The majority of the guests were young, wealthy and attractive, and obviously bent on enjoying themselves.

Dinner was a noisy affair, and afterward everyone gathered in the drawing room, where chairs had been arranged in a half-circle around the piano. Seated between Lord Strathmoore and Evelyn Bellamy, Emily felt very much the guest of honor. Evelyn had been most helpful in providing names and brief biographies of the other guests. Now as they prepared to listen, she smiled slyly. "And that handsome young man with the violin is already known to you, I think. What a lucky woman you are, my dear. I fully understand why Marcia was so intent on acquiring him as a partner for her debut. Not only is he a superb musician, but he's absolutely delicious to look at!"

As the first notes sounded, Emily laughed inwardly. She would have to remember to pass on the compliment.

"Last one! I'm free at last!" Pulling off his tie with a flourish, Stani grinned at her in the mirror.

"How can you say you're free when you look at me? Seems that would remind you that you're doomed to a life of endless toil." She turned her profile to demonstrate.

"But only as a solo artist. No more 'introducing Marcia Strathmoore-Finch' below my name."

"I thought she played very well. And you were your usual brilliant self. Oh, and I must tell you, Miss Bellamy paid you a lovely compliment." She focused on removing the studs from his shirt front. "She said that not only are you a superb musician, but you are, now what was that word she used? Oh, yes, delicious."

As she had expected, he blushed crimson. "Good grief! I thought she might be the one serious music lover in this crowd. Most of the others seemed to be more concerned with sizing up their prospects for the evening. I'm sure I saw some not-so-subtle groping in the back row. This is not our sort of crowd, love."

"Oh, I don't know. Groping with the proper partner can be nice. And tomorrow we can leave them all to their games. We are the exclusive guests of his lordship for a personal tour of the estate. Crops and cattle, darling. Sound more like our sort of crowd?" Slipping the shirt off his shoulders, she concentrated for a moment on folding it over a chair.

"At least there'll be a little reward for all this effort. The library here contains a rare Wordsworth handwritten manuscript. Marcia has promised to let me have a look at it in the morning. Apparently her great-grandfather was known for his extensive English poetry collection, so I may have a browse before we take our tour." He stood behind her, his hands running gently over her rounded middle.

"Just be sure you don't browse for too long. Lord Strathmoore is so pleased to have someone he can show off his farms to. I somehow doubt anyone else here knows a thing about organic gardening. Stani, are you listening to me?" He seemed totally absorbed in tracing the line of her neck with tiny kisses.

"Not really, something about organic something. Can't we talk gardening tomorrow? Your idea about groping with the proper partner was much more intriguing."

Turning in his arms, she laughed softly. "Miss Bellamy was so right. I am a lucky woman. And you are delicious."

♡

They were the first ones down for breakfast, joining John and Lord Strathmoore who were already discussing the day's planned excursion. Miss Bellamy was the next, followed shortly by a very perky Marcia. For a girl who had been up until close to dawn, according to her father, she was bright-eyed and eager to hear the details of the tour. She even suggested that Emily might like to see the calf barn, where she understood there was a new set of twins. She explained that she had to see the cook about a picnic lunch for some of the more adventurous guests who intended to walk to the site of a ruined abbey on the estate. "But then I'll meet you in the library, Stani. I can't wait to show you that manuscript."

As they prepared to leave, Emily decided the chill wind called for a heavier wrap, and returned to their room for her coat and hat. By the time she rejoined the others in the hallway, Stani had already gone to the library on the second floor. The earl was anxious to get started, and John assured them he would wait for Stani and catch up with them at the barns. Climbing into the Land Rover, she looked up to the windows in time to see Stani's smiling face. She waved, blowing him a kiss, then as the car bounced away toward the barns, she turned to the earl. "Stani's so excited about seeing that Wordsworth manuscript."

"I'm amazed Marcia found the thing. I was so sure I remembered my father saying he'd sold it at some point to pay off some debt or other he'd run up. Not the most level-headed, my father. I'm lucky he held on to the land."

♡

John waited in the hallway, finishing a cup of tea and reading the local newspaper. Checking his watch periodically, he realized he should have asked how long this browse of the library might take. Without any sense of direction, he mounted the stairs, thinking he'd find Stani and encourage him to get a move on.

After wandering the length of one hallway, which seemed to house several guest rooms, judging by the sounds of late night revelers finally preparing for the day's activities, he retraced his steps. Again, a series of closed doors lined the long corridor. He strolled past several without detecting any signs of life. Then from a doorway at the far end, he thought he heard muffled voices. He approached cautiously, not wanting to be caught lurking outside someone's bedroom, until the crash of breaking glass and a subsequent loud thud stopped him in his tracks. What followed were clearly the sounds of a scuffle, accompanied by two distinct voices, one notably raised in protest. John paused in the hallway, waiting for confirmation of his suspicions. He tested the knob, and found it locked. Just as he prepared to put his shoulder to the door, he heard a sound unlike anything he'd ever heard before.

Just on the other side of the door, the unmistakable voice of Stani Moss rose to what could only be termed an outraged roar. "Marcia, unlock this door. Now!"

John waited, a smile threatening to crease his face. At last the key scraped in the lock and the door flew opened. As Stani strode past, straightening his jacket with an angry jerk of his shoulders, John briefly caught sight of the Lady Marcia, standing with her hands on her hips. On the floor beyond lay a shattered lamp, an overturned chair and several books scattered around a large desk. Judging by the devastation, and the lady's furious expression, whatever she had hoped for had gone decidedly amiss.

He had followed Stani halfway down the stairs before the resounding slam of the door echoed in the hall above. "Hold up, lad. Are you all right?"

"I'm fine!" He didn't stop until they reached the ground floor. When he turned, demanding to know where Emily had gone, John couldn't hold back a grin.

"She's gone to the barns. I told her I'd bring you along. What happened up there?"

"I was attacked, that's what happened!" He ran his hands through his tousled hair, struggling to bring his breathing under control. "Just take me to the barns. I don't want to talk about it now."

"You can't go like that, son." He pointed to Stani's gaping shirt front, now minus several buttons.

Looking down, he swore under his breath. "Daft girl! I'll run up and change. Please, whatever you do, don't tell Emily!" He started back up the stairs, taking two at a time.

"I'll wait here. And Stani? While you're at it, better wash your face. That's definitely not Emily's shade." At the answering growl of exasperation, John chuckled softly. Turned out the boy was quite capable of defending himself after all.

He had gotten through the hours of bumping over farm lanes, listening with apparent rapt attention to the earl's detailed descriptions of conservation techniques and animal husbandry. Ignoring the question in Emily's eyes when he had caught up with her coming out of the calf barn, he had merely kissed her cheek and apologized for the delay. But now, as they returned to the house, heading to their rooms to freshen up before lunch, he knew she would be demanding an explanation.

"What on earth happened to you, Stani? You looked as though you'd just had the shock of your life." She turned to him as soon as the bedroom door closed behind him.

As he began, carefully choosing his words, she listened in silence. But when he reached the moment where Marcia had suddenly gone from tearful regret at their parting, to forcing him onto the top of the desk, she began to shake with laughter. "I'm sorry, darling. I know it wasn't funny!"

"It wasn't funny at all! The crazy girl had me sprawled out on the desk and was climbing on top of me, tearing my clothes off!" He raised the torn shirt in the air as evidence.

"I'm sorry!" Wiping at her tears, she waved an apologetic hand in front of her face. "Poor Stani! Are you sure you're all right?" Her expression turned to one of earnest concern, although her eyes still sparkled with amusement.

"I'm fine." He tossed his head, as if to shake off the memory. "To make things worse, there was no manuscript. She was merely laying a trap. And I walked right into it! I never even saw what was coming until she tried to kiss me. Even then, I was the perfect gentleman, trying to spare her feelings. And then she just swept the lamp off the desk and over I went. I had the oddest thought, that she should have used her hands on the keyboard the way she was using them on me. I would have sworn she had at least four, as much ground as she was covering." He sank onto the foot of the bed beside her, his voice growing husky with emotion as he went on. "When I finally escaped from her and realized the door was locked, I just snapped. I shouted at her, Emily. I mean, I yelled at the top of my lungs."

She draped her arms around his neck, burying her face on his shoulder. Staring into space he relived those last minutes in the library. He saw again the huge blue eyes, glaring up at him from the mass of wild golden hair, and the little snarl that curled that rosebud mouth. Gathering Emily to his side, he closed his eyes. And then he threw back his head and laughed. "I only wish you could have seen her face!"

Chapter Thirty-six

By Sunday morning, they were more than ready to return to the chaos of city life. As the car turned out of the gated entrance, they agreed that their weekend in the country had been much like a trip down the proverbial rabbit hole. While John congratulated Stani on finally revealing a bit of the temper that normally accompanied that hair of his, Stani himself felt he'd been to the edge of a precipice and barely escaped with his life. He admitted that the rage he'd experienced had been an entirely new emotion; but at the moment he'd realized he was locked in a room with a woman who would apparently stop at nothing to have her way, he had been more terrified than angry. He might never stop wondering what would have happened next if she had not unlocked the door, he said.

"Oh, I had that covered, lad. My shoulder might not have recovered, but you would have been rescued from the lady's clutches, I can assure you. I was just hesitating a moment to see if you could save yourself." John's laughing eyes met Stani's in the rear view mirror.

"Please don't hesitate like that again." Stani grinned suddenly. "Although, I did think I sounded quite masterful, full of righteous indignation, wouldn't you say?"

"Definitely. But it seems she's willing to let bygones be bygones."

"Yes, darling, she even gave you very nice present and a sweet little goodbye kiss. Although I thought for a minute there you were going to fight her off. That was raw fear in your eyes, if I'm not mistaken."

"Joke all you like, but you weren't there. No wonder her father gives her everything she wants. She doesn't handle rejection well at all." With a little shudder, he picked up the book that lay on the seat beside him; a leather-bound volume of Elizabeth Barrett Browning's Sonnets from the Portuguese. "I hate to imagine the significance she must have thought this would have, after. . . well, *after*."

"But the note she wrote was very friendly. 'My dear Stani, please accept this as a token of my undying gratitude and affection. You made my fondest dream come true.' Nothing threatening in that. I think she was simply overcome at the thought of never seeing you again." Emily tucked the note back into the book. "As a woman, I can fully understand how losing you would be devastating. But as your wife, I have no sympathy for her at all. All those curves don't scare me anymore."

Stani laughed, drawing her into the circle of his arm. "They scared me half to death!"

If their weekend in the country had been, as Stani put it, a trip to Wonderland, the next few days in London were a sobering return to reality. A letter from Milo outlining Stani's commitments for the next two months, with a block of three weeks in April termed "personal," convinced him they would need to leave London as planned by the following week. This necessitated making definite arrangements for Will and the care of the house in their absence, and a final visit to the obstetrician with Emily.

Will proved to be the bright spot in the otherwise rainy and hectic week. He was already settling in with Nigel, working every afternoon as well as accompanying Nigel to on-site shoots. His mornings, it had been determined, would be divided between helping Mrs. Winslow with household chores and spending time under Bertram's careful tutelage.

During their brief absence, it seemed Mrs. Winslow and Bertram had taken it upon themselves to work out a scheme for Will's immediate future. When offered the spare room in her flat in exchange for a miniscule sum in room and board, Mrs. Winslow reported that Will had accepted readily. He knew how to live with a lady, he had assured her, having shared a two-room flat with his friend Esther for years. He could be a help in the kitchen and he knew how to wash and iron as well. Informing Stani and John of the arrangement, she had smiled tearfully. "He's a lonely little soul, our Will. Just like a lot of us, I'm afraid. He'll be good company for me, and he'll come here with me to help keep things nice and clean, all ready for you when you return. Did you notice the windows, when you drove up? He insisted on washing them, same as he did when he worked for that service. He's quite handy. Once Mr. Bertram can help him with his speech a bit, you'll see how bright he is."

Bertram had learned, quite by accident, that Will loved to read. After washing the windows outside the music room, Will had asked if he might borrow a book from the assortment he'd noticed collected on the shelves in there. He had stayed up much of the night reading, and in the morning carefully returned the book to its place. When informed that he could keep it as long as it took to finish reading, he had replied that he was finished, and would like to borrow another if permitted. "Turns out he hasn't only been taking food from trash bins, he's been taking whatever reading material he could find as well. Imagine, a boy who wants to read, in the midst of the kind of life he was living. I've offered to help him with some basic mathematics and history also, but I believe if I can get him to read aloud, it may help correct his stammer. I've been looking into various methods used by speech therapists."

"Good heavens, George, it sounds as if you've taken on a project. I thought you were anxious to get back to your retirement." John had been listening with a barely concealed grin, as his old friend described with pride the discovery of such a promising pupil.

"I am, although I had hoped you might convince Stani to keep me in mind for whenever he and Emily find themselves back in London. I've quite enjoyed my time here. They're a lively pair, as it is, and with two infants, it seems to me they'll need plenty of hands to keep things under control. In the meantime, I've promised Mrs. W. I'll be available to help her out with young Will. He needs a man's influence, too, I think."

With the decisions apparently already made, Stani talked with Will to make sure he was actually in agreement. "You're not just letting them railroad you, are you? It's your life, Will. You can say no if something else would suit you better." Having always gone along with someone else's plans, Stani felt the need to spare Will the same kind of domination.

But with a huge grin, Will had assured him he was happy with his new situation. Already more at ease, his stammer was not quite so debilitating. He liked Mrs. Winslow immensely; she was motherly and funny, too. They laughed a lot while they worked. And as for Mr. Bertram, he was a bit stuffy at times, but he was smart and knew a lot that he could teach a boy who had never really been to school much. And Will wanted to learn, he said. Nigel was talking of taking him on as an apprentice, when he turned eighteen.

"So you've found your place, have you? I want you to write me letters, Will, at least once a month, and tell me how you're doing. If you need things, there's money put aside for you. Mrs. Winslow can buy you whatever you want. No more going through trash bins, all right? I'm also counting on you to keep an eye on this house. Look out for anyone hanging about, climbing the garden fence, and the like." At Will's wide-eyed puzzlement, Stani grinned. "I don't have to worry about that anymore, do I? Friends?" He extended his hand and after an instant of hesitation, Will shook it firmly.

"F-friends."

The visit to Emily's doctor had been a daunting affair, much more so than Stani expected. While he had for the first time listened through a stethoscope to the eerie, gurgling cacophony that threatened to disguise the two heartbeats, he had also listened to the doctor using words like "medium-risk" and "pre-term labor." He had cautioned that while her physician in New York came highly recommended and could certainly perceive her case differently, he felt almost certain the babies should be delivered by Cesarean section. Something about the size of Emily's pelvis and a narrow birth canal, he had said in a tone that made those things seem eminently threatening. But he had insisted that she was doing fine and that it would be safe for her to fly home and travel by car until well into the third trimester. He had also insisted, however, that she rest as much as possible and see her doctor before she made the seven-hour journey next month.

When they talked later, Stani was sure Emily had downplayed the doctor's cautionary tone. "I feel fine, and he said himself that I'm carrying them well. Not too much weight gain and my blood pressure is perfect. I'll be a good girl and rest once we're home, I promise. Don't get that dark, worried look in your eyes, darling. It's his job to remind me of the risks. He's not predicting that I'll have any problems." She had smoothed his forehead, as if to wipe away the imaginary lines of worry.

"Still, it's my job to watch out for you. And for you." He laid his hand tenderly on her swollen belly. "You two be nice to your mother, you hear? No pranks and definitely no early arrivals."

As if the doctor's visit hadn't been enough to put his nerves a bit on edge, Emily herself began to behave strangely. One minute, she was her usual practical self, organizing the packing and making final arrangements with Mrs. Winslow for the care of the house, and the next, she was silent and thoughtful, her eyes clouded with sadness. When he found her in the nursery, standing with a hand on each of the cribs, staring out the window, he knew something had her deeply disturbed.

Going to her, he put his arms around her waist and kissed her cheek. "What is it, darling girl?"

"I'm homesick, Stani." Her voice was hollow and forlorn.

"I know, I feel the same way, but we'll be home in just a few weeks. Springtime in the hills, Easter and Jack's wedding."

"No, I mean for here. For London." Tears welled as she continued to stare out at the garden below.

"But darling, we're still here." He felt lost, as if he'd missed a cue and couldn't get his bearings in her thoughts.

"I know. But we'll be gone for a long time. Always before, this was just a place we stayed. But now it's our home, and there are people here we care about." Turning into his arms, she laid her head on his shoulder and wept softly.

"Oh, my darling girl, I'm afraid this is our life, going from one place to another, leaving people behind. That's the price we pay. You're married to a wandering minstrel, remember?" He stroked her back, letting her cry.

When she finally lifted her head, she was smiling, a watery little grin. "I'm just being one of those emotional pregnant women. Hormones, I guess." She looked fondly at her rounded waistline. "Lots of hormones. I'll be fine. Although I expect there'll be plenty of tears. You might as well get used to them."

He laughed, drawing her closer. "I thought I already was."

Chapter Thirty-seven

John had finalized the arrangements for their return. After tearful goodbyes and a rainy pre-dawn drive, they arrived at the airport to discover their flight had been canceled due to weather. If they took the only available later flight, they would have to wait in the airport for six hours. Stani's immediate reaction was to delay their departure by another day. In meant going back to an empty house, unpacking the necessities and then returning to the airport early the following morning. One look at Emily's face told him he would have to do better than that. He pulled John aside and after a few minutes in negotiation with the ticket agent, returned to Emily in triumph.

"We can get a flight to Washington this morning. We'll stay the night there in a hotel, first class all the way, I promise. We'll rent a car in the morning and drive up. We'll be in New York by early afternoon. How's that?"

All would have been well, had the weather been in the least cooperative. The flight was turbulent, and Emily was unable to rest comfortably, even in the well-cushioned first class seat. She said the babies seemed to be tap dancing on her bladder, and they made numerous trips to the restroom, Stani holding on to her as they swayed up the aisle. When she finally managed to drift into a restless sleep, her head on his shoulder, he breathed a sigh of relief and tried to close his eyes for a few minutes. But as they approached the end of the flight, the attendant leaned in with a whispered word of warning. There was a thunderstorm over the DC airport, and the pilot had been instructed to circle until the storm moved off.

Out the window, Stani could see the spectacular display of lightning in the clouds below. Emily stirred against him, but thankfully continued to sleep. Across the aisle, he caught sight of John's white-knuckled hands clutching the armrests of his seat. Never a carefree traveler, Stani realized that now John must be facing his worst nightmare as the plane trembled and rocked in the turbulence. If only they had stayed in London, he thought grimly. Here he was with his very pregnant wife, and his terrified bodyguard, bouncing in mid-air over a thunderstorm when they could be safely at home, complaining about airlines that canceled flights at the first hint of rain.

It seemed to Stani that they circled over the same cloud for hours. They were offered a snack, which Emily woke long enough to eat and then promptly fell back to sleep after a brief glance out the window. John was looking increasingly green, Stani noticed, and his own head was starting to pound, most likely from clenching his jaw against the rising urge to snap at the next sympathetic flight attendant who asked if there was anything she could do to make them more comfortable. The answer should be obvious. Get the plane safely on the ground somewhere, he really didn't care where, so he could get his exhausted wife to bed.

Finally, after a descent through the cloudbanks that bounced open overhead luggage bins and caused several passengers to scream in terror, the plane touched down gently on the rain-washed tarmac. The pilot had the good grace to utter an apology and a prayer of thanks over the loudspeaker, as white-faced flight attendants collected scattered carry-on bags.

Stani had held Emily's head pressed against his chest, his body braced over her during the landing. Now as she sat up, blinking sleep from her eyes, she gazed at him questioningly. "Things got a little bit rough back there, didn't they? Or did I dream it?"

Fighting tears of relief, and smoothing the hair from her face, he tried to smile. "Just a little bit, love. Just a little bit."

Across the aisle, John had not released his grip on the armrest. "You can relax now, old man. We're back on terra firma, safe and sound." Stani reached over and laid a comforting hand on John's shoulder.

Without opening his eyes, John said softly, "Still praying, lad. Still praying."

It was mid-afternoon the following day before they finally reached New York. By then, Stani's head was banging in earnest. He had insisted they go first to his old hotel suite, where they could freshen up and rest a bit before their first visit to the loft. Emily was brutally optimistic, he thought, assuring him that she would love whatever Peg had done to the apartment. But his stomach twisted with dread at the prospect.

"Besides, darling, I need to phone Milo and check on my schedule, not to mention, you should have a good meal after that long drive. We'll just rest a while, then we'll go. Maybe Milo and Jana are available to meet us there later."

Emily caught his arm as he turned to the phone. "Stani, stop. I thought we were all past this. I've never known you to want Milo on hand for protection. Look at me. You have a migraine coming on, haven't you?" Her arms opened wide; he had no choice but to let her hold him close.

"I feel so stupid. If you're disappointed, it's my fault. I suppose it would be best to just get it over with." The soft, cool hand on his cheek momentarily eased the throbbing in his temple.

"I don't want to get it over with. I want to see our new home. The place our babies will come home to. The place we'll be a family for the first time. I'm excited, Stani, not afraid. Now let's just go. Later, you can call Milo and maybe he and Jana can come over for a visit. In our new home."

The elevator doors opened and they stood silently together, gazing into a space he would never have recognized from their previous visits. Late afternoon light streamed through the gauzy drapes, gently touching every surface. The initial impression was one of warmth and comfortable opulence. A wall of books and another of gallery-hung artwork, surrounding welcoming leather couches and elegant plaid wing chairs. A long golden pine table and ebony Windsor chairs, flanked by a huge pine cupboard filled with red and white dishes. The red Florentine goblets were displayed there, along with a set of cobalt blue plates. Everywhere the odd assortment of wedding gifts had been arranged into a décor that seemed completely intentional, as if a trained eye had selected each item to complement the others. As they wandered slowly through the space, Stani could hear Emily's sighs and soft exclamations. But she never actually said a word.

They continued to explore, and in the kitchen found a letter, placed on the new white marble counter where they would be sure to see it.

Dear Ones,
Welcome home! You'll find dinner and breakfast in the fridge, courtesy of the deli across the street. I thought you should have some

time to get acquainted with things before you had company. I'll come by tomorrow to share a few of the secrets and help you find the things I may have hidden in my effort to get the place organized for you. Please understand that every stick of furniture is on approval and anything else can be returned if you don't want to keep it. (Other than your wedding gifts, of course!)

Emily, I know how important the kitchen is to you, so I contacted your friend Sal in Charlottesville for guidance. I would have left things as they were, but once the other work was done, the kitchen seemed to belong in some other apartment! Again, everything, except the cabinetry of course, can be sent back, and even that, the contractor assures me, can be altered. In the drawer below, you will find a book of names and addresses. Every workman, every shop, every dealer I used is listed there. I've included the names of some very nice baby shops, as well. Not my area of expertise at all, I left the nursery to you, dear. But I would love to go with you to shop, if you'd like a second opinion.

Stani, the little nook in the south-facing corner is for you. I understand you are quite the composer these days, so I hope this space will inspire you.

Again, welcome home. Sorry to hear your flight was disrupted, but now that you're back on this side of the pond, I look so forward to catching up on all the news.

Love, Peg

Emily was touching the golden pine cabinets, opening doors and drawers, examining the array of utensils inside. Still, she was silent, and her expression remained one of amazement, or was it bemusement? Stani couldn't quite tell.

Drawn to a corner near the south-facing windows, he found a large antique writing desk, a music stand and the bust of Mozart. Opening a drawer, he discovered staff paper, and pencils, already sharpened. Turning, he caught sight of Emily disappearing through the door to what appeared to be a bedroom. He followed quickly, only to come to an abrupt halt in the doorway. She was standing by the bed, a magnificent carved bed with garlands of red roses painted on the arch of the headboard. It was dressed in splendor, red and gold striped pillows and a white quilted coverlet.

Emily turned to him, her eyes wide with some powerful emotion he couldn't read, tears trembling down her cheeks. He was frozen by her expression. "I'm so sorry. We'll change it, I promise."

"No! It's beautiful." She stroked the cover tenderly. "This is just like the one I used to pull you through the snow."

"What?" He was sure he'd misunderstood her barely audible whisper.

"It was on Mother's bed. I took it to the yard. It was ruined. Oh, Stani, how could Peg have known?"

"Are you saying you used a quilt like this one to take me into the house that day?"

She nodded, wiping at a tear.

Stani shook his head, staring at the quilt and imagining what it must signify to Emily. "It's just a coincidence, I'm sure."

She took a deep, shuddering breath and smiled, a smile so radiant he felt his heart twist in his chest. "I don't believe in coincidence, Stani. It's a sign, a beautiful sign that we're home."

That first night in the apartment, they spent a great deal of time just sitting together, staring out at the view of the river and the lights along the bridges. A brief visit from Milo and Jana had left Stani flushed with pleasure. While they had been admiring of the apartment, the conversation had centered primarily on their astonishment at the size of Emily's waistline, and joyful speculation on the impact of two babies on their already full lives.

"They are happy for me, truly happy. As if I had finally accomplished something." Stani laughed softly into her hair, shifting her gently across his lap.

"You have. Quite a lot, from the looks of things." She gestured grandly to take in the apartment, and her ever-increasing midsection. "Here you are, master of all you survey, about to become the father of not one, but two heirs to the throne. Did you see the nursery? I can't believe Peg had walls moved to make a room adjoining ours! And the bathroom! I have a clawfoot tub to soak in, no matter where I am! And all this luxury thanks to my brilliant, beautiful husband."

He felt the blush rising to the tips of his ears. "You really love it all? Nothing you want to change?"

"Not a thing. This kitchen is far and away the best of the three. Three kitchens! Did I die and go to heaven without noticing? And this room, Stani, this huge empty room, is so homey now. The colors, the furniture, our things all put in order, it might have been here for years. And all we have to do is unpack and live here."

He kissed her, out of gratitude and an overwhelming sense of his own good fortune. "Live here. Work here. Have babies here. You were the girl, if I remember correctly, who was less than enthusiastic about living in New York, or anywhere other than her own little valley. Would it be arrogant of me to think I might have influenced you to become such a citizen of the world?"

"Arrogant? I would think the more appropriate word would be humbled. It was no small feat to overcome my fears, you know. It must have taken a great deal of patient prayer. Of course there's the fact that I love you to distraction and can't bear the thought of letting you out of my sight. Speaking of which, I suppose I'm going to have to, aren't I?"

"Let me out of your sight? Yes, love, I'm afraid so. I do have to work. But for the next few weeks, it will just be here in the city. Then we'll go home, really home, for three weeks. After that, I will have to travel some. I've already told Milo I intend to take the summer off, no exceptions."

"Um. I'll be spoiled beyond redemption. A whole summer." As she idly stroked her belly, her lips turned up in a mysterious little smile. "I think we're having boys, Stani."

"Boys? You can't be sure, can you?" For some reason, his heart had begun to hammer against his ribs.

"No, of course not. But every time I imagine you holding them, I envision boys. Two little boys, with red hair, of course. We should think of names, make a list. Unless you already have something in mind?"

Suddenly overcome, his throat tightened and he buried his face in her hair. "Emily, how can you be so calm? When I think of two babies, I want to run out into the streets, screaming to the world that the greatest miracle of all time is happening to me. To Stani Moss."

She laughed softly. "Not your style, darling. Besides, this is not the first miracle in your life. They follow us around, remember?" Turning his face up to hers, she kissed him tenderly. "Now about names, I was toying with the idea of Andrew, and maybe Ian?"

Chapter Thirty-eight

Their life in New York had fallen into place much too simply, as John pointed out. "You always seem to attract the sort of people to fit your needs, lad. Including your wife, of course. But it seems Peg has become the perfect chum, introducing her to the right people, taking her around to the best shops, not to mention getting her the perfect housekeeper." There was a noticeable twinkle in John's eye.

"No, the housekeeper came from Jana. Although it was Peg who suggested her. Mamie has been with Jana since we moved here. But I agree, she's perfect for Emily. She's as motherly as Mrs. Winslow, but she has no interest in cooking. Emily is completely satisfied. As for Peg, it's a bit frightening, their spending so much time together. Only my wife, with her utterly unorthodox view of her fellow man, and woman, could be so at ease in this situation. But you know she and Peg are a lot alike. It's not surprising they've found so much in common."

"And it never worries you that *you* might be the thing they have most in common?"

"Of course it does. But what can I do? Between them, they're all the forces of nature rolled into one. I'm only a man, John." He grinned, in spite of himself. Sometimes, he'd decided, it wasn't worth the effort to worry about things as elemental as the friendship between two such determined and self-confident women. Better to just accept on faith that he wouldn't find himself caught in the vortex of their combined energies someday.

Today they were on their way to meet Emily and Peg at a baby furnishings shop. He had insisted that this time he wanted to be included in the choices, although he had no real idea what might be involved. Three nurseries, he decided, required at least some input from him, and Emily had already chosen the other two on her own. He had persuaded John to come along, citing the need for masculine support and pointing out that it was useless to try to avoid Peg these days. Like it or not, they were one big irregular family now, all focused on preparing for the arrival of the next generation.

After an hour of surveying the options, they ended up going with dark wood, classic spindled cribs and chests on which something called a changing table attached. "You lay the baby here to change its diaper, darling. In here, you store the diapers and other supplies. And this," Emily pointed to a large covered pail disguised by a handsome wooden barrel, "is where you place the soiled diaper." Each time she said the word there was a peculiar little upturn to her lips. Peg and John seemed to be finding the discussion a source of considerable amusement.

"And I suppose you think I can't be taught to change a diaper?" He glared at John.

"I suppose anything is possible. But I want to be around to watch the first one, that's for sure. Photographs might be appropriate, as well."

"Careful, John. He'll have you helping. With two of them, we may all be pitching in." Peg grinned, as if looking forward to an activity she had only observed from a safe distance herself. "Any luck finding a nanny yet, Emily? I was told that agency was the best."

Stani took note of Emily's grimace. The first interviews had been disillusioning at best. They had talked at length about her emotional reaction to each and decided to tell the agency to put any further candidates on hold. It was the first time he'd ever known her to be so intimidated by anyone, other than Milo.

"I'm not sure a nanny is what we need, Peg. Maybe just some nice girl to help out. It's too much to think about right now." As Emily bent over a double stroller, examining its sumptuous interior, Stani sent Peg a silent warning. Sensitive subject. Better left alone.

They finished off the furniture order, adding two Boston rockers and a wardrobe. Next they looked at bedding, and Emily was instantly drawn to a tartan in tans and soft greens. "But what if they turn out to be girls, darling? Isn't this just a bit too stern?"

"If by chance they are girls, we'll just add something floral. But really, Stani, don't you trust my instincts?" She was examining a large, brown teddy bear, pulling on one ear to test its sturdiness.

He laughed at the arch of her brows. "Of course I do. But I would not want to encounter the displeasure of two young ladies who were less than satisfied with their accommodations. A man facing the prospect of living with three women has to be a little cautious, don't you think?"

"I think we're having boys. Girls would never be this rowdy. It feels as if they're playing soccer most of the night. And wrestling, tossing each other around from one side to the other. Girls would be doing something sweet and quiet. No, Stani, these two are boys. Rough, tough, very athletic boys." Taking his hand, she laid it against her side, so he could feel for himself the activity that had kept her awake the night before. "See what I mean? Boys."

"Ah, I see. Well, lads, I bow to the superior wisdom of your mother." In a stage whisper, he went on in his best brogue, "But just in case, lassies, your papa will make it all right. Don't you worry."

Reaching out to ruffle his hair, Emily grinned. "You're going to hopelessly spoil our babies, you know? Now let's look at mobiles. I was thinking maybe carousel horses. Or farm animals."

"Any chance we might find something with a mule?"

As Emily wandered toward a display of mobiles, Stani close behind, Peg turned to John. "That much happiness is hard to fathom. Are they always like this?"

"They had some rough days in London, but I hope now they'll be just this giddy for a while."

"I envy them. To be so young and have so much life ahead." Peg's eyes were suddenly shadowed in sadness.

"Don't sound so grim. You're just a lass yourself." He knew he was dangerously close to the edge of something, but there was no denying his response to her.

With a shake of her head, she smiled up at him. "Thank you. I suppose it's just these last few months, I can't quite remember what I found so exciting in my life. Dad would be disappointed in me, I'm sure. You sounded like him just then." She dropped her eyes, a little grimace twisting her lips. "I miss you, John." He watched as a tear slipped down one cheek.

Behind him, he heard Stani calling. Later, he thought, he'd probably think of a suitably non-committal response. Meanwhile, he turned away leaving Peg to collect herself while he went back to what he knew how to do, watch out for Stani and Emily.

♡

The doctor in New York, a surprisingly young, cheerful man, was in agreement with his London counterpart. Cesarean birth, planned in advance if possible to avoid the onset of labor, would be the best scenario. Of course, babies, especially twins, often had their own ideas. He set the due date for mid-June, but advised that in most cases, a couple weeks early was normal. Given the apparent size of the fetuses, he wouldn't rule out even earlier. Again, Stani found the visit left him filled with the most helpless kind of anxiety.

"Mother Nature, darling, will work things out in her own time. We have to trust that while we'll do our part, the rest is in the hands of a much wiser being."

"I can't consider a doctor who looks more like a college student a wiser being." He tore his hands through his hair in an effort to banish his rising frustration.

Emily laughed softly, brushing the unruly curls from his forehead. "I don't mean Dr. Adams, Stani. Women have been having babies since time began. Given the world population, I'd say the process has been pretty successful. Just have faith. Now relax and give your tired wife a foot rub. These New York sidewalks are terribly unforgiving. I think my shopping days are about over, for a while at least. Peg and I picked out the most adorable layettes at Bergdorf's, two of them, of course. And just in case, we told the clerk we might want pink instead of blue, or maybe one of each. But the little boys' things are so sweet, little rompers and caps, and of course, the little nightshirts with baseballs and tennis rackets stitched on the fronts." She leaned back on the arm of the couch, closing her eyes as he stroked her feet.

"No violins or pianos? How unfair. Not every boy dreams of being an athlete, I'm sure. Why not a plow, or a test tube? Or, heaven forbid, a textbook. I can see now we'll have a great many stereotypical myths to overcome." He was scowling, staring at her belly.

"You're going to be such a wonderful father. I can't wait to see you holding them for the first time."

He paused, his hand going still. "Not right at first, surely? That wouldn't be safe, would it? I've never held an infant, Emily! I wouldn't know how to begin."

"You handle a million dollar violin every day, Stani, and you rarely even break a string. Babies are not so fragile, you know. Here, I'll show you. It's easy." She rose and padded to the kitchen, coming back with a sack of sugar wrapped in a dish towel.

"What on earth?" His look of mildly panicked dismay turned to a grin.

"Now just bend your arm, like this. Put your hand under his head, here. Now just cradle him against your chest, the same way you do me. There, now what's so scary about that?" She gazed down at him proudly, as if he'd actually mastered some new skill.

"But this doesn't move, or cry. It can't get hungry or soil its diaper.

Really, darling, I don't think it would be wise to let me hold one so small. And it won't be this small anyway, will it?" He handed back the bundle, as if it had suddenly taken on life.

"Five pounds would be a good size for a newborn twin. Don't be a coward, Stani. There will be two of them, and I can only nurse one at a time, you know?"

"Nurse?" She had forced the bundle back into his hands and he was carefully settling it in the bend of his arm again.

"I'm going to breast feed, of course. Easiest for the mother, and best for the baby. Of course, they'll have to take a bottle, too. So while I nurse one, you can bottle feed the other." She sat down beside him, watching his eyes widen at the prospect.

"You have this all planned, haven't you? Are there classes I can take? I mean, surely every father-to-be hasn't had experience?" He wanted desperately to pass the sack back to her, but felt sure she'd only find a way to refuse it.

"I'll teach you, darling. And the babies will teach you. They have a way of letting their needs be known. You'll make a wonderful father. Just wait, it will come as naturally as making beautiful music." Leaning her head on his shoulder, she sighed sweetly. Ever so gently, he shifted the sack to his other shoulder, tenderly patting its solid roundness. In that instant, he knew he was going to love fatherhood; no matter how terrifying its first few moments might be.

Chapter Thirty-nine

Spring came on in a day, it seemed. April had started out with a cold rain and a fierce windstorm. The howling around the walls of windows in the loft was almost deafening at times. And then the next day, the sun had come out and the temperature had soared. On the rooftop garden, they planted the flower boxes and Emily joked that by the time they bloomed, she'd be too busy to bother about such things. Nonetheless, she found a glider built for two in a catalog and ordered it, telling Stani they could bring the babies up here at night and introduce them to the stars. "This is our front porch, I suppose. The babies will have to learn about nature up here. I think we'll plant a patch of grass next year, when they start walking. And put out bird feeders to attract the songbirds. That way, the farm won't seem so foreign to them when we go home."

Stani listened to her with wonder, as she talked almost constantly about their lives after the babies came. She was so totally immersed in the anticipation of motherhood, and in spite of her growing discomfort, she seemed blissfully happy most of the time. A new calm had descended over her lately, a spiritual quiet that left him in awe of her. She was a Madonna, he realized, with her tranquil smile and far-away gaze. He had never loved her more. And he had never been more ready to protect her, to provide a place of peace, where she could enjoy these weeks of waiting.

They made plans to break the drive to the farm with an overnight stay at an inn outside Washington. The doctor had emphasized the need for plenty of rest. Emily experienced bursts of energy, followed by catnaps in any available chair. At night, the bed was a throne of pillows and even then she walked the floor at times, trying to relieve pressure on a nerve in her lower back. All this, she assured him, was normal. Stani rubbed her back to help her relax, and at times stroked her belly in an effort to lull the babies into their own version of calm. But as a result of her restlessness, he found himself dragging most days. He looked forward to being at home in the valley, counting on the slower pace to refresh them both.

The trip went smoothly, with a pleasant interlude at the country inn. Their rooms overlooked a hillside where apple trees bloomed and they sat until after dark on the little balcony, watching as the stars came out. The fresh air was a tonic. Emily slept for six straight hours, something she hadn't accomplished in weeks. As a result, when they arrived at the farm late in the morning, she was bright-eyed and ready to greet the steady stream of visitors that came through the gate until after supper.

Stani was anxious to meet with Bobby, to see for himself how the family was adjusting to their new life here. But the first Dixon to greet him had been Robbie Joe, who had come racing across the yard when the big car pulled in the drive. He was overflowing with news of his lessons, the names of the composers he'd been learning about and a careful listing of the music he was practicing. Laughing, Stani seated him on the porch swing with instructions to hold on until he could get his wife settled in the house. But in only a matter of minutes, Emily was in the capable hands of Angela, Martha Jean and Sara, and Stani found himself freed of all responsibility.

While Bobby helped John unpack the car, and Ruthie served iced tea to the ladies around the kitchen table, Stani returned to find Robbie waiting impatiently in the swing. "Well, young man, I take it you've been making strides. And you are doing everything your parents expect as well? School work going well? All your chores done? The letters I've had from your teacher tell me you're a very good student. In fact, she's afraid you'll soon have learned everything she has to teach you. That happened to me, you know. But there's always another teacher out there with even more to teach."

Robbie had been listening wide-eyed, barely containing his excitement. "But you haven't heard me yet!"

"Ah. Is it that important, for me to hear you play?" Stani tried not to grin at the eagerness on the boy's face. "In that case, you'd best get your instrument and show me what you've learned. I'll wait right here." While Robbie raced across the yard to the cottage, his return was more sedate, as he carried his violin and bow with care. Once on the porch, he stood straight as an arrow in front of Stani, took a deep breath and tucked his instrument with practiced purposefulness. A chill of anticipation touched the back of Stani's neck as he watched the boy raise his bow.

In a matter of a few minutes, Emily was standing in the open doorway, with the others close behind. As they listened to the sweet melody, so carefully executed, Robbie was oblivious to the rapt attention of his audience. His eyes closed, he played only for the man in front of him, and for himself. When the last note sounded, he slowly looked up to Stani for his reaction.

It would have been impossible for the boy to understand the impact of his performance. In years to come, he might grasp the effect his music had on its audience. For now all that really mattered was whether or not Stani was pleased. He remembered that moment of anxious waiting, when the music ended and he had yet to see the look of satisfaction cross the face of his listener. He smiled, forcing down the tears of pride that threatened. "Robbie Joe, that was fine, really fine. You have been working hard. I'm proud of all you've accomplished, lad." Their eyes met for an instant in an exchange of mutual gratitude. "Now how about putting down that violin and coming with me to the kitchen. I'm pretty sure I saw a strawberry tart in there. Did your mother make that?"

Obediently, the boy laid the violin on the swing. "Yes sir, she made it. But it's not a tart. It's shortcake."

"Ah, I see. And next you'll be telling me those oatmeal biscuits aren't biscuits at all, I suppose." With a twinkle in his eyes, he held the screen door open.

"You eat biscuits with butter and honey. Those are cookies. My mama baked 'em this morning, 'specially for Miss Emily. You know, people around here'll laugh at you if you don't talk right."

Their conversation continued as they passed the ladies, now gathered in the front room. Stani caught Emily's eye as he steered Robbie toward the kitchen. Her smile said it all. It was so good to be home again.

Jack and James arrived at dinnertime. Angela, who would stay the night in order to spend time with Lil when she drove out from Richmond on Sunday, served the dinner Sal had sent as a welcome home. With Martha Jean, Sara and Mike, and John, they all gathered at the dining table. Stani's eyes met Emily's as Mike said grace. The happiness he saw there was a perfect reflection of his own. They might feel at home anywhere now, but this would always be the place they had shared their first hours together, made their first memories. It would always be home in the truest sense of the word.

After dinner, while Sara and Martha Jean stayed behind to clean up the kitchen, everyone else settled on the front porch to enjoy what was left of the spring evening. Emily and Jack claimed the swing, and sat with heads close together, talking softly. Jack had been noticeably taken aback at the sight of her very rounded middle. He at first seemed speechless, but now was full of questions.

"You're sure you're up to reading at the wedding? I mean, that's still two weeks away."

"I'll be fine, Jack. As long as Stani's strong enough to haul me up to the lectern, there shouldn't be any problem. So far, being pregnant hasn't affected my eyesight." She grinned at him, loving the slightly stunned expression on his face as he looked down at her waistline.

"And you think it'll really be June? I've seen women a lot less pregnant at nine months."

"Twins will do that for you. And no, I doubt very much I'll go full term. As long as they can breathe well on their own, and they can come home with me when I leave the hospital, all my prayers will be answered." She rubbed her belly tenderly, a gesture that caught Stani's attention across the porch where he sat perched on the railing with James.

"Look at her. She hasn't even had a nap today. I know she's exhausted, but she's so glad to be home. Poor Jack, did you see the look on his face? I suppose it is a bit shocking when you haven't seen her in a while."

"It would be shocking no matter what. That's a lot of baby there, man. Are you ready for this?"

"Is any man ever ready? I'm pretty sure you just grow into the role. All I ask is that Emily and the babies are safe and well. Every time I hear the doctors talk about pre-term labor and narrow birth canals, I have nightmares. And she's so calm, as if she'd done all this before." A hand went to his hair, but he stopped the gesture. Faith, she kept saying, just have faith. "So how are things going with the job hunt in Boston? Emily's had letters from Penny, but she said they seemed intentionally vague."

"Ha! That's my girl. She thinks it's bad luck to talk about anything before it actually happens. I have a job, though. I start in June. It's not much, money-wise, but I'll be able to take classes and work at night. Counselor in a church-run club for boys. I found it through Penny's priest, as a matter of fact."

"And what about her parents? How did the visit go?" He watched as Emily and Jack left the porch, walking slowly toward the backyard arm in arm. From the smile on her face, he thought they must be sharing sweet memories.

"Great. At least I thought so. Penny still seems to think they'll oppose our marrying outside the Catholic Church. I'm trying to let her work it out with them. Maybe when I'm actually there, I'll get a better sense of things. Penny can be stubborn, you know. She's a tough little cookie." James grinned, shaking his head. "That's one of the things I love most about her, though. She's strong and passionate. She would have made a great trial lawyer."

"I've concluded most women are a lot tougher than men. And a good thing it is. Humankind would come to a screeching halt if we had to go through childbearing." He turned to watch Emily heading back toward the house, motioning to Jack to wait. "Poor girl, another trip to the loo, no doubt. I hope we can make it through the wedding. She swears there's always a tiny foot on her bladder these days."

James laughed out loud. "It sounds like you *are* going through childbearing yourself. You're a good man, my friend. I've known men who hardly seemed to notice their wives were pregnant."

He grinned, feeling the color creep up his neck. "I find it so miraculous. That's my family, the only real family I've ever had. When I look at her, I still can't quite believe we've come so far. You'll find out someday. It'll be the same with you, I'd be willing to wager. When you love a woman, the thought that she's carrying your child is overwhelming. It's all-consuming."

Emily returned to the yard, taking Jack's arm and walking slowly toward the barn. In the paddock, Stubby was watching their progress. Stani could have sworn he saw the mule blink his eyes in amazement.

"I just want to convince the woman I love to agree to marry me— when the time is right. If Penny had her way, we'd already be married. She insists she can support us, which she can. But that's not the point. I have enough pride to want to at least contribute, and until I get my masters that's not going to happen. Even then, she'll always make more money that I will. We have a long way to go, before we can figure out just how things will work. Where we'll live and how we'll live. And that's another thing we've had to argue about. Penny wants me to move in with her, live together while I'm in school. I'm not totally opposed to the idea, but I can't believe it will improve things with her parents if we do."

"Living together before you're married? That doesn't sound like either of you. How does that fit with your faith, James?"

"It doesn't, I suppose. But we're not kids, and she wants very much for us to be together now."

"Complicated. Emily would tell you to pray, to wait and listen for an answer. But I would say follow your heart. Do what feels right, what will leave the least possibility for regrets when all is said and done."

"You waited. Was it worth it?"

Again, he felt the hot blood rise in his face. "Absolutely. We went a little mad at times, but in the end, yes, it was well worth the wait. And what's more, Emily is convinced she conceived on our wedding night. How's that for a night to remember?"

At the fence, Emily was stroking Stubby's nose and smiling up at Jack. It was all he could do not to race across the yard to her, gather her into his arms and kiss her with all the passion his memories aroused. But he continued to sit on the porch rail with James, wondering how he had ever come to be so blessed.

They slept in their blue and brown bedroom that night, the window open to let in the cool spring breeze. Stani rubbed her back, while they talked softly in the darkness. Humming with contentment, Emily listened as he described his conversation with James.

"Poor fellow, he seems to have come up against a strong-willed woman. Penny strikes me as the kind who rarely backs down. Irish, isn't she?" He could just make out her profile, her lips turned up in a sleepy smile.

"Does that automatically make her stubborn?" Her voice was muffled against the pillow.

"It doesn't hurt. But it surprises me somehow that she wants him to move in with her. I'd have thought a good Catholic girl like herself would have wanted to wait."

"She didn't expect us to. I think she was disappointed that we weren't sleeping together. Penny's a very modern girl. And she's not a child. She's well past twenty-five. She knows what she wants. But they have to decide for themselves. We did what we felt was right for us and look what it got us." Turning on her back, she struggled to prop herself on the mound of pillows. When he had stuffed them behind her, finally satisfied that she was in a more or less comfortable position, he folded an arm beneath his head and lay looking up at her.

"We didn't have to worry about money, or parents who objected to our plans. It seems to me now that the road was pretty straight and smooth for us. Once you agreed to take that road with me."

She laughed softly, reaching out to touch his face. "No regrets?"

"You know I haven't. I'm the luckiest man alive and I know it." He kissed her gently, caressing the curve of her cheek with his palm. "Now try to get some sleep, darling girl. Remember, the doctor emphasized plenty of rest. You haven't had any today."

Her only response was a satisfied little sigh.

Chapter Forty

The celebration of Palm Sunday filled the church with joyous music. They watched the bright-eyed children march down the aisle waving their branches and listened to the inspiring sermon surrounded by friends who were much more like family. No matter where they worshiped, nothing could be as fulfilling to Stani as when they stood together in this little church.

Even John had seemed moved, but Stani knew better than to question him. He sensed that for John the process had been slow and subtle, but there was definitely an on-going change. He also sensed that once again Peg had captured John's attention, but that too was a subject he intended to leave unopened.

He had however, approached John on another subject. After lunch, once he had settled Emily for a nap, insisting she rest until Lil arrived, he prepared to go forward with his plan. Taking the necessary equipment from the trunk of the car, he went first to the caretaker's cottage. This might be more challenging than he anticipated, but he was going to give it his best shot. After all, a man had certain responsibilities to his sons, and no one was going to accuse him of shirking his.

Emily was dreaming. It was a bright spring day and under the new green canopy of the oak trees, a gaggle of little boys was engaged in a riotous game of some sort. She could hear the eager calls of encouragement, the excited laughter and the occasional shouts of triumph, along with what she could have sworn sounded like Stani's and John's voices, urging them on. She smiled in her sleep at the vision of running, tumbling children in her front yard.

Gradually, the sounds became so loud, she woke to the realization that she hadn't been dreaming at all. Making her way slowly to the front room, she stood at the window by the piano blinking in disbelief.

Maybe it was a dream, she decided. Surely her eyes were deceiving her?

The three Dixon boys, Robbie Joe, Wayne and Ricky, were racing across the yard in pursuit of a soccer ball. Tending the imaginary goal was Stani, now dressed in his old blue jeans and a work shirt open halfway down his chest. She could see sweat glistening on his skin, as he braced himself for the onslaught. On the edge of the likewise imaginary field, John was apparently acting as coach and referee. He had rolled up his shirt sleeves and loosened his tie, but seemed otherwise oblivious to the heat of the afternoon, as he waved his arms and shouted enthusiastically. As the ball made its way toward the goal, more by reason of the slope in the lawn than any actual contact with a player's foot, Stani dropped to his knees, easily scooping it up before his opponents could score. A tumble of little boys and a burst of shouting and laughter followed, as John helped Stani to his feet and clapped him on the shoulder. Beaming, Stani ruffled the hair of his opponents, lifting the smallest one in his arms and raising him high above his head.

Angela, who had been sitting on the porch watching, stood and cheered wildly as the boys made their way toward the house. Still not quite sure she hadn't been dreaming, Emily went to the screen door for a closer look.

"Darling, you're awake! You just missed it! Liverpool was defeated in a fine effort against Manchester United." Setting down his laughing burden, he came bounding up onto the porch.

"Stani, when did you ever play soccer?" Drawn into the hysteria of the moment, she found herself giggling as he opened the door and took her in his arms. He was sweaty and breathing hard, and there were blades of grass matted in his hair.

"Ah, a very long time ago. John tried to teach me."

"So you've decided to take it up again, all of a sudden?" With one finger, she wiped at a trickle of perspiration on his cheek.

"You said these lads, or lassies, were very athletic. It got me thinking that I'd better get in shape. I've gone awfully soft lately, you know. At one time, believe it or not, I could run three miles in Central Park and barely break a sweat." He led her to the swing, seating her carefully on the cushion.

"Really? I've always thought you were in very fine shape. Very fit indeed, especially for a classical musician." She eyed his bare chest, a wicked little smile playing at her lips.

"Ah, classical musicians. Pallid, spindly-legged creatures that rarely show themselves in the light of day." With an equally wicked grin, he buttoned his shirt. "Surely, my children deserve better."

"Did you really run in Central Park? When was this?" She turned to pick grass out of the wind-blown curls.

"After the accident. Until I realized I was only doing it to punish myself. As with other things, I went to excess." He watched as the boys gathered around Angela's tray of lemonade and cookies. "They're great kids, aren't they? Bobby says they've adjusted fine to the move."

"Punishing yourself how?" Her eyes held his gaze, insisting on an answer.

"Pushing too hard. It was all part of trying to get control. I told you I was a disaster, right up until the moment I first stepped onto this porch."

"Stani Moss was never a disaster. A little bit lost, perhaps."

"A lot lost, for sure. But no more." Catching her hand, he raised it to his lips. "All thanks to you, my love." He was considering accepting the invitation in her darkening eyes, when with a clearing of his throat, John joined them in a nearby chair, balancing a tall glass of lemonade. With some effort, he turned his gaze. "Thanks, old man. That was more fun than I remembered."

"You never had that much fun. You were always wanting to get back to that violin." John gave him a look that said clearly he'd been holding out on him all those years ago.

Ruthie appeared, leading little Emily across the yard. When the toddler caught sight of Stani, she began to pull eagerly at her mother's hand. "She wanted to come out and play with the boys," Ruthie called, laughing as Emily broke free and ran toward the porch. Climbing the steps, she made directly for the swing, holding out her arms to be picked up.

"Well, hello! Don't tell me you remember me after all these months?" Stani lifted her to his knee, his face spreading into a smile of pure pleasure. Immediately, the little hands reached to touch his hair. "See darling, I told you she finds my hair as fascinating as you do."

"Now Emily, don't be such a bother. We really just came to collect the boys. They have chores to do. Thank you for playing with them, Stani. Bobby can't do much of that sort of thing anymore." Coming onto the porch, Ruthie reached out for the little girl, lifting her into her arms.

"My pleasure. They're great lads, gave me a real workout. Any time they want a rematch, just let me know." The three boys filed onto the porch, lining up like stairsteps along the rail. "Boys, your mother says you have chores to do. Thank you for the fine match. And we should all thank Mr. Kimble here for his excellent coaching, right?"

They said their thank you's shyly, Robbie Joe acting as spokesman. "We don't play that game at our school. Thank you for teaching us." He turned to Stani, seeming to hesitate.

"Something I can do for you, Robbie?" There was a definite twinkle in his eyes.

"You said you might play your violin for Miss Emily tonight. I was just wondering if maybe I could watch?" His voice was soft, as he cast his eyes toward Emily hopefully.

"I think that would be lovely, if it's all right with your mother, of course." Emily smiled up at Ruthie, who was clearly preparing to object. "We'll make sure it's not too late."

When the Dixons had trooped back across the yard, little Emily squealing in protest at being so quickly spirited away, John rose to help Angela back up the steps with her tray. As she joined them, she was shaking her head. "What a clan! Stani, you were wonderful with them. Where did you learn to handle kids so well?

At Stani's look of astonishment, John chimed in. "Really, lad, you were hardly a child yourself. It's amazing the way they take to you. All I can say is wonders never cease around this place."

Stani blushed profusely, Emily laughed and Angela said, with a wise twinkle in her eyes, "As I always say, love turns ordinary people into the best they can be."

When they were finally alone, John having suggested that he would accept a sandwich if it were offered, Emily sighed softly. "I guess they understand we still want some time to ourselves." Linking her arm in his, she rested her head against his shoulder. "Were you really planning to play for me tonight?"

"I thought it might help you sleep; a little fresh air and soft music. Uniting in the peace of this place. Of course, we won't be alone. I suppose we'll never be alone like that again, will we?"

"Not until we're old and gray. That's all right. We'll find time, I'm sure. Angela and John were right, you know. You're a natural with children. That must be why you want so many."

"Did I say I wanted lots of children? If I survive this pregnancy, I think I want to consider carefully before we do this again. Maybe two will be enough." He closed his eyes, setting the swing moving gently.

"Oh no. We'll need girls, just to keep things fair. Isn't Emily adorable?" She snuggled closer, her arm sliding across his waist.

"Um. Yes, she is. Almost as adorable as you. Are you comfortable, love?"

"Completely."

Music drifted from the radio in the kitchen, and the porch swing groaned softly in rhythm as it moved slowly back and forth. Stani gave himself over to the quiet. There would be precious little of such peace in the weeks to come. With his wife pressed so warmly against his side, the breeze sighing in the trees and the songs of the birds melding with the music in his head, he let himself drift on a wave of contentment. Moments like these were sacred treasures, each to be counted as a gift, none to be taken for granted.

Chapter Forty-one

When Lil first caught sight of the two of them dozing in the porch swing, she wasn't sure whether to laugh or cry. Emily looked so contented, her head drooping against Stani's shoulder, and Stani's face, with his eyes closed and a little smile on his lips, was completely relaxed in an expression she'd never seen before. How could they be so happy? How could their lives be so secure that they could just fall asleep in the middle of the afternoon, with nothing better to do than cuddle together in a porch swing? She ground her teeth for a moment, knowing full well her response had nothing to do with Stani and Emily and everything to do with her own impossible life.

Lil thought she might just go into the house and leave them to their dreams, but as soon as she set foot on the porch, Stani woke with a start. Catching sight of her, he flashed that grin of his, and she had to answer with one of her own.

"What happened to the glamorous celebrity couple I left in London?" Her stage whisper finally penetrated Emily's consciousness and she slowly raised her head, blinking drowsily.

"We came home, didn't we, darling girl?" He turned her face up to his and kissed the tip of her nose. Too sweet, Lil decided, to stay annoyed with for very long.

"Oh, yes. Come give us a hug, Lil. I'm too lazy to get up." Holding out her arms, Emily smiled her welcome, her eyes still cloudy with sleep. It seemed to Lil her waistline had gotten twice as big in the past month.

"How much longer, before you need a crane to pull you up? Good grief Em, are you sure it's only twins?" They hugged, all three of them, and Lil perched on the arm of the nearby chair.

Emily laughed, looking down at her bulging middle. "It's only going to get worse. I didn't realize it was so awful until I saw everyone's face here. The same look of shock and disbelief everywhere I go. I think I heard a few gasps in church this morning."

"Stani, don't tell me you've already been in the barnyard. You've got hay in your hair."

"Not hay, Lil, grass. I've been playing soccer with the Dixon kids. I suppose it might be time to get cleaned up, before any more company arrives. Can you take care of my wife while I shower?" He stood up, shaking his hair until it curled wildly around his head. Lil had to laugh. When she first met Stani Moss, she could not in her wildest dreams have imagined him looking so disheveled and downright normal as he did now in his faded jeans and sweat-stained shirt.

"Sure. But I should say hello to Mom. Can you manage on your own for that long, Em?"

"Actually, I'd better go in, too. I'll join you in the kitchen in a few minutes." She laughed up at Stani, holding out her hands. "Take me to the loo, will you, darling?"

Over his shoulder, as he followed Emily into the house, Stani grinned back at Lil. "What man could resist such an invitation?"

They gathered in the sunroom, where a cooling breeze billowed the curtains and the scent of just-blooming roses filled the room. When Emily had settled in an armchair, her feet on the ottoman and several cushions supporting her back, Stani left them to visit.

The first topic of conversation was the nanny search. Lil asked how it was going, and Emily promptly tried to change the subject. "What's the problem, Em? I thought there would be plenty of candidates in a place like New York. Doesn't every wealthy young mother have a proper British nanny to take the babies strolling in Central Park?"

But at the sight of Emily's downcast eyes, Angela sent a warning glare. "No luck finding the right one yet, dear?"

"I don't think I want to find the right one. They were all so properly disapproving, so *knowing*. They all seemed to think they were going to be in complete charge. I want help, but I intend to take care of my babies myself." Her expression was mutinous, but her lower lip trembled ominously.

"Of course you do, dear. Maybe you need something less traditional, someone more your own age. A mother's helper, perhaps."

"That's what I told Stani. The only problem is getting someone who'll be reliable enough and willing to travel back and forth to England and Europe with us. A young woman will be more inclined to have her own life, won't she?"

"I'm sure someone will come along. Don't worry about it now. You still have lots of time."

"I'm afraid I'm just avoiding making a decision. I got so discouraged after I'd interviewed a half-dozen women who were so stern and officious, they took all the fun out of the idea. Oh, well, let's talk about something more pleasant. Lil, how's Charles doing?"

It was Lil's turn to look away. "Fine, I suppose. Busy."

"You suppose?" Emily looked to Angela for a clue, but she only shrugged, a worried shadow crossing her face.

"Oh, if you must know, all he can talk about is that Covington guy and period instruments. He sent an audition tape to him, and Covington has invited him to come to London again, to join in the revolution, as Charles calls it." Lil stood up abruptly and went to the kitchen, taking down a glass and slamming the cabinet door. Everything about her tone and her stance at the sink expressed her opinion of the authentic performance movement.

"But Lil, that's wonderful, isn't it? What an opportunity for Charles to pursue his passion." Emily suspected she might be adding fuel to the fire, but better to get on with the imminent explosion, before the kitchen suffered at Lil's frustrated hands.

"Wonderful? Charles goes off to England to make history, while I sit in Richmond and play three concerts a year, wasting my life working in a stupid music store. That's wonderful, all right."

She set the glass down hard on the counter and Angela winced. "Lil, calm down! When did all this happen?"

"I'm afraid it started when Stani introduced Charles to Matthew Covington." Emily grimaced as she struggled to get out of her chair. "Lil, please come in here and sit down. I'm sure it's not as settled as you make it sound. Has he really offered him a position in the orchestra?" She held out a hand to draw Lil closer.

With an apologetic shrug, Lil came to sit on the ottoman at Emily's feet. "Yes, he has. Charles hasn't accepted yet, but I know he wants to. I'm sorry, Em. It's not Stani's fault. And it would be perfect for Charles. It just sort of cuts me out of the picture, at least for now. I can't go with him, and there's no way I'm ever going to play that kind of music, anyway. We went to one concert, in Williamsburg, and it set my teeth on edge. I didn't tell Charles that, of course."

"Good for you. Have you told Charles you understand what an opportunity this is for him? Or that you don't want him to go without you?"

"Not exactly. I'm waiting for him to tell me what he plans to do. Right now all he does is talk about how much it would cost, and how much he wants to go. I didn't want to add to his problems."

"I'm sure there will be some way to work things out. Just be patient." Emily patted her arm encouragingly.

With a wry smile, Lil said, "Look for the signs? Isn't that what you mean?"

Stani was in the doorway, still flushed from his shower, and at those words, he laughed softly. "What signs is she telling you to watch for now, Lil?"

"Matthew Covington has offered Charles a position in his orchestra if he can get himself to London. Isn't that wonderful?" Emily continued to hold onto Lil's arm, giving it a little squeeze as she talked.

Considering the slump to Lil's shoulders, Stani asked more gently, "Is it wonderful, Lil?"

"Of course it is, for Charles. Can you believe it? Covington said he was impressed with Charles' passion. Charles! Of course, he has been more enthusiastic lately. He really loves this whole period thing. And he deserves to go."

"But?" Stani knelt by Emily's chair, looking from one face to the other.

"But it means leaving me here. I won't ask him to stay for me, but oh, Stani, I don't want to be left behind!" Nearly toppling him backwards, Lil threw her arms around his neck with a pathetic little sob.

He let her cry for a few minutes, looking helplessly to Emily and Angela. "Now, see here. I'm sure Emily's right." He set her back on the ottoman and perched on the arm of the chair. "These things have a way of coming out all right in the end. When is Charles planning to go, if he goes?"

"He has to be there the first of August, to rehearse for the fall season. But if he can go sooner, he will. It's all comes down to money. He's thinking about selling his car and asking his father for a loan. Our season is over next month, so he's free to go any time after that." Another sob threatened and she let out a little hiccup.

"And what are your career plans?"

"What do you mean?" She stared up at him in confusion.

"Are you happy with the symphony?"

"Sure. I guess. It isn't particularly exciting. Not quite like I thought it would be."

"Ah. So it wouldn't break your heart to leave it?" Now all eyes were on him, and Emily's hand had come to rest on his knee, as if ready to signal caution.

"No, but there's nothing else around. I don't want to give up the viola, if that's what you mean."

"Of course not. But there are plenty of opportunities other than an orchestra chair. Recording, for instance. Studio musicians make good money, you know. And there are studios in New York and London."

"Right, like I could ever get a job like that. I live in Richmond, remember?"

"Stani, where are you going with this?" Emily felt a tingle of premonition, a sense that she was reading his thoughts. Across the room, Angela was unusually quiet, but her black eyes were gleaming and she had twisted her hair over her shoulder in a characteristic gesture that said she was prepared to listen.

"It seems to me that Lil needs to be free to follow Charles, and we need a young woman who's free to travel with us. I think we've decided the nanny idea won't work, haven't we, love? Of course, if Lil doesn't like babies, we're out there. And then too, she couldn't stay in London all the time. She'd have to travel all over the place, stay in those awful five-star hotels with us. In between, I might be able to get her a gig now and then. I do have friends in the recording industry, you know. Stop me if this sounds too outrageous." He grinned into the wide eyes, both brown and gray, that had fixed on him in fascinated wonder.

"Oh, Stani, that's brilliant! Lil, would you consider it?" Emily's voice was husky with excitement.

Blinking as though bathed in a sudden bright light, Lil turned to Angela. "Mom, what do you think? Could I take care of babies? I mean, I've done my share of babysitting, but am I any good with them?"

With a moment's pause for dramatic effect, Angela threw out her arms to embrace them all. "Oh, Lil, I think you'd be wonderful! Emily can teach you anything you need to know. And just think of all that traveling! Stani, you're a genius!"

He blushed to the tips of his ears. "Not really. I'd already thought someone like Lil might make the perfect sort of helper for Emily. They're so much alike. I just had no idea she'd be willing to leave her present situation. It seems Matthew Covington has provided the solution to our problems. But you realize we won't be in London all the time?"

"Oh, yes. But at least I could see Charles when we are. I wouldn't be stuck back here. And you really think I'm good enough to do studio work?" Lil was visibly excited now, her tear-streaked face alight with anticipation and her thoughts obviously racing.

"I know you are. In fact, how about joining me this summer in New York? I'm recording my own compositions. Jana is playing with me. It would be nice to keep things in the family. And you did, after all, inspire me to write for the viola in the first place."

"Stani, if Lil is our mother's helper, she'll already be in New York. We'll have babies by then, remember?" She looked down at him with a teasing little smile.

"Ah, that's right. So you see it could all work its way around. Do you want some time to talk it over with Charles, and maybe think it through a bit more calmly, Lil?"

But Lil had already thought as much as she cared to. Again, she threw her arms around Stani's neck, this time with a yelp of joy. "Who needs calm? This is the most exciting thing that's ever happened to me! Thank you, Stani, a thousand times, thank you!"

Chapter Forty-two

Stani reminded himself more than once during their first week at the farm that this time had been set aside as a vacation. And while it was certainly a vacation from his normal routine it could hardly be considered free time. There was so much to do, so many people to talk with about so many varied topics. First and foremost was the ongoing care of the farm itself. He and Emily sat down with Bobby on Monday morning, after saying their goodbyes to Angela and Lil very soon after breakfast. He listened with as much focus as possible to the discussion of a plan for the next year involving the renewal of the fallow land in preparation for planting the full acreage next spring. Emily seemed to know exactly what this mysterious process involved and he watched in awe as she drew a diagram of the former plantings and listed the varieties that had produced the best results for her father.

Bobby had visited the farm it turned out, with his own father as a teenager. He recalled the organic methods J.D. Haynes had favored, as well as the careful attention to each plant which had required so much labor from just one man and a little girl. He understood fully that Emily would want to go on in the same way, as the garden was brought back to life.

"There is one thing that will have to change. Mr. Haynes plowed every year with that old mule. I'm afraid he and I are both past doing that kind of work. You're going to need a tractor, unless you want to hire someone every time you need to break ground. It would make better sense to have your own for an operation this big, if you ask me."

Stani grinned. This was the one question Bobby seemed to feel he was capable of addressing. "I suppose you can tell me what kind of tractor I need?"

"Yes sir. A little Farmall will do the job fine. It comes with every kind of attachment you'd want."

"Ah, and you know just where I can buy one?" He was aware of Emily's shining eyes watching him in amusement.

Bobby grinned back. "Yes sir. The dealership over in Mason will have everything you need."

He hesitated, wondering if there were more he should ask. "Will they take a check?"

"Oh, yes sir."

"Then I suppose we'd better go buy a tractor, hadn't we?" He rose from his chair at the kitchen table.

"Aren't you even going to ask how much it'll cost?" Bobby stood also, pushing his chair carefully under the table.

"Ah, yes. How much will it cost, Bobby?"

"Not as much as that car of yours. And by the way, that thing needs a tune-up, bad."

"Really? And where would it go for a tune-up?"

"I can do that for you, sir. I worked on all the trucks in the shop for the county. 'Course, finding the plugs for that thing might be a problem around here. I'll go in to the parts store in town and see if they can fix you up. You want to know how much that will cost?"

"Do I?"

"No, sir, probably not. But it'll cost a damn sight less than an engine overhaul."

He laughed. "Bobby, how would we ever manage without you? I only wish I understood all this better. I'm afraid tractors and cars are not things I've spent much time around. You'll just have to be patient with me, I suppose." He winked at Emily as they started for the back door.

"No problem, sir. I don't know much about what you do, either. But Robbie Joe sure seems to. I guess I'd better learn, at least a little, so I can understand what he's talking about. Let me ask you something, do you really make music on a two-hundred-year-old fiddle?"

Stani was sure he heard Emily laughing as they walked out the door.

As if his mind weren't overloading with details pertaining to the farm, there were all the events leading up to the wedding. While Emily was hostessing a bridal shower for Martha Jean at the farm, Stani was invited to join a fishing party for Jack. "But I've never been fishing in my life. I don't even know what's involved, other than a pole of some sort and water."

Emily only smiled at his concern. "You'll be fine. James will be along, and he can show you the ropes. It's just a farm pond, not an ocean. I expect it will involve more eating and talking than actual fishing. Man talk, reminiscing about the big one that got away. That sort of thing."

"Ah, just the sort of thing I know nothing about, you mean?"

"I think it's nice you were included. It shows you're part of the community now."

They were actually alone, sitting in the porch swing in the darkness. Holding her hand, he closed his eyes and pictured her as she had looked on their wedding day. "That is nice. It's what I asked for, isn't it? To be just that fellow that married Emily Haynes."

"I love you, Stani Moss." Her voice was soft next to his ear. He gathered into his arms, his hand resting on her belly. He could easily feel the flutter of tiny hands and feet and it sent a responding spasm of emotion through his chest.

"You're not going to overdo it, with all these ladies coming? I'm not sure I like the idea of leaving you for that long."

"Don't be silly. Sara won't let me lift a finger. All I'm supposed to do is put on a pretty dress and sit by the teapot. Ruthie is doing all the housework, and the food is being provided by the ladies of the church."

"The ladies who think everyone should take that walk down the aisle?"

"You have an excellent memory. For a man who's about to observe another birthday. How would you like to celebrate?"

"Just kiss me and wish me 'Happy Birthday' as I go off on my first fishing expedition. There's too much happening already to worry about my birthday." He nuzzled her neck, savoring the warm scent of her skin.

"No big celebration with string quartets and life-size posters?"

"Ha! No thank you! If you'll remember, I ran away as fast as I could." Ever so gently, he nipped at her earlobe.

"I also remember you proposed to me that night."

"Did I? How romantic of me." One finger under her chin, he turned her face and his lips covered hers. As her hands slid up his chest, she let out a little moaning sigh. Somewhere, an owl hooted and the breeze stirred the leaves overhead. The kiss was long and sweet and he knew he wanted more.

"Stani?" Her head dropped to his shoulder, her lips just touching his neck.

"Yes, darling girl?"

"This is lovely, but I really have to stand up. One of the babies is kicking me in the ribs." She giggled sweetly in his ear. "Can you help me out of the swing, please?"

Chapter Forty-three

John had found his own rhythm for what he called "rustication." Most days he rose at dawn, carried a mug of tea into the backyard and watched the sunrise in the company of the old white mule and a pair of cautiously friendly tabby cats. After a brisk walk of a half-mile or so down the road and back, he took his book, whichever of J.D.'s collection he was reading at the moment, and settled in the sunroom. By the time Stani and Emily appeared, he was ready for breakfast, and after helping Stani clear the dishes, he returned to his book until lunch. Retiring to his room after the leisurely meal, he took a long siesta, following which, he was ready for tea. On the farm, teatime was observed with a substantial serving of freshly baked fruit muffins or Emily's special cinnamon bread, washed down with iced herbal tea. Another two hours of reading usually brought him to dinnertime, and while he often helped set the table, he managed to avoid any actual duties in the kitchen beyond harassing Stani with regard to his role as assistant to the chef.

Emily was clearly happiest when bustling about the kitchen, and the resulting meals were pure pleasure to a man who endured restaurant food so much of the time. He complimented her profusely, not only with words of praise, but by cleaning his plate and accepting seconds and even thirds. Dessert generally consisted of fruit and cheese, but on one occasion she had prepared a tart filled with dark chocolate which even Stani devoured with zeal.

John had never fully appreciated what three home-cooked meals a day and ample time for rest could do for a man's soul. He found himself thinking more profoundly than he had in years, contemplating creation's mysteries in the quiet hours of early morning and late evening. Nothing disturbed his peace, no place to rush off to, no one to contact in preparation for the rushing off, no last-minute thing to retrieve after having rushed off in too great a hurry. For the first time in his life, he began to accept that he might even like to settle down someday. During the all-too-brief years of his marriage, he had savored the peace of the home his young wife had made for them. Since then, he knew he had run from that kind of peace, refusing to confront the memories of all he had lost.

Jack Deem was getting married. Jack was older than John by almost ten years. He had never been married, yet now he was entering into wedlock with the spirit of a young man in love. He and his bride were clearly passionate about one another. Their eyes, while not young and bright, were warm and speaking enough for anyone to see what they shared. Of course, Jack was a man of faith and had probably not, as John had, found comfort in the arms of women for the sake of comfort alone. But still, something in the back of his now much quieter mind seemed to be pushing forward a suggestion. Could it be that it was really never too late for true love?

The suggestion seemed to perversely call forth the image of Peg Shannon. Here, hundreds of miles from New York, John felt safe in contemplating that image, much safer than he felt in the actual vicinity of Peg herself. Since the death of her father, she seemed changed, softer, almost vulnerable. She was talking about selling the estate in Florida, even getting a smaller place in New York. Simplifying her life, she had said. She spoke with what sounded much like regret of never having had a family of her own. These changes confused John, reminding him of his former suspicions of Peg. They also unnerved him, given his response to her. He found himself wanting to take her in his arms and comfort her, knowing full well where that would lead. He was no match for her, he had learned that before. If he had been powerless then, when he had merely been intrigued and flattered by her attention, what could he expect now, when his emotions were so dangerously engaged?

All this he considered as he sat watching the sunrise, and walked the country lanes. While the books he read were interesting, he knew that through many pages, his mind was elsewhere. How had he, rational stoic that he liked to imagine himself, been captured by a pair of bright blue Irish eyes and a hearty laugh? It was all Stani's fault. All of it. He had brought Peg into John's life, he had left her there for the taking, and now he had shown by his own example how transforming love could be. As he watched Stani and Emily, so completely engrossed in one another and the future they shared, even as he watched Jack and his Martha Jean preparing to join their remaining years, John had to admit that he envied them. The joy they brought to each other, the commitment they were willing, even eager, to make, and the obvious warmth they shared, were all things he had known once. He was well aware of the cost of losing those things. But he had to acknowledge the risk might well be worth taking.

One other idea gnawed at his thoughts, in the midst of all this contemplation. It had been there for a long time, he realized. He wondered if he ought not pursue it in earnest before it was too late. As he had watched the changes in Stani, he had become convinced that for Stani at least, the quest for a spiritual home had led him to just the proper place. Never having made a firm commitment to any faith, John had believed himself satisfied to drift. Lately, each time he witnessed the effect Stani had on the lives of others, he felt a pull to know more about the power he seemed to draw on. When Stani had opened the door to Will Harrison, invited him into the unorthodox circle of his family, John had been profoundly impressed. Emily, he was willing to acknowledge, was probably some sort of saint, but Stani he knew had been as lost a soul as ever walked the earth. Nothing could have brought about these changes other than his successful search for a God to believe in.

So while Stani and Emily smiled at John's long, lazy days, they would have been surprised to know just how hard he was actually working at solving these mysteries. By the end of the first week, he had decided that one must be resolved before the other could be approached. On Good Friday, after a solemn service in the little stone church, he asked Mike McConnell if he could spare a few minutes of his valuable time. Later that evening, he drove into town and in the hour he spent in the pastor's office, his life suddenly turned a corner and the road ahead was filled with unanticipated promise.

Chapter Forty-four

Stani was relieved to see the drive empty of any visitors when he pulled through the gate. It had been a long and enjoyable afternoon, but he was tired and not particularly in the mood to smile and greet any lingering shower guests. He wasn't absolutely sure what a bridal shower involved, but then he hadn't known what to expect from a fishing party either, and he'd been pleasantly surprised. Still, he was ready to relax now, and sit in the porch swing with his wife for an hour or two.

Emily was sitting in the sunroom, her feet on the ottoman. He was pleased to note that her ankles were as slim as ever, no sign of the swelling she predicted would occur in the last weeks of pregnancy. In fact, with the obvious exception of her expansive waistline, and the enticing new curves above, she was still as slender as a reed. And more beautiful than ever. She turned her face up to him now, a smile of welcome on her lips. As always, his heart did a strange little twist, missing a quarter-beat, as he leaned over to kiss her.

"How was the shower? And how are you? Tired?" He perched on the arm of her chair, touching her hair. She had pinned it up in a loose sort of knot at the back of her head, and it fell in becoming tendrils around her face and neck.

"It was lovely. And I'm fine. How about you? Catch any fish?" She grinned, her eyes twinkling.

"No, of course not. But I learned a lot. You didn't warn me the bait would still be alive. Thank goodness for James and Mike."

She laughed, taking one of his hands. "These beautiful hands had never touched worms before, I'd bet."

"Still haven't. But it was all great fun. I heard lots of stories about the good old days. Even a couple about your father. Plenty of tales about Jack's adventures through the years. Some of the younger guys talked about how he kept them out of trouble when they were kids. Thirty years is a long time to be sheriff in a place like this. He's touched every life in the county at some point, I guess."

"Yes he has. And they won't let him retire. He said once he'd have to just pack up and sneak out of town in the middle of the night, to ever get out of office. Have you eaten?"

"Oh yes. The plan was to fry the fish that were caught, but since no one really caught any, other than a few little ones that they threw back in, we all went to the truck stop for steaks. It was surprisingly good. What about you? Can I fix you some supper?"

"No, I'm fine. I ate enough finger sandwiches and cake to hold me all night. I was sitting right by the food, serving tea, and I couldn't resist nibbling all afternoon." She reached up, stroking his face gently. "You got a little sun. I see freckles peeking out."

He wrinkled his nose. "Freckles? Please. I haven't had freckles since I was. . . ."

She smiled knowingly. "Since you were fifteen? You had them last summer, from working outside. I love your freckles. I'll always remember them from the first time you were here." A shadow crossed her face at the long ago image. Then just as suddenly, her lips curved in a mysterious little smile. "Stani, let's go outside. I have a surprise for you." He was startled by the abrupt turn in the conversation. Taking her outstretched hands, he helped her stand, drawing her close for a moment.

"You're beautiful, you know?"

"I know nothing of the kind, but it's sweet of you to say so. Now come on, let's go out back. There's something I want you to see."

Tugging on his hand, she led the way out the back door. Just beyond the circle of light from the sun room, a table stood on the lawn. Covered in a checkered cloth, it was set for two, with a single tall candle burning among flowers in the center.

"What is all this?" She was still pulling him across the grass.

"It's a moonlight picnic, the one we never really had last year. Happy birthday, darling!" From somewhere in the house, music sounded, soft strains of a Mozart sonata drifting on the night air. Now that his eyes were growing accustomed to the dimness, he could make out a loaf of fresh baked bread and a wedge of cheese, as well as a bottle of sparkling white grape juice chilling in an ice bucket. Two champagne glasses stood at the ready. Two chairs from the dining room were drawn up to the table, and he pulled one out and seated her carefully.

"This is lovely, darling girl, but you didn't move these things out here by yourself?"

"No, John did it for me. I couldn't let your day pass without at least a little celebration."

"Thank you. I'd almost forgotten it was my birthday." He watched as she opened the bottle and poured juice into the glasses.

"To my darling husband, many, many happy returns!" Raising her glass, she smiled and in the glow of the candlelight, he could see tears welling in her eyes. "I love you with all my heart, Stani Moss. Never more than now." A shiver touched his spine at the huskiness in her voice.

"Nor I you. I asked you last year to make me the happiest of men. You have done that, and so much more." He raised his own glass, touching hers. "To many more years like this one."

They sat for an hour under the stars, not saying very much, listening to the night creatures and gazing at each other in the soft light. From inside the house, the music continued to play. It finally occurred to him to wonder who was keeping the records going.

"John. He offered to leave for a while, but I asked him to stay and provide the background music."

"Speaking of John, Mike said something odd to me today. He said he had a long talk with John yesterday evening. He was impressed with what a deep thinker John is. What do you suppose prompted John to talk to Mike?"

"You." The directness of her gaze suggested he should have known the answer.

"Me?"

"All I know is John told me you had inspired him to think about things a bit differently. I gather he's been making a journey of his own recently."

"John? But he's always seemed indifferent to that sort of thing. Take it or leave it."

"Not any more. I thought he might have talked to you about it."

"John?" He knew he was repeating himself, but the idea just wouldn't take hold.

Emily laughed softly. "Maybe you should ask him. I need to go inside now, I'm afraid. You boys can clear this away while you talk things over." She got to her feet, standing over him smiling. "Come on, darling. Don't look so shocked."

"How could I have inspired John to anything? He's always been the one to show *me* the way." Rising, he took her arm and together they started toward the house. "Are you sure that's what he said, that I had done something to change his thinking?"

"I'm quite sure, Stani. Why should that be so hard to understand?

You inspire me every day."

With a look of outright disbelief, he sighed. "You know very well it's the other way around." But her only reply was another of those mystical little smiles.

In the front room, John was standing by the stereo, watching the record spinning on the turntable. As Emily went into the bedroom, she heard Stani ask hesitantly, "John, there wouldn't be anything you've been meaning to tell me, would there?"

Their voices drifted off toward the back of the house. "As a matter of fact, lad, there is something. And by the way, happy birthday."

Chapter Forty-five

As always when they came home to the valley, the days passed too quickly. Easter Sunday, with all its glorious celebration, opened the week leading up to Jack's marriage to Martha Jean. Every day seemed to hold some major event. Stani met with Robbie Joe's violin teacher on Monday, plotting the course the boy's studies would take in the months to come. They watched from the yard with the whole Dixon clan, as Bobby plowed the garden for the first time with the new tractor on Tuesday. The truck bearing the long-ago-ordered baby furniture arrived from Charlottesville on Wednesday, and all day Thursday was spent setting up the farmhouse nursery. By Friday night's rehearsal, Stani felt as though he had just completed a marathon tour, exhilarated and exhausted.

He stood with Emily at the lectern and read the scripture passages chosen from their own wedding. While Martha Jean had elected to take that walk to the altar on the arm of her brother, she and Jack would recite a prayer of their own composition together and walk out of the church as man and wife to the same joyous strains of "Simple Gifts." It was amazing, Emily said, to think they had inspired someone like Jack to step outside the traditional wedding service.

"What's even more amazing is that they decided to take this step at all. Two people who've never been married, going to the altar at their ages. That's brave."

"It's sweet. They deserve to be gloriously, deliriously happy. Just like we are. Only they won't have to worry about nurseries and layettes." Her back ached from standing so long, and one of the babies seemed to have moved permanently beneath her ribs. Every breath produced a painful little jab. More than anything, she wanted to go home and straight to bed, but instead they were expected to attend the rehearsal dinner at the cafe.

Taking note of her tired eyes, he gave in to the urge he'd fought throughout the rehearsal. "Darling, if I insisted we go home now because I'm totally fagged after all the excitement this week, would you pose any serious objection?"

She smiled, just a hint of grin, and said very solemnly, "I suppose if you're that tired, I can miss this one party. You have been working awfully hard. Let's find Jack and make our excuses. But just remember, I'm the one who gets the first back rub."

♡

There was no sweeter sanctuary than their own bedroom. The calming colors, soft lights and most of all the big sleigh bed provided the retreat they so desperately needed. Tomorrow would be a long, strenuous day, no matter how joyous. Stani listened to Emily breathing softly as she dozed in his arms, wondering how they could possibly return to the hectic pace of the coming weeks. He had concerts scheduled all over the northeast well into May. He and John would have to travel for days at a time, leaving Emily at home with only Milo and their very capable housekeeper, Mamie, to watch out for her. Jana was currently on a tour in Canada. Peg had plans to go to Florida for a few weeks to see to the closing of her father's home there. Lil would not be available for another month.

A wave of rising panic began to churn in his chest. He couldn't leave her! How would she sleep at night without him there to rub her back and arrange her pillows? What if she went into labor early? Milo would certainly not know what to do. Feeling an urgent need to get up, to pace the floor in an effort to clear his head of these terrifying images, he started to sit up, gently moving her away from him. As he lifted his arm from beneath her head, a sharp twinge of burning pain shot through his shoulder. Emily murmured something in response to his stifled groan, but thankfully, she didn't wake.

He got out of bed, flexing his arm. It had just been her weight on his shoulder, he was sure. This wasn't the first time he'd felt a little pain lately. Not always that severe, but always in the same place, just at the top of his left shoulder. He shrugged it off. It was nothing, he was sure. Not the kind of thing he'd known for so long after the accident. No numbness in his hand. No stiffness. Just that little stab every now and then.

Standing at the window, he let the breeze blow on his bare torso until he shivered in the coolness. He needed to get his mind around all that was coming in the next few weeks. If he really decided he couldn't leave her, there were concerts to cancel, travel plans to change. Maybe he could simply cut a few dates, so he wouldn't have to be away for more than a day or two at a time. Still flexing his arm, he turned back to look at her, that familiar rush of protectiveness flooding over him.

As if she sensed him watching her, she opened her eyes and smiled. "Come back to bed, Stani. You look cold."

Crawling in beside her, he stretched on his back, raising his arm and folding it behind his head, testing to see if the pain was still there. Sure enough, the same jab in the same spot. Quickly he brought his arm to his side. Gone. Nothing there now. Nothing to worry about.

Emily turned toward him, reaching out to slide an arm over his chest. "Are you okay?"

"I'm fine. Just thinking about all that's coming up in the next few weeks. Maybe I should scale back my schedule a bit. I don't like the idea of being away from you so much." Rolling on his side, he looked into her eyes, brushing aside the strands of hair that clung to her cheek.

"Don't be silly. I'll be fine. You're taking off the whole summer, remember. Are you sure that's all that's worrying you?" She was half asleep, but a concerned little frown crossed her face.

"Isn't that enough?"

"Don't worry. About anything, remember?" Her voice faded into a whisper, but he was certain he heard the word "prayer."

Martha Jean Clark and Jackson Carter Deem were married on a brilliant spring afternoon in a quiet, intimate affair with only seventy-five invited guests in attendance. The reception followed in the church social hall, featuring a three-tiered wedding cake and a brief toast with sparkling cider. By late afternoon the happy couple had departed for their honeymoon at a remote cabin in the Smokies, loaned by the bride's brother. They would be gone for two weeks, long enough for the contractors to complete the first phase of remodeling on Jack's ancestral home just outside of town.

Martha Jean had been elegant in a white lace suit with a spray of Lily of the Valley in her salt and pepper curls. Standing next to her tall, broad shouldered groom, she had seemed delicate and vulnerable, not words commonly associated with her forceful personality. As Jack bent to kiss his bride at the conclusion of the ceremony, Emily thought how handsome he was, just as he had always seemed to her as a little girl. His fair hair might not be as thick now, but his eyes still twinkled the same bright blue and his face was only made more expressive by the deep lines etched by years of hard work.

They would be happy, Emily knew. Their lives outside the home they would share might not change much, but neither of them would have to face nights alone now. She had learned how comforting it was to share a bed with someone you loved. Just to have a caring presence nearby, someone to reach out to in the darkness. Jack had lived alone in that big old house most of his adult life. Martha Jean would make it a home now; fill it with her special brand of effervescent warmth.

As Emily watched them race to the car through a shower of rice, she laughed along with everyone else. It was a joyous beginning. It was also the end of something, the final step in closing a door to the past. Jack, she knew only too well, had loved her mother for so many years, had remained single because no other woman measured up to what he idolized in her. She would never know if her father had been aware of Jack's feelings, but she herself had recognized from childhood, through some instinctive understanding of the tone in his voice, the shadow in his eyes, that Jack had accepted life without the thing he wanted most.

Emily hoped her own happiness had contributed to this day. Jack had been so dedicated to them, to her father and to herself, at least in part because of his love for her mother. Emily knew she would always have his affection, his support, but now he was finally free to live his life, free of his responsibility to see that she was happy. Just before the wedding, she had kissed him and wished him all the joy she had found in her marriage. There had been tears in his eyes for just a second, and then the familiar grin had creased his face. "You always could find happiness, Em. Even when nobody else could see it. But it seems to me now, it's found you."

When the car drove away, tin cans rattling behind, she turned to Stani and tried to smile through her tears. He held out his arms to her, gathering her close. She wished for a moment that she could find words to describe all she was feeling, and then she realized he already understood.

They spent the next five days soaking up as much peace as possible. With the wedding behind them and the farmhouse in order, ready for their return at some undetermined date in the summer, there was nothing pressing left to do. They sat on the porch and watched the Dixon children play in the yard. Together, they prepared meals which were eaten with John and whoever happened to drop by. James was a frequent visitor, checking with Bobby on farm business and then staying to drink iced tea and talk.

As she listened to James, Emily vowed to have a long heart-to-heart with Penny in the next few weeks. It was time, she thought, for her friend to face reality. James wanted desperately to make Penny happy, but asking him to compromise his values would never lead to real happiness. Whatever anxiety was holding Penny back from a total commitment, Emily believed there was nothing to do but look it squarely in the face and call it by name. Whether it was the differences in their beliefs, or the dread of her parents' opposition, or some other obstacle, there was no time like the present, before James moved to Boston, to meet it head on. Penny had never been a coward, quite the opposite. But the fear of again losing a man she loved might have made her willing to settle for less than her dream. They would have to talk, Emily was convinced. Penny needed someone, just as James had, to listen to her worries. In Penny's case, she wondered if she might not also need a shoulder to cry on.

A line of thunderstorms blew through on their last night at the farm. A spectacular show of lightning, and thunder that rattled the windows, eventually took out the electricity for a time. In the light of candles, they ate a cold supper and talked of all that had filled the past three weeks.

"Now you need a vacation, lad. There's too much to do around this place." John grinned at the tired face across the table. They had spent the afternoon packing the car, and Stani was visibly weary.

"No vacation for me. We're back on the road, old man." With a wry grin he said pointedly, "At least one of us is well-rested."

Emily chuckled. "You'll get more sleep on the road, darling. I won't be there to wake you up every two hours."

"Don't remind me. I still think I might cut a few dates." He frowned at her, running a hand through his already tousled hair.

"You're sold out everywhere, lad. Word's out that you won't play the States again for a while. Milo is positively giddy at the ticket sales. I'd think twice about canceling now."

He groaned. "Trapped."

"I'll be fine, as I keep telling you. All I have to do is sit around and gestate for a few more weeks." A particularly brilliant flash of lightning illuminated the kitchen. Stani jumped.

"See, my nerves are already shot, just thinking of you going into labor while I'm on some stage hundreds of miles away, oblivious to what's going on."

"You won't be oblivious. I'll make sure we have a system all worked out to get word to you, assuming these little guys are rude enough to start without you." She fondly patted her side, shifting uncomfortably in her chair. "Darling, will you carry a candle for me?" Her nod toward the bathroom brought him quickly to his feet.

"Excuse us, John. You see why I don't want to leave her? She needs me!"

Going to the sunroom, where he could get a better view of the spectacle, John stood watching the display in the expanse of sky across the valley. He thought of the storm that had done so much damage here last summer, the one that had injured Emily and convinced Stani not to leave her then. He understood Stani's concern, but there would always be some reason to stay home. Especially now that there would be babies to watch over. Poor lad, he would have to learn to have more faith, John mused. Then with a grin, he corrected himself. Stani had plenty of faith; he just needed to learn to rely on it more.

John knew only too well what that dark look and those heavy sighs meant. He was going to have his hands full in the next few weeks, as Stani pushed himself in front of packed audiences and worried about leaving Emily at home. But now he felt completely confident that he was up to taking on the task. He had looked to the hills, and just as promised, found the help he had so long been seeking.

Chapter Forty-six

It was ironic that now, when he needed someone to watch over the most important person in his world, he was turning to a person he had always taken completely for granted. Stani felt a twinge of guilt at the thought that in all the years Mamie had been in his life, he had never bothered to learn anything about her. He had known she was somehow related to Milo's chauffeur, Robert. He thought she must have begun cleaning the apartment for Jana not long after they settled in New York. She had definitely been there while he was still in school. He could recall her chiding him for leaving textbooks on the seldom-used dining table, remarking that if anyone ever wanted to have a meal there, they would have to eat on top of his homework. During his recovery, Mamie had come more often, maybe every day, rather than her customary two—or was it three—times a week. She had hovered on the periphery, a look of motherly concern on her face. She had apparently caught Peg's attention then. As soon as he and Emily mentioned the need to find a housekeeper, Peg had suggested Mamie. With Milo and Jana traveling so much, surely they could manage to share her for a few months.

A transplant from the deep South, Mamie Washington was the perfect match for Emily. They shared much of the same heritage, and exactly the same approach to making a home a haven. Just as Robert, who it turned out was indeed Mamie's brother, seemed to take a personal interest in them, Mamie immediately made it clear she considered herself solely responsible for their comfort. She was solicitous of Emily, and with a twinkle in her eye, assured her that "Mr. Stani" could learn to be a good daddy, as long as they told him exactly what to do.

He had tried to discourage the formality in her address, reminding her that she had known him since he was just a boy, but with characteristic frankness, Mamie had pointed out with a grin that he surely didn't wish her to call him "Young Stani" as she had back then. And just plain "Stani" would never do. He had the impression that

Mamie was proud of him, that she took personal satisfaction from his having turned out so well, after the years when she had no doubt observed his near self-destruction. And Mamie fully understood the kind of life they lived, the hours of practicing at home, the constant traveling, and of course the need for privacy. She would not have retained her position in Milo's household had she lacked discretion, Stani was quite certain.

Mamie, Stani decided, was much like the stage managers he worked with in the concert halls he'd played so many times; or like the concertmasters he saluted year after year. He knew their faces, acknowledged them as old friends, and knew absolutely nothing about their lives. Mamie had made his bed and done his laundry, cleaned his bathroom and kept his clothes in order. Personal services he had taken for granted, never giving any thought to the woman who so carefully folded his shirts and lined his toiletries in a perfect row on the bathroom vanity. Now, he was asking her to take care of Emily and his unborn children.

Of course, it was Emily who almost immediately learned the details of Mamie's life. Without even asking questions, she knew that Mamie had never been married, or had children of her own, but had raised two young nieces after the death of Robert's wife many years ago. The girls were now mothers themselves and Mamie took pride in their accomplishments and those of their children. Mamie was deeply religious, loved gospel music, and had little patience with what she considered the abandonment of morals in modern society.

"She told you all these things in between doing the vacuuming and folding the laundry?" Stani had to smile at Emily's account.

"Sort of. We have a glass of iced tea together on the roof. She doesn't think I should go up there alone. So I just suggested she join me on her break. She's not all that fond of high places, but she seems to enjoy our conversations. She told me how glad she is you've settled down and seem so happy now. Like everyone who knew you before we met, she swears you never used to laugh."

He responded with a chuckle. "I probably didn't, dark, brooding genius that I was. I wish I had taken more notice of her back then. I have a feeling she may have seen me at my worst. Hung over, or stumbling in after a night out. I should probably apologize for my behavior. It's disgraceful that I can't recall a single real conversation with her in all the years she came to the apartment."

"She doesn't seem to hold it against you. Unfortunately, people like Mamie are used to being ignored, as long as they do their jobs well.

You'll have time to make it up to her now."

He smiled at her across the dinner table. "Because now she's a member of the family? Do you ever really meet a stranger, love?"

"Not for long, if they want to be friends. And most people seem to, even in New York. I met our neighbor from the other penthouse this morning. Susan Gibson, divorced, non-custodial mother of two, and fabric designer. I saw her hanging these huge sheets of cloth on the roof, so I climbed onto the flower box and said hello."

"You climbed onto the flower box?! Emily!"

"It was perfectly safe. I stood there for a while and we chatted and then she came over for a cup of tea." She grinned. "I drank way too much tea today."

"So is she nice, this divorced mother of two?"

"Yes. Very friendly and open, told me a lot about herself. She said she went to the right schools, met the right man, married in a fairy tale wedding and had two perfect children; then one day she woke up and discovered she was living the wrong life. She gave her husband custody of the children to avoid what she calls the war of the worlds. Her father owns the apartment, and he's backing her while she tries to get recognized as a designer."

"Sounds like she told you her life's story."

"I've never known anyone like her. I guess she's the first divorced person I've ever really talked to. She doesn't seem to miss her husband at all. In fact, she says she's much happier on her own."

"Sad, but I'm sure that's what most divorced people say."

"I think she did what was expected of her, and now she's rebelling against everything, trying to establish her own identity. She was a debutante, a real high society girl. Now she wears jeans and t-shirts and looks like a hippie. I'm pretty sure she's growing marijuana on her roof."

"Oh, wonderful! There goes the neighborhood. Maybe just say hello, but definitely don't go over there. Imagine explaining to Jack how you got caught in a drug bust."

"Do people really get in trouble for smoking pot in New York? I would have thought too many do it for the police to bother."

He eyed her with an amused twinkle. "What do you know about smoking pot?"

"Stani, I went to college. I've never smoked it, but there was plenty around campus. What about you, did you smoke it, at all those parties?"

"I tried it, but whisky is much more effective, if you really want a rush. And the smoke always made me a little queasy. Let's face it, love, we're just not cool enough for that sort of thing." He began to clear the table, trying to picture his wife sipping tea with a reefer-smoking dropout. "Did you tell her anything about yourself? Or was she the only topic of conversation?"

"She never asked and I didn't offer. I don't want to be critical, but I think it's fair to say she's the center of her own universe." She got to her feet, stretching and stifling a yawn.

"Poor girl, did you miss your nap, listening to the fascinating tale of our neighbor's misspent life?"

"I'm afraid so. Let's leave the dishes and go up on the roof. It's a beautiful night. We won't have many opportunities like this." Tugging his arm, she started for the stairs.

He followed, a sudden knot tightening in his chest. Only a few days left before the touring began. She had made a convincing case for getting the work out of the way now, so that he would be free by the time the babies came. Pregnant women managed alone every day, but the mother of his twins would surely need his help, she had argued.

Sitting in the new glider, gazing out over the city, he asked her one more time, "Are you sure you're okay with my going?"

"I'll miss you horribly, but the sooner you go, the sooner you'll be home again. I suppose there will always be times I have to stay behind. It may be harder on you, if you insist on worrying about me." She snuggled close, resting her head against his shoulder. She sounded tired, her voice soft and husky.

"If you're fine, I'll be fine. How's that?"

"It's a deal. But Stani?" Her hand tightened on his arm.

"Yes, love?"

"Don't be totally fine without me, okay? I'd hate to think we could ever be really happy apart for long." He knew she was thinking of the couples who must have been happy once, but learned too easily to live without each other.

"Never fear. 'Entreat me not,' remember?"

"How could I ever forget? But maybe all couples believe their vows are for always on their wedding day."

"Jiliand Emily Haynes, I'd make the same vows every day of my life." Her response was a little sigh of satisfaction, as she turned her face to him and kissed him sweetly.

"You always say just the thing I need to hear." He could feel her relaxing against him, her breathing slow and regular.

"And now I'm going to say one more thing you need to hear. Darling girl, it's time for bed."

Chapter Forty-seven

If Emily had ever imagined pregnancy as the happiest time in a woman's life, all her illusions were now thoroughly shattered. As a student nurse, during her rotation in obstetrics, she might have had sympathy for women in actual labor, but as for the months prior to giving birth, she had probably discarded the thought of any real hardship. Oh, women complained about backaches and swelling feet. They moaned about stretch marks and weight gain. But by and large, pregnant women always seemed so happy, like smiling, waddling mother ducks. In fact, she now knew, they hardly recognized themselves and probably smiled to keep from crying, as they helplessly watched their bodies grow more grotesque with every passing week.

If it had not been for Stani, she would have given in to despair many days. But he still said she was beautiful and his eyes told her he was speaking what he believed to be the truth. At night, when he rubbed her aching back with his strong, gentle hands, when he kissed her swollen belly and talked lovingly to the babies inside, he made her feel more or less like a woman worthy of his adoration. Not that she didn't look forward to holding her babies in her arms and loving them with all her heart. But until she could also pass them to someone else's arms and walk about freely again, just for a few minutes, she knew she would not feel remotely like her old self. She dreamed of racing over the fields, the wind in her hair, her feet barely touching the ground. Then she woke and discovered herself unable to sit up in bed, having instead to roll off the side and waddle across the floor, fearful of her own image in the mirror.

Of course, she could never say anything about her feelings. She was so grateful to be successfully pregnant, after the fright of last summer. She prayed constantly that she would carry the babies long enough, that they would be born healthy and strong. She worked hard at remaining calm and taking each day in stride, not daring to wish it to be over any sooner for the sake of her own comfort. She also prayed for patience, for the strength to avoid complaining about all the aches and pains, for a smile when she felt like crying. Again, if it had not been for Stani, she doubted she could have been so cheerful. But the sight of his face, so full of excitement every time he felt the babies move, made it easy to smile in response. He was so good, so tender, and so willing to share in this with her. He wanted to know what she was feeling, so she told him, not that she was in pain, physically and emotionally, but that the babies were strong and hearty inside her, growing more so every day.

Now that she no longer had to worry about hiring some forbidding stranger to help her take care of her children in the course of their crazy life, she felt a little better. Again, it had been Stani who had conceived such a brilliant solution. Lil might not be a professional mother's helper, but Emily knew she would be willing to do whatever was asked of her, and she also knew Lil would never try to tell her how to raise her babies. The idea of some officious, overbearing woman, who had never even had babies of her own, looking down her nose at everything she did, just because she was young, and one had even implied, spoiled by wealth, was intolerable. She had cried so hard when she tried to explain her misgivings to Stani that he had declared on the spot that he would quit performing and they could just move back to the farm until the babies were old enough to start to college. She had laughed then, assuring him that there had to be some better way. Sure enough, he had come up with one.

Now if she could just remain calm, bear with this a few more weeks, they could soon get back to some kind of life. Hopefully one that did not revolve around her staying near a bathroom and carrying a load of pillows everywhere she went. Once they were born, she knew these babies would bring them nothing but joy. They would watch them grow, love them and share their amazing if completely irregular life with them every day. She could imagine what a wonder it would be for Stani to have his children, the family he so desperately wanted, right there with him, in the hotel rooms, in the cars and on the trains and planes, even some day in the concert halls. They would be so happy, a band of gypsies, carefree and loving. And she would be able to at last walk, not waddle, and stand without helping hands to lift her. He was right, she thought, they should carefully consider before they did this again. But she knew in her heart, she would be only too ready to carry more babies, just as soon as she got over having these two.

Stani had to make himself content with the arrangements they'd made. There was no alternative, and Emily assured him she would know if he was worrying and that would make her less than happy. Blackmail, he told her, plain and simple. To which she had smiled sweetly and declared it a pregnant wife's privilege.

Mamie would come every weekday morning and stay until three. Robert was exclusively available to drive Emily on any errands she needed to run, or if she just wanted to get out of the apartment for a while. Milo would take her to dinner, or bring in takeout meals, every evening. Everyone, including the building's doorman, had Stani's schedule and the list of contact numbers. The first weekend, Lil was flying in to keep Emily company and get acquainted with the apartment. The second, Penny was coming down from Boston and they planned to put the finishing touches on the nursery. There had been some delay with the furniture delivery and it was promised for that week.

"So you see, Stani, I'll have plenty of company and plenty to keep me out of trouble. Peg will be back the next week and she promised to take me to a matinee."

"Really? You're up for all that sitting in one place for so long?" He gave her wry grin. They had gotten up every hour the previous night.

They agreed that if she went into labor, he would fly home immediately from wherever he was, end of tour. According to the official due date, there were still six weeks to go. Neither of them admitted to the other that it seemed impossible she could carry the babies that long. But Emily was forcefully optimistic, and Stani knew his job at this point was to be supportive, not to express his anxieties. When they kissed good-bye, both were very near tears, forcing brave smiles and making silly comments to cover the agony of parting. Each had the thought that the next time they met, they might well be parents.

John waited during the first days for Stani to confess to the pain in his shoulder. Not that he expected the boy would just tell him outright. But he watched for an opportunity to bring up the subject when he could catch Stani off his guard. It came after the concert in Detroit. Stani as usual had wanted to change into a fresh shirt before going to the reception following the concert. When John held up the tailcoat for him, he held it just a bit too high. The resulting awkward angle brought a grunt of pain and in the mirror he could see the accompanying grimace. Their eyes met in the reflection.

"You can tell me now or later, it's up to you. But you can't avoid telling me much longer, lad."

"It's nothing, just a twinge." It was clear the pain had been enough to cause him to blanch momentarily.

John nodded. "Right. How long has it been 'twinging'?" Settling the coat on Stani's shoulders, he gave it a little pat. "Do you need a rubdown tonight?"

"No. It's not that kind of thing." Stani turned from the mirror and started toward the door, the set of his jaw suggesting he was done with the subject.

"Then what kind of thing is it? And when are you planning to see a doctor?"

"I'm not. It's nothing, I'm sure." He was gone, firmly closing the dressing room door.

John let it go then, satisfied with at least an acknowledgment of the problem. There was time, and with the demands of this tour, it wouldn't take long to get to the bottom of things, he felt sure.

The next afternoon in Cleveland, John noticed that after rehearsal Stani downed two aspirin with his tea. "Does that help?" he asked offhandedly.

"Not particularly." Immediately, Stani frowned, caught by his own frankness.

"So what sort of twinge is it?" John pretended to concentrate on unpacking, watching out of the corner of his eye as Stani flexed his arm, testing the shoulder.

"Just a little jab, at the top of the joint. Kind of a burning when I raise my arm. I'm sure it's just a strain." He tried to grin. "Maybe from that soccer match at the farm."

"That was weeks ago, son. And if that little skirmish caused it, you really do need a doctor."

"I don't have time for that now. Anyway, it doesn't affect my playing."

"Not yet." John let it drop. The look in the boy's eyes told him more than words could anyway.

In Minneapolis, after a particularly demanding performance, Stani admitted he probably should see a doctor. The pain was getting worse. It was keeping him from sleeping, waking him every time he rolled on his shoulder. Problem was he wanted to see the same doctor who'd done the surgery after the accident. He wouldn't trust anyone else. "How am I going to see a doctor in New York without Emily knowing something's wrong?"

"What makes you think you can hide it from her? She'll find out eventually anyway. I'd have thought after what happened in London, honesty would be the *only* policy."

With a sigh, Stani agreed. "We could stop off in New York on the way to Baltimore. See if you can get me an appointment then. But I won't say anything to her until I've seen the doctor. It's probably nothing, and there's no point in worrying her needlessly."

Emily was thrilled when Stani called to say he had found a few hours to come home. Her routine was starting to drag, and after all the excitement of Lil's visit, her days seemed even longer. She couldn't wait, she told him, to show him the new cradle she'd purchased. One of the antique dealers she had met through Peg had found a handmade cradle, easily large enough to accommodate two newborns. He had called on Friday just after Lil arrived, and they had rushed across town to see it. Emily had fallen in love with it on sight. Lil spent hours waxing it to a soft sheen and they had fitted it out in white eyelet bedding. Now it resided in a corner of the living room, and whenever she passed it, she couldn't resist giving it a gentle push, just to watch it rock smoothly back and forth.

Stani arrived on Tuesday afternoon, and Emily saw at once that he was tired and needed most of all to relax. There were circles under his eyes and tense lines around his mouth. After he had admired the cradle and peeked into the nursery at the newly-arrived furniture, they took a long nap together, ordered Chinese for dinner and sat on the roof watching the lights come on across the city. He said the tour was going fine, described the audiences as incredibly enthusiastic, and avoided, she was sure, telling her what it was that had him so stressed. It was probably just his concern for her. She decided not to mention that Dr. Adams had advised she could go into labor any time now. She'd made all the necessary preparations. Her bag was packed and the list of phone numbers was tucked in her purse. If it happened when Stani was still on the road, everything was in place to get him home as soon as he was needed. No reason to worry him now.

It was a sweet interlude, and then he was gone again in less than twenty-four hours. Emily tried to remind herself that there were things to look forward to. Penny would be coming in on Friday evening. They would have their heart-to-heart as promised, and Penny would help her set up the nursery. It was tempting to do it herself. But she had promised Stani she would wait. Still, it couldn't hurt to stow all the tiny clothes in the wardrobe. And maybe Mamie could help her hang the curtains. Boredom was probably something she'd never complain of again, she mused. But right now, there were far too many hours in the day to just sit and think. Besides, she would rest better once the nursery was in some sort of order. And Stani would never need to know.

Obviously, the surgeon had not agreed that the cause of his pain was 'nothing.' John studied the sleeping face in the rear view mirror. If anything, Stani seemed even more strained than before the appointment. But he had not wanted to discuss it, racing home as soon as he left the doctor's office, saying he'd have to think things over when he had the time.

As if aware that he was being watched, Stani opened his eyes and leaned forward. "Could we pull over somewhere for a cup of tea?"

A sign not far up the road advertised home style dining and John pulled in. A typical Pennsylvania Dutch building with colonial furnishings, the place was almost deserted in the middle of the afternoon. The waitress who greeted them suggested they might enjoy sitting outside and led them to a table on the brick courtyard at the rear. Songbirds chorused in the one huge oak that shaded the space, and the smell of honeysuckle was heavy on the warm air. Just the place for good man-to-man, John thought.

"Want to tell me what he said, or are you still thinking things over?"

Stani stared into the distance for a moment, his face grim. "It's a bone spur. He said it's not that uncommon after a break heals."

"What's he going to do about it?"

Another moment of studying the tablecloth and he sighed. "There's nothing to do but remove it. He injected it with some kind of steroid, but he said that only masks the pain. I'm supposed to take anti-inflammatory pills until I decide to have the surgery."

"And when will that be?" John found himself gazing into the distance now. The look on the boy's face was too hard to watch.

"I told him I couldn't possibly do it now." Running his hands into his hair, he let out another long sigh. "He said it will only get worse. He predicted it wouldn't be long before he'd hear from me. All I have to do is call and he'll set it up."

"I see. It doesn't sound like anything so serious. How long would you be laid up?"

"Six weeks. Just a few days in hospital and a little therapy after it heals. I know it's nothing compared to before. But how can I put Emily through that, right after the babies arrive? I need to be able to help her and the doctor said my arm would be in a sling for several weeks. I'm going to wait, maybe until the babies are a couple of months old. It will mean canceling some things next fall, but at least I will have been there for them in the beginning."

John had to smile at his logic. Babies, if his memories were correct, only needed more attention as they grew. Of course, Stani wouldn't know that. "Very noble in theory, lad. But truth is she'll need you to be fit later on even more than now. And how do you propose to hide this from her until the time seems right? She's bound to catch on, you know."

With a little snort, he agreed. "Just taking an aspirin gets her attention. What would you do, John?"

He thought carefully. "Hard to say. What would Emily tell you to do?"

Stani's face fell. He was defeated before he started. "You know what she'd say. Have the surgery."

"Well, there's your answer. Once she finds out, you won't have to make the choice."

Stani played with his spoon, drained his cup and stared into the distance a while longer. "Still, I think I should wait as long as I can. I'll get these concerts behind me and at least hold my sons a few times first."

John raised a brow. "Sons? For sure?"

Stani grinned. He seemed more relaxed, now that he'd made his decision. "She's positive. Haven't you noticed she's always right?"

Chapter Forty-eight

On Friday just after lunch, Stani phoned to say he had arrived in Chicago for the symphony's annual gala fundraiser. It was an honor to be on the bill, but getting there from Washington had been tricky. There was rain all over the Midwest and flights were being canceled left and right. He would go straight to the concert hall, rehearse and stay there for the dinner and concert. He would call when he finally got back to the hotel, just to make sure she and Penny were doing okay.

Mamie seemed to be coming down with a cold. At one o'clock, Emily insisted she go home and go to bed. It was against her better judgment, Mamiè argued. But in the end, she agreed that a few hours of extra rest might be what she needed to ward off an illness. With a long list of cautions against doing anything more than sitting until her company came, Mamie changed out of her uniform and left to catch the one-thirty bus.

At two-fifteen, Penny phoned from Boston. Her flight was delayed because of a storm in the Midwest and she would not arrive in New York until five now, which of course meant traffic would be at its worst. Was Emily going to be okay until she got there?

"Of course I will. I think I'll take a nap. That way we can stay up late talking, and I won't doze off on you." Emily laughed sleepily into the phone. "I can't wait to catch up on things, Pen."

She stretched on the couch, propped on all the throw pillows she could stuff behind her, and tried to fall asleep. For a while, she drifted, the silence of the apartment disturbed only by the hum of the refrigerator or a moan from the depths of the building. She mused on how even a building this size could settle and sway, making its own melody with creaking floor boards and sighing windows. Music, she thought, would be nice. But she would have to get up, walk all the way across the room, and then try to settle herself on the couch again. Not worth the effort.

At three, or maybe a few minutes after, because she thought she had heard the clock on the shelf strike the hour, the first pain woke her with a start. It didn't last long, but it was definitely a contraction. After a minute or two, she got up, looking at her watch to be sure of the time. She went to the bathroom, brushed her teeth and combed her hair. In the bedroom, she changed from the caftan and sandals, her customary at home attire these days, into a dress and proper shoes. From the wardrobe, she took her bag and set it in the living room by the elevator door. All of that had taken less than twenty minutes. The second pain came right on time. She applied the test she had learned to use in the ER, known as the 'floor test.'

If a pregnant woman believed she had started labor, calling in on a Friday afternoon when all the regular doctors had left for the weekend, the nurse was taught to ask if, during the supposed contraction, the abdomen was as hard as a concrete floor. If the answer was 'not quite,' the woman was told to wait until it was. If, on the other hand, the answer was 'yes,' she was told to come in immediately. During the second pain, Emily prodded her belly, demanding that she maintain her objectivity. There was no room for doubt; she definitely passed the floor test.

Phoning the doctor's office, she reached his answering service. He had left the office, but was on call. She waited another ten minutes, walking around the living room, tidying up the couch and getting a glass of water from the kitchen. Exactly twenty minutes after the last pain, the third hit, during which the phone rang. With very little conversation, the doctor agreed to meet her in the ER at four-thirty.

Next, she dialed Robert's number and when he answered, she said simply that she needed to run a quick errand. Robert promised he would be there for her in ten minutes, traffic allowing.

Writing out a carefully worded note for Penny, which she intended to leave with the doorman, Emily went into the bathroom and gathered several towels from the linen cabinet. Better safe than sorry, she reasoned. If her water broke in the back seat of the limo on the way to the hospital, she would be prepared. Tucking the towels under her arm, she picked up her purse, the note and her suitcase and with one last look, took the elevator to the lobby.

The fourth pain hit just as the doors opened, and she stepped out. Bracing herself against the wall, she waited until it passed, then approached the doorman in his little cubicle. She gave him specific instructions. Her friend would be arriving by taxi from the airport sometime around six. He was to hold her cab, give her the note and take her bags up to the loft once she was on her way. She described Penny carefully, petite, dark short hair, and probably full of questions.

The doorman was no green boy. He knew right away that Mrs. Moss was in labor and for some reason she was going to the hospital alone. Solicitously, he took her arm and carried her bag to the waiting car. With a speaking look to the driver, he put her in the back seat, and heard her give the man directions in her usual sweet, calm way.

"Robert, take me to the hospital, the emergency entrance, please. There's no rush. And don't pay any attention to me. I'm fine."

John got the message at six. Stani was in the banquet room having dinner with a hundred and fifty other people when a stage hand came to the dressing room with the note. Milo had called. Emily was in the hospital. Per her strict instructions, Stani was not to be told until after the concert. John was to make whatever arrangements necessary to return to New York tonight. That was all. He didn't say why she was in the hospital, if she was in labor or for some other reason. John did some quick mental calculations. She was just at eight months. Could be labor, or just a precaution. Not that it mattered, he knew. Stani was needed, and it was his job now to get him back there.

His thoughts starting to race, he felt his pulse quicken. This was just the sort of thing he liked best, having to think on his feet, face a sudden challenge and execute a plan. With a spring in his step, he tucked the note in his pocket and went in search of the house manager.

When Stani came off stage after the final curtain call, he was mildly surprised to find John standing in the wing. At first, he went on talking with the conductor, complimenting the pianist on a fine performance, and drinking the mineral water the stage hand had offered him. Gradually, it occurred to him that John was waiting for him. And then somehow he knew.

"Let's go, lad. There's a plane waiting." At Stani's wide-eyed, wordless question, John took the violin and packed it in its case, jerking his head toward an exit.

"A plane?" That was the best he could do. The other questions were lodged in his chest, whirling in his brain, forming a massive knot in his gut.

"The chairman of the symphony board loaned you his private jet.

Just stick with me, son. You'll get your breath back in a minute." Steering him out the door to the waiting car, he pushed him into the back seat and climbed in beside him.

"Labor?" Stani managed to breathe at last, as the car pulled away sharply.

"Don't know. Milo just said she's in the hospital." He handed Stani the note. It would be easier, he hoped, for him to read it himself, rather than go on with these one-word quizzes.

Little else was said as they boarded the plane. John helped him out of his tailcoat and provided a clean shirt, doing up the studs for him when he could see that the trembling fingers would never accomplish the task. The attendant on the plane, a polite young woman who had evidently been told they were on an emergency mission, offered food and drink. To John's surprise, Stani ate a sandwich and drank some tea, though he doubted the boy was aware of what he was doing. His eyes were dark and his lips tight, as if he were engaged in some intense internal discussion.

They were told the flight would last two hours and John suggested Stani try to nap. "You'll want to be awake when you get there, son."

"I'll be awake. I'll never sleep again, until I know she's all right." Turning to look out into the darkness, he folded his arms over his chest and clenched his jaw. John gave up trying to comfort him. He understood that this was just part of the process. Every man worth his salt went through the same kind of torture.

Penny had tried to stay with Emily as long as possible. They had lied, saying Penny was her sister, since only family was allowed in the labor room. But finally the nurse had insisted she leave, after giving Emily something in her IV to make her relax. They would be taking her into surgery shortly and Penny could wait in the designated area. It was after nine o'clock, and before they had given Emily the epidural, the labor pains had been less than ten minutes apart and very intense. She intended to stay awake for the C-section, so she could be sure the babies were okay, she had told the doctor in a voice that suggested there would be no argument. Penny was impressed with how calm and in control Em was. She was practically telling the nurses how to do their jobs, but they hadn't seemed offended. There had been plenty of conversation and laughter in between the contractions.

As they rolled her through the swinging doors, Emily had waved a drowsy hand, and with a lump in her throat, Penny had said, "see ya later." Then she had gone to sit alone in the waiting room. At least she could finally let go the hold on her emotions. Milo, she knew, had already gone to meet Stani and John at the airport, although he would have a while to wait. She suspected he just wanted to get out of the hospital, since he hadn't even been allowed to see Emily when he arrived. Penny had told him exactly what Emily said she wanted him to do, and he had made a phone call from the nurses' station. She had no idea what the plan was to get Stani and John home, but Milo had sent a message back to the labor room by a nurse, saying that he was to meet them at the airport around midnight.

Wiping at tears that insisted on falling, Penny tried to pray. Emily was completely confident, she knew. But Penny needed the comfort of prayers answered. She had not come to New York tonight prepared to go through such an ordeal. She had been looking forward to unburdening her own worries and benefiting from Emily's sound council. Instead, she'd been handed a note by a doorman who clearly questioned whether she was up to the job, and then had to stare down an admissions nurse who most closely resembled a bulldog. As if by telepathy, Emily had asked her attending nurse to page her "sister," and Penny had heard her name sounding over the loudspeaker. With a glare at the bulldog, she'd been ushered back to Emily's cubicle.

Emily had confessed that her experience in the ER had prepared her for the need to bend the rules. Besides, she chuckled, her face growing red as another contraction came on, she needed a sister tonight more than any other time in her life, even if she had to invent one. They had held hands and Emily had assured her that everything was going normally. The doctor certainly seemed in no hurry to get her into surgery, and then it turned out he was also attending two other patients, dashing in to check on Emily every now and then. He was young and smiling, asking when Stani would make it in, as if they had all the time in the world to wait for him. Penny at one point wanted to scream at him that it wasn't Stani having labor pains, to just get it over with. But Emily had been so patient that she was instantly ashamed of herself. She thought Emily might actually be glad Stani wasn't there, so that when he did arrive, it would all be over and the babies would be there for him to see.

Watching the clock, Penny realized no one had told her how long this might take. She was hungry and her neck ached from hours of tension. She should try to find a vending machine, or at least a coffee pot somewhere. It was after eleven when she finally met the doctor coming out of the waiting room. He'd been looking for her, he said with a grin, to tell her she was the proud aunt of twin boys. Healthy, hearty boys, each weighing in at a little over five pounds. "So much alike I thought for a minute I was just seeing double." The doctor had looked a lot like a kid who'd just won his first ballgame, Penny thought, triumphant and a little giddy. But he'd put a very sympathetic arm around her shoulders when she'd dissolved into relieved tears. Then she realized he hadn't said anything about Emily.

"She's doing fine. Her blood pressure dropped for a few minutes, but we got her stabilized quickly. She'll be in recovery for a couple of hours. But the babies will be down in the nursery in thirty minutes or so. Why don't you go say hello? You'll recognize them right away. They have red hair." He grinned again, and turned to go back through the swinging doors. Fortunately there was a chair nearby, because Penny found her knees shaking and knew she would have to sit a minute or two. She had to get her head around all this. Emily was now the mother of twins. Boys. Identical twin boys. With red hair. It was just a little too much to take in, after the night she'd had. But after a few minutes of weary contemplation, she was ready to move on to the next step. She headed off to ask directions to the nursery. She would be the first member of the family to greet them, she realized, so she put on what she hoped was her proudest 'auntie' smile as she went.

Milo was waiting outside the hangar, talking with Robert next to the car. He immediately held out his hand. "Congratulations, my boy. By now, I'm sure you're a father."

"What do you mean? You don't know for sure? You just left her there alone?" Why was it that Milo could rile him, even at a time like this?

"They wouldn't allow me to see her, Stani. But her friend—Penny is it?—was coming out with regular updates. All was going well, and they were planning to do the surgery an hour or so ago. By the time we get you to the hospital, it should all be over." Milo was urging him into the car, that confident smile on his face, as if he could personally ensure everything was all right.

John put a steadying hand on Stani's arm as he slid in next to him. "I'm sure it's all fine, lad. It's not as if Milo could be of much use there." In the front seat, Milo was saying something to Robert about Emily. Stani tried to listen, but there was a roaring in his ears, as if the sound of his own breathing were echoing in his head.

"She's cool as a cucumber, Miss Emily is. Just got in the car and said, sweet as you please, 'Drive me to the hospital, Robert. And there's no need to rush.' Went right in on her own, told them who she was and what she wanted. Next thing I know, she's already gone back with the doctor. Cool as a cucumber, yes, sir." Robert sounded decidedly proud and pleased with his role in the night's events.

Stani wanted to ask questions, but somehow the words refused to form. Eventually, he hoped, he would learn exactly what had happened tonight. Right now he just needed to keep his head together until he could see her for himself. Once he looked into her eyes, held her hand, he would be all right.

John had to hand it to Milo. He seemed to know just what he was doing once they arrived at the hospital. He went straight to a woman sitting behind a glass window, spoke in his usual ingratiating manner, and in the next few minutes, not one but two doctors came out to talk to Stani. John tried to listen closely to what they were telling the boy, because he knew in his present state of mind, most of it was going right past him. The only thing of real importance, it seemed to John, was the repeated assurance from both Emily's doctor and the babies' pediatrician that everyone was doing fine. Emily was still in the recovery room, but the babies were in the nursery ready for them to see.

A nurse led them through the maze of corridors, Milo striding along behind them with a definite bounce in his step. John was staying close at hand, keeping a watch on Stani's face. He was pale and had yet to smile. The thought crossed John's mind that he hoped the lad wasn't about to pass out. He had the look of man in shock, truth be told.

Penny was standing by the big picture window, and when she heard them coming, she turned with a huge smile for Stani. "Well, it's about time! Your boys have been asking when their father was going to put in an appearance." She stepped aside and beyond the glass, under the bright white lights of the nursery, a row of identically blanketed infants in identical little clear boxes could be seen. A nurse wearing a surgical mask had obviously recognized the new arrivals. With a smile in her eyes, she pushed two of the boxes forward on their rolling carts, until they were right next to the window.

It was then that Stani finally appeared to realize just what had happened tonight. He let out a sound that seemed to contain a sob, a laugh and a huge sigh of relief. His face broke into a smile that stretched its expressive limits. With Milo on one side and John on the other, he stared unblinking at the incredibly tiny infants, each wrapped in a blue blanket. While making the appropriate expressions of admiration, John felt himself fighting a rush of unmanly emotions. Penny, on the other hand, was weeping openly, with big tears sliding into her smiling lips.

One of the babies was crying, its face red and wrinkled with the effort, while the other slept, its tiny features smooth and pale. Nothing but their heads was visible outside the blankets. Each wore a white cap, like a miniscule toboggan, and the nurse removed them with a flourish, as though unveiling a pair of trophies. Sure enough, both tiny heads were covered in soft fuzz the color of new copper.

"Well, my boy, what do you think of your sons?" Milo had held back longer than John would have expected. He was obviously bursting with pride.

"Beautiful. They're beautiful, aren't they?" His eyes were fixed on the two infant forms, as the nurse held up first one and then the other, unwrapping them and showing off fingers and toes. "They're so little, but look, they're breathing all on their own! Emily was worried they'd need to be in incubators at first. But they're fine. Look at them, John!" Without turning, Stani urged him closer. "Look at them!"

"I see them, lad. They're as fine as anything I've ever seen. That fellow on the left is a bit cranky, but I suppose he'll calm down like his brother soon enough." He chuckled as the baby angrily flailed his arms about at being so rudely exposed.

Penny spoke up. "Oh, don't let him fool you, he was screaming just as loudly earlier. I could hear him through the glass. What I want to know is how you're going to tell them apart. I've been staring at them for thirty minutes, and I can't see one thing different about them."

"Emily will be able to tell. She says there's always some little thing, a freckle or a birthmark or something. She read up on it, just to be prepared in case they were identical. And they are, aren't they? One is supposed to be bigger than the other, but I can't see any difference." Stani still hadn't taken his eyes off the babies. Now returned to their beds both were squirming about and scrunching their faces in a variety of grimaces and smirks.

"I don't think a couple of ounces are going to show, son. What are you planning to call them?"

"We have a few choices picked out. Emily wanted to meet them first, before we decided. To be sure the names suited them." He seemed distracted, his attention still riveted on his sons.

A nurse came up and spoke to Milo, then stood waiting, an indulgent smile on her lips.

"Stani, Emily is in her room now, if you want to see her. I took the liberty of arranging for a suite, so you can stay with her if you like." When Stani finally turned from the window, Milo looked down at him with a flicker of concern in his eyes. "I knew you wouldn't want to leave her, and you need to get some rest, my boy."

The nurse led Stani away, leaving the two of them to stand with Penny and watch the ongoing display. Each movement, each wave of a hand, or turn of a head seemed worthy of note. John wondered if the nurses assumed this odd threesome to be members of the same family. But then, in spite of their various connections to Stani and Emily, they were in fact the family these babies would grow up with, a family just as loving and proud as any other. Grandparents, aunts and uncles came in an assortment anyway, and as long as they filled their roles with appropriate measures of love and support, how could it matter by what route they came to the jobs? No one could worry that these two wee lads would lack for anything, with an impresario for a grandfather, a lawyer for an aunt and an ex-copper as uncle. Not that they would care, John mused. All they needed to know was how much they were treasured for the miracle of their own tiny selves.

There was a nurse in the room, checking the flow of various tubes and charting her findings. She looked up with a smile and touched Emily's arm. "You have a visitor, dear."

Her eyes opened, heavy-lidded and clouded with sleep, and ever so slowly it seemed to Stani, they turned his way. For some reason, he had frozen in place, just inside the door, fighting for control before he could go to her. But when she saw him and smiled, his legs took him in two strides to the bed, and he clasped the hand she held out, raising it to his lips.

"Have you seen them?" Her voice was soft and hoarse.

"Yes. They're beautiful."

She smiled again, her eyes closing, giving up the fight. "You said your sons would be handsome."

"So I did. I was wrong. These lads are the most beautiful things I've ever seen, aside from their mother, of course. How are you feeling, darling girl? I hear you had quite a night." The nurse pushed a chair close behind him and he sat down, still holding her hand.

"She's just had something for pain, so she may be in and out for a while now. There's a couch over there, all made up for you when you want to get a little sleep yourself. Just ring if you need anything." Quietly, the door closed behind her and at last they were alone.

There was so much he wanted to say, how desperately grateful he was, how wretchedly sorry that he hadn't been there, and most of all how much he loved her. But the sight of her face, so pale and drawn, the deep circles beneath her eyes, and the sound of her soft, shallow breathing held him in terrified silence. The doctor had assured him that she was fine, just a little tired after the ordeal of labor and the surgery. There had been some problem with her blood pressure after the delivery, but again he had been told that was nothing to be concerned about, just a reaction to one of the drugs.

With an overwhelming wave of all the emotions he had experienced in the past hours, he dropped his head on the sheet, pressing her hand to his cheek. Sobs, silent and painful, tore through his chest. He had no idea how long he struggled there, fighting for breath and acknowledging his need for this kind of release. When her hand came to rest in his hair, her fingers twining in the same way that had always made his nerves jangle with desire, he lifted his face. She was watching him with the tenderest of smiles.

"Poor Stani. You've had a rough night, haven't you? But you're here now. We're all here now. Tell me about them. I didn't get to see them, you know. I stayed awake through the whole thing, and then I passed out before I could see them." Her voice was so low he strained to catch her words.

"They're identical, two little red-faced, bright-eyed, very feisty boys. They each weigh a little over five pounds, and, I hate to say it, but they both appear to have red hair." She smiled, her eyes closed again. "They're perfect, darling. All ten fingers and toes. A matched pair. Penny is afraid we'll never be able to tell them apart."

"Penny was great. She stayed with me the whole time." Her lids fluttered, but clearly the weight was too much.

"I'm so glad she was here." He wiped away tears with his free hand, shaking off the returning urge to cry.

"We lied. We said she was my sister." A hint of a grin curved her lips.

He chuckled. "Did you?" He couldn't resist touching her hair, smoothing it off her forehead.

"Stani, don't leave, not for a while. Please." She shifted slightly on the bed, a frown crossing her face.

"I'm not leaving at all, darling girl. Milo got you the VIP suite, so I can stay with you. I must admit, Milo can be very thoughtful at times."

But she was asleep, the frown still shadowing her face. He sat for a long while, just staring at her. For the first time, he noticed that she was incredibly slim again, her body strangely flat where the huge bulge of baby had been. He fought the powerful need to take her in his arms, making himself content with holding her hand, twining his fingers in hers. Exhausted, he thought briefly of stretching out on the couch for just a few minutes, but then Emily sighed and he knew he wouldn't move from the bedside.

The nurse came in, and he realized he'd dozed, sitting in the chair. She checked the tubes, peered under the sheet for a minute or two and then, with a sympathetic smile, left just as quietly as she'd come. Through the slats of the blinds, he could see the first glow of sunrise. Today would be his first day as a father. He had no idea what that might entail, but his heart skipped a beat at the thought.

Chapter Forty-nine

By eight that morning a stream of nurses had come and gone, each doing some mysterious thing to Emily which required his leaving the room. On one such occasion, as he stood waiting in the hallway, John arrived with a suitcase.

"Thought you might still be asleep."

"What do you mean 'still'? I never went to bed. Thanks for this, though. I think a shower might be just the thing." He was a sight, he knew, in his wrinkled tux shirt, which had somehow lost two of its studs.

"How's she doing?" John leaned against the wall, prepared to keep him company.

"I can't tell. These nurses are doing something to her all the time. I think she's okay. She slept most of the night, or what was left of it. She hasn't seen the babies yet, and she's getting pretty anxious. One nurse said the doctor has to see her first, but he's in another delivery."

"Relax, lad. That's the way of hospitals, wait and wonder. I stopped by the nursery and both your little ones were sleeping." John grinned, a proud twinkle in his eye. "By the way, I took Penny to your place last night, in case you're wondering."

"Oh my gosh! I never even gave her a thought!"

"Don't worry. She was ready to get some sleep. Being in a labor room was a new experience for the girl. She swears she'll never have children now." Again he grinned, seeming to say these young people were a constant source of amusement.

The nurse came out, signaling that Stani could go back into the room. Eying John, she asked if he was family. "Yes. Can he go in?" Not waiting for permission, he pushed John through the door.

By now, Emily was wide awake. Her color was much improved and she was sitting up higher in the bed. Her hair had apparently just been brushed and she had changed into one of her own nightgowns. When she caught sight of John, she smiled and held out her hand. "Uncle John, how are you this fine morning?"

With a laugh, he kissed her cheek. "I'm a sight better than this lad here. Did you have to keep him up all night?"

"He is a fright, isn't he?" She reached up to touch the stubble on Stani's cheek. "Why don't you get cleaned up, darling? I'd hate for our babies to see you looking so scruffy. John can keep me company while you shower."

It was an order, he knew. Obediently, he took his bag and headed for the bathroom. As he prepared to shower, he listened to her quizzing John about the babies. With a grin and a shake of his head, he accepted that their sons would be the only topic of conversation for the foreseeable future.

The doctor finally arrived at nine, looking by now completely exhausted. He had delivered four babies in the past twelve hours, he declared, including their two. He was headed home, as soon as he checked Emily over. Again, Stani left the room, standing at the door hoping to catch what the doctor was saying to her. When the nurse beckoned to him to rejoin them, the doctor was just washing his hands in the bathroom sink. His first words were all Stani really needed to hear.

"She's doing fine. I think we can have the nursery send up the babies now. Just remember not to overdo, Emily. And if you need the pain meds, take them. Martyrdom is not a virtue, not on this ward. The nurses will get you up later for a little walk. You probably know the routine as well as they do, but try to let them take care of you. Please?" His weary grin produced a nod from Emily.

"I'll try, I promise. Just let me hold my babies, and I'll be the model patient."

"Ha! No nurse is ever a model patient." He gave her a little pat on the knee and started for the door. "You have your work cut out for you, so get some rest while you can. I'll see you in the morning."

It seemed another eternity before the doors at last opened to admit two nurses pushing two little beds. The look in Emily's eyes, as she sat forward with a grimace to get a better look, brought a lump to Stani's throat and the threat of more tears. That was love, he knew, in its purest form that lit her face as the first baby was placed in her arms. The infant was making soft gurgling sounds, its tiny fingers reaching out over the edge of the blanket as if to touch her. Deftly, she unwrapped him, examining him as if he were the rarest treasure. Stani couldn't take his eyes off her, marveling at the way her hands controlled the little body, even as it wriggled and squirmed. His wife as mother was a fascinating new being, more beautiful than he had ever seen her.

He realized with a jolt that the nurse was now holding the other twin, waiting as if she expected him to take it from her. "Here, Father, there's one for you, too." Her eyes twinkled, as she held the bundle toward him.

"Go ahead, Stani, just like we practiced." Now Emily was watching him, as she cradled the baby in the bend of her arm. He mimicked her pose, and to his dismay, the nurse deposited the second twin unceremoniously in his arms. The baby stared up at him, the dark eyes seeming to take his measure.

Removing the little white cap, the nurse chuckled. "No doubt where he gets that hair. You two enjoy your babies. We'll be back in a while. And if you want to try nursing them, go ahead. All they've had so far is a little sugar water." The nurses were gone, leaving the four of them alone for the first time.

"Do you like them, darling?" Her little smile said she was teasing, but his protest rose immediately.

"Like them? They're the most amazing things I've ever seen. But they're so tiny. I didn't expect them to be so tiny." He touched the coppery fuzz with the tip of his finger, and Emily laughed softly.

"I told you they'd have red hair. Isn't it wonderful? My three red-haired men."

He continued to examine the infant, as it seemed to solemnly return his gaze. "Do you think he can see me? I thought babies couldn't actually see at first. He certainly seems to be giving me the once over." He glanced up and his breath caught in his throat. Emily had opened her gown and was urging the baby to nurse with a stroke of her finger on his cheek. He watched with wonder as the baby responded, and was soon making soft, satisfied little noises as it nursed. He wanted to tell her how moved he was at this new sight, but words would have been an intrusion on the mystical moment between mother and child. Looking back to the infant resting so naturally in the bend of his arm, he acknowledged that fatherhood was going to be the most powerfully emotional experience he'd ever known. This bursting sensation in his chest was love, he now knew, and nothing in his life before could have prepared him for the fierceness with which it flowed through him.

Emily was smiling, a serene little smile that now brought to mind a Renaissance Madonna. The baby's tiny hand circled the tip of her index finger, and she said softly, "He has hands like you, darling. Look how long their fingers are." With the greatest care, he uncovered a hand and laid his own finger against the palm. In response, the baby grasped it with amazing strength, and made a little cooing noise, as if pleased with his efforts.

"Son, that's quite a grip you have there." The words came so easily, without any thought, and Emily laughed softly. She was bundling her twin back in his blanket, carefully placing him on the bed beside her. He was sleeping peacefully, his lips still pursed from nursing.

"I dreamed of how you'd look, holding our child. Oh, Stani, I love you so much." There were tears rolling down her cheeks, and he longed to wipe them away. But the baby in his arms squirmed and made a sudden mewling sound of discontent.

"What did I do wrong?"

"Nothing, darling. Hand him to me. He just wants to be fed, too."

So it went, that first morning of fatherhood. Every hour brought some new experience, all of which Emily handled with complete competence. She was calm and patient, explaining everything to him carefully, training him to be her assistant, she laughed. By the time the nurses came to take the babies back to the nursery, he felt decidedly more confident in his new role. The father of twins, she assured him, learned quickly, or ran away. And she knew very well, she said as she closed her eyes and drifted off to sleep, that he had no intention of running anywhere.

It had not occurred to him that she would be in so much pain. When the nurse came to get her up, and she walked to the bathroom for the first time, he was crushed by the slow, halting steps and the way she hunched over, holding one hand to her abdomen. By the time she returned to the bed, it was clear she was exhausted. The nurse offered her an injection, but she refused, asking instead for something milder.

"Emily, the doctor told you not to be a martyr. Shouldn't you have something that really helps?"

"No. I'll be fine. Don't look so worried. I have at least twenty stitches, Stani. They're going to hurt a little bit. But I don't want drugs. I want to be able to enjoy my babies when they come back. Be a love and get me some water, will you? Who would have thought going to the bathroom could be such a marathon?" With an unconvincing smile, she shifted on the bed, struggling to adjust the pillows behind her.

"Here. Let me. And don't tell me about pain, love. I screamed like a baby myself, every four hours after I woke from my drug-induced nirvana. Drugs, my darling, are not just for sissies, you know. And I'll feel better if you're not in so much pain."

But she was not to be persuaded, he learned quickly. And each time the babies were brought to her, she seemed to improve. Motherly love, he decided, was the reason women were so much tougher than men. Just the sight of her children eased whatever distress she felt, and brought that beatific smile to her lips. In between visits, she slept, deep, renewing sleep, a look of studied satisfaction on her face.

Penny came to visit early in the afternoon, reporting that she had been hard at work on the nursery. She had also made all the calls on the list, spreading the news to the valley. "Lil will be on a plane in ten days, ready to start work, she said. And Jack cried, Em. I mean he was so choked up Martha Jean had to take the phone to get the details. There are already gifts being delivered to the apartment from all over the place. Word sure must have gotten out fast."

The hospital room was rapidly filling with flowers, as well. When Milo appeared a few minutes later, the reason became clear. After kissing Emily and clapping Stani on the shoulder, he declared that the babies were by far the most remarkable sight he'd ever seen. "I released a statement to the press this morning, Stani, announcing the birth. I wasn't sure what to do regarding the last two concert dates. Will you cancel, or can you tear yourself away?"

"Cancel," he said firmly. Emily immediately laid a hand on his arm.

"No, darling. It would be a shame to disappoint so many people. I'll be here for at least ten days. By the time I'm home, you'll be finished. Don't cancel, Milo. He'll go."

With a sigh of resignation, Stani nodded. "My wife has spoken. Apparently, I'll go." Emily might be confined to a hospital bed, but she was no less in charge. If he had ever doubted the strength of her will, he was now convinced nothing could hold her down for long.

By Wednesday, when he left for Philadelphia, Stani had decided fatherhood was his true calling. He loved everything about caring for his boys. Even diaper changing, after the initial shock, had proved a pleasant sort of bonding time, as he refined the art of talking nonsense to the baby to take his mind off the task at hand. Feeding time was magical. While Emily nursed one twin, he bottle fed the other, and they sat together, the four of them, in the sweetest kind of family circle. Of course, the mysterious technique of burping had been a challenge, and once mastered could still produce that less than desirable regurgitation. But he had learned to protect his clothes, and the sound of a little belch near his ear gave him enormous satisfaction.

With each passing day, and night—the babies came for feedings every four hours around the clock—he felt increasingly confident. With Emily close by, of course. The thought of being left alone with the twins still gave him pause. But he was sure in time he would be able to handle even that. It was difficult to grasp the idea that these babies would be his forever. He tried to imagine having them with him everywhere he went, always there to be loved and cared for. Everything about family life was an unfolding mystery to him, but he was certain he was going to love it.

They had named the twins with very little debate. Emily's first choices had been Ian and Andrew, and Stani had agreed completely that these lads seemed well suited for the names. "Neither of them looks like a 'Ludwig' or a 'Felix', for sure," Emily had said as they stood over the little cribs studying the identical sleeping faces. Second names took a bit more thought, and after overriding her suggestion of Stanley for one of them, they decided on Ian Patrick and Andrew Haynes. They tested the names, saying them in various tones, from fondest greetings to sternest warnings.

"Now which is which, do you think?" Stani had yet to see any significant difference in the twins, relying on the tiny wrist bands to tell them apart. At the moment, his sons were still "Moss, Emily, #1" and "Moss, Emily, #2."

"Number One should be Ian, I think. He is the first born, and I always think the names in that order somehow. So this is Ian, and this is Andrew." She touched each of the babies on the head to make the naming official. "There, that was simple enough."

"What will not be so simple is keeping them straight once they outgrow those little armbands."

"Oh, really, Stani, they're not that much alike. Look, Ian's ears are larger, and Andrew has a wrinkle on his nose. And Ian's eyebrows have more arch. Andrew has a tiny freckle, here on his cheek. I'm sure as they grow we'll be able to see more and more differences." Even Emily didn't sound completely confident.

"I'd be in favor of some sort of mark, maybe a discretely placed tattoo just to be sure we don't send Ian to Cambridge when it was really Andrew who was meant to go." He was rewarded for his foolishness by a tinkling laugh and a warm kiss.

"I'm so glad you're the father of my children. No one else would be half so much fun." He helped her back to bed, happy to see she was moving more comfortably. She was quickly returning to her old self, her color normal and the dark circles gone from beneath her eyes. Leaving her would have been impossible otherwise, he knew.

"So my total ineptitude hasn't discouraged you?"

"You're a natural. Those violinist's hands are perfectly suited to handling tiny newborns. And the way you talk to them, I could listen all day. I think my father must have talked to me like that. Jack said he read to me from Shakespeare, while I was still in my crib. I loved the way you explained to them what you were playing for these concerts." The faintest hint of a frown crossed her face. "They're going to miss you, while you're gone. I'm sure they'll wonder why their Papa isn't here." The frown dissolved into tears.

"I thought you wanted me to go! I would gladly have canceled." He perched on the edge of the bed, taking her in his arms.

"I know. I'm just being silly. Hormones again." She wiped at her tears, producing a shaky smile. "We'll be fine. We have an entire hospital staff at our beck and call. It's just been so nice having you here."

When the time came to say goodbye, Stani fought his own tears, and lost. It was Emily who comforted him, as he watched the little cribs roll through the door. "They'll be fine, darling. And when you get back on Sunday, we can all go home together."

"But I won't be here for their circumcisions. What if something goes wrong? I read that it can, you know."

She laughed, ruffling his hair. "Nothing will go wrong. It's not as if you could stand there and watch. It's all done without any ceremony whatsoever. Now stop looking for things to worry about. Go. Make a lot of people very happy, and then come back home to us." Taking his face between her hands, she kissed him with undisguised longing. "I love you, Stani Moss. Now go, before my hormones get the better of me again."

John was waiting in the hallway, and he laid a bracing hand on Stani's shoulder. "She'll be fine. And so will you, once you get your mind on something besides those babies."

With a wry grin, he shook his head. "No, John. There's never going to be anything else on my mind again. Even the music will have to take second place to them."

They stopped by the nursery for one last torturous look. Ian was sleeping, one hand tucked under his cheek, while Andrew was squirming in his crib, his tiny legs stretching beneath the blanket. "See, already they're showing their personalities. Ian tends to be easy going, but Andrew shows more ambition. I think Andrew may be the dominant twin. More like his mother, you know. He'll be the one to take charge."

John heaved a sigh, steering Stani away from the nursery window. "You know all this after five days? For a man who'd never even held a baby, you certainly have taken to fatherhood, lad. Now do you think you might focus on that violin again for a few days? I hear the house in Philadelphia is standing room only. Wouldn't want to give them a second-rate performance."

When he talked to her on the phone, he could picture her with the babies. When he closed his eyes to sleep, vivid images of them were etched against his eyelids. Everywhere he looked, in the hotel lobbies, in restaurants and on the streets, there were women pushing baby carriages, couples with small children in hand, even a double stroller with two little boys reaching over the sides of their seats. Had there always been so many babies in the world? Had he been blind until now? He watched with interest, taking note of the various equipages, wondering what Emily would say to the sort of sling he saw one woman wearing, a tiny head just visible over its folds.

To his surprise, he played with an intensely focused passion. His longing to be somewhere else translated into greater depth of emotion; yet at the conclusion of the piece, his mind went immediately back to his family. What were they doing now, how much formula had the bottle fed twin taken (always a source for concern, as Andrew clearly preferred mother's milk), and how was Emily's incision tonight? He phoned from the hotel the minute he returned, and to his dismay, realized he'd wakened her.

"I'm so sorry, love. I forgot how late it is." But she was full of forgiveness, answering his questions in a voice husky with sleep. "John says I'm obsessed with all things baby now. I went shopping. Aren't traveling fathers expected to return bearing gifts?"

"You went shopping? How sweet. Not that they need a thing. But of course, they'll expect you to bring them something." She laughed softly. "Stani, they're only a week old. You don't have to spoil them yet."

"And what about you, can I spoil you?" He pictured her there in the soft light of the hospital room, her hair spread over the pillow, her eyes dark and smoky.

"Oh, I suppose so. You didn't buy me something too, did you?"

"You'll have to wait and see. Now go back to sleep, darling girl. Oh, and Emily?"

"Yes, Stani?"

"Have I told how much I love you and our boys?"

"Yes, you have. But I'll never get tired of hearing you say it."

Chapter Fifty

Going home was an occasion for the entire family, odd assortment that they were. After John had packed them in the limo, Robert drove them to their building. The doorman, who had put Emily in the car to go to the hospital, beamed at them as he held the door and watched them make their way into the lobby. The new parents each carried a tiny blue blanket-wrapped bundle, while John lugged two diaper bags stuffed with going-home supplies. Robert followed with an impressive load of baggage, a far cry from the one little suitcase Emily had carried out just ten days earlier.

They had barely settled the twins in their cradle when the buzzer began to sound. First Milo with Jana, just returned from Canada and eager to meet the babies at last. Then Peg—who by now had named herself "Auntie Shannon"—her arms full of yet more gifts. The one thing she did best, she declared, was shop. The fascinating new world of New York's finest baby shops had become her playground. As everyone hovered over the cradle, talking in studied whispers, Emily met Stani's gaze across the room. Each knew that time was limited. The babies had thus far observed a strict schedule and would soon be ready for changing and feeding. And they were not accustomed to such an adoring audience.

While Emily prepared formula in the kitchen, Stani went to the nursery, searching out the necessary supplies. Sure that diapers were at the ready and the two rockers were in place, he checked his watch. If they were true to form, the twins should be about to make their needs known.

Meeting Emily in the hallway, he stopped long enough to gather her into his arms and kiss her gently. "Welcome home, darling."

"Welcome home, yourself." With a little wave, she passed on to the nursery.

Sure enough, Andrew began to cry, his unmistakably strident voice startling the group gathered around the cradle. Ian joined in with his customary whimper, which Stani knew would quickly build to a crescendo if ignored. Two angry little faces and four thrashing fists garnered soothing comments from the ladies, but Milo was clearly alarmed. As Stani lifted the first twin—this time Andrew would be the one to nurse—he laughed at Milo's horrified expression.

"Don't worry, it's not as bad as it sounds. A clean nappy and a good feeding, and he'll be a perfect little gentleman again." Nestling the baby on his shoulder, he started for the nursery. "Come along, lad. Mother's waiting."

He returned shortly for Ian, who by now had reached his full vocal potential. He chuckled at the furious tone of the baby's wail. "Sorry son, you'll just have to make do with your Papa this time." Collecting first the baby and then the bottle, he looked at the three astonished faces and grinned. "You didn't think I had it in me, did you? Now if you'll make yourselves at home, we'll be back in a bit. Unless one of you would care to change his diaper?"

♡

Emily was determined to keep to a strict routine, just as they had done in the hospital. It would at least allow her to catch a nap several times a day. If Stani could help her feed the babies at night, he could get some extra sleep while Lil filled in during the day. Surely three people could meet the needs of even the most demanding of infant twins. Of course, the babies were not all that demanding, she insisted. They were really very content, free of problems like colic or diaper rash. But they knew exactly when they wanted to be fed, and their tolerance for less than immediate attention was still very low.

She was so impressed with the way Stani had taken instantly to fatherhood. His fascination with everything the babies did kept him at the ready; he never seemed to tire of the steady round of changing and feeding. And he had a real gift for calming them, cradling them on his chest and talking softly. He said it must be the resonance that soothed them, but Emily was sure it had to do with the sweet tone in his voice. Already he had decided that Ian had more of his personality, contemplative and retiring, while Andrew was the robust, innovative type. It would be Andrew, he predicted, who spearheaded any schemes, while Ian would follow along, just to please.

"In other words, my son, Andrew, will get your son, Ian, into trouble. Is that what you're saying?" She looked at the infant sleeping in her arms, trying to picture a rough and tumble little boy leading his brother on some mischievous adventure.

"I wouldn't have phrased it quite that way, but I do think Andrew has more of your strong character and creative mind." Stani laid his cheek against the fuzzy little head resting on his shoulder. "Some of us are just followers, darling, who need braver souls to lead us forward."

"Nicely put. But you have to admit, they look like you. Already, I can see that strong jaw and those high cheekbones. It's too soon to be sure, but I think their eyes will be brown, as well." Carefully, she rose and laid Andrew in the cradle, then held out her hands for Ian. "Time for a nap, Papa. For all of us."

Reluctantly, he passed the baby to her. "I have to get some work done, darling. I promised Milo I'd go down to the office and look over the fall bookings. Europe awaits, remember?"

"I suppose. Right now that seems a very long way off. Don't be gone long, please?" She had already stretched on the couch, her eyes half closed. Stani was amazed by her ability to fall asleep whenever the opportunity presented. He had not yet acquired the skill.

"I have a couple of errands to run, but I won't be long. Where did Lil get off to?"

"Groceries. She has to learn the city way of shopping. No huge supermarkets here. So I gave her a list and a map and she headed off with the cart. Hopefully she won't end up lost." Still under the spell of actually residing in the Big Apple, Lil had been restless to get out and experience life in Manhattan. Emily had made it part of her duties to shop for groceries and rather than putting her in the car with Robert to run her errands, had bought the requisite folding wire cart for her to haul her purchases home in. Good practice, Emily said, for real life in New York.

Stani chuckled. "I wouldn't worry about Lil. She's another one of those brave leader types. I'm impressed with how much she's willing to take on. She and Mamie may come to blows over who does what, though."

"Mamie can handle her." Her voice was slurred as Stani bent to kiss her forehead.

"Sweet dreams." As the elevator door closed, he felt a twinge of sadness. Leaving them, even for an hour or two, left him anxious and distracted. So great was his focus on enjoying every minute of their infancy, he could easily neglect the work that would ensure his sons the best life he could provide. He shook his head, the same thought once again crossing his mind. How could any father walk away from his child? How could *his* father have walked away and never looked back?

He had believed after meeting Jamie Moss that he would never give him another thought. He had satisfied his life-long need to see his father; had recognized that while there were similarities, they were really just strangers with no common history or bond. But since the birth of his sons, he had more than once recalled the face of the man who had by some genetic accident passed on his red hair, his talent with a fiddle and his love of whisky. At some point in time, someone must have laid his son in his arms. How could it be that he had not possessed this overwhelming, all-consuming instinct to love and nurture him? Stani had never really known the details of Jamie's departure, but he knew it had been some time during his own first year of life. What kind of man would walk out on his wife and infant son, without any promise of support? What kind of man never worried if his child was safe and well, never had any desire to watch him grow or hear his first words? Jamie had admitted following Stani's career through the years, but he had never once tried to contact him. Where was the heart in a man who felt no connection with his own son, no interest in his well-being?

The bitter memories served one purpose. Stani now knew without a doubt that he was not his father's son. He was convinced that while he might have inherited some things from Jamie, he could never for even a moment consider abandoning his children. Rather, he would die trying to do his best for them, protect them and secure them from the hardships of life. The sensation of a tiny form resting over his heart—a memory he would carry with him wherever he went now—was enough to remind him that the sole purpose of his life was to love and provide for his family. Loving Emily had opened his heart, preparing him to join her in this life. Perhaps that was the difference; perhaps Jamie had not loved Stani's mother enough. He could forgive him, but he would never really understand him. Especially now that he knew what fatherhood felt like.

With these heavy thoughts still in his mind, he sat down with Milo to go over the European tour dates. To his surprise, Milo had put a great deal of care into the schedule. He pointed out that he had allowed for the possibility of Emily remaining in one city longer, while Stani traveled and performed in the region. In Italy, she might stay in Rome, while Stani went on to cities to the north and south. In Germany, she might remain in Frankfurt, in France she might like to stay in Paris. Not that he wouldn't make provisions for her to travel with Stani, but Milo thought they might like some options.

"I wonder if so much moving around might not be unsettling for the twins. This first tour it might be wise to allow for adjustments as we go along." There was no mistaking the note of protective concern in Milo's voice.

They agreed on the more flexible arrangements, talked about the need for accommodations for Lil and the probability that she would be recording with Stani later in the summer. As the talk wound down, Milo leafed through the papers on his desk, drawing a single sheet from the stack.

"This was brought to my attention. When I noticed you favoring your arm, I felt there might be something you had neglected to tell me in all the recent excitement." He laid the bill from the surgeon on the desk.

Stani felt himself blush. He had not anticipated having to explain to Milo his need to see the doctor. "It's nothing."

"Really? Why would you look so guilty if it were nothing? Stani, if you need to protect Emily from some problem, I fully understand. Your confidence would be safe with me."

He considered for a moment downplaying the situation. But as John had said, it would all come out eventually. In fact, the effect of the steroid injection was already beginning to wear off. His days of deception were numbered.

"A bone spur has developed at the site of the injury. I'll need to have surgery to remove it."

Milo seemed to take a moment to absorb the information. "When?"

"When I decide I can't stand the discomfort any longer. Right now seemed the worst possible time."

"Will you be recovered in time for these concerts? I can't in good conscience schedule dates I know you might not be able to make."

"I'm aware of that. If I go ahead soon, I'll be fine by late September. It's a matter of telling Emily and that seems unfair. She has her hands full, without having to take care of me."

A little smile crossed Milo's face. "What seems fair to you may seem dishonest to her. If I know anything about Emily it's that she would expect you to be honest with her."

Stani groaned. "You're right, of course. I'll tell her soon, and we'll have to decide together when the time would be right."

Again, Milo smiled. "Don't wait too long, my boy. She'll only be more upset if she thinks you've been hiding this from her. And I would imagine she can be quite a force to reckon with if displeased."

Stani had to grin. "You have no idea."

Stani gave the conversation with Milo a great deal of thought. Most intriguing was the idea that Milo had made such an effort to see that he and his family would have the best possible experience when he returned to touring. He hadn't expected that. But then he could not have anticipated any of the considerations Milo had given them, from the gift of the loft apartment, to his insistence on paying for the luxury hospital suite. Emily had said numerous times that he failed to give Milo proper credit. He had to acknowledge that the tension between them had almost disappeared. There had been a time in the past when the discovery that he had hidden something from Milo would have led to an argument, with Stani automatically going on the defensive. Instead, Milo had invited his confidence and been sympathetic to his position. The conversation had been genial, man to man, a rare thing between them at any time in their history.

The other thing that continued to turn in his thoughts, as he made his rounds and started for home, was the realization that he had to confess to Emily. Hiding something from her, no matter the reason, was too painful. As it was, he was taking medication on the sly, carefully avoiding lifting his arm in her presence, and praying she wouldn't—with that special sixth sense of hers—discover that he was in pain. He had argued the case for waiting at least until the twins were a month old, but even he recognized the reasoning seemed weak. Milo had been right. She would be even more upset when she learned he had hidden the truth. Everyone, including Milo, knew what a force his wife could be, and that he was no match for her.

Chapter Fifty-one

There was one downside to the joy of parenthood. It played havoc with a marriage. There was too much happening—around the clock—too many people bustling in and out, to permit a loving couple to spend any time actually loving each other. One or the other of them always seemed to be holding, feeding or changing a baby. Lil was on hand, Mamie was busily doing her job, Peg seemed to drop by at least once a day, and John was always hanging about, just in case he was needed. The loft was a space of over three thousand square feet, with numerous rooms aside from the huge living area. But other than locking themselves in a guestroom, they could never hope to be alone together for long. The nursery opened onto their bedroom, necessitating modesty and decorum at all times. Stani found himself longing for that summer at the farm when they had never seen another soul for days on end. Just an hour alone, without fear of interruption, would have been bliss.

How was he ever going to find the right moment to make his confession, with so much going on? He needed time to explain, to deal with whatever emotional fallout his news might bring, and most of all to come up with some sort of plan with Emily's help. If one of the babies needed her, she would race away from him in mid-sentence, he was sure. Or if Lil walked in on them, she would demand to know what had brought Emily to tears. And he shuddered to think of Peg getting involved. Emily was force enough; he certainly didn't need Peg bullying him, too.

So he waited, praying for the right moment. He wondered, though, if God might be leaving this one up to him. A lesson he needed to learn, or perhaps a form of penance, which he would have to suffer through alone.

The twins were three weeks old. He could hold on another week, until after their first visit to the pediatrician's office. Once the doctor confirmed what they could see for themselves, that the babies were flourishing, he would make time, find the opportunity, and get it over with. She would forgive him, he knew. It was getting through the actual moment, seeing that look in her eyes, the one that said she was disappointed in him, that terrified him.

Stani woke late in the morning, his shoulder aching. Emily had gotten up at dawn, he remembered, telling him to stay in bed. It was Lil's turn to feed this morning. But when he'd rolled over to go back to sleep, the ache had started. It had persisted through his fitful nap, and now he knew there would be no more sleeping.

There was no sound from the nursery, or anywhere else in the apartment that he could detect. Going into the bathroom, he took the bottle of pills from their hiding place in his shaving kit, swallowed two and turned on the shower. A long, hot, pounding shower would help, he was sure. As the steam clouded the glass doors, he flexed his arm, testing its limits. Not good. The doctor had been right. He couldn't take much more, knowing relief was available.

He heard Emily come into the bathroom just as he turned off the water. He could see her through the fogged glass, apparently searching for something on the counter, pushing around bottles of baby shampoo and lotion. Grabbing a towel, he wrapped it around his waist and opened the shower door. As her hand came to rest on the big brown pill bottle, he caught his breath, waiting for her to push it aside in her search. Instead, she picked it up, reading the label, her head tilted at a curious angle.

Slowly, she turned to him. It struck him that her intensely pained expression was on a par with what he might have expected at the discovery of a whisky bottle tucked in his sock drawer, or a letter from a secret lover in his coat pocket. Holding the bottle toward him, she said softly, "Stani, what is this?"

He was in no position to answer, standing there dripping wet and nearly naked. With his heart pounding, he reached for his robe. "Let me get dressed, and I'll explain."

But she lifted the robe from the hook, holding it behind her. "Tell me now." Her gaze, steady and searching, seemed to freeze him in place.

"Now?!"

She studied the label again. "You saw a doctor on May tenth? Why?"

"My shoulder." He felt much like a prisoner, standing before his accuser.

"What's wrong with your shoulder?"

"Emily, please let me get dressed. We have a lot to discuss." He started to step out of the shower stall, but she was blocking his path.

"What's wrong with your shoulder?" Her voice was quivering, but her chin came up, her eyes defying him to tell less than the whole truth.

He took a deep breath, shivering a little, whether from fear or the cold water evaporating on his skin, he couldn't be sure. "Bone spur."

Her expression unreadable, she stared at his shoulder, as if she could see the offending growth. "How bad?"

"I'll have to have surgery."

"Is that all?"

"Isn't that enough?" To his dismay, his voice cracked.

Without another word, she put her arms around him, pressing her body full length against his. "Oh, Stani! Why on earth didn't you tell me?" The thought crossed his mind that she was getting wet, but the feel of her hands running over his shoulders, the nearness of her face to his, silenced any warning. Twining her fingers in his hair, she kissed him, a sob rising in her throat. He wasn't sure just what it all meant, but he was willing to follow her lead. Wrapping her in his arms, he pulled her even closer. Somewhere on the periphery of his consciousness, he heard a baby crying. Andrew, judging by the tone. But Emily didn't react. She kissed him more deeply, her exploring hands sending his pulses racing.

The sound of Lil's footsteps in the nursery, barely audible over the baby's squalling, finally caught her attention. But she didn't release him. She stood still, listening until Lil's voice, soft and soothing, could be heard and the baby's crying quieted. One more incredibly sweet kiss and she looked into his eyes. There were tears coursing down her cheeks, but she smiled. "You should get dressed. You'll catch cold standing here, you know."

"You're not angry?" He wasn't quite ready to let her go.

"I'm furious. After you get dressed, I expect a full explanation. Now, hurry. I don't have long before Ian wakes up and wants to nurse." She turned and went into the bedroom, leaving him to stare after her, his knees suddenly weak and his heart pounding.

Emily was sitting on the edge of the bed studying the pill bottle, when he joined her.

"This is the surgeon who repaired your shoulder?"

"Yes." Sitting beside her, Stani braced for the next phase of questioning.

"How long have you had pain?"

"Two or three months. It wasn't bad at first, but it gets worse, he says."

"Right. When does he want to do the surgery?"

"Any time. He said to call him when I was ready."

"But you were holding off because of me and the twins?"

"You already have so much to do, it didn't seem fair for you to have to take care of me too."

"So you were sneaking around to take these. You realize you're supposed to take these with meals? You could be giving yourself an ulcer." Finally, she looked up at him. She didn't look furious, he thought. She looked guilty.

"I don't take them very often."

"Call the doctor." She tossed her head and straightened her shoulders in that way that said so clearly she had decided on a plan of attack.

"What? You mean now?"

"Call the doctor. Make an appointment. I want to talk to him, too."

"But we can wait a little longer. At least until after you and the babies have your checkups."

With a sigh, she reached up and touched his face tenderly. In a patient tone she might have used with a reluctant child, she said, "Stani, you've waited long enough. It's very sweet of you to be so self-sacrificing, but if you put this off, it will only interfere with our plans for the fall. I'm assuming he told you six weeks of recovery including therapy?"

"That's right. How did you know?"

"I'm a nurse, remember?"

"You really think we can handle this right now? He said my arm will be in a sling for a couple of weeks at first. How will I help you with the babies?" As if on cue, Ian's whimper sounded in the nursery.

"You'll still have one good arm. Last time I checked, the boys barely weighed six pounds each." She smiled at him, laying her hand gently on his shoulder. "You'll be all healed long before they hit ten pounds."

"There's one other thing. The recording. We'd have to reschedule that to later in the summer."

"That's a small thing compared to a European tour, isn't it? Or maybe you could go ahead with it in the next few weeks. Lil and Jana are both in town now. I don't know what else would have to be adjusted. It's just a thought. But in the meantime, call the doctor."

She kissed him, a quick punctuation to the conversation. In the nursery, Ian's voice was rising to an insistent squall. At the door, she turned back. "And Stani?"

"Yes, love?"

"Don't you ever, ever hide anything like this from me again. What kind of wife does that make me, if my husband hides things from me?" Tears were brimming, a look of supreme sadness turning her eyes a dark, smoky gray.

He went to her, took her in his arms and kissed her gently. "The most cherished of wives, darling girl. I was only trying to protect you."

She considered the idea for a moment, caressing his shoulder as though to soothe the imagined pain. Then she met his eyes, her lips turning up ever so slightly at the corners. "Just make very sure you never try to protect me like that again. Okay?"

Chapter Fifty-two

Lil had found moving to New York City an unexpectedly and almost disappointingly painless transition. Of course, without all the support from Emily and Stani and their friends, she knew it would not have been anything like this easy. From the start, when she'd arrived primed and ready to go to work, they had insisted on her getting acquainted with the city, sending her out with the driver Robert, or with John, on simple errands designed, she suspected, to put her at ease in her surroundings. Peg Shannon, who seemed to drop by almost every day, had taken her shopping, pointing out the best places to find this or that, although Peg seemed to think Lil had unlimited spending money and very sophisticated tastes. But going around with Peg had been fun, and while Lil wasn't quite clear on her connection to Emily and Stani, she enjoyed her company a lot.

Lil had protested to Emily that she wasn't doing enough actual work, which had brought on an unexpected fit of laughter at first. But then together they had drawn up a list of her duties and a schedule of what the twins' routine demanded. She was given a wire shopping basket on wheels and sent to the grocer's, the butcher's shop and other places each day with a detailed list of the items Emily wanted for meals. She had her place on the feeding schedule, although she never had to get up at night, the way Emily and Stani did. Other household chores, including taking charge of the twins' laundry—which the housekeeper, Mamie, seemed to think *she* should do each day—and cleaning the nursery, took up a good part of her day. She was on hand to help at bath time, mainly to observe as Emily bathed and Stani dried each baby. And she cleaned up the kitchen after dinner, while the babies were taken for their evening journey to the roof with their parents.

Watching Emily and Stani with their newborns was more fun than Lil could ever have envisioned. While Emily was her usual totally efficient self, Stani gave the impression of being on a huge adventure, with every tiny thing those babies did a source of entertainment. He wanted to be holding one or the other of them all the time. Mamie had scolded him, telling him he was going to regret spoiling them, and then she had laughed that deep, musical laugh of hers and said that's what babies were for, spoiling. Mamie seemed to be a part of the family, just like John and even Peg. They had all apparently known Stani for years and joked with him about how he had changed since becoming a husband and father. As far as Lil was concerned, Stani Moss was just about as perfect as a man could be and she doubted she'd ever be able to kid around with him like the others did. He was still the musical genius she'd first idolized, and now he was also the world's most devoted family man. And he was just as handsome as he'd always been, never more so, she decided, than in the middle of the night, nodding over a baby as he rocked it back to sleep.

Then there was all Stani had done to help Charles. Without even being asked, he had contacted Matthew Covington to learn what Charles would need in order to join the orchestra forming in London. There would be little in the way of income, at first anyway, for a position in an orchestra performing nothing but period music on antique instruments. Charles might be kept busy, but he would not be making a living wage with Covington. He would need a place to live and some sort of added income if he were to survive at the beginning.

Stani had phoned Charles, encouraging him to apply for a grant from the Haynes-Moss Foundation. And he had offered him room and board at the townhouse in London. Mrs. Winslow, he felt sure, would be delighted to see to his needs, once he made the move. Lil had been afraid Charles might refuse the offer, but in the end, he had applied for the grant and made his commitment to go to England.

They had played their last concert together in the hall where they'd met. Lil doubted Charles would find the occasion as emotionally charged as she did, but he had surprised her with a dozen red roses and a note reading "For my darling Lil. You are my inspiration." Not quite sure what he meant, she had nonetheless been encouraged by the gift. She still struggled to define their relationship. When she had Charles' attention, when she could intrude on his obsession with the offer from Covington, she felt he really cared for her, as he said he did. Since that day in London, when he had kissed her on the street, he had certainly been more demonstrative, more openly affectionate. But even at that, much of the time, she felt she was competing with his one true love, music. They had made no plans for a future together. Charles pointed out that at this point in time, he barely had the means to support himself. He seemed satisfied to say he loved her, without feeling there was anything more needed to keep her stringing along.

If she hadn't believed he was the only man for her, she would have been insulted. But there was no doubt. Charles was just what she had imagined for herself, a talented, dedicated musician who respected her as an equal. That he was not particularly romantic or exciting, she gave little thought. She would wait as long as it took, until one of them could make enough money for them to be together. In the meantime, this new job offered all kinds of possibilities and she was not at all unhappy. She fantasized about a future with Charles, dreamed of a time when they would love and laugh together the way she saw Emily and Stani do every day, although she wondered if Charles could ever be as affectionate as Stani was. While he had proven himself capable of more passion than she'd ever expected, most of the time he was the same shy, absentminded Charles. But that was after all, she told herself, the man she'd first fallen in love with.

Around the apartment, Emily and Stani were certainly not the least bit shy about showing their affection for each other. Lil was always coming up on them hugging and kissing, or looking as if they had just finished a passionate encounter of some sort. While she might blush or look away, they never seemed embarrassed. Of course, she had to remind herself at times, they were still practically newlyweds. And they never could keep their hands off each other, since that first time she'd seen them together on Christmas day at the farm. She supposed that after a while, she would get used to it. John teased them a lot about all that lover-like behavior. A sense of humor was apparently the best way to handle that type of thing, or just try to ignore it, if possible.

But the morning Emily came into the nursery, the front of her dress soaking wet, Lil couldn't resist asking what on earth had happened to her. Stani had been in the shower earlier, and she wondered if he had pulled Emily in with him, something that wouldn't have surprised her at all.

"Stani has to have surgery." The explanation hardly seemed to fit the question.

"What? When? And what does that have to with your clothes being wet?"

Emily had picked up Ian and carried him to the rocking chair. As she opened the front of her bodice, she seemed to be struggling for calm. Once the ever-present shawl was draped over the nursing baby, she said softly, "That doesn't matter. I just kissed him, while he was wet. He's been keeping it from me, Lil. His shoulder's been hurting for months, but he didn't want to worry me." The look in Emily's eyes made Lil's heart beat a little faster.

"How serious is this surgery?" She sat down in the rocker next to Emily's.

"Not very. There's a bone spur where his shoulder healed after the accident. It isn't really anything very major. But he's going to need me to take care of him, and I'm going to need your help, Lil."

Just when she'd been wondering if she was really needed after all, Lil understood that things were about to change. Emily seemed to be thinking out loud, planning as she talked. There were doctor's visits, and other things to be taken care of before the surgery, and afterwards, Emily would want to stay with Stani in the hospital until he was released. Lil would need to be in charge of the twins, with help of course. Peg, and maybe John, would be on hand. Emily would need someone to bring the babies to the hospital, so they could nurse at least once a day. And once Stani was home, he wouldn't be able to help out the way he had been.

Watching the worried look on Emily's face, even as she cuddled the baby and rocked him back to sleep, Lil searched her mind for the best way to reassure her. "We'll manage fine, Em. It'll be good practice for me, for when we go to Europe. I have to learn to handle them both by myself at some point, anyway. Besides, you and Stani should be able to go out once in a while, get away by yourselves." She'd been thinking they might want to go to dinner or just get out for an hour or two, but so far, all they'd done together was hang around the apartment.

Emily smiled, that funny, knowing little smile of hers. "Lil, you're a lot wiser than I give you credit for. We do need to get out. I think I might take my husband out to dinner tonight, in fact. I've been neglecting him, I'm afraid."

***

Stani wondered why he had ever hesitated to tell Emily about the pain in his shoulder. From the moment she found out, she became a woman on a mission. Not only had she set about organizing their lives so that he could have the surgery as soon as possible, but she also seemed dedicated to proving to him how much she loved him, as if there had been any doubt in the first place. But apparently she felt she had somehow neglected him since the babies' arrival. Now she was bent on pampering him, preparing special meals to ensure he would be in the best possible shape for surgery and insisting he rest more, ignoring his protests that he loved getting up to feed the twins at two in the morning. She arranged times for them to go out, just the two of them, even if simply for a walk around the neighborhood, or a cup of tea on the roof while the babies were napping. And much to his astonishment, she made love to him. While it was still too soon after the delivery to "resume relations" as the hospital discharge orders referred to the act, Emily was determined to find every possible method of pleasing him, taking him to bed at any available hour, regardless of Lil just down the hall. He told her he was beginning to feel like a kept man, subject to her every whim.

"That's fine, just as long as you enjoy my whims too. And you do, don't you Stani?" They had locked the bedroom door at eight o'clock, leaving Lil still cleaning up the kitchen. Emily had that suggestive little gleam in her eyes, one he recalled all too well from the early months of their marriage, as she proceeded to turn down the bed and plump his pillow. Coming to stand in front of him, she concentrated on unfastening each button, her eyes focused on his face as she slipped the shirt off his shoulders. Taking his hands, she led him toward the bed.

"Emily, it's a bit early for bed, isn't it? I'm not in the least sleepy," he teased.

"No. It's never too early, if the time is right." And apparently, the time was more than right. His wife, Stani had to acknowledge, was the most intriguing of lovers, intensely sweet one moment, and fiercely insistent the next. If he had ever fancied himself an experienced seducer, Emily had proven that in spite of her innocence, she was far more creative. There was no limit, it seemed to the variety of ways she could arouse him. And now, as if she felt she owed him something for his silent suffering, she brought them all into play.

"You realize I'm being hopelessly spoiled? When the boys are big enough to run around the house at all hours, we'll never find time for this sort of indulgence." The lights low, his wife in his arms, he was pleasantly drowsy and thoroughly at peace with the world.

"Nonsense, parents still find time to be lovers, darling. Otherwise, every family would have only one child. Even my parents, at their ages and in spite of my mother's health, managed to enjoy a very active love life."

He eyed her sharply. "And just how would you know that?"

She met his gaze with one of those wise, wide-eyed stares. "I slept right across the landing from them, Stani."

He considered pursuing the subject further and thought better of it. "Ah, I see."

"Intimacy is after all not limited to one act, you know." She nestled her head on the pillow next to his, sighing contently.

He let out a laugh that he only hoped Lil wouldn't hear. "So you have proven beyond any doubt, my love."

Chapter Fifty-three

When it was all over, everyone agreed things had gone quite smoothly. All the various doctors' visits, including the twins' first inoculations and Emily's six-week checkup, had fit into the time frame before Stani's surgery. After much consultation, the recording session had been rescheduled for the end of August. The first annual meeting of the foundation board had taken place in the loft, with the board members assembled around the dining table. The numerous scholarships and grants had been awarded over tea and cinnamon bread, the atmosphere enlivened by the presence of Ian and Andrew at the table in the arms of their parents.

Penny had come to New York to help celebrate the twins' first month birthday, and Emily had finally found time to have that heart to heart talk with her. The situation was more complicated than a simple difference of opinion over when and where Penny and James might marry. James had moved to Boston for the job and to finish his degree. But if he and Penny were to overcome the ever growing number of barriers to their happiness, it would take considerable compromise on both sides, not to mention a lot of prayer and patience.

When Penny left to return home, it was with the understanding that everyone in the Moss household would be holding out for a happy resolution and that Penny herself would wait and watch for signs as to what to do next. She was to take the message to James that "love binds all things in harmony." Stani and Emily agreed that their friends were facing an uphill battle, in spite of their love for each other. They also agreed that what they had seen as obstacles to their own life together had been nothing in comparison to what some couples had to overcome.

The surgery was scheduled for the last week in June. With Lil in charge at home, assisted by Peg, Mamie and John, everything seemed in order. Refusing to leave Stani, Emily had worked out a schedule that allowed for each of the twins to be brought to the hospital for feeding, Lil assigned to transport the baby with John doing the driving.

Milo again arranged for a suite, which would allow them the privacy and comfort he insisted they deserved. In his press release, Milo had downplayed the surgery as minor, emphasizing the upcoming European tour and recording release. Always concerned about speculation in the press, he had felt it best to anticipate rather than react to any adverse publicity.

Milo and Jana met them at the hospital on the morning of the surgery, planning to sit with Emily during the procedure. "You don't need to be alone, my dear. I know this is just a simple operation, but three hours is a long time to wait." Emily thought the look in Jana's eyes must reflect the memories of that night he'd returned to New York after the accident, when they had waited for so many hours while Stani was in surgery.

For her own sake, Emily had tried to put aside what every nurse knew could happen during the most routine of surgeries. But this was very different from preparing a patient to send to the operating room. This was her husband, the most essential being in her life. If only she didn't know so much, hadn't seen so much, and could enjoy the bliss of ignorance. Even the surgeon had been more forthcoming with details, knowing her experience. She supposed he believed her immune to his blunt description of the procedure, but the images that came unbidden to her mind left her more anxious that she would ever have admitted to Stani.

They had talked the night before about the plans they'd made for the coming weeks. He had held both babies, one in the bend of each arm, and explained to them why he had to be away for the next few nights. They were under orders to behave like perfect little gentlemen, he reminded them, which prompted Andrew to gurgle a response. Ian had watched his father's face with his usual solemn consideration, and then smiled a tiny, one-sided grin. "So happy to see you understand me, lads," he had said, but Emily could see the tears welling in his eyes as she took the babies from him.

Already drowsy when she kissed him and walked beside the gurney to the surgical suite, he had smiled and held her hand. He had given Milo and Jana strict, if slightly slurred, instructions not to tell tales of his misspent youth during the wait, and Emily thought he must see how worried they looked. It was foolish, she told herself, to try to ignore the natural anxiety before any kind of surgery. Worse still to pretend he would not be in pain, would not experience the usual post-operative unpleasantness. But this was not some life-threatening illness; this was a simple fix for a common problem. So when the gurney stopped at the door, and she bent down to kiss him one last time, she said softly, "You have a nice nap. I'll be right here when you wake up. I love you, Stani Moss." Smiling her brightest, most adoring smile, she waved him away. And then, as soon as the doors swung closed, she turned to the wall for a long, indulgent moment and let the tears come.

The three of them sat in the comfort of Stani's room, happy to avoid the hard, worn chairs in the surgical waiting room. Milo was the first to speak, as if he needed to unburden his mind. "At least there's no snow this time. Do you remember, Jana, how treacherous the streets were that night?"

"I only remember how cold it was. Why do hospitals always keep the temperature so low?"

Emily tried to picture them sitting alone in the overnight hours. "How long was he in surgery, do you remember?"

"Almost three hours. Then the recovery room. It was morning before he was in his room and we could see him. But of course, he was asleep for days after that. New Year's Day, he finally woke up." Jana stared out the window, her face a sad blank as she talked, shaking her head gravely at the memories. "He was so confused. He couldn't remember, but he didn't even ask questions about what had happened."

Milo looked at his wife, the same sadness in his eyes. "Even when we told him, I don't think he quite understood the extent of his injuries. I don't think he really wanted to know."

It occurred to Emily, as she listened to the story of those first days unfold, that they had suffered a great deal, and that Stani had never understood all they must have gone through. He had talked about how lonely and afraid he had been. But it was clear to her, as they recalled that time, that they had been terrified for him.

"Without Peg here, I don't know how we would have managed. And John too, of course. It took all of us to care for him. Even after he came home, he needed us all. Do you remember how hard it was for him to stand alone? John was the one who got him back on his feet. He would take him out walking at night, in the cold. John did everything for him, even helped him shave and dress." Jana glanced at Milo, as if to be sure he remembered the details as she did.

Emily walked to the bed, straightening the sheets and smoothing the pillow, picturing Stani as he had smiled at her earlier. The image was suddenly overlaid with his face, battered and bleeding as it had been when she had first seen him in the snow. She turned back to Milo and Jana. "I wondered, every day, how he was, who was taking care of him. He was never out of my thoughts, for weeks. But I knew that somewhere there were people who loved him, who were waiting to give him everything he need." In spite of herself, tears tightened her throat.

Without moving, Milo looked up to meet her eyes. For a moment he seemed to hesitate, carefully considering his words. "You saved his life, Emily. You saved him and sent him back to us. For that we will always be grateful. But we should be even more grateful for what you've done for him since. You've made him happy. No one had ever done that before."

There was nothing to say. Hearing those words from Milo, after listening to them talk of the weeks following the accident, closed the door on any doubts she could have had. They loved him as much as she did, and they were all a family, Stani's family.

The door opened and the doctor strode in, mopping at the sweat on his face. Milo and Jana got to their feet, standing next to Emily in support.

"Everything went well. That was a good sized spur. He'll be fine in a few weeks, good as new." At the collective sigh of relief, he looked at Milo. "Nothing like last time, eh? He made an amazing recovery. I was almost certain he'd never play again." Turning to Emily, he asked if she wanted to go to the recovery room.

"No, I'll wait here. I'm sure he can manage without me. I have a baby coming to be fed shortly." In fact, her knees were trembling and she desperately wanted to sit down and collect herself before Lil arrived.

"He'll be in recovery for another hour or so. Good seeing you again." The doctor shook Milo's hand and was gone. But his words were still echoing in Milo's head, judging by his horrified expression as he turned to Jana.

"Now he says that. He never told me that, I swear. I would never have pushed him so hard if I had thought he might not be able to play again." He seemed to be searching his mind for something he had missed.

But Jana laid her hand gently on his arm, looking up into his face. "It's all right, dear. He would have pushed himself just as hard, even without you. It was for Stani to decide, and for God to provide the means, if he was meant to go on playing. Even you could not have made it so, if it were not meant to be."

Lil brought Andrew to nurse, but he seemed to sense Emily's anxiety. He was fussy and in the end, Lil gave him the bottle she'd brought just in case, Emily looking on with an unusually grim stare. "I guess I can't hide anything from them, can I? Maybe after Stani's awake and I see for myself he's all right, I'll be a little calmer. I tell you, Lil, I never thought it would be so hard. Now I understand why families are always so nervous, even over the simplest things. Human nature, I suppose."

Before Lil left, they brought Stani back into the room. He was asleep, but as soon as Emily could fuss over him, checking all the tubes and smoothing his hair, Lil could see she felt better. When John came in, he stood by the bed for a few minutes with a very stern look on his face, until he seemed satisfied that Stani was doing well. Poor Stani, Lil thought, so many people hovering over him. Milo and Jana both looked like they might cry, and earlier today, out of the blue, Peg had actually broken down. Or maybe it should be lucky Stani, to have so many people caring so much. Looking at his sleeping face, Lil had to admit even she felt a little teary. Some people were just born to be loved, and if there was ever such a person, it would have to be Stani Moss.

It would have been impossible, Stani thought, not to make comparisons to that first time. The same hospital, the same doctor, even the same sense of having lost time somewhere. And he dreamed of the girl with the gray eyes, floating next to him, her voice so close to his ear. But now that voice was speaking words of love, and her hand, soft and cool, was stroking his forehead. It should have been lovely, having her all to himself, hovering nearby, coming to his bedside at the slightest sound. Instead, it was agony.

Something was playing havoc with his head. The slightest movement brought on a staggering wave of dizziness and nausea. And his shoulder throbbed, the pain seeming to radiate throughout his body. There was nothing to do but remain absolutely still and wait for the drugs to kill the pain and dull his senses. He drifted, aware of people coming and going, afraid to breathe too deeply or even think about opening his eyes. For what must have been hours, he prayed for relief, fought the urge to heave, and most of all longed for the strength to look into her eyes and smile. He knew she was anxious. He could sense her tension every time she touched him. He so wanted to tell her he was fine, but the effort would most likely prove him a liar.

Sometime late in the evening, when the flow of traffic had ceased and the lights in the room were low, he slowly opened his eyes and discovered that the ceiling was no longer whirling above him. Cautiously, he let his gaze move to where he thought he had felt her presence, at the left side of the bed. She was sitting in a chair, her head nodding, one hand laid next to him on the sheet. Very carefully, he took a breath and whispered, "Hi."

Instantly, her head came up. "Hi. How are you feeling?" Her hand went to his hair; the gentle stroking of her fingers was for the first time comforting. He began to feel more hopeful.

"Okay. Not so queasy now." It took a lot of effort, and produced the tiniest twinge in his stomach.

"Poor darling. Anesthesia can do that to you. Just stay still." Standing up, she checked the IV flow and looked under the hospital gown at the dressing on his shoulder. "You're doing fine, you know. The doctor says you'll be up and around tomorrow and probably go home the next day. How's the pain?"

"You sound just like a nurse." He tried a little grin. She was so beautiful, haloed by the soft light. His eyes followed her as she moved around the bed.

"I would hope so. But answer the question, please. You haven't had any meds in hours now. Don't go too long." She glanced at her watch in a very nurse-like manner.

"Drugs are for sissies, or so my wife seems to think." Much better. Finally, his head was behaving normally.

"I had babies to feed. You have no such excuse." She pushed the call button pinned next to him on the pillow. "I'm ordering your medication. If you wait, the pain could bring back your nausea. We wouldn't want that, would we?" Clasping his hand, she put her fingers on his wrist. He was sure his pulse accelerated at her touch.

"No, darling nurse, we wouldn't." Closing his eyes, he held the image of her face, looking down at him with that sweet little smile. "How are my boys?"

"Just fine. Probably being spoiled beyond redemption. Auntie Shannon is spending the night at the apartment. Milo and Jana went over there for dinner. I don't imagine any one of them let our poor babies languish in their cribs for long." The door opened and a nurse came in with a syringe; telepathy, he assumed. The well-remembered burning surged up his arm and in seconds, he was drifting again.

"Emily?" It could have minutes or hours later, he wasn't sure.

"Yes, darling? What do you need?"

"You. You are real this time, aren't you?"

"Yes, Stani. This time, I'm no dream. Just try to make me fade away. You won't get rid of me that easily." He felt her lips on his, wished he had the strength to raise his arm and pull her close, and then drifted off again.

By the time Stani was released from the hospital, Emily had made up her mind. They were going home. Just as soon as the stitches were out, and the surgeon could give her instructions for his therapy, she was packing up her family and heading south. New York City in the summertime was not a place to be if there were other options. Everyone who could, who had a beach house, or a mountain home, left after the middle of June. They had the perfect place for Stani to recuperate, and she intended to get them out of town as quickly as possible.

Her husband was a model patient. As long as he had a baby or two nearby, he was happy. He sat for hours, his foot on the rocker, watching the twins sleeping in their cradle. In spite of the sling that held his left arm immobile, if she placed a baby in the crook of his right arm, he could hold it comfortably, carrying on lengthy conversations about anything and nothing with his sons. She told him he should consider himself fortunate to have such good companions. They rarely argued with him and only occasionally fell asleep during his lectures.

"At least they don't run off and leave me. Can't you just sit down with me for a bit? Why do we pay all these people to help you, if you insist on doing it all yourself?" He had watched her darting in and out of the room all morning, and each time she passed him, he longed to pull her down beside him on the couch.

Obediently, Emily took a seat next to him, glancing into the cradle to assure herself that one or the other twin was not going to require her immediate attention. "What can I do for you, sir? Do you need a pain pill? You haven't had anything since breakfast." She made a move as if to rise, and he quickly slid his arm around her waist.

"No. I don't need a pill. I need a wife. This wife, if you don't mind. What is all this bustling about in aid of, anyway?"

"Packing. Or at least organizing to pack. We now have at least ten times the amount of stuff. It will take a van to haul all of this to the farm." Settling in at his side, she laid her head on his shoulder. "But it will be so good to be home, won't it? Cool mountain breezes and quiet, lazy afternoons."

He chuckled. "Lazy? Aren't you the mother of my twins? No one seems to have time for lazy anymore."

"But in the country, the pace will be slower. The house is smaller. And I think I'm much calmer there, not so driven. New York has a way of making you pick up the pace, no matter what you're doing."

"I think Lil may be a little disappointed that we're leaving so soon. She's really taken to big city life." Shifting his position, he pulled her closer, nuzzling her hair. He was feeling much more himself, and watching his wife, with her wonderfully womanly shape, was driving him a little mad.

"She'll get to spend some time with Charles before he leaves. I know she's looking forward to that." Her hand found its way into his shirt, idly exploring.

"How are you going to manage? John is planning to make his annual trek to his sister's in Ontario. Lil is going to Richmond. You'll be stuck with me and two infants. Are you sure you're up to it?"

"Of course, I am. How can you doubt it? I told you once we country girls know how to take care of our men." Turning up her face, she touched her lips to his cheek.

"Ah, yes. So you did." Just as his mouth closed over hers, the buzzer announced a visitor, Ian began to whimper and the telephone rang. Stani groaned. "Maybe at the farm, we won't have quite so much traffic? You answer the door, I'll get the phone." He gently set the cradle rocking with his foot, reaching for the telephone on the table beside him. "But just remember, at some point, we get to run away together, right?"

Laughing, Emily went to the elevator. "In eighteen years or so."

Chapter Fifty-four

The letters arrived the day before their planned departure. John was in Milo's office, plotting the travel arrangements for the European tour. When the secretary laid the two envelopes on the desk, both of them instantly recognized the handwriting. Milo picked up first one and then the other, giving John a look that spoke volumes. Taking the silver letter opener, he slit open the first envelope.

What reason would Stani's mother have to be writing now? They hadn't heard from her since that visit over a year ago. John was sure she hadn't contacted Stani. He would have told him. The look on Milo's face, as he scanned the letter, gave little indication of its contents. When he had finished, he passed it to John with raised brows. "What do you make of this?"

She had been ill, she wrote, and had done a lot of thinking. She wanted Milo to know that she was writing to Stani to ask for forgiveness. She had seen the magazine article and knew he was going to be a father soon. There were things she wanted him to understand about the past, about what she had done. She hoped Milo would not think her ungrateful for all he had done, but she needed to explain herself to Stani, before it was too late. She had not, she said in closing, told Stani how seriously ill she was. That would not be fair to him. But if her doctor was being truthful with her, she could not expect to live beyond the end of the year. Time was short, and she hoped very much to see her grandchild, if at all possible.

John read the letter through twice, his heart sinking lower at each word. Just when Stani was recovering from this surgery, when he was so happy with his family, and they were about to set off for Virginia, this unwelcome voice would be calling him back to the past. He wondered just what she had said to him in the other letter.

"He doesn't need this. It will only open old wounds for no purpose." He handed the letter back to Milo.

"He'll feel he owes it to her, if she asks to see the babies. I know Stani. He's never really accepted her for what she is." Milo stared at the unopened letter. "Will you take this to him, and stay with him when he reads it? Don't let him do anything rash, John. She can wait until he's in London in September. He's in no condition to go running over there now."

When John arrived at the loft, they were just finishing lunch. He had taken the two of them, the day before, to the surgeon's office. Stani's shoulder was healing up just fine, the doctor had said. Emily was going to be his therapist, and they had laughed that she was always the best therapy for whatever ailed him. Now, as they sat over the remains of a Chinese take-away, the two of them were talking softly together. From the high color in Emily's face, he could imagine what the subject of the conversation had been.

"Well, old man, are you ready to start packing the car? Robert will be bringing the limo first thing in the morning, but we can load up my car today. Or at least you can. Being a cripple has its advantages at times." Something in his face must have given him away. Stani's grin faded and he sat waiting, a question in his eyes.

"This came for you at the office. Milo asked me to bring it over." He handed Stani the envelope, wishing he could somehow warn him of its contents.

Stani opened the letter, Emily watching silently. Grim lines tightened around his mouth as he read, but otherwise, his expression never changed. Slowly folding the single page, he rose and went to look down on the cradle, where both babies were sleeping soundly. "Read it, John. Maybe it will make sense to you."

She said she knew he was about to become a father, and thought this might be a good time to try to explain her actions all those years ago. Once he had children, he might understand that sometimes parents had to make difficult choices, in order to do the best for their child's future. She did not regret letting Milo Scheider take charge of his career, or even that she had given him guardianship, but she knew now that she should have stayed involved. It wasn't that she hadn't been interested, but it had seemed kinder to let Stani settle in one place, rather than shifting him back and forth. She had thought then he would only be more confused if she remained in his life. There was no excuse for just letting him go without any explanation, she said. And there was no way to make up for the missed birthdays, or the absence of Christmas presents. Most of all, she felt now, she had failed him when he was injured in that horrible accident. She should have accepted Milo's offer to come to New York. She should have been there for him. He had turned out so well, become a good, kind man, so generous with his money and his time. She couldn't take any credit for all of his successes, but she wanted him to know how proud she was of him. She hoped someday he would find it in his heart to forgive her for never having been the kind of mother he deserved.

She closed by saying that the next time he was in London, she hoped he'd get in touch. She would very much like to meet his wife and child. That was all. No mention of her illness, no urgency in the request. Immediately, John wished he had followed his urge to destroy the thing, before it could do its inevitable damage. Worse still, he knew more than this letter told, and he hated keeping the truth from Stani. As with all secrets, it would come out eventually, and do even more harm then.

"I have to say I'm surprised. I would never have expected her to be so open." It was a lame response, but he needed to buy a little time to gauge Stani's reaction.

"I can't understand why she felt she had to say this now. Maybe the thought of being a grandmother finally thawed her a bit. But what she said about the accident—did you know Milo offered to bring her to New York? And that she declined?" There was that look, the result of deception. It cut to the quick, seeing his eyes go dark like that. John took a deep breath and went to stand beside him, waiting for some kind of inspired response to come to mind. He was keenly aware of Emily, still at the table, waiting to be included, no doubt.

"I knew. By the time you were well enough to understand, we all decided there was no point in telling you. It wasn't as if you were asking for her."

"Of course not. I'm surprised Milo even thought of such a thing. Did he think I was going to die?" His hand went through his hair, that tight look settling over his face. John glanced at Emily, silently inviting her to step in any time.

"No. But everyone was so worried about you. It seemed the right thing to do, to contact her. I wasn't in on the decision, but I could understand it. Listen, lad, this is just a letter. She's probably had a mid-life attack of conscience, hormones or some such thing. After you've had time to absorb it, it won't seem so important." John was pretty sure his tone wasn't going to convince Stani, and the look on Emily's face was growing increasingly suspicious. He was a lousy liar, especially when he was covering someone else's lie. His inclination was to go ahead and tell Stani everything, but something held him back.

"May I read it, Stani?" Emily's voice was already full of tears. Not surprising, given the look on Stani's face.

He blinked, as though he'd forgotten she was there. "Of course. But I have to tell you, I can't even recognize her in that letter. It doesn't sound like her at all." He continued to stare down at the babies, while Emily took the letter John held out to her. When she had finished, folding it carefully and placing it on the table, she went to stand behind Stani, wrapping her arms around his waist, resting her head on his shoulder.

Thinking they might do better alone, John started to leave. But immediately Stani called him back. "There has to be more to it. Just seeing a few pictures in a magazine can't have prompted her to write all that."

"She wrote to Milo, too. Maybe you should talk to him." That might be simpler. But would Milo tell him the truth, knowing what his reaction might be? "In the meantime, I should start packing the car." He turned to the stack of bags by the door. "Emily, which of this lot goes now?"

She whispered something in Stani's ear, turning to follow John to the elevator. "I'll go with you. To supervise."

Stani seemed to come back to the present, a frown on his face. "Emily, you're not supposed to lift yet."

"I said supervise, darling, not carry." She blew him a kiss, as they got on the elevator. "Just watch the babies. They won't sleep much longer." As soon as the doors closed, she turned to John, and he knew by that direct gaze, there would be no lying to her. "What do you know? Obviously, more than was in that letter."

"She told Milo she had been ill, that she's dying. She said it wouldn't be fair to tell Stani."

"How can it be fair not to tell him? You think she's just trying to clear her conscience?"

"Probably. Why else would she say all that now? There've been years at a time when he never heard from her. Even before they left London, he rarely saw her. I didn't think it bothered him back then. He never talked about her. But after the accident, when he was struggling to deal with things, she was on his mind a lot. He said he was always trying to please people because he had never been able to make her happy."

Emily was silent until they reached the lobby, a look of intense concentration on her face. John wondered if she might not be praying. When at last she looked up at him, he could see the determination in her eyes. "He has to be told, John."

"And what if he wants to go running over there? None of you are ready for a trip like that."

"We'll have to see what he wants to do. He's more sensible than that, I think. But the important thing is not to keep a secret from him. We promised each other, no more secrets. Even if the result is painful, the truth has to be told."

"Will you tell him? It might be easier coming from you." But he already knew she would do it. Emily had made the decision—judging by the way she squared her shoulders and gave her head a little toss— to do what was right, and then stand by Stani no matter what his reaction.

Emily waited until they were in bed. The twins were asleep, and Lil had gone out with Peg to a concert, a going-away treat. She knew it had been on his mind all evening. He'd been quiet and distracted, even when they were bathing the babies and getting them ready for bed. The tight lines around his mouth had never eased, since he had first read his mother's letter.

In the simplest way she could think of, she told him he had been right, there was more that had prompted his mother to write to him now. In her letter to Milo, she had told him she was ill, gravely ill. Stani grimaced, as if he'd taken a blow, but he didn't say anything. Emily went on to tell him they didn't know the nature of her illness. But she had indicated in the letter that she had six months left.

"John and I agreed you needed to be told. Your mother apparently thought it would be unfair, but I was sure you wouldn't see it that way." He was staring at the ceiling, the knotting muscle in his jaw the only betrayal of whatever emotion he was fighting.

"Thank you." His voice was flat. "I wondered, you know, if it might not be something like that. It would take something life-changing for her to say those things to me." He closed his eyes, but she knew he was thinking hard.

"You so rarely talk about her. I'm not sure I know what you really feel for her." Curling closer, she laid her arm across his chest, her cheek pressed against his hair.

"I don't think I feel much at all. Except disappointment. I suppose every child has the expectation of certain things from their mother, and I was always disappointed. It seemed that she was never quite happy with me. Even when I started to play the violin, and everyone else seemed to be pleased, it wasn't quite enough for her. Maybe it was because my father played the fiddle. If I had shown some other talent, maybe she would have been happier. She just couldn't seem to praise me for doing something well without pointing out some other shortcoming. Do you know that's probably why I hated my hair? She would say things, complain about it, as if it were a bad thing to have red hair, as if it were my fault that it curled." She could feel the pain spreading through his body.

"She made it so clear what a burden I was, how much she had sacrificed for me. If she bought me new shoes, the first scuff I put on one was an indication of my ingratitude. When I outgrew my clothes, she would make a fuss about having to replace them so soon. Have you ever noticed how frequently I say 'thank you'? It's a reflex, from as early as I can remember. I wanted to be sure she knew how grateful I was. Milo told me once that I said 'thank you' before anyone even did anything for me, just in case. I don't think my mother was a cruel woman; but she needed to blame someone for her own unhappiness, and I was the only one available. It seemed as if she held me responsible for her miserable life. Even when I was just a little boy, I knew it was all somehow my fault." His voice finally broke. Holding him closer, her own tears flowing, Emily pulled his head to her shoulder and stroked his hair. It was a long time before he spoke again. "What should I do? Please, just tell me what to do."

"What do you want to do?"

"I want to go back to the moment before John handed me that letter. I want to pretend I don't know anything about it, that I never read those things she said. The fact that she's ill doesn't seem as important as what those words did to me."

"What did they do to you?" She continued to run her hand over his hair.

"They made me wish I could love her. But I can't. Not after all this time. I can forgive her. But I can't feel anything for her but this sadness. I was glad she let me go to live with Milo. I didn't miss her at all, after a while. I just put her out of my mind. I was pretty sure she never missed me."

"Do you feel you owe her anything at this point?" Emily raised herself on one arm, looking into his eyes.

"No." He hesitated, returning her gaze. "Maybe. I mean, she is still my mother. And she has reached out to me, finally. Do *you* think I owe her anything?"

"I think you owe it to yourself to follow your conscience. If she is sick, there may not be a chance in the future to change your mind. You need to be sure you don't have any regrets when all is said and done." Reaching out, she stroked his face, and he smiled.

"Watching out for me, are you?"

"Of course. You're all that matters. That may sound unfeeling, but it seems to me your mother gave up any claim to you a long time ago. Even if she regrets that now, I expect it's too late to undo the damage."

"But it wasn't the fact that she gave me up that hurt so much. It was what went before. As I said, I was happy to go with Milo and Jana. It may not have been a perfect life, but it was certainly happier than I would have had with her. At least they were satisfied with me, as long as I did what they wanted. Milo always encouraged me to work harder by first telling me how special I was. He made me believe in myself. For the first time, I wasn't a burden to anyone."

The memory of those hours while Stani had been in surgery came back to her. "Stani, they love you so much. They talked about the accident that morning while you were in the operating room. If you could only have seen their faces, you'd never doubt how much they care."

"I don't doubt it anymore. I know how blessed I've been. I have a family, one of my own now and the one I've picked up along the way. I don't need my mother's approval. But if she needs something from me, I don't think I can withhold it."

"Somehow, I expected you to feel that way." She laid a kiss on his cheek.

"I suppose I could write to her, tell her when I'll be in London. I thought about sending her a photograph of the twins. Would that be enough, do you think?"

"It's more than she asked for. Would it make you feel better if we could find out more about her condition? John suggested contacting Bertram and having him do a little snooping. But I didn't want him to without your permission."

"Maybe. I'd at least like to know how serious it is, and if there's anything she needs. Milo sent her money for years, I know. But I have no idea what her situation is now that she's married. If money would help, I could certainly do that much."

In the nursery, one of the babies began to cry and was very soon joined by his brother. "I'll go. You try to get some sleep." Emily threw back the covers and slid her feet into her slippers.

"No, I'll help you. Those lads have a way of putting everything in perspective for me. They never let me forget what's really important."

Settling his arm in the sling, he gave her a weary smile. "I suppose they got that from their mother, didn't they?"

Chapter Fifty-five

Their first road trip was accomplished in just the gypsy-like fashion Emily had always imagined; a convoy of two cars—one a limousine—with vast quantities of luggage, plenty of helping hands and no shortage of laughter. By morning, Stani's mood was much improved and he stood chatting with the doorman, good-naturedly supervising the last-minute scramble to pack the cars. When the process was more or less completed, he and Emily bundled into the back of the limo, the twins in their car beds on the seat opposite and a hamper full of baby gear tucked on the floor at their feet. "Remember when we found the back of a limo romantic?" Emily settled herself next to a bulging diaper bag, making sure Stani had enough room to comfortably rest his arm on the pillow she'd provided.

He chuckled, stretching his legs past the hamper. "Fond memories, my love. I'm beginning to think I should consider one of those huge touring buses. If entire rock bands can pack themselves into those things for months on end, surely we could manage for a few days. Are you sure the boys are all right in those cots? They're used to being together so much of the time in the cradle." He leaned forward to check on the babies for the third time.

"They'll let us know if they're not happy, Papa. Now relax. I think Robert and John have finally gotten everything crammed into the trunk. We might just get out of the neighborhood by lunch time at this rate."

Lil stuck her head in the open window. "Cozy?"

"Oh, yes. How about you? Did John leave you any leg room? The back seat is packed to the roof, I know." Emily was making a vain attempt to stuff the diaper bag into a space next to the hamper.

"I'll manage. The bathtub had to go in the trunk. That's what all the rearranging is about. Now at least I can let my seat back a few more inches. Either of you need anything before I wedge myself in for takeoff?"

"Are we leaving today, or is this just a trial run?" John leaned in, a grin on his sweat-streaked face.

"Let's go! My wife will be needing to eat lunch in another hour."

"Oh! That reminds me, where did we put the picnic hamper?"

As John started toward the trunk, Stani called to him. "Never mind. It's here on the seat next to Robert. Now let's go! The twins will be ready for kindergarten before we ever get out of New York!"

The trip was again broken at the inn outside Washington where they had stayed in the spring. The innkeeper, who remembered them well, was amazed at the twins. "Two peas in a pod. And red hair, too. Fine boys you have there, folks."

"Unfortunately, they require ten times their weight in luggage." John was hauling the suitcase labeled "Overnight Necessities" to the stairs. "Please tell me they don't need a bath tonight. The tub is packed under half-a-dozen other bags now." Without waiting for an answer, he headed up to their rooms.

"Poor John. Do you think he'll get used to it as time goes on?" Emily was carrying Ian's car bed, while Lil followed with Andrew's. Both babies were staring up in fascination at the passing view, each with a fist crammed in his mouth.

"He'd best get used to it. We have all of Europe to traverse, and the bags aren't going to get any lighter. Of course, by then, I'll be a bit more help. Isn't there anything I can carry in one hand?" Stani was watching in frustration as the caravan proceeded up the staircase.

"Yes, sir. The picnic basket's on the front seat. That should be light enough, since it's empty now." Robert passed, a grin on his face, bearing the hamper from the back seat. "This is the last of it, I think." From the bottom step, he glanced back at Stani. "At least those little boys aren't running around under foot yet. Just wait, things'll get a lot more exciting once they start walking."

The twins were so intrigued by their new surroundings that they refused to nap. Taking them to the big front porch lined with white rocking chairs, Stani and Emily sat with them for much of the late afternoon, savoring the quiet and the fresh breeze from the surrounding hills.

"This is more like home, lads. Clean air and not a car horn to be heard for miles." With Andrew cradled in his right arm, Stani rocked slowly, fighting his own drowsiness.

"We should make arrangements with Pastor Mike for their baptism, as soon as we can. And I suppose we have to make the decision about godparents." Emily stroked the springy fuzz on Ian's head, laughing softly as it refused to stay in place. "I think the curl is starting to come in their hair. Right now, it just pops right back up, as soon as it's combed down."

"They'll need to see a barber before long. At least I can teach them how to control it, so they won't suffer the way I did. Poor lads, I apologize again for passing that cruel gene to yet another generation. Notice, Mummy, that already the only thing people notice is the color of our hair. Not our obviously superior intellect or our exceptional strength. No, only our red hair!"

Emily laughed. "Stani, they're barely two months old. Only a doting father is going to see anything but a couple of small, squirmy babies with sprouts of red hair. To almost everyone, newborns look pretty much alike. At least ours have something to set them apart. And you know how much I love red hair. It's always been one of my favorite things about their father." She gave him a long, warm look, and he grinned, his color rising.

"Did you hear that, boys? Your mother fancies me."

"Are you talking nonsense to these lads again? I never thought I'd see the day Stani Moss would sit around cooing to a baby." John joined them, a tall glass of iced tea in hand. "Well, it's all unpacked. Lil is taking a nap, Robert has gone off to gas up the limo, and this old man is going to rest."

With a speaking glance at Emily, Stani turned to John. "We've been thinking about godparents. The twins will be baptized while we're at home this time. We'd be honored if you'd act as godfather for one of them."

John hesitated, clearly surprised at the idea. "You don't think I'm too old?"

"I told you he'd say that." Emily grinned. "No, we don't, obviously."

"Then I'd be the one who's honored. Which one?" He gazed from one baby to the other, apparently trying to judge which he might be best suited for.

"Ian, we think, has more Stani's personality. He's a bit more reserved, more introspective. We thought he'd be the one for you." Emily held the baby up, and as if to substantiate his mother's claims, he gurgled sweetly.

"All right, Ian, it's a deal. But if you turn out to be the ruffian, that will be just fine, too. I would have given anything to see this one here take a few more tumbles." He jerked his head toward Stani. "Still and all, he's turned out all right." He held up his glass in a salute to the tiny baby who watched him with dark, serious eyes. "Well, Ian, my boy, we'll have to see what the future holds for us, won't we?"

Stani laughed. "Now who's cooing at babies?"

The sight of the farmhouse, in the deep afternoon shade of the oaks, was as welcoming as it had ever been. To no one's surprise, there were cars lining the driveway, including the sheriff's cruiser. As they began to extricate themselves from the cars, the screen door opened and with Jack leading the way, friends and neighbors streamed out. Three Salvatores, two McConnells, Myrtice Green from the post office, and even Mr. Harris from the bank, along with Martha Jean and Ruthie, clustered around the limo, all speaking in hushed whispers, peering into the windows with great caution.

When the first car bed was removed, Andrew was greeted with admiring oohs and ahhs, until it became clear that he was wide awake and ready to be passed to someone's waiting arms. He waved his arms, kicked his legs, and indicated his desire for attention with a series of angry squalls. When Ian followed, lifted from his cot by Emily and passed to Stani's waiting arm, he too decided to treat the welcoming committee to a proper display of his vocal abilities. Stani grinned, as various motherly types attempted to soothe his sons. "Feeding time, I'd say. Not to mention, Ian smells suspiciously as though he needs a clean diaper, Mummy. That's a two-handed job, I'm afraid."

Gradually, they made their way into the house, the train of baggage following; and while Emily and Sara took care of the diaper changes, Lil went to the kitchen to prepare bottles for both babies, her brother Joey going along to supervise.

"Here, Jack, you do the honors. This is Andrew Haynes Moss. Andrew, this is my godfather, making him your honorary grandfather. Now be a good boy, because he is, after all, the law in these parts." Emily placed the baby in Jack's arms, along with a bottle and a blanket for his shoulder. "Don't want him to spit up on your uniform." She stood back and watched as Jack studied the now content Andrew. "Do you like him?" she asked softly.

Struggling to contain his emotions, Jack smiled down into the wide, dark eyes. "I like him just fine, Em. Just fine."

Across the room, Lil had placed Ian in her mother's arms, and

Angela was gazing teary-eyed at his red, angry little face. Handing her the bottle, Lil said with a laugh, "Here, Mom. This usually quiets him down. He's the calmer one, believe it or not."

Standing next to Angela's chair, Stani leaned over to the baby. "This is Ian Patrick, who normally has a very charming way with the ladies. Ian, be nice. This is your grandmother Angela, one of the many formidable women in your family."

"Oh, Stani, he's just exactly like you. Look at those fingers. A string player if I ever saw one." At the introduction of the bottle, Ian's protests were silenced. He stared up into Angela's face, a tiny frown still creasing his brow. Then, as if deciding to accept her as a member of his growing entourage, he smiled around the nipple, a miniature version of his father's famous flashing grin. "Hello, Ian Patrick. Can we be friends, after all?"

Everyone hovered over the babies as they were fed, and like the perfect infants their parents knew them to be, they fell asleep under the many pairs of admiring eyes. When Lil and Emily had taken them into the nursery and settled them in their new cribs, iced tea and cookies were served on the front porch. The conversation first centered on the twins' remarkable resemblance to their father, then the demand for the details of their birth and every milestone since. Finally, there were concerned questions about Stani's shoulder.

"I'll be good as new in a few weeks, but it's been ever so nice to have my private nurse hovering over me. Since these lads came along, I've had to share her with them. And they can scream a lot louder than I'm permitted to."

Laughing, Emily added, "So, of course, I decided this was the perfect time to come home, with Stani needing time to recover, and the twins so anxious to meet everyone here. Although, if I had known how much trouble it is to move two tiny babies a few hundred miles, we might still be in New York. But I suppose it was good training. I need to learn how to pack lighter."

John raised his glass. "Hear, hear!"

The Dixon children were spotted coming across the yard, Robbie Joe leading little Emily by the hand, Ricky and Wayne running to keep up. From the front door of the cottage, Bobby waved. "Here comes my brood." Ruthie was passing around the platter of cookies for seconds, and looked up with a proud smile.

Lil stared at the line of children approaching. "Can you imagine traveling around the world with that many kids?"

Sitting in the swing side-by-side, Emily and Stani exchanged smiles. Taking her hand, Stani said with a satisfied sigh, "Oh, I'm sure it could be done."

Late that night, in the quiet of their bedroom, Emily sat in the dim lamplight nursing Andrew. On the bed, Stani reclined against a mound of pillows, Ian nestled on his chest. Already asleep, the baby's tiny fist curled trustingly around his father's little finger. Through the open window, the chorus of night creatures could be heard, and a soft breeze stirred the curtains.

"It's heavenly, isn't it?" She looked over at him, her lips curving in a contented smile.

"Perfect." He closed his eyes, letting the calm wash over him.

"Peace. Quiet."

"You. Me. Our boys." Emily gently laid Andrew on the sheet next to Stani and buttoned her gown. Carefully, she slid in next to him.

"How's your shoulder tonight? Can I get you something to help you sleep?"

"I'm fine. What about you? You must be exhausted."

"Happy. Thankful to be home again. And yes, I'm a little tired." Leaning over, she kissed his cheek. "I'm going to put these two to bed, and then I'm going to spend a few minutes just loving my husband, if that's all right with him?"

His eyes opened, as a slow smile spread over his face. "An offer I can never refuse."

When she had put the babies in their cribs and turned out the lights, she stretched beside him, her head on the pillow next to his.

"I've been thinking," he said softly, "about my mother. I want John to find out more, if he can."

"Okay. And then what?"

"I'm not sure. I'm praying that I'll know what I'm supposed to do. Where is my responsibility in this? I'm expecting some kind of sign, I suppose."

"I'll pray for that too. In the meantime, can you enjoy being here, try to relax and let yourself heal?"

"My shoulder's healing just fine."

"That's not what I mean. Let your heart heal. That little boy you talked about the other night is still hurting, Stani. He still feels unloved and unwanted. I hear that every time you talk about your mother. But you are loved, darling. And you are wanted. If she didn't make you feel that, there was something wrong with her, not with you."

In the darkness, he turned to her, burying his face in her hair. She held him closer, wrapping herself around him. "It's unfair of her to intrude like this now. I want to do what's right, but I refuse to let her take me back there. I'm a man, a husband, a father now. Everything I wanted to be. I have so much to be thankful for, so much to be happy about. Why has she chosen now to unburden herself to me?"

"Maybe because she needs you to forgive her, to release her. She doesn't know you're happy. Tell her. That may be all she needs to be at peace with herself."

He was quiet for some time. When he spoke, there was an eagerness in his voice, as if he had suddenly found direction. "I can do that. If that makes her feel better about our past, I can certainly tell her how happy I am now. I can even show her, if necessary. Would you go with me to see her? Could we take the babies to her?"

Rising on one elbow, she looked down into his eyes. "Of course we could. Is that what you want?"

"If that's all it would take to put her mind at rest, it would be the thing to do, don't you think? I can write to her, tell her we'll come to visit her in September. If John learns that we need to go sooner, we can try to work that out." He pulled her closer. "Thank you. For showing me what I should do. And for loving me."

She kissed him, a long tender kiss that grew deeper as he responded. "Don't thank me, Stani. You never have to thank me for loving you. The pleasure is all mine."

Stani wrote to his mother, a brief letter that focused on the present rather than the past. He said in closing that he did not feel there was anything to forgive. He had a good life, full of blessings and all the happiness a man could hope for. His career gave him great satisfaction, and along the way his life had been filled by people who loved and supported him. He promised to visit in September when they were in London, so that she could meet his wife and twin sons. By the way, he wrote, they are identical, and both have red hair. Emily was thrilled that all her men were redheads.

John wrote to George Bertram, telling him of the situation and suggesting he make some very discreet inquires as to the nature of Stani's mother's illness and financial situation. Providing her address, he also pointed out that neighbors were always a good source of information where illness was concerned. Nosy, or caring, either way they usually managed to learn the details.

Milo wrote to Stani's mother, reminding her that Stani was a married man with a great deal of responsibility now. It would be better for him to continue to provide whatever help she needed, rather than involve Stani. He asked her to inform him of the nature of her illness and what, if any, treatment options might be available. Stani, he knew, would want her to have every advantage. "He is a fine man," he wrote in closing, "one we can all be proud of. Stani himself has turned his life in unforeseen directions, found a deeply grounded faith in God, and developed far beyond anyone's expectations. He has dedicated himself to serving others, helping wherever opportunity arises. While he continues to grow as a musician, his life is about much more than music now. We never saw, in that gifted little boy, the potential for Stani to become a great man. But in the years to come, he may well be known as much for his character as for his music."

When Milo read over his letter, he was surprised by the tone and the direction he had taken. Something had prompted him to tell her the things she might never know otherwise. And he had needed, for himself, to be the one to tell her. He had taken her son, raised him as his own, but Stani had proved to be much more than the musical superstar Milo had envisioned. They should both be proud of the man, who in spite of them, had turned out so well.

Chapter Fifty-six

Emily had been right, of course. Life on the farm, even for a brief interlude, provided the renewal and the healing Stani needed. On their own with their sons for the first time, they settled into a routine that allowed them to love and laugh in a way they had not done in months.

"I know we need help when we're traveling and when you're working, but isn't it wonderful to pretend we can take care of ourselves for a while?" The babies were napping on a quilt in the middle of the sunroom floor, while Stani read in a chair nearby. The aromas of rosemary and lemons from the roasting chicken and spiced apples from the baking tarts filled the air as she opened the oven door. "Stani, wouldn't it be nice to be like this all the time? I often wonder if real people, the ones who have regular jobs and mortgages, I mean, really appreciate what they have?"

"Don't tell me you want me to take you away from the drudgery of our celebrity lifestyle so soon?" He chuckled, closing his book and gazing out at the cloudless sky above the barn.

"Oh, not really. But I miss being alone with you. Remember last summer, all the time we had alone?" She came to stand in the doorway, looking down on the sleeping babies.

"I remember, all right. I remember nearly going mad with desire and working very hard at jobs I'd never done before, and being happier than I'd ever been in my life." He reached for her, drawing her into the circle of his arm. "Have I told you that you are much too slender and alluring for a woman who only recently gave birth to twins?"

"Um, yes. Last night, and the night before, if I remember correctly. It's a good thing I'm such a good nurse. Otherwise, you'd have already damaged your chances for a full recovery. You have to be more mindful of your shoulder, my darling, and curb your passion just a little bit." Ruffling his hair, she pulled away and went back to the kitchen. "By the way, when you were out for your walk, Robbie Joe came over to remind you that he has a lesson this afternoon. Is that the third or fourth reminder?"

"He's anxious to show me how much he's learned. His teacher wrote that he works harder than any student she's ever had, even at the university level. The boy is insatiable, apparently."

"Reminds me of what Milo said about you. You wanted to do more and more, and he couldn't hold you back. Is Robbie really that talented, do you think?"

"Yes, although he has to develop more technique. He learns, but his style hasn't emerged yet. I may take some time to work with him, if he seems willing. How soon can I start to play again?"

"When it doesn't cause you any pain. Stani, please don't push yourself. We came home so you could have some peace to recover. And I want us to spend as much time being a family as we can, while we're here. Once you get back to work, I know how it will be. You'll be running here, there and everywhere." She slammed the oven door closed and turned to him with a frown.

"If I had two free arms, I'd hold you and tell you how beautiful you are when you're angry. And then I'd kiss you like this, until you forgot all about how annoyed you were with me." When he caught her to his side, she willingly offered her face for his kiss with a little gurgling laugh.

"I'm not annoyed. Well, maybe a little bit. What would it take to make you relax for more than a few hours? What's driving you so these days?" Gently pushing him onto a bar stool, she began to set their lunch on the counter.

"I have much too much music in my head. All the pieces I want to record. Delaying the session has me frustrated. Plus, there's a new melody, something that just started and I want so much to play it. This is nothing like as difficult as the recovery after the accident, but not being able to play puts me on edge." He picked up a sliver of chicken, and popped it in his mouth. "But, as long as you take such good care of me, I'm sure I'll survive. What sort of relaxation did you have in mind for this afternoon?"

"I thought we might take the babies into town. We could roll them along Main Street, introduce them to everyone, and then go to the cafe for dinner with Jack and Martha Jean. Plus, I thought it might be nice to show them the window." A shadow darkened her eyes as she looked up at him, and he realized how much this visit must remind her of her parents. Bringing her babies here for the first time would of course be bittersweet.

"I think that's a lovely idea. And we can talk with Mike about the baptism, if he's free. Have you decided for sure how we're going to solve the godparents dilemma?"

"Yes. It came to me last night. John and Penny for Ian, and James and Lil for Andrew. That way, if things didn't work out for them, Penny and James wouldn't share a godchild. But we can still have both of them as godparents. Does that sound right to you?" She helped him load his plate, cutting up the chicken for him.

"Perfect. Have you written to them, or are you going to call?"

"Call. I want to be sure when they're both free to come down. And I'll call Lil tonight. She and Charles were going to Williamsburg to a concert last night. She said she's determined to get used to authentic performance if it kills her." With a chuckle, she settled on the stool next to him. "We really are so lucky. Why did I ever think anything could interfere with our being together?"

"Ah, I can answer that one. You thought our worlds were too far apart, we had nothing in common, and worst of all, I'd soon become bored with you. Tell me, darling girl, do I ever seem bored?"

"No, Stani. Not in the least." She gave him a sweet, warm smile, filled with all sorts of beguiling promise. From the sunroom, the sound of one baby's contented gurgling was soon joined by that of a second's far less contented squall. "Oops. So much for that. It's feeding time, Papa."

As he gulped down the last of his lunch, Stani shook his head and laughed. "Not bored, oh no, never the least bit bored!"

It was all finally arranged. After several attempts to catch James at home, Stani spoke with him on Sunday evening. Penny and Emily talked for almost an hour, ending with a promise to finish the conversation when Penny came for the baptism. Lil said simply that she'd been hoping to be asked. The date was set and everyone informed.

"Do you really expect Milo and Jana to make the trip?" Emily had written to everyone in New York, making certain they understood that their attendance would be welcome, but was not required.

"He said they would. And of course, Peg has already made plans. She'll be in Florida next month and will make the trip from there. Expect elaborate gifts, my love. Peg has a new project, spoiling our sons." Stani gazed down at the babies, nestled in their cots under a shared canopy of mosquito netting. "They're growing so fast. I think they're getting huge, until I see them next to other children. Emily has certainly taken a liking to them."

"It's the red hair, I'll bet. But you're still her favorite. I love to see her with you. We really do have to have a daughter next time." Emily was browsing a cookbook, as she sat next to him in the swing.

"Next time? You're not thinking of next time yet, are you?" He tried to keep the alarm out of his voice. "Emily, I think we should wait a year or two, shouldn't we?"

"That's fine, if that's what it takes. As long as I'm nursing, I shouldn't conceive. What do you say to shellfish for dinner? The market had some beautiful scallops this morning. I could run back into town and get some."

Stani blinked. From pregnancy to shellfish, his wife had the most disconcerting way of leaving him breathless. "Fine. But I mean it about waiting, Emily. You still have a lot of healing to do, the doctor said. Maybe we should take other precautions."

"Don't worry, darling. Those things have a way of happening in their own time. You watch the boys. They should be fine until I get back." Dropping a little kiss on his lips, she was headed through the house and out the back door to the car.

Stani was left with his jangled thoughts. He should have known she would rebound from the trauma of childbirth much faster than he did. He had not forgotten the anguish of seeing her so pale and fragile, nor had he recovered from his dismay at her pain after the C-section. All normal, he knew, but nonetheless, he was not ready to put her through it again anytime soon. Not to mention the months of watching her deal with the pregnancy itself. No, he would insist on waiting a year or two. With a sigh, he acknowledged he had little or no say in the matter, if Emily made up her mind.

He dozed a bit, the warmth and quiet of the afternoon settling over his senses. Gradually, he became aware of voices, of someone calling, at first playfully, and then with increasing urgency. He turned toward the sound to see Ruthie and Robbie Joe crossing the yard.

"Have you seen our Emily anywhere? She was asleep on the porch, and now we can't find her. She has to be hiding somewhere. She just learned to play hide-and-seek-from the boys." In spite of her tone, Stani could see the alarm in Ruthie's eyes. "She's started climbing lately. She's fearless about heights." Her gaze went to the fence, as if she pictured the toddler scrambling over its rails.

They continued to call, Bobby coming from the house to join in the search. Eventually, all the Dixons were fanning out, Bobby heading into the woods behind the cottage. Stani glanced at the twins, still sleeping in their cots and called to Robbie Joe, who had started down the drive toward the gate.

"Robbie, will you watch the twins for me? I'll help your folks look. Does Emily have a favorite hiding place?"

"She went into the barn one time chasing after one of those old cats. You know how the door's always open."

Stani's heart lurched. Stubby was in the paddock. Surely, tiny Emily was not brave enough to go near him. He headed around the house, slipping his arm back in the sling. It was a nuisance and he more and more frequently took it off, but Emily insisted he keep it handy. It slowed his progress, as he tried to race toward the barn.

Stubby was standing in the shade of his stall, his eyes half closed. There was no sign of little Emily anywhere near the paddock.

Stani peered into the interior of the barn, waiting for his eyes to adjust after the brightness of the sunlight. "Emily? Are you hiding in here?" He felt a little foolish. Surely, she couldn't have walked all this way in her game.

He went in, his eyes adjusting to the dimness. "Emily? Come out, sweetheart. This is no place to play." He looked behind stacks of feed bags, checked each of the empty stalls, finally glancing upward to the loft.

And then he spotted her, halfway up the ladder to the hayloft, her little sandals planted firmly on the rung. From the loft above, one of the cats peered cautiously over the edge. Emily turned to look down at Stani, and her smile slowly turned to a look of apprehension as she realized the distance she had climbed. She whimpered, her tiny, dimpled hands gripping the rung more tightly even as her feet began to move uncertainly.

For a terrified moment, his heart caught in his throat. "Emily, don't be afraid. Just stay right there." Stani evaluated the ladder. It hadn't been in use for years. Would it hold his weight if he tried to climb after the child? "Stay there, sweetheart. I'm going to get you down." By now, her eyes were wide and tearful, and the whimpering had turned to hiccoughing sobs.

He looked around helplessly for something else to climb on. For just a moment he considered running for help, but leaving her was unthinkable. "All right, Emily, I'm coming to get you. Don't move, okay?" He stripped off the sling, mounted the bottom rung and raised himself off the floor. The wood beneath his foot creaked ominously and then splintered. Quickly, he set his foot on the second rung, pulling himself up with his right arm. Again, the wood threatened to give way, and Emily cried out, as if she knew her rescuer was in peril.

"It's all right, sweetheart. I'm coming." He tried to lift himself to the next rung, the effort drawing a groan as his weight pulled at the incision on his shoulder. Looking up, he saw that Emily's feet were now dancing anxiously on the rung above him. "Be still, Emily. Don't move."

It was over in an instant. The barn door opened wider, flooding the space with sunlight. Ruthie and Bobby ran in together, stopping in their tracks at the sight of Stani dangling on the ladder, their little girl just above him. With a heart-rending shriek, Emily let go her grip on the rung. Stani launched himself backward, reaching out as she dropped toward him. He would never recall just how she ended up clutched to his chest, her arms clinging to his neck as they tumbled to the floor. The searing pain in his shoulder was breathtaking, but he scarcely noticed until Ruthie had lifted the sobbing child from his arms and Bobby had helped him to his feet. Ruthie and Emily were both crying, Bobby was asking him if he was all right, and he had the distinct impression that he was floating somewhere above the scene.

He heard her voice before he saw her, standing in the doorway, her eyes wide and dark as she called his name. He tried to smile, to reassure her, but the floor seemed to be tilting precariously and there was an odd, muffled roaring in his ears. Someone said he should sit down and he found himself on the pile of feed bags, his head forced between his knees by strong, gentle hands.

"It's all right. He's just a little light-headed. He'll be fine." She sounded so certain, he was almost convinced himself. Very softly, as if only for his ears, she asked, "Stani, how badly are you hurt?" Was he hurt? He didn't think so. Just the pain in his shoulder, and the spinning sensation in his head, but otherwise, he thought he must be all right.

"I'm fine, love. Really." His voice sounded hollow, far away. He tried to look up at her, but she pushed his head down again.

"Take deep breaths, darling. It's just the shock." He stayed there, her cool hand on the back of his neck, for what seemed a long time. The sounds began to fade away, the voices explaining what had happened, the gradually quieting sobs, and he thought they must be alone.

"The twins! Who's with the twins?" His head came up this time, and she smiled with relief.

"Robbie Joe is watching them. They were still asleep when I got here. Do you think you can make it into the house now?" She had stripped back his shirt at some point, and was studying the incision. "I think you're okay. I know it must have hurt. You almost fainted."

"Emily's all right?" He struggled to his feet, his legs feeling less than reliable.

"She's fine. They've all had a bad scare. Here, take my arm. Go slowly, now. I don't want to have to call them back to help me pick you up." Cautiously, she led him into the yard. "Okay?"

"Fine. But I think I might like to rest for a bit. That was more excitement than I needed this afternoon." He felt slightly ill, and the ground was pulsing before his eyes in rhythm with the pain in his shoulder. He heard himself explaining breathlessly, "No matter about my arm, I couldn't let her fall, you know." They were through the door, and he sank into the nearest armchair, settling his head back against the cushion. Again, he seemed to be floating away.

She brought ice for his shoulder, and a cool cloth to cover his eyes. He could hear her voice murmuring soothing things, but the words didn't quite sink in. Eventually, he was aware that the twins were in the sunroom, too. He opened his eyes, beginning to feel stronger. The pain was subsiding.

"Hi. A little better now?" Sitting cross-legged on the floor, she was nursing Ian. Andrew lay at her side on the quilt, and she held a bottle for him with her free hand. "These boys of yours refused to be put off. How are you feeling?"

"Rather like I took a swift blow to the gut."

"More like a blow to that shoulder. I'm going to call your doctor, as soon as these two are happy again. I think you're okay, but I want to make sure."

"I'm fine. I thought I could climb up to her, but the rung broke and left me hanging. Then I guess I hit the floor pretty hard." He closed his eyes, recalling the eruption of pain.

She laid Ian beside his brother and came to take another peek under his shirt. "It looks okay." Then suddenly her voice broke and she bent over him, drawing his head to her chest. "Oh, Stani, I'm so proud of you. But you could have been seriously injured. Did you even think about that?"

"There was no time to think. It all happened too fast." He leaned into her arms, loving the feel of her fingers in his hair. The pain was still there, but it was nothing compared to the comfort of his wife's tender attentions.

"You realize you saved a child's life?" He could taste her tears as she turned his face up and kissed him.

"I did what anyone would do. Now do you think I might have

something to drink, and maybe one of those pain pills? I feel very much like a sissy just now."

"You're no sissy, my darling. You're a hero." She kissed him again and he wondered, if every man were so grandly rewarded, there might not be more acts of incidental heroism committed every day. If he never played the violin again, it would have been worth the sacrifice just to feel that precious little girl safely in his arms. But to hear his wife calling him a hero was a reward far beyond anything he'd ever hoped to merit.

Chapter Fifty-seven

By the end of the week, the word had spread. Stani Moss, who had come home to the farm to recuperate from recent surgery, had risked his own safety to snatch the Dixon's little daughter from certain death. It was the topic of conversations all around the courthouse square.

Jack brought them a copy of the twice-weekly county newspaper which contained a letter to the editor titled, "Good News Still Happens." It addressed the issue of the preponderance of negative news; political scandals and sensational press reports unfit for family dinner-table conversation. The writer said he wanted to see if the paper would actually print an uplifting story of heroism with a happy ending. Surprisingly, the details were accurately recorded, names and all. There was even a line regarding the amazing coincidence that Moss's wife, the former Emily Haynes, had delivered the Dixon child in a dramatic Christmas Eve birth and that the little girl was named for her.

"Seems Bobby told the tale at the hardware store when he went to buy lumber for a new ladder. It was repeated at the coffee shop, the post office and the bank. Who knows exactly where he heard it, but old Thad Adkins, who used to publish a little paper over in Macon years ago, got wind of it, went around to everyone to get the details and wrote this to the county editor, who I hear was a mortal enemy of his, back in the day. Jerking his chain, so to speak."

It seemed to Stani that Jack was much too pleased with this unexpected publicity. He read the report, his color rising steadily. "He makes it sound as if I did something extraordinary. Anyone would have done the same." He passed the paper back to Jack. "Thank goodness this didn't happen in New York. It would have been picked up and spread like wildfire through every rag on the stands."

The following day, Milo phoned. There had been a call from one of the wire services, asking him to substantiate the story that Stani had saved a child's life. What on earth was going on down there? And was Stani all right?

"I'm fine, a little sore, but fine. How could they have gotten wind of this?"

"It seems the Washington papers picked up some human interest piece from a local paper down there. At least they had the decency to call me. What happened, Stani? Surely you didn't actually jump off a ladder?"

"I'm afraid I did. Have you seen the story? The letter in the local paper was pretty accurate, other than making me out to be some sort of hero."

Emily chimed over his shoulder. "He *is* a hero, Milo. Bona fide!"

"Do you want to make a statement, Stani?"

"Good heavens, no. Can't you handle it? Just tell them the story has been exaggerated and everyone is fine. Won't it just go away if we ignore it?"

But Milo was never one to ignore good press. "Stani, for once they want to report something positive, that actually happened, and they have an accurate account of the story. It would be foolish to just ignore it. Let me make a statement, at least substantiating the story that's already out there."

In the end he agreed, but the idea made him grossly uncomfortable. It was one thing to have his music discussed in the press, but this was much too personal. He was still trying to decide if he had been chosen to take part in a miracle, or just been in the right place at the right time. Putting the incident on the same page with the debate over the rising price of gasoline made it seem somehow trivial. It was Emily who pointed out that the story would most likely inspire others, restoring someone's lost faith in human nature.

"Besides, Stani, it will be old news in a day or two." The twins bathed and put to bed, they had retreated to the porch where the only light was a soft glow from the single lamp in the window. The deep stillness of the warm night seemed to call for soft spoken conversation.

"I hope so. This is supposed to be our time, and I resent the intrusion, especially from gossip mongers." He took his arm out of the sling, which Emily had insisted he wear until the soreness subsided, and gathered her close. "Kiss me and tell me you love me, even if I decline the title of hero."

His lips closed over hers before she could protest. Although still a bit stiff and bruised, he was feeling much more himself and he intended to take advantage of every opportunity for these sweet private moments. All too soon, first Lil and then John would be returning, and then the influx of guests for the baptisms would be upon them. "Dance with me?" he whispered in her ear.

"What? Are you sure you're up to it?" He could see the shadow of her smile as she searched his face.

"Maybe not a tango, but I'm sure I can manage a nice, sedate waltz. We haven't danced in months, and this is the perfect night for it."

She put on the recording and joined him under the oaks, going into his arms with an embarrassed little laugh. "What if someone's still up in the cottage? They'll think we've lost our minds."

"Let them. I think we still have the right to dance in the moonlight. There's nothing immoral or illegal about it. Besides, all the lights are out, and I have it on authority from Robbie Joe that a nine o'clock bedtime is strictly observed. It's well past ten now." He circled across the lawn, relishing the astonishing lightness of her as she floated with him. "You haven't forgotten how to sweep me away, darling girl. Remember the first time we danced?"

She giggled. "I remember the outraged housekeeper you were so rude to."

"See, I'm not always a model of civility. There's a downright unpleasant side to my nature, too."

She tossed back her head and laughed, a musical chime that echoed in the trees overhead. "I've yet to see it, if it exists. You are the least unpleasant person I've ever known. In fact, you're unnaturally good-tempered, not to mention, as Lil would put it, drop-dead gorgeous." She drew closer and pressed her cheek against his.

He was the one to laugh now. "Please, ma'am, you'll make me blush with such outrageous flattery."

"Not flattery, darling. That's a direct quote. You will always be Lil's ideal, no matter how much she may be in love with Charles. She's never quite forgiven me for snaring you first."

"Did you snare me? I thought you held me at bay far too long." He nuzzled her neck, inhaling the sweet scent of soap and warm skin. They circled the grass, moving ever more slowly, until at last they stood swaying gently near the gate. Eventually, she led him toward the fence, leaning against the rail and gazing back at the house.

"There was another summer night, you know, when I stood here and told myself that you were never going to be a part of my life."

"Really? When was that?" He had again gathered her into the circle of one arm, and was preoccupied with lifting her hair and kissing the nape of her neck.

"The night I saw that magazine story about your recovery. I couldn't stop staring at your picture, and I had to give myself a good stern lecture. I was going to be very, very happy with my life here, all alone."

"It doesn't seem to have worked out quite that way. Thank heavens. Emily?"

"Yes, Stani?"

"The music has stopped. Do you think we should go in and check on the twins?" As she turned in his arms, she let out a sigh, briefly finding his lips in the darkness.

"I'm sure we should. But just for a little bit longer, hold me." She clung to him, her hands caressing his shoulders.

He complied with her request, not quite sure of the change in her mood. "What's troubling you, love?"

"For just a minute I realized what I would have missed if you had never come back for me. What a horribly lonely life I would have condemned myself to. Thank you for not letting me send you away."

He turned her face to the light, gazing into her eyes. "Don't ever thank me, darling girl. As a very beautiful woman told me recently, the pleasure is all mine."

The telephone started ringing the next day. Everyone had seen the articles in the various papers and demanded to hear the story first hand. After talking to Peg, John, Penny, Angela and Lil, they felt all of the most important people had been satisfied that Stani had survived the rescue without suffering any harm. They agreed enough was enough. Packing up the twins they went down to the springs, the site of a once grand resort where in the last century the wealthy had spent their summers enjoying the cool mountain air and the healing sulfur waters. Spreading a blanket in the shadow one of the remaining sentinel chimneys, they laid out a picnic of fruit and sandwiches. They took off their shoes and waded in the bubbling springs, dangling the babies' tiny feet in the clear, cold water. Emily told them the names of the birds and the flowers, touching their toes to the tickling blades of grass. Stretched in the shade of an ancient elm tree, listening to the gurgling responses of his sons to their mother's soft voice, Stani eventually drifted in and out of sleep.

With the babies fed and safely in their cots beneath the net canopy, Emily joined him, sitting cross-legged and drawing his head onto her lap. "Peace?"

"Absolute. I knew once that story got out, we wouldn't have any. Oh, well, it will pass in a day or so, as you said. In the meantime, maybe we should unplug the phone. We can't just run away from home." He opened one eye and grinned up at her. "Can we?"

"No, we can't. We're somebody's parents now, remember? Aren't they adorable, in their little sun hats? I guess I'm not supposed to say so, since I'm their mother, but I think our babies are exceptionally beautiful. Of course, the fact that they look absolutely nothing like me makes it a little less boastful, don't you think?"

"I think you may boast all you like. You did, after all, carry them for eight months. And who knows, they may grow up to look more like you. There's always hope."

"No, these two are definitely like you. Maybe when we have a daughter, she'll take after me."

"Back to that, are we?" He sat up and in one swift move, pushed her down and stretched beside her. "Is motherhood so appealing that you want to stay pregnant all the time?"

She laughed, winding her arms around his neck. "I wouldn't mind. At least I have a wonderful maternity wardrobe now." Pulling his head down, she kissed him, her fingers weaving in his hair. Very soon, they were engaged in an increasingly warm embrace, with Stani's shirt somehow cast aside in the process. So engaged in fact, that the big brown sheriff's cruiser had already come to a halt next to their car before they realized they had company.

Standing in the open door of the cruiser, Jack grinned. "Don't mean to interrupt, but I thought I might find you two down here." As they righted themselves, both laughing and blushing profusely, he approached the blanket, casually choosing an apple from the remains of their meal. "Thought you might like to know there was a TV crew poking around town this morning. Thankfully, Myrtice called me when they came in the post office asking for directions to the farm. I told them you had packed up and gone to Florida for a week."

Emily blinked at him. "Why Florida?"

"It was the best I could think up on short notice. They seemed to buy it. I made sure they headed back down the highway, but I wanted to warn you." He grinned again, eying the shirt snagged on a nearby sapling, flung by eager hands only moments earlier.

"Thanks, Jack. Sorry to be so much trouble." Stani squinted up at him, struggling for some semblance of dignity.

Pausing to peek under the netting, Jack gazed down at the babies for a moment, shaking his head and chuckling fondly. "No problem. Well, I'll be getting back now. You two enjoy your afternoon." Turning, he started toward the car. "Oh, and Em? Don't forget the chiggers are bad down here this time of year. I wouldn't roll around in the grass too much, if I were you."

They were sure they heard him laughing out loud as he drove away.

Stani insisted they begin the exercises the surgeon had ordered. After all, he pointed out, any soreness in his shoulder now was more likely the result of his fall to the barn floor, rather than from the surgery. "I have to start some time, darling. And all these hot soaks you've made me endure have eased out all the stiffness. Of course, if you'd agree to join me, I'm sure they'd be twice as therapeutic." Over the rim of his mug, his eyes twinkled suggestively.

"Fine. We'll start the exercises. But slowly. I know you. You push too hard." She arched her brows, drying her hands on her apron. "First, I have to measure your range of motion. Although judging by your recent amorous endeavors, I'd say it's pretty good." Now it was her turn to grin, as she ran her hand over his shoulder and down his arm.

"Am I allowed to kiss my therapist, or would that be bad form?" He stood patiently as she lifted his arm at various angles and degrees. When he seemed satisfied with the process, she wrapped her arms around his waist.

"Now you may kiss me. But don't think I do this with all my patients. Only the ones who father my children are so privileged." She closed her eyes, waiting for his kiss.

"Not to refine too much, but just how many of us are there?" Before the last word was out, she had pressed her lips over his, barely containing her laughter. It was that position that Lil found them, as she came through the back door.

"Welcome home," she said to announce herself. Two pairs of startled eyes turned her way. "What? I thought I was supposed to come back to work today. Have you two even looked at a calendar since you've been here?"

With their days alone ended, Emily looked for ways to create private moments. Walks, naps and trips to town provided excuses to get away together. They took the babies into the backyard in the mornings and sat near the flower beds, watching the butterflies and the occasional hummingbird, pointing them out to their ever-more-alert sons. Now two and half months old, with shining dark eyes and enchantingly lop-sided smiles, they were a constant source of pleasure to their parents. Gone were the tiny, fragile newborns; Ian and Andrew were now chubby, dimpled babies with sturdy arms and legs that seemed in almost constant motion during their waking hours. They had developed a vocabulary of expressive coos and gurgles, and each possessed a hiccoughing laugh that invited the listener to join in.

The first time they were treated to the sound of their father playing his violin, both twins went suddenly silent and still, as if mesmerized by the strange, new experience. But once the novelty wore off, they could eat, sleep and cry to the music, apparently immune to its effect. Stani lamented the fact that his sons seemed so totally unimpressed with what others judged to be his considerable ability. "You don't suppose they'll always have so little regard for music, do you? Wouldn't that be a terrible irony?"

"Don't fret, darling. I doubt many three-month-olds care much for Beethoven. Try Brahms, or maybe Mozart. Let them develop their ears slowly. It's not as if they won't have plenty of years to learn to appreciate what you do." In the cool of early evening, Stani perched on the railing with J.D's violin. The babies were nearby in their cots, their legs waving in the air, completely fascinated with the recent discovery of their toes, while Emily lounged in the swing. "What will you play for us tonight, Papa?"

Considering for a moment, as if listening for some distant sound, Stani put the violin to his shoulder and began to play. The melody was intensely sweet and tender, with a decidedly highland character. Closing his eyes, he lost himself as the tune progressed, to such an extent that when it came to an end, he slowly looked around as if surprised by his surroundings.

Emily was smiling at him, a warm look of wonder in her eyes. "That was exquisite, Stani. What was that?"

"Lullaby. It's been in my head for weeks. Did you like it?"

"I loved it, but more importantly, I think your sons liked it. Look."

Both babies had fallen asleep with identical expressions of blissful repose on their faces. Ian had one hand laid over his heart, while Andrew had flung both arms wide. The music they had inspired had obviously been well-received.

Chapter Fifty-eight

John reached the farm on Monday evening, the first of those scheduled to arrive for the baptisms. He had spent two weeks in Canada with his sister, returning to New York for what he called his real vacation. "Doing absolutely nothing, no loading, no lifting, and definitely, no driving. I never left my hotel unless I could walk to my destination." He was clearly pleased to see the twins, holding each one and enjoying a private conversation as he assessed their growth and development. "Say what you will, Stani, they're more like you all the time. Three pairs of those penetrating eyes may be more than I can handle."

Early the first morning, he found Stani in the kitchen alone. No time like the present he decided, to get the unpleasantness out of the way. Bertram had sent his report, John told him. The investigation had been simple enough. A house in the same block as his mother's had been up for sale. Posing as a potential buyer, Bertram had encountered a knowledgeable neighbor, and after a nice, long chat, had come away with a good deal of information. Stani's mother had been diagnosed with colon cancer in the early spring. She'd undergone surgery and a series of treatments, but the prognosis was not encouraging. Until very recently, that is. Her husband had told the neighbor that an experimental therapy, only recently approved for cases such as hers, had offered them an unexpected ray of hope. An old friend of his wife's was offering to help with the considerable expense, and she had decided to go through with the treatment.

With a suspicious frown, Stani asked, "An old friend?"

"Milo. I asked him point blank."

Stani visibly tensed. "Milo. I should have known he would try to intercede. He's never wanted me to give her money."

"He made a deal with her, a long time ago. He would take care of her. He never believed you owed her anything. At any rate, that's what we know so far."

Shaking himself from obviously heavy thoughts, Stani agreed. "I suppose she'll stay in contact with Milo. I'll talk to him while he's here. I should at least share in the expense."

John laid a hand on Stani's shoulder. "That's fine, lad. Just don't lock horns over this, for heaven's sake. The two of you arguing over who's going to help her would be wrong in so many ways."

With a flicker of a wry smile, Stani shrugged. "I'm sure you're right. Emily and I have decided to visit her as soon as we get to London. Hopefully, she'll be able to enjoy the visit."

"Speaking of Emily, where is she this morning? I was sure she'd be down here cooking up some sort of sumptuous breakfast." Taking a blueberry muffin from the plate on the counter, John looked around for other evidence of Emily's culinary efforts.

"She's in the garden, gathering our lunch. She should be in shortly. Missed her cooking, have you?"

"Missed a lot of things. Tough as this job is at times, it's not anything I'd give up for the solitary life. This trip to Europe should be all kinds of fun." The back door opened and Emily paused, setting her brimming bucket on the floor.

"Good morning, John. I wondered if we'd see you before noon." She was wearing a pair of worn overalls—now wet with morning dew and splattered with mud—and a sleeveless plaid shirt. As she kicked off her clogs by the door, Stani had the thought that she was by far the most adorable farmhand he'd ever seen. "I suppose you boys would like some breakfast? Stani, you know how to prepare bacon and eggs. Where are your manners, letting John stand hungry in our kitchen?"

Speechless, he stared with widening eyes as she unbuttoned the overalls, letting the straps fall from her shoulders. "Emily!"

She paused, holding the garment at her waist. "What?" With a grin she let it drop, revealing pristine khaki shorts beneath. "Really, Stani. I wouldn't just strip in front of John. Not without at least warning him." Stepping out of the overalls, she hung them on a hook by the door and came into the kitchen, her eyes sparkling. Immediately, Stani caught her in his arms, planting a kiss on her smiling lips.

"I'm never quite sure what you might do next, love."

"Never boring?"

"Never."

John stood watching, a grin splitting his face. "It's nice to see some things never change."

Stani was spending an hour with Robbie Joe each morning, sometimes listening, sometimes playing for him, encouraging the boy to hear and understand more about technique and style. They communicated well, he thought, although he had to remind himself that most of the language of music was still new to Robbie.

When Emily caught sight of them late in the morning, each with violin in hand, heading across the yard to the barn, she called out the window to Stani, "What on earth are you doing?"

Turning, he grinned. "Acoustics!" he called back.

"I think he's having too much fun playing teacher. They've been at it for hours." John was still sitting at the kitchen table, keeping Emily company while she washed the vegetables she'd picked earlier.

"He says he's learning too. They're quite a pair." She paused as the sound of strings drifted from the barn. "I'm almost surprised Stani's even willing to go in there now. After what happened, he says he'll never put his foot on a ladder again."

"But he's all right? The shoulder's healed properly now?" John had hesitated to ask Stani, sure of the answer he'd get.

"He seems fine. If it had happened earlier, the result could have been far worse."

"Quite a thing he did, catching that little girl. Another of those valley miracles he's always talking about?"

She turned to smile at him over her shoulder. "I'd say. Of course the publicity was a little bit unpleasant for him. But it's finally died down. It never occurred to me the word would get out like that. All because an old newspaper man got wind of a good story."

John went to stand in the doorway, watching as Stani and Robbie emerged from the barn. They were talking intently, Stani waving his violin and bow expressively as he walked. "Have a care there, lad! That fiddle can't be replaced, you know!" Chuckling, he turned back to Emily. "First time it's ever been played in a barn, I'd wager. What was the point, do you think?"

Coming through the back door, Stani was explaining to Robbie, "So you can hear how clear the tone is, vibrating off the wood. It would be very different if the walls were covered in something softer or even if they were made of stone." The boy was listening with rapt attention to the end of the lecture. Stani pointed with his bow toward the plate of muffins, indicating Robbie should help himself. "Pity we don't get that kind of clarity in the studio. Emily, you should hear it out there. It's like a cathedral. It's truly amazing."

She grinned at him as she dried a glossy red pepper and placed it on the counter. "Maybe you should build a studio down here. I read not long ago about some folk singer converting a barn for that purpose. Of course, Stubby might not care for all the company."

He blinked at her, his eyes suddenly focused on some distant vision. "Do you think we could? I mean, would other musicians be willing to travel down here, just to record with me? And we'd need a technician. I know a good bit, but I'm not an expert. The equipment would cost a lot, if we got the best, state-of-the art, you know. But it would be worth it, if we could convince other artists to use it, too. I might even make a little money from it eventually." The words tumbled as rapidly as his thoughts, until he hesitated at the astonished look in Emily's eyes. "Just an idea, darling." He grinned sheepishly.

"It's brilliant, Stani! John, isn't it brilliant? Imagine, having your own studio, right here. We could spend more time here then." Throwing her arms around his neck, she kissed him soundly.

"You mean you think we could do it? What about Stubby? We can't just put him out of his stall." Stani's color was high, his eyes shining at her response to his fit of madness.

"We could build him a little stable all his own, on the other side of the paddock. It's not as if we're going to ever use all that space for livestock again. We'd need a good contractor to do the work. Maybe Bill Stichman could do it. He's always up for new ideas." Her own eyes shining, she was obviously caught up in envisioning the project.

Robbie Joe, perched on a stool at the counter, had been trying to follow the excited discussion. "You mean you want to make music in that old barn?" The frown on his face suggested he feared his mentor had suddenly lost his mind.

"I mean I want to make recordings in the barn, Robbie. As it is now, I have to go to New York or London to record my music. It costs a lot of money and the sound isn't nearly as fine as what we could get out there. Of course, we'd have to get rid of the cobwebs and the dust." Turning to John, he asked, "What do you think Milo would say to the idea?"

With a grin, John replied, "Pretty much the same thing the boy said, until you explain it to him. But if you want it, lad, I suspect he'll come around to see it your way. Just be sure to include the bit about it making money."

Chapter Fifty-nine

"I'm afraid this is going to be almost as hectic as the week of our wedding. The dinner guest list has grown to a frightening number. I'm not sure where everyone's going to sit." Emily was staring at the dining room table as if she could somehow will it to expand.

As he came through the door from the kitchen with Andrew in his arms, Stani said softly. "Let me put this little lad to bed, and I'll see if I can help you. Why don't we just have a picnic on the lawn?"

She was still standing there when he returned and it struck him that she looked very tired, even a bit pale beneath her tan. Then there were the dark circles under her eyes, and the telltale downward tilt of her mouth. Emily, he feared, was headed for a whirlwind.

"You're not wearing yourself out with all this are you? Why don't we try to make it an early night and start fresh in the morning?" He held out his arms and she sagged against him

"That sounds lovely. I'm too tired to think. I just hate the idea of everyone balancing plates of gooey pasta on their laps all over the house. And it would be nice for us all to sit down together somewhere."

He urged her toward the bedroom, as she continued to think out loud. "I've been wondering if we won't have to add onto the house sometime soon. We need more bedrooms, and definitely another bathroom. When the twins get too big for the nursery, they'll need their own room."

Switching off lights as he went, Stani chuckled. "They have a few more months, darling, before they outgrow their cribs." He followed her through the door, where she paused, turning back as though she'd forgotten something.

"I meant to measure the lace tablecloth, the one my mother loved so much. I don't think it's big enough if we put all the leaves in the table."

He stopped her progress by wrapping his arms around her waist. "Emily, my love, the tablecloth will still be there in the morning. I'm putting you to bed, before you dissolve into a pool of exhausted tears." She opened her mouth to protest, then abruptly closed it again. As he had anticipated, her eyes filled.

"You're right, of course. I'm sorry." Laying her head on his shoulder, she took a long, ragged breath. "Hormones."

"Really? I would have sworn it was just the eighteen-hour days, two demanding babies and a needy husband. Hormones, too? Poor darling."

He helped her into her nightgown, turned down the covers and when she was finally stretched on the bed, he gently rolled her onto her stomach and began, with long, slow strokes, to rub her back. Immediately, he was rewarded with a soft hum of gratitude.

"You, my darling girl, try to do too much. I thought when Sal offered to cater it would take some of the load off you. Obviously you've found something else to fret over. Now how can I convince you to relax and enjoy our sons' big day?"

She made a muffled response to the effect that she'd try harder.

"And you must leave all the housework to Ruthie. Promise?"

Again she mumbled a reply, but this time he thought he detected resistance.

"Emily, it's too soon for you to be doing heavy work. I was with you in the doctor's office, remember?" He had worked his way up to her shoulders and gently lifted her hair away from her neck. The temptation was too great. Ever so lightly he touched his lips to the soft skin.

"I'll be good, I promise." She rolled over and smiled up at him, her lids drooping. "Now come to bed. Please."

"Only if you swear you'll let me get up with the babies in the morning. I'll even make your breakfast. I can't have the mother of my sons all hollow-eyed and weepy on Sunday."

He quickly undressed and turned out the lights. By the time he slid into bed beside her, she was almost asleep. But she turned into his arms, nestling her head in the bend of his shoulder. "You're so sweet to me," she whispered.

He fell asleep to the rhythm of her breathing, pondering the mystery of a life that constantly stayed one step ahead of his best efforts. There were so many things, so many people, to attend to. With his head full of music so much of the time, he forgot too easily his responsibility to at least support his wife in all the mundane but essential details of their complicated existence. His last thought was that he needed help, some practical soul to point him toward a solution to the pasta-balancing dilemma on Sunday. That would be a start, he hoped, toward taking away those dark smudges beneath her beautiful gray eyes.

Stani was as good as his word. At the first whimper from the nursery, he was up and on the job. Andrew woke first, and he had downed a bottle before Ian's demands became loud enough to disturb his mother. Taking them one at a time to the sunroom, Stani settled them in their favored spot near the door, making certain the quilt was spread where he could watch them as he worked in the kitchen. They couldn't exactly move about yet, but they had learned to turn their little bodies in circles by digging in with their heels, so that occasionally they collided, resulting in a confusion of waving arms and legs. With one eye on the now content babies, and the other on the bacon frying on the range top, he turned his mind back to the problem of accommodating the dinner guests on Sunday.

Jack was the first to come to mind. He might have the answer, or if not, Martha Jean might be enlisted. Sara McConnell was another possibility. Although Angela was surely the one to take charge in most instances, Stani was reluctant to call her. She, along with Sal and Joey, would be bringing the food early Sunday morning. He felt it would be too much to ask for any more assistance from that quarter. Of course, Bobby might be able to help arrange something. He was certainly handy with a hammer if there was anything to be constructed.

As he cracked eggs, casting an eye toward the twins, he decided to talk to Jack first. He would understand the need to keep Emily from overextending herself better than anyone else. As soon as she had eaten breakfast and had a nice leisurely shower, he would call Jack for advice.

Lil appeared just in time. The tray was ready, complete with linen napkin and the best china from the dining room. "Ooh, are you in the doghouse, Stani?"

"No. But Emily was so tired last night I thought she deserved a little pampering today. If you can watch the boys, I'll take this to her. Help yourself to some breakfast." Carefully balancing the tray he headed toward the bedroom, painstakingly navigating through the dining room and past the stairs. The bedroom door was ajar and he backed slowly through, peering into the dimness. He set the tray on the ottoman and crept closer to the bed. "Breakfast is ready, darling girl. Are you awake?"

She sat up slowly, gazing around the room, stretching her arms over her head. "What time is it? Are the babies awake?"

"Yes, awake and fed and lounging in the sunroom. Lil's on duty." He arranged the pillows behind her and placed the tray over her lap. "They were most co-operative this morning. Otherwise, I'm afraid you would have had to settle for tea and toast."

She looked over the tray and smiled. "Oh, Stani, this is beautiful. And thank you for the extra sleep. I feel much better this morning." She tucked into her eggs with a zeal that made him chuckle.

"I've been giving some thought to our dining dilemma. Would you trust me to try to arrange something?"

Her fork paused in mid-air. "You want to take that on? Stani, that would be wonderful, but what do you have in mind?"

"Something that would allow us all to sit down at one table. Informal, but elegant enough to suit the occasion. I was thinking the front lawn would be the most likely place. It worked so beautifully for our wedding reception." He waited for some sign of agreement. It came in the form of a beatific smile, complete with a sparkle of tears.

"That sounds lovely. But how will you ever pull off something like that?"

He was disappointed by her lack of confidence, although admittedly it matched his own. "I have a few ideas. Trust me, if I feel I'm in over my head, I'll let you know in plenty of time. I'll make sure we don't all end up sitting on the grass. How's that?"

Again, that smile, and she reached out to tenderly stroke his cheek. "That's perfect."

The first guest scheduled to arrive was Penny. She was coming alone on Wednesday, planning to stay at the parsonage. James would follow on Friday evening. Penny had promised to be at the farm from dawn 'til dusk each day. Milo and Jana intended to drive down from New York on Thursday, and Peg was flying in from Florida on Thursday night. The three of them had opted to stay at the Rivhanna Resort, as they had done for the wedding, but promised to be on hand every waking hour. Stani could foresee a great deal of coming and going, disturbing the comfortable routine they had established and, no matter how well-meaning, turning his home into a three-ring circus.

After phoning Jack, who promised to come by later in the morning, Stani went in search of Bobby. At the very least, the front yard would need mowing and raking. He would ask Bobby to be on hand when Jack arrived. The more heads the better, he thought. He was pleased to see that Emily was sitting on the quilt, playing contentedly with the babies. There was no sign of last night's anxiety. He gave himself a cautious little pat on the back. Maybe he was learning, if slowly, to do his job properly.

In the end, the dining issue was simply resolved, but it evolved into a group effort in which Stani considered he had played a very small part. He could only hope the weather co-operated, and Emily was pleased with the result. In the meantime, he prepared himself to act the larger part of gracious host, doting father and attentive husband. As he had explained to Jack, Emily had done enough, giving birth to the twins, nursing him through surgery and getting them all to Virginia. It was his turn to carry the load for few days, or suffer the emotional consequences. Jack had smiled knowingly and wished him luck.

Chapter Sixty

The weather in early August typically turned hot and dry. Crops required irrigation and livestock grazed beneath the shade trees, taking advantage of the cooling waters of farm ponds for an occasional wade. But as the week of the twins' baptism advanced, the air was heavy with humidity and clouds gathered every afternoon, threatening thunderstorms and rain. Stani was increasingly anxious that the plans so easily formulated would be dashed by a fickle turn of nature.

By the time Penny arrived on Wednesday afternoon, Emily's spirits seemed to have recovered. She declared that no matter how haphazard the event might be, the presence of their friends and their honorary families would make for a happy, and most certainly a memorable day.

As dinner wound to a close that night, without any preamble, Penny announced offhandedly that she and James had decided to be married. They had set a tentative date and were making their plans. Her announcement was followed by a brief stunned silence broken only by the sound of a distant and notably strident train whistle.

"But that's wonderful! When and where?" Emily had clearly been taken by surprise, which struck Stani as odd. Something in Penny's voice made his skin prickle ominously.

"Sometime in the next few weeks. We're going to elope, just go somewhere, find a judge and get married." Penny's gaze was slightly defiant, as she met Emily's across the table.

"Penny, no! Is that what you really want?" She hesitated, and it occurred to Stani that they might need some privacy. He sensed rising emotions on both sides. Lil's wide eyes were going from face to face, as if she were trying to decide which might burst into tears first.

"Maybe we should leave you girls to visit. John, how about a hand with the cleanup tonight?"

Pushing back his chair, he tried to signal his fears with a subtle jerk of his head. Unfortunately, John was totally absorbed in his dessert, a tart filled with native blackberries and topped with rapidly melting ice cream. Stani tried again. "I thought we might take the twins for a little stroll down the drive. After that dinner, you should need a bit of exercise."

At last catching the hint, John followed him into the kitchen. "Problems?"

"I just think they may need some time for girl talk." He turned with a grin. "It may be cowardly, but Emily's as much girl as I can handle."

Packing the twins in their carriage and eying the sky for any sign of an approaching storm, Stani set off slowly down the drive. Two pair of wide, dark eyes stared up at him, as they bumped gently over the gravel. "You see, lads, there are times when the best thing a man can do is get out of the house."

"I thought James and Penny were well on their way to married bliss, after that dashing proposal. What's the problem?" John was keeping pace, his eyes on the vista beyond the gate.

In as simple terms as he could manage, Stani tried to explain the many obstacles to what should have been happiness for two deserving people. "I suppose every couple who falls in love faces some compromises, but they have more than their share. Not to mention the fact that both have suffered a great deal in one way or another. When I first met James, he was still a pretty lost soul. And from what Emily says, Penny must have grieved for years after her fiancé was killed. She dedicated herself to helping her family, and now they are the greatest barrier to her happiness. Ironic."

"It sounds as if they've made up their minds to go ahead in spite of it all."

"Yes, but if I know anything about Penny, she would have wanted to be married in the Catholic Church. And with James being the son of a Presbyterian minister, that poses another problem. I hope they haven't just thrown over their convictions to rush into marriage. James said Penny wanted to live together, and he had refused."

"Good heavens. 'The course of true love never.' Is this going to upset Emily? I got the feeling she was already tottering on the brink. She's been through a lot, lad, what with you having surgery and then flying off that ladder."

Stani grimaced, pausing in his stride to adjust the blanket covering the babies' churning legs. "I know. And I'm sure this won't help. Maybe in trying to support Penny, she'll pull herself together." In the distance, the first rumble of thunder sounded. "Wonderful! Let's get back to the house. I'm afraid it may be a stormy night, inside and out."

But by the time they returned, just as the first raindrops began to fall, Emily, Penny and Lil had settled on the front porch, iced tea glasses in hand, and were deep in discussion over the details of the upcoming wedding. Emily greeted his bewildered look with an enthusiastic toast.

"We've come up with the most brilliant idea, darling. Actually, it was Lil who thought of it first. We're going to have a wedding on the roof."

"What?" The image of a wedding party clinging to the farmhouse's sloping roof, with a be-robed judge poised on one of the dormers, brought him to blinking halt.

"In New York. The first of September. If Penny and James were going to elope, they might as well elope to someplace special." Emily patted the cushion beside her.

"They wanted you two as witnesses anyway, and it would be a lot easier for them to come to you, rather than haul the twins somewhere to meet them. And Penny even knows a judge in Manhattan. Then they can have a nice, romantic weekend honeymoon right there." Lil was clearly proud of her inspiration.

Still a trifle perplexed at the turn of events, Stani took his seat on the swing, studying Emily's face to be sure she was really pleased with this plan. "It sounds as if you have things all sorted. Penny, are you certain James will be agreeable to this plot you girls have hatched?"

"I don't know why not. His only stipulation was that he not be required to wear anything more formal than jeans. And that you would be there, of course." Amazingly, Penny seemed elated, her face stretched wide in a characteristic smile again.

Emily took his hand, and he thought he detected a warning in her grip. "Then I propose we take everyone somewhere special to eat afterward, and I'm sure we can find a nice bridal suite for you, as a wedding present. That's my paltry contribution." The rain was coming down in earnest and a gust of wind sent a cool spray onto the porch just then. "I say we adjourn to the house, before we're all soaked." As everyone made the move, Stani held Emily back, a question in his eyes.

"It's complicated. I'll tell you later. But this is the best way. At least they'll have a day to remember, with people who love them." Her face was shadowed by the growing darkness, but he was sure he saw a tear or two.

Babies bathed and fed, Penny headed back to town, and John and Lil engaged in an ongoing game of Monopoly, Emily and Stani retreated to their bedroom. Outside, rain continued to pour and the occasional flash of lightning, with the accompanying rumble of thunder, added to the coziness of the room. Stretched on the sheepskin rug with the twins between them, Emily tried to explain what had taken place earlier.

"It seems the Catholic Church requires a form to be signed stating that although one or the other of the couple is a non-Catholic, the children of the marriage will be raised in the church. That was the final straw." She was gently tickling Andrew's upturned feet, watching him grin and swat aimlessly toward her hand.

"James refused to sign?"

"No, Penny did. She says she wants her children, if she ever has any, to be free to choose. She makes the valid point that they should experience both their parents' churches and decide for themselves."

Stani picked up Ian, who was almost asleep, and settled him tenderly on his chest. "So a civil ceremony was the only option? Why not marry in James' church?"

"The compromise is that they won't marry in a church at all. That way, no one can use that as a reason to be offended. Penny says she thinks her parents will eventually accept the marriage if they do it this way. We talked about reading some scripture, and they had already considered using the prayer of St. Patrick. It would certainly be appropriate for an Irish Catholic girl like Penny. When Lil suddenly popped up with the idea of having it on the roof, Penny burst into tears." She paused, fighting down her own emotions. "I knew you wouldn't object, so I just ran with the idea."

"Of course. You're sure it will work the same way for James?"

"If I know James, and I've known him a long time, he just wants to do things the simplest way possible. I think he really wanted us to be there, so this should be fine with him. Thank goodness they were planning to do it soon. We leave for England the following week."

Stani groaned softly. "One more thing for you to do, organizing a wedding, in the middle of packing. I'll be recording, remember, and so will Lil. That leaves everything on your beautiful shoulders."

Emily tossed her head, and taking a deep breath, smiled into

Andrew's bright eyes. "We can handle it, can't we Andrew? Besides, there's only so much to do for the wedding. A few flowers, maybe some recorded music. We can have the cake with the dinner you so generously offered. Of course, the loft will be in chaos, with all the packing, but maybe Mamie can help me get things organized." She lifted the baby high over her head. "You, my darling boy, don't look at all sleepy. Do you realize you have another busy day tomorrow? What say we go to the nice dark nursery and rock ourselves to sleep?"

She left Stani stretched on the rug, stroking Ian's warm little back and gazing up at the ceiling. The sound of the storm was far from comforting. He could picture lakes of water on the lawn and dripping trees overhead. "Ah, well, laddie, we can only do what we can do. Your Papa is no match for Mother Nature. The good thing is, you'll never mind, whatever we do for dinner on Sunday, will you? But it would be awfully nice to make your mother happy." The baby gave a little sigh and snuggled closer. Stani grinned as the springy red hair brushed his chin. "Time for bed, eh? I couldn't agree more. Have to be in top form for your Grandfather Milo tomorrow. Maybe if you and your brother could be at your most charming, he'll agree that building a studio in the barn is a brilliant idea. It certainly couldn't hurt if you'd soften him up a bit for me."

Emily was standing over him, laughter in her eyes. "Rallying the troops? Poor Milo, he doesn't stand a chance against the three of you." She took the baby from him. "Come along, darling boy. It's a perfect night for me to snuggle with your papa for a while." With a look that sent a chill of anticipation down his spine, she turned toward the nursery. "You'd better be in bed when I get back. I owe you a back rub, remember?"

After what evolved into much more than just a massage, he lay for quite a while listening to the rain. Emily was curled against him, but he sensed that she was not asleep, either. When she reached up to stroke his face, letting her fingers pass over his lips, he smiled into the darkness. "If we're tired and cranky in the morning, it will be all your fault, you know?"

"No apologies. We have too few opportunities as it is. I was just swept away by the sight of my husband in the role of father."

"Ah, was that what did it? Well, in that case, you'll have plenty of opportunities. It's a role I mightily enjoy, although lover still holds first place." He turned on his side, pulling her closer.

"Are you really concerned about Milo objecting to the studio? Or is there something else?"

He hesitated, reluctant to spoil the moment. "Bertram found out more about my mother's illness. She has colon cancer. It turns out Milo is paying for her to have some sort of experimental treatment."

"And that bothers you?"

"I should be the one to pay for something like that. But John thinks it would be wrong to challenge him on it. Apparently Milo has some long-standing arrangement with her."

"That would make sense. After all, Milo has you to thank for much of the money he's made over the years. I can understand his feeling some obligation to support your mother. It would fit with his idea of fairness."

"What a bizarre history we have. Everything seems to have developed in these odd, concentric circles around me. He didn't adopt me, but he certainly sees himself as my father. She didn't give me up entirely, but she completely abandoned any relationship with me. Somewhere along the way, the two of them seem to have formed this unholy partnership and left me totally in the dark. I have no idea what's gone on between them."

"Is it important now?"

With a long sigh, he buried his face against her shoulder. "I suppose if I wanted to know, I'd ask him, wouldn't I? I've always stayed away from the subject of what happened back then, for fear of learning things I didn't want to know."

She held him, idly stroking his hair. "There are a lot of things better left in the past. It's only what you do now that really matters. John's right. Arguing with Milo over your mother would be senseless. He's following his conscience, I imagine."

He couldn't help smiling. "I seem to remember telling you that when you got to know Milo, you'd understand why he sent you that check. Now it seems you understand him better than I do."

"I understand that he loves you, and that's all that matters to me, even though he may show it by writing large checks and pushing you harder than you might like. Taking care of your mother was probably his way of paying a debt of gratitude."

"Amazing. You make him sound positively benevolent. I would have thought he was paying her so he could have more control over me."

"Either way, you turned out to be the man you are, so he can't have done too much harm. He's proud of you Stani, and that's what you wanted, isn't it?"

He was silent for a time, and she wondered what he was thinking.

When he finally turned his face up to look into her eyes, he was smiling. "You not only saved my life, you made sense of it. Have I told you what a miracle worker you are?"

"Yes, I think you have. But you give me too much credit. Your heart was leading you in the right direction, that first time you came here."

"And you just gave it a little push, is that it?"

With a sleepy little laugh, she wound her arms around his neck. "Something like that."

Chapter Sixty-one

They woke to brilliant sunshine and a soft, warm breeze stirring the rose bushes beneath the window. The twins had slept through the night, and were more than ready to be changed and fed. By the time Stani could venture outside to check on any damage, the day was rapidly growing hotter. While Emily prepared breakfast, he took his mug of tea and walked toward the paddock, bent on having his morning chat with Stubby. But very quickly, he was distracted by the sound of industry coming from the barn.

Peering inside, he found Bobby hard at work. Looking up with a grin, he put down his tools and brushed the dust from his hands. "Figured I'd start in here, in case it rains some more. We can move them out front when they're done." He stood back to eye his handwork. Two long panels, hinged together to form a square, rested on two sets of sturdy saw horses. "What do you think, big enough?"

"It looks perfect. Do you think the yard will dry out if we don't get more rain?"

"It might. But if not, we could always lay down tarps, sort of like rugs. That way the folks wouldn't get their shoes muddy. We'll work it out, as long as it isn't raining on Sunday. Pity this old barn is so dirty. This would make a nice place for a party, if it was cleaned up good."

Stani looked around. Other than a veiling of cobwebs and the scattered layer of feed and straw on the floor, it wasn't that bad. The wooden walls and ceiling gleamed softly with age, and the light from the open stall doors highlighted the warmth of the space. "Bobby, you're a genius!"

"What?" Bobby frowned at him. "I was just thinking out loud. It would take a heap of work to get this place cleaned up."

"How large a heap? How many hands would it take?"

Rubbing his chin, Bobby started out cautiously, as if recognizing the risk in such a venture. "Well, I suppose with Ruthie and Robbie Joe, me and you, maybe Mr. Kimble and some of the others, we could get it done in a day or so. We'd need some good brooms and mops, maybe open all the stalls and let the breeze blow through to freshen the air, and it might clean up pretty nice. You really want to try to do it, don't you?" Bobby's spreading grin said he did too.

"I'm going to make a phone call. If Martha Jean thinks it would work, we'll do it." He was out the door and headed for the house when another thought struck. Stubby. The paddock was an unsavory mess. Turning back, he stuck his head in the barn door. "What about the paddock? How can we make that presentable with all this mud?"

Again, Bobby grinned. "A load of straw might help. We'll worry about that after we get all the rest done. Meanwhile, I'll move old Stubby downwind to the other end of the paddock. He won't like it, but I'll tell him it's for Miss Emily, and maybe he'll oblige me."

When Emily realized the barn was the scene of some sort of extraordinary activity, she went to investigate. The surprised expression on the half-dozen faces that looked up when she entered, not to mention the strong scent of sanitizing cleaner and the cloud of dust in the hayloft stopped her in her tracks. "What on earth, Stani? You aren't working on the studio already, are you?"

He congratulated himself on his quick recovery. "That's exactly what we're doing. I thought if we spruced the place up a bit Milo would be able to visualize the recording studio better." He hoped the emphasis in his voice would clue the others. To his relief, John chimed in.

"The dirt and dust might have put him off. You know how fastidious he is. Cleaned up a bit, he should be able to see what Stani's thinking of doing in here."

Emily eyed him suspiciously, but he thought the look said more that she thought he'd lost his grip, rather than indicating she might have a clue what was really in the works. "Can I help?"

"No, no, love. You have plenty to do inside, I know. I thought you were planning to make trifle for Milo." He started to walk her out the door, hoping to distract her. "Besides, I'm going to be ravenous by lunch time. Any chance of something hot and maybe some fresh baked bread?" That might keep her busy for the next several hours. With yet another skeptical glare, she started toward the house.

"Be careful, Stani. Don't forget your shoulder." Pausing, she turned back for one last look.

"Don't worry, love. It's fine. I thought I proved that last night." He laughed as she blushed and ducked in the back door.

Back inside the barn, John greeted him with a wry grin. "Quick thinking, lad. But judging by the look she gave you, she thinks you've gone just a bit over the edge. And what do you plan to tell her when she asks what you've organized for dinner on Sunday?"

"Ah, well, I'll come up with something. I only promised to tell her if things weren't working out. Since that's not the case, maybe she'll accept that I have everything under control." Even he wasn't impressed with his answer.

"Right. Let me know how that goes. Meanwhile it will take an army tramping through here to get everything in place. How do you propose to get that past her?"

Again, he waited for inspiration. "Diversion of some sort? Maybe I can convince her to go shopping or visiting, or something."

Bobby spoke up. "We need a plan, a schedule, so things get here in time. When's Mrs. Deem coming out? She'd be the one to set it all up. Then you'll know when to get your wife out of the house."

They talked as they worked, sorting through the various phases of the project bit by bit. By the time Martha Jean arrived just after lunch, under the pretense of bringing out some dresses for Emily to consider for the big day, they had come up with several possible scenarios. While Lil sat in judgment on the dress selection, with instructions to drag it out as long as possible, Martha Jean declared the need for a bite of lunch, which Stani graciously offered to serve her. And then, he suggested, as they headed toward the kitchen, she might be interested in his latest project. He'd love to get her opinion on the layout for the new studio.

"I think he's gone a little mad with this whole idea. It's all he talks about. I hope he hasn't forgotten that we still have things to do before Sunday." Emily met Lil's eyes in the mirror.

"I wouldn't worry. Now turn around. I like that, but maybe the blue one would be cooler. Is Stani going to wear black? Surely, he could find something a little more cheerful. Although, if you wore white, it could look pretty cool in the pictures. Are you having a real photographer, or just a bunch of people taking snapshots?" She rattled on, wondering if Emily wasn't too smart to fall for all this. But it was kind of exciting, being part of a conspiracy. If they pulled it off, she was pretty sure Emily would be thrilled. Of course, she'd probably also cry. Lil knew she'd been on the edge of a meltdown lately, and Stani surprising her with something so sweet would be just the thing to set her off.

On Thursday afternoon, when Stani was preparing to announce his plan to create a state-of-the-art recording studio in the old red barn, Emily served tea in the front room; a proper English tea complete with sandwiches, scones and a luscious trifle made with sponge cake and more of the native blackberries, picked that morning from the hedge along the fence line. With the twins situated on a quilt in the middle of the floor where everyone could easily admire them, the six adults gathered for some much needed refreshment. Not only were Milo and Jana weary from the long drive, but Stani and John had been hard at work in the barn much of the day. Lil had been enlisted to help Emily in the kitchen, while also making sure the twins were clean and fresh for the arrival of their grandparents.

After his first cup of tea, Milo was sufficiently revived to turn the conversation in a totally unexpected direction. Taking an official-looking envelope from the breast pocket of his jacket, he drew out its contents with a flourish. "I have something of a surprise for you, Stani. You've been summoned by Her Majesty the Queen."

With a distracted frown, Stani responded simply, "What?"

"The Queen. Your presence has been requested at a charity gala at Buckingham Palace in November."

"What?" His color deepened and he squinted across the room at Milo.

"I said the Queen has requested your presence at the royal residence. You are to perform for Her Majesty's charity gala on November twelfth of this year." Milo's response suggested that he thought Stani hadn't understood him over the noise of the general conversation. He spoke slowly and distinctly, but again, Stani's only response was a question.

"Why?"

"I assume she wants to hear you play before she approves your nomination to the New Year Honours List." This time Milo smiled, a twitch of a grin playing at the corners of his mouth.

"What?" Everyone had stopped talking, pausing to tune in the one-sided conversation.

"Stani, really, have you suddenly grown hard of hearing? I said this letter is from the Queen's secretary, requesting your performance at a benefit concert at Buckingham Palace on November the twelfth of this year. Furthermore, I have it on good authority that you are to be named to the New Year Honours List. You have been nominated for a CBE."

Once again, Stani frowned and, carefully setting his cup on the table nearby, asked, "Why?"

John spoke up. "Let me take this one, Milo. Because you're a British citizen, and in the course of your career thus far, you've contributed a barge-load of cash to the national economy. As a result, you're probably well on your way to a knighthood by the time you're forty. This is just the first step." Stani listened in silence, then turned his questioning gaze back to Milo.

"I might have phrased it a bit differently, adding that you are being recognized for your service to music, and most likely also for your charitable efforts, but yes, John has summed it up nicely."

Everyone started to talk at once. Jana exclaimed softly that it was a great honor for someone so young. Lil asked if he would have to be called "Sir Stani" now. John replied in the negative. And Emily simply walked across the room to her husband, who was showing every sign of going into shock, and kissed him soundly.

"Congratulations, darling. Aren't you thrilled?"

Stani looked accusingly at John. "You knew about this, didn't you?"

"Of course. I had to unsnarl the logistical nightmare of getting you two to London from Paris and back to Brussels in forty-eight hours, not to mention getting Lil and the twins moved along as well. I've enlisted Bertram to do the security detail in London."

Running a hand through his hair, Stani looked at the faces around the room. "I don't know what to say."

"You'll have to say yes. Milo's already accepted on your behalf. Of course, I guess you could still refuse the CBE if you wanted to." John was still grinning, watching the color rise in Stani's face. "But I'd take the medal, if I were you. Better form."

"What exactly is a CBE?" Lil wanted to know.

"Commander of the Order of the British Empire." Stani pronounced the words softly, as if echoing some long-ago lesson.

"Sounds like a big deal. What do you have to do, after you become a 'Commander of the Order of the British Empire'?" In her best British accent, Lil imitated Stani's reverent tone.

"Nothing. Just hang the medal on the wall. If you march in a parade, you won't have to go last. I hear the MBE's bring up the rear." John's description brought a giggle from Emily.

"I can't see you marching in any parades, Stani. But it's a wonderful honor I'm sure. Milo, will we have to go to the Palace again for him to receive the award?"

"Oh, yes. It's considered quite a huge media event."

Emily poured fresh tea into Stani's cup and passed it to him. "Drink this. You look as though you might need it."

He grinned up at her, finally seeming to come to grips with the news. "Never in my wildest dreams did I expect anything like this."

"Well, you should have, my boy. If rock and roll bands, even the very scruffiest of them, can be awarded honors, then why shouldn't someone like you be recognized? You've represented your country most admirably all over the world, and as John so aptly put it, generated a barge-load of revenue in the process. I quite anticipated this day would come." Milo's tone implied this was just another of his carefully planned maneuvers, calculated to advance Stani's career.

His eyes still wide with the shock of it all, Stani gazed down at the twins. Andrew was studying his toes, his chubby little legs waving in the air, while Ian was staring up at Milo, apparently hanging on his every word.

"Did you hear that, laddies? Your papa gets to play for the Queen. Although I doubt that impresses you nearly so much as it should."

"Well, it certainly impresses their mother. But before we get too far ahead of ourselves, wasn't there something *you* wanted to tell Milo about?" Emily was concerned the news had thrown Stani into such a state he might have forgotten his mission.

Stani drew a deep breath, ran a hand through his hair and seemed to pull his focus back to the present. "Ah, yes. Nothing quite so spectacular, Milo, but I have a proposition to make. It may sound a bit far-fetched at first, but bear with me until you've had a chance to hear what inspired me."

Quickly captivated, Milo listened closely as the plan was outlined. Stani got his violin and they adjourned to the barn, with John trailing along. It was over half an hour before they returned, and by the eager expressions on both faces, it was plain that Milo had been convinced. The conversation became so animated that Emily and Lil gathered up the twins and, with Jana, retreated to the front porch.

"What a pair! Now Milo will talk of nothing else. He's always been interested in having his own studio. Stani has made yet another of his dreams come true." As Jana settled herself in a chair, balancing her tea cup on the broad arm, she laughed softly. "My dear, you should never worry that life will be dull with Stani. He's enough like Milo that his mind never rests. He's always creating something."

Draping the netting over the babies' cots, and giving her little ones a smile, Emily agreed. "He's brilliant, isn't he? Wait until you hear the lullaby he's written." Her eyes sparkled as the voices inside rose enthusiastically. "At least they're in agreement. I'd hate to think of the volume if they weren't!"

Chapter Sixty-two

Stani had never known the kind of satisfaction he felt as he watched the progress in the barn. If he could actually succeed in keeping Emily in the dark until the project was completed, all the better. It became an obsession, involving whispered phone conversations, clandestine meetings, and enlisting everyone available to distract her as people came and went, conveying everything from dishware to furniture past the house. Fortunately, the one window in the nursery faced the woods. He encouraged everyone to ask for a visit to the little room, complete with a viewing of the twins' wardrobe, which gave ample time for a vehicle to creep past the house and park out of sight behind the barn. Proud mother though she was, Emily began to question all this interest in baby clothes. But when even Milo spent a half-hour inspecting the nursery, looking over all the books and toys that awaited the babies in the future, she decided her sons must be as fascinating to everyone else as they were to their parents.

With Peg's arrival on Friday morning came yet another surprise. While there had been some discussion about what the twins would wear for their baptism, nothing had been decided. Emily was leaning toward the white rompers trimmed in blue piping. Stani favored the blue and yellow plaid outfits with matching caps that he said made the babies look as if they were going golfing. Lil secretly thought they looked adorable in the mint green overalls she had purchased for them in Bergdorf's, but kept that opinion to herself. But Peg had outdone them all this time, as it turned out.

An immaculately wrapped box, with a gold and silver label that spoke to the expense of the contents, was opened to reveal a pair of white lawn christening robes. The style was definitely masculine, with tailored collar and cuffed sleeves, and each featured a row of tiny pearl buttons down the pleated front. The robes were elegantly long and sparkling white. Clearly, Peg had intended to dress the babies in the very finest money could buy.

"These are fit for royalty, Peg. Good heavens, they may have been intended for just that. Is that a royal warrant on the label?" Stani held up the box top, his tone almost, but not quite, disapproving.

"Of course. That was exactly my point. Your sons are little princes, Stani. They should be dressed like royalty. I had a friend of mine in London pick these up for me. I know the babies are Americans, but their father is still British. Please tell me *you* like them, Emily."

Studying the garments, hesitant to touch them and spoil the delicate fabric, Emily glanced questioningly at Stani. "I love them, Peg. I've never seen anything so. . . so. . .exquisite. Aren't they wonderful, darling?"

"Of course they are. I appreciate the sentiment, Peg, but you shouldn't have gone to so much trouble." Still not certain how to accept such an excessive gift, Stani sensed he might be on the wrong side of the argument.

"But since we have these, Stani, surely they would be the perfect thing. Nothing else we've considered would be as appropriate." At last Emily tucked a finger into one tiny cuff. He knew he'd been overruled.

"Well, Stani, what do you say?" The challenge in Peg's voice was tempered by a hint of a teasing smile.

"What can I say, but thank you? However, Auntie Shannon, next time you're tempted to spend so much, please try to control the urge. No diamond studded rattles or gold plated tricycles, please." He gave her quick kiss on the cheek and carefully replaced the box top. "Now, if you'll come with me for a few minutes, I want to show you my latest project."

"Stani, surely that can wait. At least let Peg visit with the twins first." Emily gave him a disapproving frown.

"There'll be plenty of time for that. She owes me a few minutes, after running roughshod over my desire to raise my sons like ordinary boys. Royal warrants indeed. What brought on this sudden royal invasion? I suppose you know about the Honours list and the Royal command performance, too?" With a firm hand on Peg's arm, he led her out the back door. When they were out of earshot, leaving Emily standing at the kitchen table shaking her head in bewildered amusement, Stani whispered, "I need a huge favor."

By Friday night, Emily was wondering if she shouldn't go ahead and prepare for the dinner on Sunday herself. It seemed Stani had forgotten all about it in his obsession with the plans for the studio. He talked of nothing else in the little time she spent with him. He was constantly in the barn with one or the other of their guests, and had gone so far as to enlist Bobby to begin some of the preliminary work. She was sure that had been the sound of a power saw and some other sort of machine coming across the yard for several days. Anxious as she was over the dinner arrangements, she hesitated to ask Stani if he'd forgotten. Her emotions were already slightly raw, and if he confessed to his failure, she was pretty sure she'd fall apart on the spot.

After everyone had gone, late on Friday night, she began to search the cabinets, setting out sufficient china, silver and glassware for twenty-four. The silver needed polishing, so she carted the chest into the kitchen, hoping to work off her anxiety on the knives and forks, rather than let it build up any further. She had just located the polish and taken out the first stack of forks when Stani came in from the barn.

"What are you doing, love?" He wrapped his arms around her waist and peered over her shoulder.

"What does it look like? I'm getting things ready for Sunday."

"I thought you were going to leave that up to me." He laid a tender kiss on her neck.

"I haven't seen any sign that you were doing anything. You've been so busy with other things." She tried very hard to keep her voice even, but there was no disguising the underlining tremor.

"I thought we agreed that if I wasn't having any success, I'd let you know. Actually, my plans are falling into place nicely." He took the fork from her hand and turned her to face him. "Don't you trust me, darling girl?"

She looked away, fighting to control her expression. "I guess."

"You guess? What sort of answer is that?" He put a finger under her chin, gently forcing her to meet his gaze.

"I thought you might have forgotten, with everything that's going on."

He kissed the tip of her nose. "You thought I had forgotten that I made you a promise? Have I ever been guilty of that before?"

"No." Her lower lip quivered dangerously.

"And I haven't forgotten now. You wouldn't want to spoil my surprise just yet, would you?"

"Surprise?"

"Yes. I have a little surprise for you, but it's not quite finished yet. If you can be patient just a bit longer, I think it will be well worth the wait."

Her eyes filled and she slid her arms around his neck. "I'm sorry. I didn't mean to doubt you. You're sure everything's under control?"

"Positive. Now, put these things away. We won't need them. Anyway, it's way past your bedtime, isn't it? How are my boys?"

"Sleeping like angels. Do you realize they are finally sleeping through the night now?" Wiping at a stray tear, she smiled at him. "You really have something planned for Sunday?"

"Of course I do. Now can we go to bed? The twins may be sleeping all night, but they still wake up very early. And have you noticed they insist on breakfast the minute they're awake? That particular trait they definitely inherited from you." Guiding her through the door, he turned out the light. Time was running short, he knew. She was very close to the edge. He would catch her, but he hoped her tears would be tears of joy, if they had to fall at all.

On Saturday morning, just after they had finished breakfast, Peg's rental car came through the gate.

"Good heavens, why is she here so early? I would have expected her to sleep in today." Stani was watching from the front window, Ian in his arms.

"No idea. She didn't say anything last night about coming this morning." Emily laid Andrew on the couch beside her and buttoned her robe. "This little man is a glutton, Papa. He's draining me dry, every time. I think we're about ready for something solid." She tickled the pink soles of his feet, which were waving in the air as usual. "No more newborns. You're big boys now, aren't you?"

Raising Ian to his shoulder, where the baby nestled sweetly, Stani grinned. "Not all that big, Mummy. When they're too big to hold with one hand, I might agree." He stepped out on the porch to meet Peg.

"Good morning! How are my two favorite men? Oh, Stani, let me hold him. Ian, right? Look at that hair. He looks as if he's been caught in a whirlwind." Taking the baby, Peg tried to smooth the springs and sprouts of pale red hair.

"He may be, if we're not careful," Stani said under his breath with a speaking nod toward Emily.

"Right." Going past him into the house, Peg announced brightly, "Emily, dear, I had the most exciting idea last night. I want to go shopping."

Emily, just rising from settling Andrew on the floor, blinked at her in disbelief. "Shopping? Where?"

"On your charming town square. I would absolutely love to explore all those adorable little shops. And we can take the twins, show them off. I told Milo we'd meet them for lunch in that sweet little cafe at noon. Now get yourself dressed and I'll pick out something for the babies to wear. Come on, Stani, you'll help me get them ready, won't you?" She was off, Ian in her arms, still talking as she headed for the nursery. "You'd like that, wouldn't you my little darling? Auntie Shannon will find some nice little something to buy for you and your brother, just wait and see."

With a shake of her head, Emily sighed. "I guess we're going shopping. What on earth put that idea into her head?" She tried in vain to imagine any possible lure the humble "little" merchants of her "little" town might have to entice a world-class shopper like Peg Shannon.

With a shrug that suggested he would never attempt to understand what motivated Peg, Stani picked up Andrew. "Better get ready, you two. And if I were you, darling, I'd wear comfortable shoes."

It was a rare sight, the elegant lady in her designer linen pantsuit and Emily in jeans and sandals, pushing the carriage in and out of every shop in the town's four-block shopping district. They even stopped in at the post office for a chat with Myrtice Green. Peg made a purchase at every stop, including the careful selection of a cast-iron skillet at the hardware store. Her chef, she declared, had been lamenting the condition of the one in the brownstone's kitchen. She browsed the racks at Martha Jean's, and Emily thought it a shame that only the high school girl who helped out on Saturdays was on hand to experience a shopping professional like Peg. Martha Jean would have loved a shot at a sale like that. As it was, Peg bought an evening sweater for Emily, a soft white mohair with pearls sewn on the collar. The perfect thing, she said, for those cool nights in Eastern Europe. They left the little clerk staring after them in awe, as Peg paid with a hundred dollar bill, the smallest thing she had left in her ostrich skin wallet.

By the time they met Milo and Jana at the cafe, the trunk of Peg's car was full of her day's haul. The twins had been perfect companions, napping for a time and then cooing appropriately when admired by passersby. But now they were hungry and in need of dry diapers. One by one, Emily took them to the restroom, changed them and, handing

Andrew off to Peg with a bottle, settled with Ian in the sagging armchair in the tiny ladies' lounge. As the baby nursed, she chuckled to herself. What kind of mischief was Stani up to? Surely, he was responsible for sending Peg on this charade of a shopping trip. It had been fun, she had to admit, watching Peg pretend fascination with the very ordinary wares in the shops, stretching the limits of her imagination to come up with an excuse for each of her purchases. Other than the sweater, and the stuffed Scottish terriers she'd bought for the twins, none of the things in her trunk could possibly have appealed to her.

He was definitely on some sort of mission to keep her away from home today. She would have to pretend surprise when she got back to the farm and discovered his secret. Maybe he had set up a tent in the front yard, or added a dining table in the front room. Or perhaps he had simply arranged for everyone to have dinner at the church social hall. Whatever it was, she would reward him generously for his efforts. If nothing else, this ridiculous excursion had lifted her sagging spirits. As she joined the others, she realized Stani's family had come to his aid in whatever he was plotting. They were even going so far as to proclaim enthusiasm for the burgers and fries she'd recommended they order for lunch. With a little wink at her babies, she tucked into her meal, wishing Stani could see the urbane threesome, sitting elbow to elbow with a room full of Saturday diners; farmers in bib-overalls, their wives in their second best home-sewn dresses, a crew of high school boys, red faced and sweaty after a morning of training for the upcoming football season, and four house-painters, resplendent in their spattered coveralls, who had paused after hours of working in the sun. If Milo's nose seemed just a trifle offended by the various human odors mingling with those of grilled onions and cabbage soup, he nonetheless graciously praised the spirit of country folk, declaring they certainly knew how to make the most of their time. "Hard work is its own reward, as they say," he stated to no one in particular. "No doubt that's one of the reasons Stani finds this part of the world so appealing."

Jana laughed softly. "That and the fact that he found this beautiful girl hidden away here. All work and no play, as they also say, dear."

When she returned home, Emily found Stani on the front porch with James and Penny. There was no indication that he had done more all day than shower and dress. Relaxed and smiling, he helped her put the twins down for a nap, admired the gifts Peg had bought for them, and settled back in the swing. The party continued until almost dinnertime, when Milo and Jana took their leave, followed shortly by Peg. Talk turned to the wedding plans, with James expressing his gratitude for what he termed Emily's genius.

"It wasn't even my idea. Lil came up with it." It occurred to Emily that Lil was nowhere to be seen. In fact, she had been absent all afternoon.

"No matter who thought of it, it has made my sweetheart very happy, and that is after all the ultimate goal. For that I owe you a great big thank you." He looked up to Penny, from his place on the floor at her feet, with an adoring grin.

"I told them you'd love the plan. I don't think I could have dreamed up anything so romantic. Of course, if it rains, we'll just have to settle for getting married in the living room. But at least the view is still spectacular. Wait until you see this place, James. It's like looking at a drive-in movie screen from your easy chair. Windows all around, with a view of all the bridges over the Hudson. Someday, maybe we'll have a place like that."

He laughed, but Emily could see his discomfort. "Maybe not quite that fancy, honey. The place you have is grand enough. Old P.B. has his own bedroom, after all. Not every old tabby can say that."

"I know. But it's nice to dream. I really never thought I'd have the luxury of my own apartment. I used to imagine myself living back in my old bedroom, working as a public defender for little or nothing. And I'd still be happy with that, you know."

"That's my girl. Keep your priorities straight. Now don't you think we should let these nice people have a little time to themselves? My mom's frying chicken for dinner. We don't want to be late for that. My dad'll grab both drumsticks, if I'm not there to stop him." Unfolding his long legs, James got to his feet and offered Penny his hands.

"We'll see you in the morning. I'll have my camera loaded and ready. I know you have a real photographer coming, but I want lots of snapshots to put on my refrigerator." Penny leaned over and gave Emily a hug, then did the same for Stani, whispering something in his ear. Emily thought it sounded suspiciously like "Get it over with."

They ate dinner in virtual silence. Emily's eyes kept going to the window, as if she were waiting for something to suddenly appear on the lawn. During the babies' bath time, she warmed up a bit, but as soon as the twins were fed and tucked into their cribs, the silence resumed. Stani tried to open a conversation about the schedule for the morning, what time they needed to be at the church for a few pictures and how they would need to adjust the twins' feeding schedule. But other than a halfhearted response, she hardly seemed to be listening.

She sat down at the kitchen table, leafing through a cookbook, her face growing ever sadder. Stani resisted as long as he could. "Emily, darling, come with me." He took the book out of her hands and pulled her to her feet. When she looked into his eyes, tears started to well.

"Where are we going?"

"To the barn." Turning, he pulled her along, his heart beginning to race.

"The barn? Stani, I don't want to talk about the studio tonight. Haven't you spent enough time on that for a while?" She pulled back, digging in her heels.

"Just come with me. There's something you have to see." He tugged harder, and she followed, but he could sense the glare fixed on the back of his head.

When they reached the barn door, he stopped her. "Wait here, just for a second."

He could see that she was again on the verge of tears. "Stani, please. Can't this wait until tomorrow?"

He opened the door just enough to get in, holding on to her hand and reaching for the light switch. As the lights came on, he drew her into the barn. "Surprise!"

The space was awash with soft light. Where bare bulbs had hung from the high ceiling, now two huge brass chandeliers sparkled with dozens of tiny lights. The ceiling itself was tented with streamers of baby blue and white crepe paper, and ropes of the same twisted streamers festooned the rail around the hayloft. In the middle of the now pristine and polished concrete floor sat a long oval table draped in blue and white gingham, topped by Lilianne's lace tablecloth. Twenty-four honey pine ladder-back chairs were lined around the table and each place setting of blue transfer ware included a linen napkin and silver flatware. In the center of the table, a huge blue and white tureen held an arrangement of yellow roses, white Queen Anne's lace and trailing honeysuckle. At the side of the space, near the former stalls, a long buffet table sat at the ready.

Stani watched as she slowly took in the sight, her eyes gleaming and her lips parted in a silent gasp. He gently explained that the table was Bobby's creation, the chairs came from a now defunct restaurant in Baxter, the light fixtures were left-overs from the remodel of Jack's house, and the dishes had been purchased from several antique shops in the area. Lil had arranged the flowers, spending hours searching the meadows for enough to fill the tureen. The silver was on loan from the church social hall, and of course, the tablecloth was the one she had hoped to use in the first place.

When she turned to him, tears streaming down her face, he thought he might cry himself. "Do you like it, darling girl? Everyone has worked so hard to make this happen for you."

One great sob and she came into his arms. "It's the most beautiful thing I've ever seen," she gasped. Clinging to him, she showered him with little kisses, sobbing broken questions in his ear. "How on earth did you do all this? How did you get it all in here without my seeing? Who found all these things on such short notice?"

Stani laughed, holding her at arm's length. "I had an army of helpers, my love. I could never have done this on my own. Bobby and Ruthie and even Robbie Joe, Martha Jean and Jack, and most amazingly, John, all cleaned up the place. Penny and James helped set the table this morning, and of course, Milo and Jana and Peg ran interference for us. Sara and Mike went all over the county hunting things. Mike found the chairs and Sara finally found the last of the plates this morning."

Wiping at her eyes, she looked again from floor to ceiling. "Who came up with the decorations? They're so beautiful."

"That would be Martha Jean. Originally, we were going to set it up under the trees in the front yard, but the rain got me worried. Then Bobby said this would make a nice place for a party, if it were cleaned up. That was the moment of inspiration, I think. It caught everyone's imagination. You almost spoiled things when you walked in on us that first morning."

"I thought you'd become obsessed with the studio. It never occurred to me this is what you were doing. Oh, Stani, it's the sweetest thing you've ever done for me!" Taking his face in her hands, she kissed him, the kind of long, tender kiss he had hoped for. When she finally let him speak, he protested.

"Surely not the sweetest? But certainly the most elaborate. I've never schemed so hard in my life. I wanted so much to have it all completed before you saw it."

"Sending Peg all over town shopping was inspired. It was worth worrying about what you were up to, just to watch her going through all that pretense. And if you could only have seen them sitting at lunch with all the locals, you'd have died laughing. Oh, Stani, I'll never forget this, never!" Another kiss and he was sure it was time to adjourn to the house. But Emily wanted to walk around the room, touching things and admiring the transformation of the rustic space. The floor was amazing, the walls were gorgeous, and even the "old barn" smell was gone.

"So you think it's suitable for our guests?" He tried to gather her into his arms, but she was still exploring.

"Oh, yes. They'll be as impressed as I am. Oh, but I guess most of them have already seen it, haven't they? In that case, they should all be able to appreciate the fruits of their labors. How am I ever going to thank everyone for all their hard work?" Her face was suddenly serious again.

"Just smile, love. They all want you to be happy, that's why they did it. Of course, there is one old friend who isn't quite so pleased with the arrangement."

"Who?"

"Stubby. He's tethered down at the far end of the paddock for the time being. He might appreciate a little attention tomorrow."

Laughing, they turned out the lights and walked across the yard. Beneath the canopy of stars, she stopped and pulled him around to face her. "How could I ever doubt you? You'd do almost anything to make me happy, I think."

"Not almost, darling. Anything. Well, anything legal. I might draw the line at theft or murder, unless I felt it was truly warranted. But you deserve all I can do and more. Now come in the house, Emily. I think you might show your appreciation better in the privacy of our bedroom. I'm pretty sure I can feel Stubby glaring at us all the way across the yard."

From her bedroom window, Lil watched them go to the barn. Stani practically had to drag Emily down there, but when they came out, they were laughing and obviously the surprise had had the expected effect. She would have loved to go downstairs and hear Emily's reaction, but her sunburned nose was slathered with cold cream. She had spent most of the morning picking flowers in the fields, getting repeatedly bitten by some kind of bug and blistering her nose. She'd be a sight tomorrow, but it had been worth it in the long run. Her contribution, aside from helping keep Emily in the dark, was the centerpiece on the table, and if she did say so, it was gorgeous.

Tomorrow she would become Andrew's godmother. She had a lot to live up to, given the tradition of godparents in her family. Her mother had been so central a part of Emily's life, and Lilianne had done the same for her when she was alive. While Lil had been just thirteen when her godmother had died, she had grieved the loss of that warm, loving support. It had been Lilianne who had taken her side when, at age eight, she had chosen her instrument over her mother's adamant objections. A tiny little girl with a great big viola, Angela had argued, would never be taken seriously. Better the violin, her own first instrument, or maybe even the flute. But Lilianne had encouraged her to follow her impulse, saying if the musical voice she wanted was the viola, she should have it. Even Angela would not argue with her best friend.

Lil heard Stani and Emily laughing downstairs, heard their bedroom door close and knew they wouldn't be going to sleep any time soon. They were insatiable, she thought. Before anyone knew it, there'd be another baby coming along. Emily was already talking about a little girl.

Climbing into bed, careful not to set her bug bites itching, Lil turned her mind to the next few weeks, to all that would have to be accomplished in the short time left before they headed off for Europe. Her first recording session, a wedding, and the mountains of packing for an extended trip. Not to mention visits to the pediatrician for the twins, and the shopping trip Peg had promised her, for what she described as a wardrobe suitable for a member of Stani Moss's entourage. With the salary they were paying her, plus her earnings from the session, she would actually be in a position to buy the things Peg picked out.

When they got to London, Charles would be waiting. They would be living in the same house, and Emily had promised she'd have plenty of time off to spend with him. Lil pictured herself, in her sophisticated new clothes, going out with Charles to meet his new friends. She would pretend enthusiasm for this authentic music movement, although it still sounded painfully discordant to her. Stani had predicted she'd learn to appreciate it eventually, so maybe she would. Meanwhile, she would support whatever Charles wanted to do. If Stani and Emily were an example of a truly successful couple, doing whatever made the other one happy had to be the top priority.

As she drifted into a restless sleep, her nose still stinging and the occasional urge to scratch entering her dreams, Lil had the foggy realization that her life was about to take yet another in a series of unexpected twists. Mother's helper, world traveler, studio musician and now godmother; none of these roles had been in her plans a year ago. Thanks to Stani Moss, and of course to Emily, too, her little dreams of playing the viola for her living had been blown into a much larger life than she could have imagined for herself. To think it had all started that night in a smoky ski lodge was to give herself too much credit, but she would never forget that first sight of Stani, leaning against the wall looking lost and uncomfortable. Amazing how he had found his way from that boy to the man he was now. Somehow, in his journey, he had taken them all along with him; and as far as Lil could see, the end was nowhere in sight.

Chapter Sixty-Three

While they had decided to break with tradition in their wedding ceremony, Emily and Stani chose to follow the baptismal service to the letter. They met with Pastor Mike, selected the scriptures to be read and beyond that, left everything to him. If, in the future, when they could speak for themselves, the twins turned out to be either conservative or creative in their religious views, at least their parents had not set them on a path in either direction.

As if inspired by his knowledge of these new parents, Mike opted to make the service somewhat more personal than usual, anyway. In his sermon, he talked about the nature of families, citing the example of Jesus' own relationship with his eclectic mix of disciples and followers. He mentioned parents who, like Abraham and Sarah, had started their family much later in life than considered practical. He gave credit to the many couples who had raised children not their own. He talked about the value of mentors, and teachers, the duties of godparents and family friends in the lives of both the child and his parents. In short, he pointed out, a family was comprised of many more than father, mother, sister and brother; and family members were bound together, not so much by common genes or history, as by love and mutual respect. Through baptism, these infants would be welcomed today into the household of faith, the church. Let that welcome serve as a reminder of the bond that joined all the members of that household, a bond that must surely go beyond that of mere flesh and blood if the church were to serve its purpose in ministering to a suffering world.

When the service concluded, with the circle of friends gathered around the babies and their parents, it was clear to everyone what Pastor Mike had been referring to. Here was a fresh-faced young girl, and an equally stern-faced middle-aged man, a trim, petite woman in a stylish business suit, and a tall, gaunt man in blue jeans, his hair flowing to his shoulders, all reaching out to lay hands on the infants as the final blessing was given. The focused devotion of all the members, as they smiled, or in some cases wept, was evidence of precisely the point of the pastor's message. If a family was indeed a unit held together by love, respect and dedication to the common good, then these two tiny red-haired boys had been blessed with the finest.

The party in the barn went on well into the afternoon. Large quantities of rich food, overlapping conversations and general high spirits fueled the guests' enthusiasm well past dessert. At some point the twins, stationed in their cots near their parents at the head of the table, expressed their desire for a nap. At their mother's urging, their reluctant father was persuaded to play his violin, lulling them to sleep with the music he had composed just for them. When they'd been carted off to the quiet of their nursery, the party continued, the music growing livelier with encouragement from everyone around the table.

When, well past five o'clock, the last car pulled through the gate, Emily collapsed into an armchair in the sunroom, declaring that it had been the best party ever, except of course for their wedding reception.

"I think it may have as much to do with the caliber of our guests as with any efforts on our part. They seem to have a gift for celebration, no matter what the occasion."

She laughed as she slid over to make room for him beside her. "They do love to party, don't they? I saw not one bored face around that wonderful table. And only our babies tired of the festivities. No one wanted to be the first to leave." Kicking off her shoes, she wiggled her toes. "Thank goodness Penny and James had a plane to catch, or we might still be at it."

Stani pulled off his tie, carefully folding it before dropping it to the floor. "Should we be helping Sal and Joey pack up? Angela disappeared upstairs with Lil, I noticed. Martha Jean said to leave the dishes soaking, but I think I should at least haul them up to the house tonight."

"Oh, no you don't. Those washtubs are heavy. Maybe after dark, we could just sneak down there and wash them ourselves." She laid a protective hand on his shoulder. "You're sure you didn't do anything too strenuous? Bobby said you were planning to muck out the paddock, until he stopped you. Really, Stani, you need to take better care of yourself."

Drawing her head to his chest, he kissed her hair. "Not to worry. Next week I go back to the life of a pampered concert artist. No more farm-hand for a while."

"Pampered? Don't I wish? I know what your schedule looks like, remember? The next four months will be grueling. I suppose this week I could force you to rest, but somehow I expect you'd find a way to get past me. If I tied you to the bedpost and stood watch, would it keep you in bed past sunup?"

He grinned, contemplating the proper response to such an appealing proposition. Just as he was about to reply, the back door opened and John came in, carrying the violin.

"Nice show, lad. Can I pack this thing up for a while, or are you planning an encore?"

"Put it away, John. I hadn't even intended to play today."

"But the boys wanted to hear their lullaby, Papa." She nestled closer, her arm sliding across his waist.

"They would have been happy with a music box rendition of 'Twinkle, twinkle, little star.' Their mother's the one who demands that I play at every opportunity. I begin to think you like my music, darling, although I seem to remember you said it had nothing to do with your attraction to me." He tried to kiss her, but she turned her head and protested.

"I told you I'd love you even if you were a plumber. But since you aren't, there's nothing wrong with showing off your real talents." Finally joined in a long, sweet kiss, Stani was aware of John still standing over them.

"Yes, John? Something else?"

"Oh, no. Just enjoying this tender little scene. I keep wondering when you two will tire of this sort of thing."

"Ha! Not in your lifetime, my friend. Not even in ours. Right, darling girl?" But Emily had rested her head on his shoulder and was very close to falling asleep. "Here, love, before you drift off let's get you to the bedroom. A nice little nap before supper is what you need."

Watching as Stani led her away, her bare feet shuffling wearily across the floor, John chuckled to himself. He wouldn't be back, he was sure. At least not for a while. With a little lilt to his stride, he went into the kitchen. It had been a day to remember, sacred and jubilant; but then with those two, every day made some sort of memory. He had just been saying to Peg, when he put her in her car, that if not for them, he'd be a sour old man by now. Grinning, he recalled that she had replied he was not old, and certainly far from sour. In fact, he was one of the sweetest men she'd ever known. So thoughtful and kind, and the way he talked to those babies, well, she said with a twinkle in her eyes, she only wished someone would speak to her in that tone of voice.

Pouring himself a glass of cold tea, he started toward the front of the house. Stani was right, a nap before supper, then a nice long sit on the front porch tonight. This country life was fine, but he was about ready to get back in harness, pack this lot up and hit the road again. Too much leisure time gave a man the notion that settling down might be nice, but it was just a notion. He couldn't afford to dwell on it long, because for some strange reason it always made him think of one certain woman. And she was not, he was pretty sure, the settling down kind.

Stani had managed to help Emily out of her dress before she'd fallen face down across the bed in her slip. Taking off his shoes and shirt, he joined her, turning on his side where he could see her profile on the pillow. In the cool dimness of the room, he thought back over the day. There were so many things he wanted to fix in his memory, including the way she had looked today. There would be pictures, he knew, but would they capture the way he had felt as the day had unfolded?

They had gone early to the church to meet the photographer from Charlottesville who had taken their wedding pictures. He had been thrilled with their choice of black and white, Stani in a black linen suit and Emily in a crisp white dress trimmed in sharp black. The babies had started the day dressed in simple white rompers. Emily had put something in their hair, so that the wispy copper crowns had settled into soft curls. They had posed for a number of informal shots before the christening robes were added. At that point, the photographer had moved them to the narthex, positioning them before the stained-glass window. It was there that Stani had first recognized how spiritually charged the day would be. He wasn't sure what Emily might be feeling, standing next to the window dedicated in memory of her parents, but he had been almost overcome by what he could only call a presence, an energy that surrounded them, as they stood, each holding a baby, haloed by the sparkling light.

The pictures would capture their proud smiles, the waving arms of the babies, the moment when Andrew had reached up to touch his mother's face in what seemed a loving gesture. They had eventually been joined by friends and family, posed with first small groups and then one giant assemblage clustered beneath the window. After the service, they had posed at the font with Pastor Mike in his robes and all four godparents gathered around.

But there had been moments during the service which no camera could record, and it was those he especially wanted to remember. The scripture reading from the First Letter of Peter, which he had selected. "You are a chosen race, a royal priesthood, a holy nation, God's own people, in order that you may proclaim the mighty acts of the One who called you out of darkness into God's marvelous light." The verse had reminded him of his own journey through darkness and the moment he had felt that call to something better.

Mike's sermon had surprised him, and the references to their lives and the people who filled them had touched Stani deeply. He had thought briefly of his mother, wondered about the day of his own baptism, but then his mind turned to the present, as he handed Ian to Mike, then watched as Emily did the same with Andrew. In that brief ceremonial gesture, they had committed their sons to a life which had taken him so long to find for himself. It was a relief to think that they might not search and stumble as he had.

But possibly the most powerful moment had come, not in the church, but in the barn. When Mike had been asked to bless the meal, he had taken a moment to address those at the table. He reminded them that in a barn the world had first welcomed the Christ Child. In a barn, the King of Kings had arrived in the form of a tiny baby boy. In a barn, the savior of the world had slept in his mother's arms, and in a barn, the Prince of Peace had received the adoration of shepherds and kings. Today, he said with a smile, two little lives were celebrated as they joined the family of faith. He could think of no more fitting place for that celebration than in a barn.

For Stani, those words had consecrated the space for all time. When he made music here in the future, it would be for him just as if he were performing in a church; the same sense of spiritual intimacy would be present, he was sure.

As he watched the faces around the table later, he wondered how they might have been touched by what they had seen and heard. He hoped they would all remember this day as not only a celebration of Ian and Andrew, but of themselves as well.

Emily sighed and opened her eyes. Turning, she came into his arms, and he pulled her very close. "It was a wonderful day, wasn't it?" she whispered.

"Wonderful. In every way. Are you happy?"

Her answer was a kiss, warm and slow at first, then growing more and more insistent. His heart lurched in his chest, as her hands, cool and soft, drifted across his skin. His wife in his arms, the afterglow of an emotional day fueling his passion, he forgot the place or the hour. And then from the nursery, the soft discontented whimpering, followed a measure later by a yowl of displeasure, shattered the moment, setting his heart hammering to a very different beat. Footsteps sounded on the stairs as Lil and Angela came racing to the rescue.

Stani reached for his shirt, as Emily slipped into her dress, and their eyes met across the bed. With a soft laugh, she whispered, "Later."

Chapter Sixty-four

As always the final week at the farm was harried. They met with the contractor about the proposed stable and the work to be done in the barn. Stani was adamant that nothing be done that might alter the acoustics. Milo would schedule a visit from a technician who would assess the equipment needs. Bobby was placed in charge as general contractor and instructed to contact the New York office with any questions, which would be relayed to Stani wherever he happened to be.

"You mean to do all this from Europe? Sounds like it would be kind of slow, writing back and forth like that." Bobby had made drawings and taken down detailed instructions as they'd talked, sitting at the kitchen table.

"Not writing, phoning. I'll be just a call away, Bobby, no matter what you need. Just keep in mind I'll be six or seven hours ahead of you time-wise."

Bobby grinned, his eyes lighting up much the way his children's might. "Wow, telephone calls from Europe. I never thought I'd be working for somebody who makes a living traveling all over like that. 'Course, I never thought I'd be in on building a record studio, either. Wonder what Mr. and Mrs. Haynes would say, if they could see the gardens growing again and hear music coming out of the barn? You sure have brought a lot of changes to this old farm."

Across the kitchen, he heard Emily laugh softly. "I wonder that myself sometimes, Bobby. But I'm pretty sure they'd be right in the middle of all these changes." She turned to look out the window, and Stani knew without a doubt that she was fighting sudden tears.

Turning back to Bobby, who was carefully stacking his notes preparing to leave, he held out his hand. "The truth is, my friend, this old farm has made a lot of changes in me. We know how fortunate we are to have you and Ruthie here to take care of things. And I mean it, anything you need, for the farm, the studio, or for your family, you just call me." They shook on it, and he walked through the sunroom to let

Bobby out the back door.

Silently, he went to stand behind her, wrapping her in his arms and laying his cheek against her hair. "Do you really think they'd approve of all this?" he asked softly.

"I know they would. I think sometimes how much I'd love for them to know you, to see our babies, to know how happy I am. And then I get this feeling, almost overwhelming at times, that they do know. They would love what we're doing here."

"I know how important it is to you to stay true to what they started here. You'd stop me if I got carried away and started down the wrong path?"

She smiled, turning in his arms. "I would. But I never worry about that. This is *our* home now, remember? I made you a full partner. You love it just as much as I do. I may miss it a little bit more, only because I'm not as good at leaving things behind as you are yet. But I'll learn." Tears sparkled in her eyes. "Just be patient with me?"

He held her there in the kitchen, the slanting rays of the sun touching every surface with gold. From the back of his mind, a thought was pushing its way forward. "You'd love it if we could be here all the time, wouldn't you?"

Against his neck, she said softly, "Of course I would, but that's not remotely possible, I know. And I love our other homes, too. I'm just being silly. Hormones, I guess."

He chuckled, holding her closer. "Then what's my excuse?"

They hoped to be back after Thanksgiving, but the plans were not definite. Milo had received requests for several special appearances in Britain during December. Home for the holidays might mean staying in London. "I can't plan that far in advance, given the way things keep changing. This is what I warned you about, the demands on my time."

"Or as Milo sees them, opportunities. I won't mind Christmas in London, as long as I have my men with me. We'll just see where this adventure takes us." She was packing the twins' clothes, carefully folding little shirts into a suitcase. Stani gave her a close look, suspicious of her resilience.

"Is that what it is, really, an adventure? No regrets?"

"None. I'm actually anxious to get started. There's so much to get done in the next three weeks, a recording for you and a wedding for me, not to mention what it will take just to get us on the plane to

London. We'll need every waking hour and all the extra hands we can find to get it all done." She closed the suitcase and snapped the locks with finality. "I've decided to take a new approach. We'll travel as light as we can, as long as we can, and laugh a lot along the way. How's that for a motto?"

He laughed. "That deserves to be put to music. A traveling song fit for a vagabond crew like ours."

"We can't afford to wear ourselves out lugging stuff around. I'm dedicating myself to streamlining our lives. We do have three houses, after all. There's no need to carry everything from one to the other. And hotels have most of what we need, anyway. So other than our clothes, and some essential baby equipment, we should be able to manage. As soon as we get to New York, Peg and I are going shopping for more sensible things to accommodate the twins' needs. Surely, we aren't the only ones who fly around the world with babies."

He took a moment to frame an argument on the logic of this proposed shopping partnership. "So Peg is going from the most elaborate and expensive, not to say fit for nobility, to the most practical? This I have to see."

Emily said her goodbyes with a minimum of tears, had a long visit with Stubby regarding his new accommodations and an equally long visit with Ruthie about the care of the house. On the morning of their departure, when Robert arrived with the limo, she was overseeing the luggage piled on the front porch, giving orders to the three Dixon boys, who had volunteered to help load. There was no sign of sadness as the last of the bags disappeared into the trunk. Again, the twins were tucked into their car beds, Lil wedged into the front of Stani's car with John at the wheel, and with one last walk through the house, she declared herself ready to go.

Stani thought she might have been fine, if she had not looked out the rear window to wave to the line of children hanging on the fence. With Ruthie holding on to little Emily and the boys perched like stair steps along the rail, they were waving wildly and shouting their farewells. It was the sight of the house behind them, he knew, that broke her brave resolve. So many memories, old and new, were framed in those walls. It would always be her first love, the one thing left of her life before. Fully understanding, he held out his arms and she lay against him, crying softly.

"It's all right, you know. I would be concerned if you *weren't* sad at leaving."

"I'm not sad about leaving. I'm sad about not knowing when we'll be back. Always before I could imagine what it would look like when I came back, what season. This time I can't." She sniffed against his shoulder.

"Well, maybe you could just imagine it in every season. You said once it's always the same, always welcoming you back. It's in good hands, darling. They know how much you love it." He wasn't sure his words made her feel any better, but she stopped crying. He held her until they had reached the highway, and she lifted her head, wiped her tears and in that profound way of hers, straightened her shoulders.

"I think next time we come, we won't plan any big events. We'll just come to rest, the way we always thought we would. And maybe we won't tell everyone we're coming." He could see she was thinking aloud, gazing out at the distant ridges on the horizon. "Yes, that would be the best way. I don't want the farm to become just a place for celebrations, as nice as they are. I want it to be home, the way it always has been." Turning, she looked into his eyes. "Do you think we could do that, just come home to be at home?"

"I think if that's what you want to do, we can do it. But darling girl, it will always be a place to celebrate. It's the place our life together began. Where we came to know and love each other. It's where our sons were conceived. It's the first place I learned to call home. I can't help but celebrate those things."

She looked very thoughtful for a moment, clearly weighing what he had said against her own needs. Then with a smile that lit her eyes and finally lifted her lips in that mysterious little upturn, she said, "Oh, Stani, when you put it that way, it's no wonder every time we come home there's a party!"

Epilogue

Their first anniversary still to come, and already they were not just two, but a family of four. Stani had never dreamed of such a thing, never dared imagine the kind of joy and contentment he had found with Emily and their sons.

The weeks at the farm, the essential, earth-bound existence there, had given him a vision of the life they could have, if he only had the courage to make the choice. Emily insisted they could be happy any place, and he knew she was capable of convincing herself and everyone else of just that. But in his heart he knew that *this* place, sheltered in the safety of the hills, was where they would find their best life. How to move the formidable mountain of his career aside and bring them into that life, he as yet had no idea.

Still, he was more and more confident that the way would become clear. There was so much to be accomplished in the coming weeks and months, commitments to fulfill and people to please. He would do what he had promised, to others and to himself. But beyond that, he envisioned a turning in the road, a new direction for their lives. Nothing clear or focused yet, only a vague outline of what might be. In his heart, he felt the rightness of it; the call to follow that turning toward whatever God had been preparing him for. At the same time, he sensed the danger, the possibility of faltering or even failing in an unfamiliar landscape. A shadowy path that appeared to lead toward a bright future might well be filled with hidden perils.

Whatever lay ahead, he would welcome the challenge. Whatever might be required of him, he would find the courage if in the end he could live out his life with the woman who had taught him to love, here in this place he had learned to call home.

Next in the Miracle at Valley Rise Series

Offered For Love

Chapter One

John Kimble quietly exited the elevator, scanning the dimly lit apartment for signs of life. At this hour of the morning, he'd assumed someone would be up and about, but the stillness in the luxuriously appointed loft was disturbed only by the rapidly moving clouds visible beyond the walls of plate glass and a rumble of distant thunder. He brushed raindrops from the shoulder of his jacket and strode soundlessly across the polished floor, placing the bundle of newspapers gently on the white marble counter. His eyes traveled around the kitchen, noting the meticulous arrangement of utensils, the symmetric lineup of cookbooks beneath the cabinets—everything in perfect order, as always.

He congratulated himself on his still keen powers of observation. He might be more baggage handler than bodyguard these days, but a good copper never forgot his training. Now, giving the kitchen another sharp scan, he spotted the evidence. The first clue to the absence of all life in this ordinarily bustling home was to be found in the sink, where two bottles stood on end, drained of their contents. A canister of formula stood on the counter nearby, alongside a measuring cup and spoon, both showing traces of congealing white residue. John grinned. Another long night.

He helped himself to a muffin from the glass-domed cake stand, poked about in the refrigerator until he located the orange juice, and took a stool at the counter. Nothing pressing to do today, he could wait. There were things he needed to talk to them about, plans to finalize, a few tidbits of news to share, and one small bombshell to drop. Taking a big bite of the slightly stale muffin, he poured juice and opened the first newspaper.

It was a good photograph, a little grainy, but a very true likeness of both of them. Emily had looked especially lovely in that simple black dress, set off by the strand of heirloom pearls she favored above all the jewelry Stani had gifted her with in the past year. And of course, he had been his usual elegant self, wearing white tie and tails and a ridiculously broad grin on his handsome face. It had been a stunner of a party, even by Peg's standards. The added treat of a surprise performance by the most sought after ticket on the classical music circuit had been the icing on the cake. The camera had captured the moment when Emily had stood beaming at his side as Stani acknowledged the standing ovation from New York's wealthiest devotees of the arts. John smiled at the picture, as proud as any parent of their offspring. It had been a fitting homecoming, a triumphant return to Stani's world.

And then they had apparently come home to babies who wanted to play all night. Four-month-old twins Ian and Andrew must have been waiting up for their parents, demanding the attention they so richly deserved. Their Papa might have been the star of Peg's party, but they were the main attraction here, no matter the hour.

John studied the photo a moment longer, then opened the next paper. This shot was just as good of Stani and Emily, and it was especially flattering to Peg. Not that she hadn't looked her typical perfection; sleek and sophisticated in a white silk gown with diamonds sparkling at her ears. Those earrings were mesmerizing, the way they caught the light, much like the spark in her blue eyes when she laughed. He had been foolish enough to fall beneath their spell for just a moment. And he had paid the price.

From somewhere in the vicinity of the bedrooms he heard the shuffle of bare feet, accompanied by a stifled groan. Stani, now far from elegant in wrinkled jeans, a limp shirt hanging open to his waist, was blinking blindly at the gray sky beyond the windows.

"Good morning, sunshine. Wondered when you were going to put in an appearance." John grinned as Stani halted halfway across the room, letting out a startled grunt.

"How long have you been here?" The shuffle resumed as he ran a hand through his wild auburn curls. "I didn't even hear the elevator."

"I noticed. Rough night? Not that there was much of it left when I dropped you off."

Stani filled the kettle at the tap and set it on an eye of the range, taking a moment to adjust the flame. "The little scamps have gotten their days and nights turned round again. Lil said they'd been asleep until eleven, but they were bright-eyed and ready to play when we got home. Now, of course, they're sleeping like angels." Taking two glasses from the shelf, he poured juice. "Emily's up, but I told her I'd start breakfast. What brings you around here so early?"

"It's past ten, lad. But that's beside the point. I come bearing news." He shoved the papers across the bar in Stani's direction. "I know how you crave publicity."

"Huh! I thought we were just putting in an appearance last night. Thanks so much for conspiring with Peg. When I saw the violin, I could have gleefully rung your neck, my friend." He looked down on the photograph of the pair of them and grinned. "She looked spectacular, didn't she? I'm still amazed at how gorgeous she is, even when I see her every day."

"Who's gorgeous?" Crossing the room, her sandals clattering on the hardwood, Lil Salvatore balanced an overflowing basket of laundry on one hip. Her free hand clutched a pair of identical teddy bears which she unceremoniously deposited on the floor near a heap of other toys. "I thought you two were never going to get up. I've got work to do, you know? While the babies are still asleep, I thought I might actually get caught up. We *are* rehearsing tonight, aren't we? Or is your social life going to put us on hold again?" Setting her basket on a bar stool, she gathered her long, black curls into a knot at the back of her head and gave Stani a sharp look. "You're burning the candle at the wrong end, or something like that." She picked up a freshly laundered diaper and snapped it open emphatically.

"Don't worry, Lil. Last night was the only social engagement on our calendar. There's no room for more of that kind of nonsense!" Emily swept into the room on Lil's heels. John mused that she looked far better put together than the other two, neat as a pin in a flowing sundress, her dark hair tied smoothly into a ponytail. Despite the gloomy weather, she seemed to bring a burst of warmth and light into the room. "But it was fun, wasn't it, darling?" Going immediately to wrap her arms around Stani's waist, she leaned her cheek on his shoulder. "And you were wonderful, as always."

"Hmm. I was duped. I should have suspected when you insisted I get all rigged out." Before he could voice further complaints, Emily took his face between her hands and kissed him.

"Made for good press, though. Nice shot of the three of you." John held up the photograph, arching his brows.

Lil took the paper, studying the column next to the photograph. "Hostess extraordinaire Peg Shannon entertained a glittering company last evening at a fundraiser for her latest pet project, the Haynes-Moss Foundation. Included among the guests were Stani and Emily Moss, just returned to the city from their Virginia estate. Moss, who was persuaded to perform after dinner, appears to have fully recovered from recent surgery. He is reported to be recording a long anticipated collection of original compositions, and will begin the second leg of a European concert tour this fall." Lil wrinkled her nose. "Estate? When did the farm become an estate?" Mocking an elegant accent, her head cocked regally to one side, she said, "We've just returned from Valley Rise, my godsister's estate, you know. Delightful little place."

Emily laughed softly. "A 'farm' won't do, not for the world's premier fiddle player, Lil. Now who wants breakfast? I'm starving!"

As she briskly threw together an omelet, Stani buttered bread for toast. "I take it there's not a sound from the nursery? Shouldn't we wake them up, so they don't sleep all day?"

The simultaneous protest from Lil and Emily brought a grin to his face. "No? But who will I play with, if they sleep all the time?"

"Stani Moss, don't you dare wake them! I need at least another hour before I have to feed and dress them. Peg is coming after lunch and we're taking them shopping."

John blinked. "You're taking the twins shopping? What would be the point in that?"

"They need to help us pick out things for the tour, equipment. We're going to use them to test things like carriers and swings and such."

He exchanged bemused glances with Stani. "Ah, that makes sense, I guess. When did you say Peg will be here?"

"By one. She said she was sleeping in, but I got the idea there was something else on her agenda. You wouldn't know anything about that, would you?"

John avoided her sparkling gray eyes. "Not a thing. Why should I?"

"I just happened to notice that the two of you disappeared after all the other guests had gone. Stani was even wondering if we should call a cab."

He considered the obvious opening. Was it wise to tell them on an empty stomach? The thought of it still made his own gut churn a bit. "I. . .that is *we* had a little chat. She was telling me about. . .some changes she's been thinking of making." He felt the hot blood creep up his neck. Three pairs of eyes, gray, black and brown, focused on him, pinning him to the spot. "If you must know, she asked me to marry her."

Emily let out an involuntary gasp, but otherwise, there was no response beyond wide-eyed expectation. Lil dropped the diaper she was folding and perched on a barstool. Across the counter, Stani put down the butter knife and took a long ragged breath.

"Don't worry, I declined the honor. I do, after all, have to take you lot to England in two weeks. That was actually a very convenient excuse." He turned his gaze to Stani, whose expression was resolutely blank. "Nothing to say, then?"

After a long moment, during which he opened his mouth and then closed it again, Stani shrugged. "What can I say? Except that for Peg to even use the word marriage must tell you something. As far as I know, she's never even considered such a thing for herself."

Emily sat their plates on the dining table and silently, they took their places. "People change, don't they?" she asked softly.

"Ah, but that's the heart of the matter, right there. Do they really change, deep down, or do they just pretend in order to get what they think they want?" John took a tentative bite of his omelet, toyed with a piece of toast and finally took a sip of tea. "I asked her straight-out if she expected me to trust that she'd ever settle down with one man. I also told her I'm not about to give up this job, so she'd either have to be ready to follow me around, or spend much of her time on her own. Which comes full circle to the matter of trust."

Stani's color deepened. Lil, watching with keen, questioning eyes, saw it immediately. She looked briefly to Emily. "Peg has a history with men, I take it?" she ventured cautiously.

Emily apparently felt it would be best coming from her. "Yes, including Stani." Both men looked away. Stani groaned under his breath and John took another long drink. Emily went on. "It was a very long time ago. Peg is a good friend. I know it sounds odd, but knowing Peg, you can understand. She lives life according to her own rules. Stani, darling, don't look so embarrassed. Lil would find out eventually. But right now, we're discussing Peg's proposal to John. And I for one find it very encouraging that she wants to get married."

"More to the point, do *I* want to get married? It would pose any number of problems, even if she were just some ordinary woman, and we all know that's not the case. Peg's life is bigger than the both of us, I'm afraid. The high society, the fund-raising, the kind of money she throws around; all that would hardly make for going home after a long day's work to a nice cozy supper and an hour or two of quiet. Not that I have much of that anyway. No, I just don't see it. She's dreaming if she thinks either of us can chuck in our lives and start a new one, and mixing the two would be disastrous."

Stani softly cleared his throat, shifting in his chair. "Somewhere in the discussion, there would have to be some mention of love, wouldn't there?"

John drained his cup and studied the table top. "It's been a long time since I even thought of loving a woman. I loved my wife when we were little more than kids, in the way that you do that first time. That was over twenty years ago. All I know is Peg's gotten in my head, but does that mean I love her?"

No one had an answer, but the communal silence was somehow comforting. Emily eventually got up and took the empty plates to the kitchen. Lil left to check on the twins briefly, returning to report that they were still asleep. Stani appeared to be lost in thought, as John sat staring at him, seeming to read his solemn face.

"You just said 'not now,' and left it at that?" Stani's hushed voice broke the silence abruptly.

"I said I didn't think it could work. She took it pretty well. She did say she'd show me she could settle down." John gave a little snort of ironic laughter. "I find it hard to imagine what her version of settling down might be."

Stani raised one brow. "Come to think of it, she hasn't been seeing anyone for a while. At least not publicly, the way she always has before. Discreet as she is, there was always some indication of who she was with. She never kept it a secret."

"Except for you." He said it softly, but the effect was profound.

"That was different. That would have raised too many eyebrows, even for Peg." Again, Stani colored and shoved his fingers through his hair.

Emily laid a hand on the table between them, as if to put an end to the debate. "Look, you two, there has to be some way to resolve the past, once and for all. Stani, after all, is happily married, with Peg's blessing. John, if Peg is willing to change in hopes of being with you, why should what happened all those years ago matter?"

Again, no one had an answer. John pushed back his chair, stood up and looked down at Stani. "It's not as if there's any rush. We're going to Europe, right, lad? And four months is a long time in anybody's life. I'd as soon leave it where it is."

"Emily's right, though. At some point, we have to get past this. It certainly seems Peg has put it behind her."

"But, as she also pointed out, Peg lives by her own rules."

About the Author

Karen Welch was born in Richmond, Virginia and grew up in nearby Amelia County. After a twenty year sojourn in North Florida, she now lives in Southeast Kansas with husband John and children and grandchildren nearby.

Contact Karen at welchkaren@Yahoo.net and follow her on Facebook at Author Karen Welch for updates on the *Miracle at Valley Rise Series*.

Made in the USA
Charleston, SC
03 October 2012